A SHORT HISTORY OF THE GREAT WAR

Copyright © 2006 BiblioBazaar
All rights reserved
ISBN: 1-4264-2180-X

Original copyright: 1920,
LONDON

A. F. Pollard
M.A., Litt.D.
FELLOW OF ALL SOULS COLLEGE, OXFORD
PROFESSOR OF ENGLISH HISTORY IN THE
UNIVERSITY OF LONDON

A SHORT HISTORY OF THE GREAT WAR

With Nineteen Maps

BIBLIOBAZAAR

A SHORT HISTORY OF THE GREAT WAR

CONTENTS

CHAPTER
I.	THE BREACH OF THE PEACE	9
II.	THE GERMAN INVASION	23
III.	RUSSIA MOVES	38
IV.	THE WAR ON AND BEYOND THE SEAS	50
V.	ESTABLISHING THE WESTERN FRONT	66
VI.	THE FIRST WINTER OF THE WAR	86
VII.	THE FAILURE OF THE ALLIED OFFENSIVE	107
VIII.	THE DEFEAT OF RUSSIA	123
IX.	THE CLIMAX OF GERMAN SUCCESS	139
X.	THE SECOND WINTER OF THE WAR	157
XI.	THE SECOND GERMAN OFFENSIVE IN THE WEST	172
XII.	THE ALLIED COUNTER-OFFENSIVE	189
XIII.	THE BALKANS AND POLITICAL REACTIONS	205
XIV.	THE TURN OF THE TIDE	222
XV.	HOPE DEFERRED	240
XVI.	THE BALANCE OF POWER	256
XVII.	THE EVE OF THE FINAL STRUGGLE	272
XVIII.	THE LAST GERMAN OFFENSIVE	288
XIX.	THE VICTORY OF THE ENTENTE	307
XX.	THE FOUNDATIONS OF PEACE	329

LIST OF MAPS

1.	THE GERMAN INVASION OF FRANCE	22
2.	THE BATTLES OF THE AISNE	66
3.	THE CAMPAIGNS IN ARTOIS	76
4	THE DARDANELLES	100
5.	THE RUSSIAN FRONT	135
6.	THE BALKANS	140
7.	MESOPOTAMIA	163
8.	THE CAUCASUS	169
9.	THE ATTACK ON VERDUN	180
10.	THE BATTLE OF THE SOMME	195
11.	THE RUMANIAN CAMPAIGN	209
12.	THE CONQUEST OF EAST AFRICA	226
13.	THE BALTIC CAMPAIGNS	248
14.	THE BATTLES IN FLANDERS	262
15.	THE ITALIAN FRONT	271
16.	THE BATTLES OF ARRAS AND CAMBRAI	275
17.	THE LAST GERMAN OFFENSIVE	306
18.	THE CONQUEST OF SYRIA	318
19.	FOCH'S CAMPAIGN	327

CHAPTER I

THE BREACH OF THE PEACE

On 28 June 1914 the Archduke Francis Ferdinand, heir-presumptive to the Hapsburg throne, was shot in the streets of Serajevo, the capital of the Austrian province of Bosnia. Redeemed by the Russo-Turkish war of 1876-7 from Ottoman rule, Bosnia had by the Congress of Berlin in 1878 been entrusted to Austrian administration; but in 1908, fearing lest a Turkey rejuvenated by the Young Turk revolution should seek to revive its claims on Bosnia, the Austrian Government annexed on its own authority a province confided to its care by a European mandate. This arbitrary act was only challenged on paper at the time; but the striking success of Serbia in the Balkan wars of 1912-13 brought out the dangers and defects of Austrian policy. For the Serbs were kin to the great majority of the Bosnian people and to millions of other South Slavs who were subject to the Austrian crown and discontented with its repressive government; and the growing prestige of Serbia bred hopes and feelings of Slav nationality on both sides of the Hapsburg frontier. The would-be and the real assassins of the Archduke, while technically Austrian subjects, were Slavs by birth, and the murder brought to a head the antagonism between a race becoming conscious of its possibilities and a government determined to repress them. The crime gave a moral advantage to the oppressor, but the guilt has yet to be apportioned, and instigation may have come from secret sources within the Hapsburg empire; for the Archduke was hated by dominant cliques on account of his alleged pro-Slav sympathies and his suspected intention of admitting his future Slav subjects to a share in political power.

For some weeks after the murder it bade fair to pass without a European crisis, for the public was unaware of what happened at a secret conclave held at Potsdam on 5 July. It was there decided that Germany should support to the uttermost whatever claims Austria might think fit to make on Serbia for redress, and she was encouraged to put them so high as either to ensure the domination of the Balkans by the Central Empires through Serbian submission, or to provoke a war by which alone the German militarists thought that German aims could be achieved. That was the purport of the demands presented to Serbia on 23 July: acceptance would have reduced her to a dependence less formal but little less real than that of Bosnia, while the delay in presenting the demands was used to complete the preparations for war which rejection would provoke. It was not, however, against Serbia that the German moves were planned. She could be left to Austria, while Germany dealt with the Powers which would certainly be involved by the attack on Serbian independence.

The great Power immediately concerned was Russia, which had long aspired to an outlet into European waters not blocked by winter ice or controlled by Baltic States. For that and for the less interested reasons of religion and racial sympathy she had fought scores of campaigns against the Turks which culminated in the liberation of most of the Balkans in 1878; and she could not stand idle while the fruits of her age-long efforts were gathered by the Central Empires and she herself was cut off from the Mediterranean by an obstacle more fatal than Turkish dominion in the form of a Teutonic corridor from Berlin to Baghdad. Serbia, too, Orthodox in religion and Slav in race, was more closely bound to Russia than was any other Balkan State; and an attack on Serbia was a deadly affront to the Russian Empire. It was not intended as anything else. Russia was slowly recovering from her defeat in the Russo-Japanese war of 1904-5 and from the revolutionary outbreaks which had followed; and there was little doubt that sooner or later she would seek compensation for the rebuffs she had suffered from the mailed fist during her impotence. Conscience made Germany sensitive to the Slav peril, and her militarist philosophy taught her that the best defence was to get her blow in first. Her diplomacy in July was directed towards combining this advantage with the appearance, needed to bemuse her people and the world at large, of acting in self-defence.

But Russia was the object of Germany's diplomatic activity rather than of her military preparations. It was thought that Russia could not mobilize in less than six weeks or strike effectively in less than two or three months, and that that interval would suffice for the crushing of France, who was bound by treaty to intervene if Russia were attacked. The German mobilization was therefore directed first against France, defence against Russia being left to second-line German troops and to an Austrian offensive. The defeat of France was not, however, regarded by Germans as a mere incident in a war against Russia; for it was a cardinal point in the programme of the militarists, whose mind was indiscreetly revealed by Bernhardi, that France must be so completely crushed that she could never again cross Germany's path. To Frenchmen the war appeared to be mainly a continuation of the national duel which had been waged since the sixteenth century. To Great Britain it appeared, on the other hand, as the forcible culmination of a new rivalry for colonial empire and the dominion of the seas. But these were in truth but local aspects of a comprehensive German ambition expressed in the antithesis Weltmacht oder Niedergang. Bismarck had made the German Empire and raised it to the first place as a European Power. Europe, it was discovered, was a small portion of the globe; and Bismarck's successful methods were now to be used on a wider scale to raise Germany to a similar predominance in the world. The Serbian plot was merely the lever to set the whole machinery working, and German activities all the world over from Belgrade and Petrograd to Constantinople, Ulster, and Mexico were parts in a comprehensive piece.

But while the German sword was pointed everywhere, its hilt was in Berlin. Prussia supplied the mind which conceived the policy and controlled its execution; and in the circumstances of the Prussian Government must be sought the mainspring of the war. The cause of the war was not the Serbian imbroglio nor even German rivalry with Russia, France, or Britain. These were the occasions of its outbreak and extension; but national rivalries always exist and occasions for war are never wanting. They only result in war when one of the parties to the dispute wants to break the peace; and the Prussian will-to-war was due to the domestic situation of a Prussian government which had been made by the sword and had realized before 1914 that it could not be maintained without a further use of the sword. That government was the work of Bismarck, who had been called to power in 1863 to save the Hohenzollerns from subjection to Parliament and had found in the Danish and Austrian wars of 1864 and 1866 the means of solving the constitutional issue at Berlin. The cannon of Königgratz proved more convincing than Liberal arguments; and the methods of blood and iron, by which Bismarck, Moltke, and Roon conquered Denmark, Austria, and France and annexed to Prussia the greater part of German soil, impressed upon Germany a constitution in which the rule of the sword was merely concealed behind a skilfully emasculated parliamentary system. The Reichstag with its universal suffrage was the scabbard of the Prussian sword, and it was because the sword could not do the work required of it while it lay in the scabbard that it was drawn in 1914.

Since 1871 the object of every Prussian Government had been to reconcile the German people to the veiled rule of the sword by exhibiting results which, it was contended, could not otherwise have been secured. Historians dwelt on the failure of the German Parliament at Frankfurt to promote a national unity which was left for Prussian arms to achieve, and philosophers deduced from that example a comprehensive creed of might. More material arguments were provided for the man in business and in the street by the skilful activities of the Government in promoting trade, industry, and social welfare; and the wealth, which would in any case have accrued from the removal of the tariff-walls and other barriers between the thirty-nine independent States of Germany, was credited to the particular method of war by which the unification had been accomplished. No State had hitherto made such economic progress as did the German Empire in the generation after Metz and Sedan, and the success of their rulers led most of the German people to place implicit reliance on the testimony those rulers bore to the virtue of their means. The means did not, however, commend themselves to the rest of the world with equal conviction; and an increasing aversion to the mailed fist on the part of other countries led to what Germans called the hostile encirclement of their Fatherland. Gradually it became clearer that Prussian autocracy could not reproduce in the sphere of world-ambitions the success which had attended it in Germany unless it could reduce the world to the same submission by the use of similar arguments.

But still the Prussian Government was driven towards imperialistic expansion by the ever-increasing force of public opinion and popular discontent. It could only purchase renewed leases of autocratic power at home, with its perquisites for those who wielded and supported autocracy, by feeding the minds of the people with diplomatic triumphs and their bodies with new markets for commercial and industrial expansion; and the incidents of military domination grew ever more irksome to the populace. The middle classes were fairly content, and the parties which represented them in the Reichstag offered no real opposition to Prussian ideas of government. But the Social Democrats were more radical in their principles and were regarded by Prussian statesmen as open enemies of the Prussian State. Rather than submit to social democracy Prussians avowed their intention of making war, and war abroad would serve their turn a great deal better than civil strife. The hour was rapidly advancing two years before the war broke out. The German rebuff over Agadir in 1911 was followed by a general election in 1912 at which the Social Democrats polled nearly a third of the votes and secured by far the largest representation of any party in the Reichstag. In 1913, after a particularly violent expression of militarism called "the Zabern incident," the Reichstag summoned up courage for the first time in its history to pass a vote of censure on the Government. The ground was slipping from under the feet of Prussian militarism; it must either fortify its position by fresh victories or take the risk of revolution. It preferred the chances of European war, and found in the Serbian incident a means of provoking a war the blame for which could be laid at others' doors.

The German Kaiser played but a secondary part in these transactions. It is true that the German constitution placed in his hands the command of the German Army and Navy and the control of foreign policy; but no paper or parchment could give him the intellect to direct the course of human affairs. He had indeed dismissed Bismarck in 1890, but dropping the pilot did not qualify him to guide the ship of state, and he was himself in 1906 compelled to submit to the guidance of his ministers. The shallow waters of his mind spread over too vast a sphere of activity to attain any depth, and he had the foibles of Frederick the Great without his courage or his capacity. His barbaric love of pomp betrayed the poverty of his spirit and exhibited a monarchy reduced from power to a pageant. He was not without his generous impulses or exalted sentiments, and there was no section of the British public, from Mr. Ramsay Macdonald to Mr. Rudyard Kipling and the "Daily Mail," to which one or other of his guises had not commended itself; it pleased him to pose as the guardian of the peace of Europe, the champion of civilization against the Boxers, and of society against red revolution. But vanity lay at the root of all these manifestations, and he took himself not less seriously as an arbiter of letters, art, and religion than as a divinely appointed ruler of the State. The many parts he played were signs of versatile emotion rather than of power; and his significance in history is that he was the crest of a wave, its superficial froth and foam without its massive strength. A little man in a great position, he was powerless to ride the whirlwind or direct the storm, and he figured largely in the public eye because he vented through an imperial megaphone the fleeting catchwords of the vulgar mind.

After Agadir he had often been called a coward behind his back, and it was whispered that his throne would be in danger if that surrender were repeated. He had merited these reproaches because no one had done more than he to inflate the arrogance of his people, and his eldest son took the lead in exasperating public opinion behind the scenes. The militarists, with considerable backing from financial and commercial groups, were bent on war, and war appeals to the men in the streets of all but the weakest countries. The mass of the people had not made up their mind for a war that was not defensive; but modern governments have ample means for tuning public opinion, and with a people so accustomed as the Germans to accept the truth from above, their rulers would have little difficulty, when once they had agreed upon war, in representing it as one of defence. It is, however, impossible to say when, if ever, the rulers of Germany agreed to attack; and to the last the Imperial Chancellor, Bethmann-Hollweg, struggled to delay if not to avert the breach. But he gradually lost his grip on the Kaiser. The decisive factor in the Emperor's mind may have been the rout in 1912-13 of the Turks, on whom Germany had staked her credit in return for control of the Berlin-Baghdad route; for the free Balkan confederation, which loomed on the horizon, would bar for ever German expansion towards the East. The Balkan States themselves provided the German opportunity; the Treaty of Bukarest in 1913 entrenched discord in their hearts and reopened a path for German ambition and intrigue. Austria, not without the usual instigation, proposed to Italy a joint attack upon Serbia; the offer was not accepted, but by the winter of 1913-14 the Kaiser had gone over to the party which had resolved upon war and was seeking an occasion to palliate the cause.

The immeasurable distance between the cause and the occasion was shown by the fact that Belgium was the first to suffer in an Austro-Serbian dispute; and the universal character of the issue was foreshadowed by the breach of its neutrality. Germany would not have planned for two years past an offensive through that inoffensive, unconcerned, and distant country, had the cause of the war been a murder at Serajevo. The cause was a comprehensive determination on the German part to settle international issues by the sword, and it involved the destinies of civilization. The blow was aimed directly or indirectly at the whole world, and Germany's only prospect of success lay in the chance that most of the world would fail to perceive its implications or delay too long its effective intervention. It was the defect of her self-idolatry and concentration that she could not develop an international mind or fathom the mentality of other peoples. She could not conceive how England would act on a "scrap of paper," and never dreamt of American participation. But she saw that Russia and France would inevitably and immediately be involved in war by the attempt at armed dictation in the Balkans, and that the issue would decide the fate of Europe. The war would therefore be European and could only be won by the defeat of France and Russia. Serbia would be merely the scene of local and unimportant operations, and, Russia being the slower to move, the bulk of the German forces were concentrated on the Rhine for the purpose of overwhelming France.

The condition of French politics was one of the temptations which led the Prussian militarists to embark upon the hazard. France had had her troubles with militarism, and its excesses over the Dreyfus case had produced a reaction from which both the army command and its political ally the Church had suffered. A wave of national secularism carried a law against ecclesiastical associations which drove religious orders from France, and international Socialism found vent in a pacifist agitation against the terms of military service. A rapid succession of unstable ministries, which the group system in French parliamentary politics encouraged, militated against sound and continuous administration; and in April 1914 a series of revelations in the Senate had thrown an unpleasant light upon the efficiency of the army organization. On military grounds alone there was much to be said for the German calculation that in six weeks the French armies could be crushed and Paris reached. But the Germans paid the French the compliment of believing that this success could not be achieved before Russia made her weight felt, unless the Germans broke the international guarantees on which the French relied, and sought in Belgium an easier and less protected line of advance than through the Vosges.

For that crime public opinion was not prepared either in France or England, but it had for two years at least been the settled policy of the German military staff, and it had even been foretold in England a year before that the German attack would proceed by way of Liège and Namur. There had also been military "conversations" between Belgian and British officers with regard to possible British assistance in the event of Germany's violation of Belgian neutrality. But the Belgian Ministry was naturally reluctant to proceed far on that assumption, which might have been treated as an insult by an honest or dishonest German Government; and it was impossible for England to press its assistance upon a neutralized State which could not even discuss it without casting a slur upon the honour of its most powerful neighbour. Nor was England bound by treaty to defend the neutrality of Belgium. She had been so bound by a treaty concluded during the Franco-Prussian War; but that treaty expired in the following year, and the treaty of 1839, which regulated the international situation of Belgium, merely bound the five great signatory Powers not to violate Belgian neutrality without obliging them individually or collectively to resist its violation. It was not in fact regarded in 1839 as conceivable that any of the Great Powers would ever violate so solemn a pledge, and there was some complacent satisfaction that by thus neutralizing a land which had for centuries been the cockpit of Europe, the Powers had laid the foundations of permanent peace. But the bond of international morality was loosened during the next half-century, and in the eighties even English newspapers argued in favour of a German right-of-way through Belgium for the purposes of war with France. It does not appear that the treaty was ever regarded as a serious obstacle by the German military staff; for neither treaties nor morality belong to the curricula of military science which had concluded that encirclement was the only way to defeat a modern army, and that through Belgium alone could the French defence be encircled. The Chancellor admitted that technically Germany was wrong, and promised full reparation after the war. But he was never forgiven the admission, even by German jurists, who argued that treaties were only binding rebus sic stantibus, while the conditions in which they were signed remained substantially the same; and Germans had long cast covetous eyes on the Congo State, the possession of which, they contended, was inconsistent with Belgium's legal immunity from attack in Europe.

The opposition of Bethmann-Hollweg and the German foreign office was accordingly brushed aside, and the army made all preparations for an invasion of France through Belgium. The diplomatists would have made a stouter resistance had they anticipated the attitude England was to adopt. But the German ambassador in London, Prince Lichnowsky, failed to convince his Government that there was anything to fear from the British Empire. Mr. Lloyd George has claimed it as one of the advantages we derive from the British press that it misleads public opinion abroad, and a study of "The Times," the only British newspaper that carries much weight in foreign countries, may well have persuaded the German Government in 1914 that eight years of Liberal administration were not likely to have provided England with the means, or left it the spirit, to challenge the might of Germany. She was known to have entered into no binding alliance with France or Russia; the peace had never in all their history been broken between the two great Protestant Powers; and, while there had been serious naval and colonial rivalry and some diplomatic friction, relations in 1913-14 seemed to have entered calmer waters. Germany had been well satisfied with the efforts and sacrifices England had made to prevent the Balkan crisis from developing into a European war; and Lichnowsky was successfully negotiating treaties which gave Germany unexpected advantages with regard to the Baghdad railway and African colonization. On the eve of war the English were hailed as cousins in Berlin, and the earliest draft of the German official apology, intended for American consumption, spoke of Great Britain and Germany labouring shoulder to shoulder to preserve the peace against Russian aggression. The anger of the Kaiser, the agitation of the Chancellor, and the fury of the populace when England declared war showed that Germany had no present intention of adding the British Empire to her list of enemies and little fear that it would intervene unless it were attacked. Any anxiety she may have felt was soothed by the studied assumption that England's desire, if any, to intervene would be effectively checked by her domestic situation. Agents from Ulster were buying munitions to fight Home Rule with official connivance in Germany, and it was confidently expected that war would shake a ramshackle British Empire to its foundations; there would be rebellions in Ireland, India, and South Africa, and the self-governing Dominions would at least refuse to participate in Great Britain's European adventures. In such circumstances "the flannelled fool at the wicket and the muddied oaf at the goal" might be trusted to hug his island security and stick to his idle sports; and the most windy and patriotic of popular British weeklies was at the end of July placarding the streets of London with the imprecation "To hell with Servia."

The object of German diplomacy was to avoid offence to British susceptibilities, and the first requisite was to keep behind the scenes. The Kaiser went off on a yachting cruise to Norway, where, however, he was kept in constant touch with affairs, while Austria on 23 July presented her ultimatum to the Serbian Government. The terms amounted to a demand for the virtual surrender of Serbian independence, and were in fact intended to be rejected. Serbia, however, acting on Russian and other advice, accepted them all except two, which she asked should be referred to the Hague Tribunal. Austria refused on the ground that the dispute was not of a justiciable nature; and the meagre five days' grace having expired on the 28th, Austrian troops crossed the Save and occupied Belgrade, the Serbians withdrawing without resistance. Meanwhile feverish activity agitated the chancelleries of Europe. The terms of the ultimatum had been discussed by the British Cabinet on Friday the 24th, and the British Fleet, which had been reviewed at Spithead on the previous Saturday, was, instead of dispersing at Portland, kept together, and then, on the 29th, dispatched to its war stations in the North Sea. Simultaneously the German High Seas Fleet withdrew on the 26th to Kiel and Wilhelmshaven. Russia replied to the Austrian invasion of Serbia by mobilizing her southern command and extending the mobilization, as the hand of Germany became more apparent, to her northern armies. Sir Edward Grey made unceasing efforts to avert the clash of arms by peaceable negotiation, and proposed a conference of the four Great Powers not immediately concerned in the dispute—Germany, France, Italy, and Great Britain. Germany, knowing that she would stand alone in the conference, declined. The dispute, she pretended, was merely a local affair between Austria and Serbia, in which no other Power had the right to intervene. But she refused to localize the dispute to the extent of regarding it as a Balkan conflict between the interests of Austria and Russia. Austria was less unyielding when it became evident that Russia would draw the sword rather than acquiesce in Serbia's subjection, and on the 30th it seemed that the way had been opened for a settlement by direct negotiation between Vienna and Petrograd. At that moment Germany threw off the diplomatic disguise of being a pacific second to her Austrian friend, and cut the web of argument by an ultimatum to Russia on the 31st. Fear lest the diplomatists should baulk them of their war had already led the German militarists to publish in their press the unauthorized news of a complete German mobilization, and on 1-2 August German armies crossed the frontiers. It was not till some days later that war was declared between Austria and any of the Allies; the war from first to last was made in Germany.

Throughout that week-end the British Cabinet remained in anxious conclave. The Unionist leaders early assured it of their support in any measures they might think fit to take to vindicate Great Britain's honour and obligations; but they could not relieve it of its own responsibility, and the question did not seem as easy to answer as it has done since the conduct of Germany and the nature of her ambitions have been revealed. A purely Balkan conflict did not appear to be an issue on which to stake the fortunes of the British Empire. We were not even bound to intervene in a trial of strength between the Central Empires and Russia and France, for on 1 August Italy decided that the action of the Central Empires was aggressive and that therefore she was not required by the Triple

Alliance to participate. There had in the past been a tendency on the part of France to use both the Russian alliance and English friendship for purposes in Morocco and elsewhere which had not been quite relished in England; and intervention in continental wars between two balanced alliances would have found few friends but for recent German chauvinism. It might well seem that in the absence of definite obligations and after having exhausted all means of averting war, Great Britain was entitled to maintain an attitude of benevolent neutrality, reserving her efforts for a later period when better prepared she might intervene with greater effect between the exhausted belligerents.

Such arguments, if they were used, were swept aside by indignation at Germany's conduct. Doubts might exist of the purely defensive intentions of France and Russia; each State had its ultra-patriots who had done their best to give away their country's case; and if Russia was suspect of Panslavist ambition, France was accused of building up a colonial empire in North Africa in order to throw millions of coloured troops into the scale for the recovery of Alsace-Lorraine. But no such charge could be brought against Belgium. She had no interest and no intention but to live in peace with her neighbours, and that peace had been guaranteed her by international contract. If such a title to peace was insecure there could be no security for the world and nothing but subservience for little nations. The public sense which for a century had been accustomed to welcome national independence wherever it raised its head—in Greece, the Balkans, Italy, Hungary, Poland, the South American Republics—revolted at its denial to Belgium in the interest of German military aggression; and censure of the breach of international contract was converted to passion by the wrong wantonly done to a weak and peaceful by a mighty and ambitious Power. Great Britain was not literally bound to intervene; but if ever there was a moral obligation on a country, it lay upon her now, and the instant meeting of that obligation implied an instinctive recognition of the character of the war that was to be fought. Mixed and confused though the national issues might be in various quarters, the war, so far as concerned the two Powers who were to be mainly instrumental in its winning, was a civil war of mankind to determine the principle upon which international relations should repose.

That issue was not for every one to see, and there were many to whom the struggle was merely national rivalry in which the interests of England happened to coincide with those of France and in which we should have intervened just the same without any question of Belgium's neutrality. Whether it might have been so can never be determined. But it is certain that no such struggle would have enlisted the united sympathies and whole-hearted devotion of the British realms, still less those of the United States, and in it we might well have been defeated. From that division and possible defeat we and the world were saved by Germany's decision that military advantage outweighed moral considerations. The invasion of Belgium and Luxemburg united the British Empire on the question of intervention. Three ministers alone out of more than forty—Lord Morley, Mr. John Burns, and Mr. C. P. Trevelyan—dissented from the Cabinet's decision, and the minority in the nation was of still more slender proportions. Parliament supported the Ministry without a division when on 4 August England declared war.

Had we counted the cost? the German Chancellor asked our ambassador in Berlin on the eve of the declaration. The cost would not have affected our decision, but it was certainly not anticipated, and the Entente was ill-prepared to cope with the strength displayed by Germany. The British Navy was, indeed, as ready as the German Army, and the command of the sea passed automatically into our hands when the German Fleet withdrew from the North Sea on 26 July. But for that circumstance not a single division could have been sent across the sea, and the war would have been over in a few months. Nor was the British Army unprepared for the task that had been allotted to it in anticipation. It was the judgment not only of our own but of Allied Staffs that an expeditionary force of six divisions would suffice to balance German superiority in the West; and that force, consisting of better material better trained than any other army in the field, was in its place in the line of battle hundreds of miles from its base within three weeks of the declaration of war. The real miscalculation was of the respective strength of France and Germany, and no one had foreseen that it would ultimately require three times the force that France could put in the field to liberate French soil from the German invader. The National Service League would have provided us with a large army;

but even its proposals were vitiated by their assumption that these forces were needed to do the navy's work of home-defence, and by the absence of provision for munitions, without which sending masses of men into battle was sending them to useless slaughter. Time was needed to remedy these miscalculations, but time was provided by our command of the sea, about which there had been no misjudgment and no lack of pre-vision. We made our mistakes before, and during the war, but neither Mr. Asquith's Governments nor that of his successor need fear comparison with those of our Allies or our enemies on that account; and it is merely a modest foible of the people, which has hardly lost a war for nearly four hundred years, to ascribe its escape to fortune, and to envy the prescience and the science which have lightened the path of its enemies to destruction.

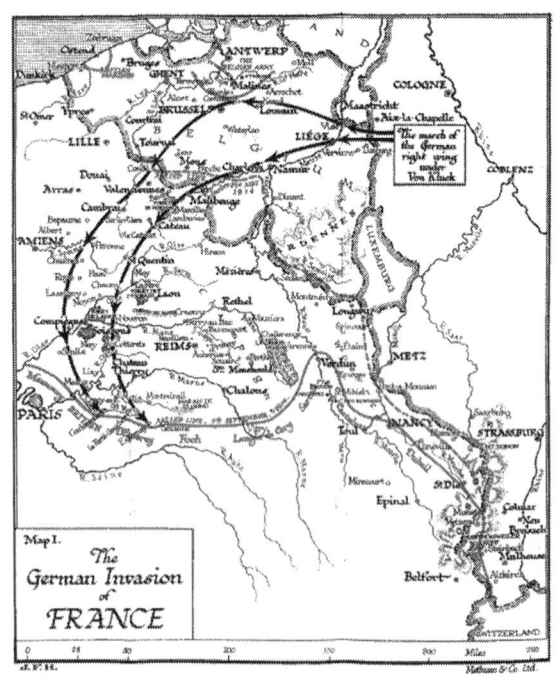

The German Invasion Of France

CHAPTER II

THE GERMAN INVASION

Germany began the war on the Western front before it was declared, and on 1-2 August German cavalry crossed the French frontier between Luxemburg and Switzerland at three points in the direction of Longwy, Lunéville, and Belfort. But these were only feints designed to prolong the delusion that Germany would attack on the only front legitimately open to warfare and to delay the reconstruction of the French defence required to meet the real offensive. The reasons for German strategy were conclusive to the General Staff, and they were frankly explained by Bethmann-Hollweg to the British ambassador. There was no time to lose if France was to be defeated before an effective Russian move, and time would be lost by a frontal attack. The best railways and roads from Berlin to Paris ran through Belgium; the Vosges protected more than half of the French frontier south of Luxemburg, Belfort defended the narrow gap between them and Switzerland, and even the wider thirty miles' gap between the northern slopes of the Vosges and Luxemburg was too narrow for the deployment of Germany's strength; the way was also barred by the elaborate fortifications of Verdun, Toul, and Nancy. Strategy pointed conclusively to the Belgian route, and its advantages were clinched by the fact that France was relying on the illusory scrap of paper. Her dispositions assumed an attack in Lorraine, and her northern fortifications round Lille, Maubeuge, and Hirson were feeble compared with those of Belfort, Toul, and Verdun. Given a rapid and easy march through Belgium, the German armies would turn the left flank of the French defence and cut it off from the capital. Hence the resistance of Belgium had a great military importance apart from its moral value. To its lasting honour the Belgian Government had scorned the German proposal for connivance even in the attractive form which would have limited the German use of Belgian territory to the eastern bank of the Meuse.

Haste and contempt for the Belgian Army, whose imperfect organization was due to a natural reliance on the neutrality which Germany had guaranteed, accounted for the first derangement of German plans. The invasion began towards Visé, near the Dutch frontier where the direct road from Aix to Brussels crosses the Meuse, but the main advance-guard followed the trunk railway from Berlin to Paris via Venders and Liège. It was, however, inadequately mobilized and equipped, and was only intended to clear away an opposition which was not expected to be serious. The Belgians fought more stubbornly than was anticipated; and aided by Brialmont's fortification of Liège, although his plans for defence were not properly executed, they held up the Germans for two days in front of the city. It was entered on 7 August, but its fall did not give the Germans the free passage they wanted; for the forts on the heights to the north commanded the railway, and the Germans contented themselves with bringing up their transport and 11 2 in. howitzers. Brialmont had not foreseen the explosive force of modern shells, and two days' bombardment on the 13th-15th reduced the remaining forts, in spite of their construction underground, to a mass of shell-holes with a handful of wounded or unconscious survivors. The last to be reduced was Fort Loncin, whose gallant commander, General Leman, was found poisoned and half-dead from suffocation. He had succeeded in delaying the German advance for a momentous week.

No more could be done with the forces at his disposal, and the German masses of infantry were pouring across the Meuse at Visé, towards Liège by Verviers, up the right bank of the Meuse towards Namur, and farther south through the Ardennes. The German cavalry which spread over the country east and north-east of Brussels and was sometimes repulsed by the Belgians, was merely a screen, which defective air-work failed to penetrate, and the frequent engagements were merely the brushes of outposts. Within a week from the fall of Fort Loncin half of Belgium was overrun and the real menace revealed. Belgium was powerless before the avalanche, and its only hope lay in France. But the French Army was still mobilizing on its northern front, and its incursions into Alsace and Lorraine did nothing to relieve the pressure. The Belgians had to fall back towards Antwerp, uncovering Brussels, which was occupied by the Germans on the 20th and mulcted in a preliminary levy of eight million pounds, and leaving to the fortifications of Namur the task of barring the German advance to the northern frontiers of France. Namur proved a broken reed. The troops which paraded through Brussels with impressive pomp and regularity were only a detail of the extreme right wing of the invading force; the mass was advancing along the north bank of the Meuse and overrunning the whole of Belgium south and east of the river. On the 15th an attempt to seize Dinant and the river crossing above Namur was repulsed by French artillery; but there was apparently no cavalry to follow up this success, and the Germans were allowed to bring up their heavy howitzers for the bombardment of Namur without disturbance. It began on the 20th, and, unsupported by the Allied assistance for which they looked, the Belgians were panic-stricken; on the 23rd the city and most of the forts were in German hands though two resisted until the 26th. The Germans had not, as at Liège, wasted their infantry in premature attacks, and with little loss to them, a fortress reputed impregnable had been captured, the greater part of the southern Belgian Army destroyed, and the provisional plan of French defence frustrated. The fall of Namur was the first resounding success of the Germans in the war.

Its loss was not redeemed by the French offensive in Alsace and Lorraine. On 7 August a weak French force advanced through the Belfort gap and, finding still weaker forces to oppose it, proceeded to occupy Altkirch and Mulhouse, while a proclamation by General Joffre announced the approaching liberation of the provinces torn from France in 1870. It was a feeble and ill-conceived effort to snatch a political advantage out of a forbidding military situation. German reinforcements swept up from Colmar and Neu Breisach, and on the both the French were back within a few miles of the frontier, leaving their sympathizers to the vengeance of their enemies. More legitimate though not more successful was the French thrust in Lorraine. It had other motives than the political: it would, if pushed home, menace the left of the German armies in Belgium and disturb their communications; and a smaller success would avert the danger of a German advance in Lorraine which would threaten the right of the French on the Meuse. Accordingly, Generals Pau and de Castelnau, commanding the armies of Alsace and Lorraine respectively, ordered a general advance on the 10th. At first it met with success: the chief passes of the Vosges from Mt. Donon on the north to the Belfort gap were seized; counter-thrusts by the Germans towards Spincourt and Blamont in the plain of Lorraine were parried; Thann was captured, Mulhouse was re-occupied, and the Germans looked like losing Alsace as far north as Colmar. German Lorraine seemed equally insecure, for on the 18th Castelnau's troops were in Saarburg cutting the rail and roads between Strassburg and Metz. The Germans, however, were not unprepared: their Fifth Army, under the Crown Prince Rupprecht of Bavaria, came down from Metz and fell upon the exposed French left, which was routed with great losses in guns and prisoners on the 21st. Not only did the invasion collapse, but the Bavarians pushed across the French frontier nearly as far as Toul and occupied Lunéville, compelling also a French retreat from the passes of the Vosges. General Pau had soon to follow suit and retire again from Mulhouse and all but the south-west corner of Alsace.

The operations in Alsace and Lorraine had dismally failed to discount the advance of the Germans through Belgium or even to impede the march of their centre through Luxemburg and the Ardennes. At the end of three weeks France was still in the throes of mobilization: the original scheme of defence along the Franco-German frontier had been upset by the German attack through Belgium; and second thoughts had fared little better at Namur. The shortest line of defence after the Germans had broken through at Liège was one running from Antwerp to Namur, and the shortest line is imperative for the weaker combatant. But the Germans were well across it when they entered Brussels, and with the fall of Namur the hinge upon which depended the defence of the northern frontier of France was broken. It was to an almost forlorn hope that the British Army was committed when it took its place on the left of the French northern armies at Mons to encounter for the first time since Waterloo the shock of a first-rate European force. But for its valour and the distraction caused by the Russian invasion of East Prussia, Paris and possibly the French armies might not have been saved.

It was a meagre force for so great a responsibility, but far from the "contemptible little army" it was falsely believed to have been called by the Kaiser. The men were all volunteers who had enlisted for seven years' service with the colours as against the three years' service of the Germans and the French; and on an average they had seen far more actual fighting than the Germans, who contemptuously dismissed this experience as colonial warfare. If in the science of tactics and strategy the British was inferior to the German Army, its marksmanship and individual steadiness were unequalled; and under anything like equal conditions British troops proved themselves the better men. But the conditions were never equal during the first two years of the war owing to the German superiority in numbers and in artillery; and there was a third cause of inequality due to the different military systems of the two countries. Universal service enabled Germany to select the ablest men—at least from the middle and upper classes—to officer and command her armies. In England before the war only an infinitesimal fraction of her youthful ability found its way into the army. Independent means and social position rather than brains were the common qualifications for a commission; and what there was to be said for such a system so long as fighting was mainly a matter of physical courage and individual leadership lost its validity when war became a matter of science and mechanical ingenuity. The fact that four of the six British army-commanders (Plumer, Byng, Rawlinson, Cavan) in the West at the end of the war were old Etonians, testifies to more things than their military skill; and it was a characteristic irony that from first to last the British armies should have been commanded by cavalry officers in a war in which cavalry played hardly any part.

The commander-in-chief was Sir John French, who had made his reputation as a cavalry leader in the Boer War and had been chief of the imperial staff since 1911. As inspector-general of the forces from 1907 to 1911 he had a good deal to do with Lord Haldane's reorganization of the British Army, and as chief of the staff he was largely responsible for the equipment of the Expeditionary Force and the agreement with the French Government with regard to its dimensions and the way in which it should be used. He was the obvious general to command it when it came to the test. With similar unanimity the popular voice approved of the appointment of Lord Kitchener as Secretary of State for War on 5 August. The Expeditionary Force consisted of three army corps, each comprising two divisions, and a cavalry division under Allenby. The First Army Corps was commanded by Sir Douglas Haig, the youngest lieutenant-general in the army, and the second by Sir James Grierson, its most accomplished student. Unhappily Grierson died suddenly soon after the landing, and he was succeeded by Sir H. Smith-Dorrien, who, like French, had made his name in South Africa. The Third Corps, under Sir W. Pulteney, came later into the field. The embarkation began on 7 August, less than three days after war had been declared, and the Government showed a sound confidence in our little-understood command of the sea when it risked the whole of our effective fighting force by sending it across the Channel to assist the French and thus abandoning the defence of British shores to the British Navy. By the 16th the transportation had been accomplished without a hitch or loss of any kind. It was an achievement which even domestic faction failed to belittle until time itself had effaced it from popular recollection.

From Boulogne and from other ports the troops were sent up to the wavering line of battle along the Franco-Belgian frontier. They came not to win a victory but to save an army from disaster. The mass of French reserves were in Lorraine or far away to the south, and the safety of the French line on the northern front had depended upon the assumed impregnability of Namur and an equally fallacious underestimate of the number of German troops in Belgium. Three French armies, the Third, the Fourth, and the Fifth, were strung along the frontier from Montmédy across the Meuse and the Sambre to a point north-west of Charleroi, where the British took up their position stretching through Binche, Mons, and along the canal from Mons to Condé. Far away to the south-west was a French Territorial corps in front of Arras, and at Maubeuge behind the British centre was a French cavalry corps under General Sordet. The French staff anticipated a defeat of the German attack on these lines and then a successful offensive, and military critics in England even wrote of the hopeless position of the Germans under Von Buelow and Von Kluck thrust far forward into a cul-de-sac in Belgium with the French on their left at Charleroi, the British on their right front at Mons, and the Belgians on their right rear before Antwerp. The German calculation was that the Belgians had been effectively masked by a corps detached north-westwards from Brussels, that the Duke of Württemberg and Von Hausen had troops enough to force the Meuse, drive in the French right, and threaten the centre at Charleroi, and that Von Buelow could cross the Sambre and Von Kluck encircle the British flank. The strength which the Germans developed in Belgium and the extension of their right wing are said to have been an afterthought due to the intervention of the British Expeditionary Force; but the original German plan required some such modification when the presence of British troops lengthened the line of French defence.

The first two army corps, under Haig to the right and Smith-Dorrien to the left, were in position on Saturday the 22nd hard at work throwing up entrenchments and clearing the ground of obstacles to their fire. That day was more eventful for the French, and it is not quite clear why they were not assisted by a British offensive on their left. On the right, the Third and Fourth French armies under Ruffey and Langle de Cary had advanced from the Meuse to attack the Germans across the Semois. They were severely checked and withdrew behind the Meuse, while an unsuspected army of Saxons under Von Hausen attacked the right flank of the Fifth French army under Lanrezac which lay along the Sambre with its right flank resting on the Meuse. The fall of Namur in the angle of the two rivers made Von Hausen's task comparatively easy, and the Fifth army, which was also attacked by Von Buelow in front, fell back in some confusion. A breach was thus made in the French line, and Von Hausen turned left to roll up the Fourth and Third armies of Langle de Cary and Ruffey; they, too, in their turn retreated in some haste, and the Germans were free to concentrate on the British. They had cleared their left and centre of danger, and Von Kluck was able on the 23rd not only to face our troops with superior forces in front, but to outflank them towards the west and bring Von Buelow down upon them from Charleroi on the east. He had at least four army corps with which to crush the British two, and our 75,000 men were spread out on a line of twenty-five miles thinner far than the French line just broken at Charleroi. Finally, owing to defective staff-work and the confusion of the French retreat, they were left in utter ignorance of what had happened, and faced the German attack as if they were part of one unbroken front instead of being a fragment round which the tide of battle surged, and under the impression conveyed to them on their arrival at the scene of action that their opponents numbered little more than one or at most two army corps.

Fighting began at 12.40 p.m. on Sunday the 23rd with a bombardment from between five and six hundred German guns along the whole twenty-five miles of front. It did surprisingly little damage in spite of the spotting by German aeroplanes; and when the German infantry came forward in massed formation, they discovered that their shelling had had no effect upon the moral of our troops or the accuracy of their rifle-fire. The Germans fought, of course, with obstinate courage and advanced again and again into the murderous fire of our rifles and machine guns and against occasional bayonet charges. But their own shooting went to pieces under the stress, and the frontal attack was a failure. Success there could not, however, ward off Von Buelow's threat to our right flank, and under the converging pressure Binche and then Mons itself had to be evacuated. But it was the long-delayed news of the French defeat and withdrawal on the whole of the rest of the line, coupled with more accurate information about the size of the German force, that determined the abandonment of the British position. Sir John French had to hold on till nightfall, but orders were given to prepare the way for retreat. The weary troops were to have a few hours' rest and start at daybreak. Their retreat was covered by a counter-attack soon after dawn by the First Division on the right which suggested to the Germans that we had been strongly reinforced and intended an offensive. Meanwhile Smith-Dorrien moved back five miles from the Canal, and then stood to protect the withdrawal of the First Division after its feint attack. It was a heavy task, and the 9th Lancers suffered severely in an attempt to hold up the Germans at Audregnies. But by Monday afternoon Haig's First Army Corps was back on the line between Maubeuge and Bavai, and Smith-Dorrien fell into line from Bavai westwards to Bry.

The design was to offer a second battle in this position, and entrenchments were begun. The fortress of Maubeuge and the Sambre gave some protection to the British right, but the Sambre was only of use in front if the Meuse was held by the French on the right and Von Kluck could not outflank on the left. Neither of these conditions was fulfilled: Von Kluck had seized Tournai and captured the whole of the French Territorial brigade which attempted to defend it, while the Meuse had been forced and the three French armies were in full retreat. A battle on the Maubeuge-Bry line would invite an encirclement from which the British had barely escaped at Mons, and the retreat was reluctantly continued to Le Cateau. Marching, the First Army Corps along the east of the Forest of Mormal and the Second along the west, our troops reached at nightfall on the 25th a line running from Maroilles through Landrecies and Le Cateau to Serainvilliers near Cambrai; but they had little rest. About 10 p.m., amid rain and darkness, the Germans got into Landrecies. In the fierce hand-to-hand struggle which ensued, the individual resourcefulness of our men gave them the advantage, and the Germans were driven out by detachments of the Grenadier, Coldstream, and 1st Irish Guards. They were simultaneously repulsed at Maroilles with some French assistance; but daybreak saw a third and more powerful attack delivered on Le Cateau. Sir John French had told Smith-Dorrien the night before that he was risking a second Sedan by a stand. But Smith-Dorrien thought he had no option. For eight hours on the 26th his men, reinforced by Snow's Division, but outnumbered in guns by nearly four to one, held their own, until another envelopment was threatened by Von Kluck. Fortunately the struggle had apparently exhausted the Germans; Sordet's cavalry had ridden across Smith-Dorrien's front and protected his left from envelopment; and the remnants of the three divisions were able to withdraw. The retreat was harrowing enough, and the 1st Gordons, missing their way in the dark, fell into the hands of the Germans and were all killed, wounded, or taken prisoners. But Le Cateau had taken the sting out of the German pursuit, and touch was at last regained with French forces to the east, with a newly-formed corps under D'Amade to the west, and with a Sixth French army which Maunoury was collecting on the Somme. On the evening of Friday the 28th Smith-Dorrien reached the Oise between Chauny and Noyon and Haig at La Fère. The First Army Corps had marched by Guise; the loss of a detachment of Munsters by misadventure early on the 27th was redeemed by the defeat on the 28th of two German columns by two brigades of Allenby's cavalry led by Gough and Chetwode. That night the Expeditionary Force had its first real sleep since Sunday, and next day there were no marching orders.

The British Army had saved itself and a good deal else by its courage, skill, and, above all, its endurance. But there was much that was lost in men, material, and ground. The fortification of the French frontier south and west of Mons was obsolete, and the country had been denuded of troops save a few Territorials in the process of mobilization. Maubeuge was the only fortress that made a stand, and Uhlans swept across Belgium as far as the Lys and down upon Lille and Arras with the object of cutting communications between the British Army and its bases at Boulogne and Dieppe. Some resistance was offered at Bapaume, where the arrival of a British detachment delayed the German advance until Amiens had been evacuated and the rolling stock removed. But the threat was sufficiently serious to induce Sir John French to move his base as far south as St. Nazaire at the mouth of the Loire, and the Germans could, had they been so minded, have occupied the Channel ports as far as the Seine. But they were not calculating on a long war or a serious contest with British forces for the control of Flanders, and their object was to destroy the French armies and dictate a peace at Paris before the autumn leaves began to fall.

They seemed to be making excellent progress towards that end. Sir J. French, indeed, took a sombre view of our losses at Le Cateau, and apparently it needed a visitation from Lord Kitchener on 1st September to retain the British Army in co-operation with the French. The fall of Namur, the battles of Charleroi and Mons, and the defeat of the French on the Semois were followed by the rout of Ruffey's and Langle's armies on the Meuse. They stretched north-westwards from Montmédy by way of Sedan and Mezières down the Meuse towards Dinant and Namur. But their left flank had been turned by Von Hausen's victory and the fall of Namur; and on the 27th Von Hausen, wheeling to his left, rolled up the French left wing while the Duke of Württemberg and the Crown Prince attacked all along the front. Ruffey had to seek safety in the Argonne, while Langle's army made for Rethel on the Aisne. On the 28th Longwy, the last French fortress north of Verdun, capitulated after a stout resistance. The defence of the frontier had collapsed, and the hopes that were entertained of resistance along the upper Aisne and thence by Laon and La Fère towards St. Quentin, proved delusive. Lanrezac's Fifth army turned on the 29th between Vervins and Ribemont, and near Guise inflicted on the Germans the most serious check to their advance. This reaction was not helped by the British retreat on Lanrezac's left, and its principal value was to protect that withdrawal. Nor was it better supported on the right. The Third and Fourth French armies were too severely hustled in their retreat to make a stand, and the reserves were still far away to the south. On the 28th-29th the Aisne was forced at Rethel, and Reims and Chalons were abandoned to the enemy; and La Fère and Laon followed on the 30th.

The British fell back from the Aisne and the Oise through the forests of Villers-Cotterets and Compiègne towards the Marne. At Néry on 1 September a battery of Royal Horse Artillery was almost wiped out, and the guns were only saved by a gallant cavalry charge of the 1st Brigade; and on the same day a hard rearguard defence had to be fought by the 4th Guards Brigade. On the 3rd they reached the Marne, but it too was abandoned farther east without resistance, and on the 5th the Expeditionary Force was concentrated behind the Grand Morin. A retreat, upon the successful conduct of which depended the existence of the Force, the security of France, and the cause of the Entente, had been successfully accomplished by the skill of its commanders and still more by the fortitude and unquenchable spirit of the men. The French, too, showed a steadiness in misfortune for which their enemies had not looked; their reverses had been more severe, and their preparation less complete than our own, and a high morale was required for armies to react against such a run of ill-success with the effectiveness that was presently displayed upon the Marne.

A public on both sides of the Channel which was unfamiliar with the elements of military science and history, looked, as soon as it was allowed to learn the facts about the German advance, for the investment of Paris and regarded the French capital as the objective of the German invasion. But Napoleon's maxim that fortresses are captured on the field of battle was even truer in 1914 than it was a century earlier; for only the dispersal of the enemy enables an army to bring up the heavy artillery needed to batter down modern fortifications, and the great war saw no sieges worth the name because, the armies being once driven off, no forts could stand prolonged bombardment by the artillery which followed in the victor's train. The cities that suffered were not isolated units, they were merely knotty points in the lines of battle, and there could be no siege of Paris so long as Joffre's armies kept in line along the Marne or anywhere in contact with the capital. There was therefore no change of plan and no mystery when Von Kluck's right veered in the direction of its advance from south-west to south and then south-east. It was both avoiding an obstacle and pursuing its original design of outflanking the Entente's left. Not that Paris was without its strategic value. It and the line of the Seine impeded the encirclement, offered a nucleus of resistance, and provided a screen behind which could be organized a blow against the right flank of the deflected German march. Still, there was no certainty that Joffre could hold the Marne, and the French Government took the somewhat alarming precaution of removing to Bordeaux.

The presence of the British on the French left, the spectacular threat to Paris, and the comparative proximity of these operations to our own shores have possibly led to too great an emphasis being placed upon Von Kluck's attempt to outflank the left, or at least to too little weight being attached to the German effort to turn the right in Lorraine. The Crown Prince was in front of Verdun and the Kaiser himself went to stimulate the Bavarians at Lunéville and Nancy, and it was not the imperial habit to bestow the light of the imperial countenance upon scenes of secondary importance. Lunéville had been occupied on the 22nd after the French failure on the Saar, and on the 23rd fighting began for the Grand Couronné de Nancy defended by Castelnau. The line of battle stretched from St. Dié to Pont-á-Mousson; but although the fiercest attack was still to come, the German thrust had been decisively checked at Mirecourt before Joffre determined to stand on the Marne. At last the French seemed to have a security on their right flank, the lack of which had proved fatal at Charleroi and on the Meuse. Paris on the one wing and Nancy on the other forbade the threat of encirclement which had hitherto compelled retreat; and the French armies were also at last in touch with their reserves.

There were other elements in the situation to encourage resistance The momentum of the German rush was somewhat spent in its rapidity, and the Germans were to illustrate the defect in their own maxim that the essence of war is violence; for violence is not the same as force and often wastes it. Moreover, the Russian invasion of East Prussia, if it did not actually compel the transference of divisions from France to the Eastern front, diverted thither reserves which might otherwise have appeared on the Marne or released the troops detained until 7 September by the siege of Maubeuge. Assuredly Joffre seized the right moment when on the 4th he decided to strike his blow. Two new armies of reserves had come into line, Foch's Ninth and Maunoury's Sixth; and two old armies had new commanders, the Third with Sarrail instead of Ruffey and the Fifth with Franchet d'Esperey instead of Lanrezac. In the east Castelnau and Sarrail stood almost back to back along the eastern and western heights of the Meuse above Verdun. On Sarrail's left was Langle's Fourth army behind Vitry, and the line was continued westwards by Foch behind Sezanne and the marshes of St. Gond. Next came D'Esperey's Fifth at La Ferté-Gaucher, and cavalry linked his left with the British guarded by the Crecy forest. Thence north-westward stretched across the Paris front the new Sixth army of Maunoury.

As early as 31 August Von Kluck had turned south-east at a right angle to his south-western march from Brussels to Amiens; but he had not thereby replaced his enveloping design by a stroke at Joffre's centre. For he thought he had disposed of the British at Le Cateau and of Maunoury on the Somme, and that D'Esperey's Fifth had thus become the flank of Joffre's forces. He was merely curving his claws to grip, and by the night of the 5th he had crossed the Marne, the Petit Morin, and the Grand Morin, and his patrols had reached the Seine. It was a brief and solitary glimpse of the river on which stood the capital of France. The battle began, like that of Mons, on a Sunday, the 6th of September reached its climax on the 9th, and was over by the 12th, The fighting extended in a curved line from Meaux, which is almost a suburb of Paris, to Lunéville, which is almost on the German frontier; and Joffre hoped that this line was too strong to be broken, and could be gradually drawn tighter until the head of the German invasion was squeezed out of the cul-de-sac into which, in the German anxiety for a prompt decision, it had been thrust. The German object, of course, was, as soon as Von Kluck discovered that Maunoury's new and the British returning armies forbade the enveloping plan, to break the line where it bent the most, that is, towards the south-east, and the weight of attack was thrown against Foch and Langle in Champagne. The business of those two generals was to stand fast while the right flank of the Germans was exposed to the counter-offensive of Maunoury and the British.

Von Kluck had committed the error of underrating his foes, and assuming that they had been broken beyond the chance of reaction; for to march across the front of an army that is still able to strike is inviting disaster, and Joffre had at last been able to shift his weight from east to west to cope with Von Kluck's unexpected attack through Belgium. Maunoury's army debouched from Meaux and began fighting its way to the Ourcq, a little river which runs southwards into the Marne at Lizy, while the British emerged from the Crecy forest and drove the Germans back to the Grand Morin. D'Esperey made headway against the bulk of Von Kluck's army between La Ferté-Gaucher and Esternay, while Foch held his own against Von Buelow and Von Hausen's right, and Langle against the Duke of Württemberg. Sarrail's Third army had, however, to give a little ground along the Meuse. The morrow's tale was similar: most progress was made by the British, who drove the Germans across the Grand Morin at Coulommiers, and thus enabled D'Esperey to do the like with Von Kluck's centre. On the 8th, however, Maunoury was hard pressed by Von Kluck's desperate efforts to deal with this sudden danger; but reinforcements poured out from Paris, the British gained the Petit Morin from Trilport to La Trétoire, while D'Esperey carried victory farther east and captured Montmirail. By 11 a.m. on the 9th Von Kluck's army was ordered to retreat, thus exposing Von Buelow's right, and giving Foch his opportunity for the decisive stroke of the battle.

It consisted of two blows, right and left, and both came off late on the 9th. Maunoury's counter-attack on the left had compelled the Germans to weaken their centre. Not only was Von Buelow's right exposed, but a gap had been left between his left and Von Hausen's right, possibly for troops which were detained at Maubeuge or had been diverted to East Prussia. Nor was this all, for his centre was bogged in the famous marshes of St. Gond. Foch struck hard at Von Buelow's centre, right, and left, and by the morning of the 10th he had smashed the keystone of the German arch. Meanwhile, on the 9th Maunoury had cleared the Germans from the Ourcq, the British had crossed the Marne at Chângis, and reached it at Château-Thierry, and D'Esperey farther east. Von Kluck now received considerable reinforcements which

Von Buelow needed more, and the latter's rapid retreat made even reinforcements useless for holding the Ourcq. It was equally fatal to success against Langle and Sarrail, and on the 10th the German retreat became general. By the end of the week the Germans were back on a line running nearly due east from a point on the Oise behind Compiègne to the Aisne, along it to Berry-au-Bac, and thence across Champagne and the Argonne to Verdun. They had failed in Lorraine as well, where the climax of their attack was from the 6th to the 9th. Castelnau then took the offensive, and by the 12th had driven the Bavarians from before Nancy beyond the Meurthe, and out of Lunéville and St. Dié.

The German right had fallen back thirty-five miles and the centre nearly fifty; but the retreat was not a rout, and the losses in guns and prisoners were meagre. The first battle of the Marne was important by reason of what it prevented the Germans from doing, rather than by reason of what the Allies achieved, and they had to wait nearly four years for that precipitate evacuation of France which it was hoped would follow upon the German repulse from the Marne in September 1914. Nevertheless it was one of the decisive battles and turning-points of the war. The German surprise, so long and so carefully prepared, had failed, and the knockout blow had been parried. The Allied victory had not decided how the war would end, but it had decided that the war would be long—a test of endurance rather than of generalship, a struggle of peoples and a conflict of principles rather than duel between professional armies. There would be time for peaceful and even unarmed nations to gird themselves in defence; and the cause of democracy would not go down because military autocrats had thought to dispose of France before her allies could effectively intervene.

CHAPTER III

RUSSIA MOVES

The first month of the war in the West had coincided more nearly with German plans than with Entente hopes, but both Germany and the Western Allies agreed in miscalculating Russia. The great Moltke had remarked early in his career that Russia had a habit of appearing too late on the field and then coming too strong. The war was to prove that to be a fault of democracy rather than of autocrats, and Russia intervened with an unexpected promptitude which was to be followed in time by an equally unexpected collapse. The forecasting of the course of wars is commonly left to military experts, and military experts commonly err through ignoring the moral and political factors which determine the weight and distribution of military forces. The soldier, so far as he looks behind armies at all, only looks to the numbers from which those armies may be recruited, and pays scant regard to the political, moral, social, and economic conditions which may make havoc of armies, evoke them where they do not exist, or transfer them to unforeseen scales in the military balance. Russia appeared to the strategist as a vast reservoir of food for powder which would take time to mobilize, but prove almost irresistible if it were given time. Both these calculations proved fallacious, and still less was it foreseen that the reservoir would revolt. The first misjudgment deranged the German plans, the second those of the Allies, while the third upset the minds of the world.

The outbreak of war found Russia with a peace-strength of over a million men, a war-strength of four millions, and reserves which were limited not by her population but by her capacity for transport, organization, and production of munitions. Her Prussian frontiers were guarded by no natural defences, but neither were Prussia's. Nature, it has been said, did not foresee Prussia; Prussia is the work of men's hands. Nor had Nature foreseen Russia, and men's hands had not made up the deficiency. Mechanical means had remedied the natural defects of Prussia's frontier, but not those of the Russian; and Russia's defence consisted mainly in distance, mud, and lack of communications. The value of these varied, of course, with the seasons, and the motor-transport, which atoned to some extent for the lack of railways, told in favour of German science and industry, and against the backward Russians. Apart from the absence of natural defences, the Russian frontier had been artificially drawn so as to make her Polish province an indefensible salient, though properly organized it would have been an almost intolerable threat alike to East Prussia and to Austrian Galicia. But for her preoccupation in the West, Germany could have conquered Poland in a fortnight, and Russian plans, indeed, contemplated a withdrawal as far as the line of Brest-Litovsk. As it was, the German offensive in Belgium and France left the defence of Prussia to the chances of an Austrian offensive against Lublin, a containing army of some 200,000 first-line and 300,000 second-line troops, and the delays in Russian mobilization.

Two of these proved to be broken reeds. Russian troops were almost as prompt in invading East Prussia as German troops in crossing the frontiers of France and Belgium, and by the end of the first week in August a flight to Berlin had begun. The shortest way from the Russian frontier to Berlin was by Posen, and it lay through a country peopled with Poles who were bitterly hostile to their German masters. But it was impossible to exploit these advantages at the expense of deepening the Polish salient with its already too narrow base, and the flanks in East Prussia and Galicia had first to be cleared. Under the supreme command of the Grand Duke Nicholas, who in spite of his rank was a competent professional soldier, and the more immediate direction of Rennenkampf, one of the few Russian officers to emerge with enchanced reputation from the Japanese War, the Russians proceed to concentrate on East Prussia (see Map). On the east Gumbinnen was captured after a battle on the 20th, and the important junction of Insterburg occupied by Rennenkampf, while on the south Samsonov on the 21st turned the German right, threatened Allenstein and drove the fugitives, as Rennenkampf had done, into the lines of Königsberg. East Prussia lay at Russia's feet, and something like a panic alarmed Berlin. The Teutonic cause was faring even worse in Galicia and Poland. Austria had a million troops in Galicia, but her offensive under Dankl towards Lublin only produced a strategic Russia retirement, while Ruszky and Brussilov overran the eastern borders and menaced Lemberg.

Fortunately for the Germans their own right hand proved a stronger defence. The incompetent General von François, who had been driven into Königsberg, was superseded by Hindenburg, a retired veteran of nearly seventy, whose military career had made so slight an impression on the German mind that his name was not even included in the German "Who's Who." Nevertheless he had commanded corps on the Prussian frontier, and even after his retirement made the study of its defence his hobby. He knew every yard of the intricate mixture of land and water which made up the district of the Masurian Lakes, and had, unfortunately for Russia, defeated a German financial scheme for draining the country and turning it into land over which an invader could safely march. Within five days of Samsonov's victory, Hindenburg, taking advantage of the magnificent system of German strategic railways, had collected some 150,000 men from the fortresses on the Vistula and concentrated them on a strong position stretching from near Allenstein south-west towards Soldau, his left resting on the railway from Eylau to Insterburg and his right on that from Eylau to Warsaw. In front of him were marshes with the ways through which he was, but Samsonov was not, familiar; and the railways enabled him to threaten either of the enemy's flanks.

Samsonov was practically isolated. Rightly ignoring the strong defences of Königsberg but wrongly getting out of touch with Rennenkampf, he had pushed on, thinking there could be no serious resistance east of the Vistula and hoping to seize the bridge at Graudenz. Hindenburg made a feint on his right, but pushed his real outflanking movement along the railway on his left. But the feint was enough to outflank Samsonov's left and close the retreat towards Warsaw. It also diverted his reserves from his centre and from his right, which on the 27th was cut off from a possible junction with Rennenkampf. A gallant attempt by Gourko to relieve him on the 30th came too late. The only exit was along a narrow strip of land between the marshes leading to Ortelsburg, and here between the 28th and the 31st the Russian forces were almost annihilated. Less than a third escaped, and the loss of guns was even greater. Over eighty thousand prisoners were taken, and the Germans who had missed their Sedan in the West secured a passable imitation in the East. Samsonov perished in the retreat. The Russian censorship suppressed the news, and what was allowed to come through from Germany was treated in Entente countries as a German lie. For more than a fortnight little was known of a victory which, save for Allenby's four years later, was the completest in the war. The relief in Berlin was immense; Hindenburg became the popular idol, Field-Marshal, and Generalissimo of the Teutonic armies in the East; and a little village, which lay behind Hindenburg's centre, was selected to give its name to the battle and to commemorate a national revenge for that defeat at Tannenberg five centuries before when the Slavonic kingdom of Poland had broken the power of the Teutonic Order in Prussia.

Russia, however, was a different power from the Teutonic Order, and Austrian generals were not Hindenburgs; Ruszky and Brussilov, too, were better leaders than Samsonov, and though Rennenkampf had to evacuate East Prussia before Hindenburg's advance, the Austrians were driven like chaff before their enemies in Galicia. The object of Russian strategy was to straighten the serpentine line of the frontier for military purposes. Hence, while pushing forward her wings in East Prussia and Galicia, she would merely stand on guard or withdraw in the Polish centre, and the Germans encountered little opposition when they seized Czenstochowa and Kalisch and pushed towards the Warta, or the Austrians when they advanced by Zamosc towards the Bug. The advance in East Prussia was also represented as a chivalrous attempt to reduce the pressure in France by a threat to Berlin, and the real Russian effort was the sweep westwards from the eastern Galician frontier, where the Second Russian army under Ruszky and the Third farther south under Brussilov were already threatening the envelopment of Lemberg (or Lwow[1]) and the Austrians under Von Auffenberg. Ruszky, formerly like Foch a professor in a military academy, was perhaps the most scientific of Russian generals;

---

1   Pronounced and sometimes spelt Lvoff.

Brussilov showed his strategy two years later at Luck;[2] and Radko Dmitrieff was a Bulgarian general, now in Russian service, who in the Balkan wars had won the battle of Kirk Kilisse and helped to win that of Lule-Burgas. There was not an abler trio in any field of the war.

By the end of August Brussilov had captured Tarnopol and Halicz and forced the successive rivers which guarded the right flank of Lemberg and Von Auffenberg's forces and protected their communications with the Carpathian passes; and on 1 September the battle for the capital of eastern Galicia began. It lasted for nearly three days, and was almost as decisive as that of Tannenberg. Brussilov's outflanking movement was continued with success, but the coup de grâce was given here, as at Charleroi and the Marne, by isolating a central group and thus breaking the line. Thrusting forward his right, Ruszky outflanked Lemberg and interposed between Von Auffenberg and the Austrian army in Poland. On the 3rd Lemberg was evacuated, and the retreat, which was for a time protected by the entrenched camp at Grodek, gradually became more disorderly. Over 70,000 prisoners were taken, mostly, no doubt, Czecho-Slovaks and Jugo-Slavs who had more sympathy with the Russians than with their Teutonic masters, and masses of machine guns and artillery. The victory was brilliantly and promptly followed up. While Brussilov pressed on to Stryj and the Carpathians, Ruszky and Dmitrieff beat Von Auffenberg again at Rawa Ruska near the frontier on the 10th, and Ivanoff, who had taken command in Poland, drove Dankl and the Archduke Joseph Ferdinand from the line they held between Lublin and the borders. The whole of the Austrian forces fell back behind the Vistula and the San, Von Auffenberg finding safety in Przemysl, and others a more temporary refuge at Jaroslav, while the van of the retreating army did not stop short of Cracow. The German detachments in Poland had to conform, and by the middle of September Poland had been cleared as far as the Warta, and Galicia was defenceless, save for invested Przemysl, as far south as the Carpathians and as far west as the Dunajec. The days of the Marne were even more sombre for the Central Empires on the Vistula and the San.

---

2   Pronounced Lutsk: the Slavonic "c" = "ts" "cz" = "ch" and "sz" = "sh."

Their gloom was relieved by the halo which shone round Hindenburg's head. Rennenkampf was gone and all the faculties of the University of Königsberg conferred degrees on the victor to celebrate its escape. Reinforcements were sent to the frontier, and on 7 September Russia was invaded. The object of the offensive is not clear except on the assumption that Hindenburg's strategic acumen was defective, and that he thought he could turn the Russian right by an advance across the Niemen. But the difficulties were insuperable and the distances were vast. Even if he got to Kovno it would need far greater forces than he possessed to cover and control the illimitable land beyond; and between him and success lay swamps more extensive then the Masurian Lakes and the heavily fortified line of the Narew. He was, indeed, in his turn falling into Samsonov's error, and seems to have been saved from his fate mainly by the prematurely successful Russian defence. He was allowed to reach the Niemen at various points between Kovno and Grodno, but was unhappily prevented from committing his fortunes to the eastern bank by the Russian artillery, which repeatedly destroyed his pontoons as soon as they were constructed. Lower down on his right an attempt on the fortress of Ossowiec proved equally futile, because the Germans could find no ground within range solid enough to bear the weight of their artillery. The inevitable retreat began on the 27th, and it was sadly harassed by the pursuing Russians, especially in the forest of Augustowo, where Rennenkampf claimed to have inflicted losses amounting to 60,000 men in killed, prisoners, and wounded. By 1 October the Russian cavalry was again across the German frontier, and Hindenburg was called south to attempt in Poland to frustrate the Russian advance on Cracow which his turning movement in the north had failed to check.

The call was urgent, for the conquest of Galicia portended disaster to the Central Empires. Cracow was a key both to Berlin and Vienna; its possession would turn the Oder and open the door to Silesia, which was hardly less vital to Germany than Westphalia as a mining and manufacturing district. It would also give access to Vienna and facilitate the separation of Hungary, and all that that meant in the Balkans, from the Teutonic alliance. Even without the loss of Cracow, that of the rest of Galicia was serious enough; her oil-wells were the main sources of the German supply of petroleum, and her Slav population, once assured of the solidity of Russian success, would throw off its allegiance to the Hapsburgs and entice the Czecho-Slovaks on its borders to do the same. These prospects were not visionary in September 1914. Jaroslav fell on the 23rd and Przemysl was invested. Russian cavalry rode through the Carpathian passes into the Hungarian plain, and west of the San patrols penetrated within a hundred miles of Cracow. In her own interests as well as in those of her ally, Germany was compelled to throw more of her weight against the Russian front. The German and Austrian commands were unified under Hindenburg, and having failed on the north he now tried to stop the Russians by a blow at their centre in Poland. Here Ruszky was now in command, while Ivanoff with Brussilov and Dmitrieff as his two lieutenants controlled the armies in Galicia.

Like every German general Hindenburg believed in the offensive being the best form of defence, and like all Germans in the advantage of waging war in the enemy's country. His plan of attack was a concentric advance on Warsaw along the three railway lines leading from Thorn, Kalisch, and Czenstochowa, combined with an effort to cross the Vistula at Josefow while the Austrians kept step in Galicia, relieved Przemysl, and recovered Lemberg. There was even a movement southwards from East Prussia which captured Mlawa, but it was only a raid which did not hamper the Grand Duke's contemplated counter-offensive. Warsaw had obvious attractions; Josefow was selected because it was far from Russia's railway lines but near to Ostrowiec, the terminus of a line which led from the German frontier; and the object of crossing the Vistula was to take in the rear the great fortress of Ivangorod lower down, and then to get behind Warsaw. The Grand Duke had divined these intentions, while he concealed his own by misleading the Germans into a belief that he proposed abandoning the Polish salient and retiring on Brest. His real plan was to stand on the east bank of the Vistula save for the defence of Warsaw which lies upon the west, and to counter-attack round the north of the German left wing under the guns of the great fortress of Novo Georgievsk. Rennenkampf was brought down to command this movement, while Ruszky took charge of the defence at Josefow.

On 10 October Hindenburg's centre moved out from Lodz and on the 15th the battle was joined all along the Vistula. Warsaw was vigorously defended by Siberian and Caucasian troops, aided by Japanese guns. The battle raged from the 16th to the 19th, when the planned surprise from Novo Georgievsk forced back the German left and threatened the centre before Warsaw. Ruszky was still more successful with his stratagem at Josefow. The Germans were suffered to construct their pontoons, cross the river, and make for the railway between Warsaw and Lublin. Then on the 21st the Russians came down upon them with a bayonet charge, and not a man is said to have escaped across the river. Next day the Russians also crossed at Novo Alexandria lower down, and a general attack drove the Germans back to Radom on the 25th and thence from Kielce on 3 November. Threatened by Rennenkampf on the north and Ruszky on the south, the German centre had to abandon Skierniewíce, Lowicz, and then Lodz, destroying every vestige of communication as they withdrew and lavishly sacrificing men in rearguard actions to protect their stores and their equipment.

Ironically enough the chief success of Hindenburg's offensive was achieved by the Austrian subordinates he had come to help. Ivanoff was a bad substitute for Ruszky, and Dankl temporarily retrieved the reputation he had lost the previous month. Jaroslav was recovered, Przemysl was relieved and abundantly revictualled for a second and a longer siege, and an attack on Sambor bade fair to put the Austrians once more in Lemberg. But the German defeat in Poland compelled an Austrian retreat in Galicia. Przemysl was reinvested and the Russians resumed their march with quickened pace on Cracow. This time they threatened it first from the north of the Vistula, and on 9 November their cavalry, pursuing the Germans, was at Miechow, only twenty miles from Cracow. Moving more slowly through Galicia while Brussilov occupied the Carpathian passes, Dmitrieff pushed his cavalry into Wielitza south-east of the city on 6 December, and on the 8th he fought a successful action in its outskirts. Farther north the Cossacks had occupied Nieszawa, a few miles from Thorn, on 9 November, and on the following day a Russian raid across the Silesian frontier cut the German railway from Posen to Cracow. It was high time that the Germans turned the weight of their offensive from the Flanders front and the Channel ports to parrying the Russian menace on their East.

Austria was in no happier case. Her invasion of Serbia which had opened the flood-gates of war had been almost submerged in the torrent, and the punitive expedition she had planned had brought punishment mainly upon herself, and that not merely at the hands of Serbia's powerful patron, but at those of the little people who were to be chastised. The early fighting was of a desultory character, and Austria's two first-line corps having been withdrawn to meet the Russians, the Serbs and Montenegrins made a combined effort on 12 August to invade Bosnia and capture Serajevo. No great progress was made, and on the 16th the Austrians retaliated with the capture of Shabatz in the north-west corner of Serbia. But next day the Serbs routed a large Austrian force in the neighbourhood, and the Crown Prince Alexander followed up this victory by another on the 18th against the Austrians on the Jadar, who were seeking, in cooperation with those at Shabatz, to cut the Serbs off from their base. The result was that by the 24th the Austrians were practically cleared out of the country, and Vienna announced that the punitive expedition, which had cost 40,000 casualties and fifty guns, had accomplished its object.

A second attempt to achieve it was, however, provoked by the invasion of Bosnia with which the Serbs had supplemented their victory, and by their capture of Semlin in order to stop the Austrian bombardment of Belgrade. On 8 September the Austrians launched an attack across the Drina which forms the boundary between Serbia and Bosnia, and the battle raged till the 17th. Again the Serbs were victorious, though they made no impression on Serajevo and the Austrians retained a foothold on the eastern bank of the Drina; and for six weeks Serbia was left in comparative peace. But at the end of October the entrance of Turkey into the war and the relief afforded to Austria's troops farther north by the increasing activity of Germany in Poland and Galicia encouraged another effort; and under General Potiorek the Austrians began a more ambitious campaign. The Serbian frontier constituted a sharp salient which was indefensible against a superior force, and the Austrians exploited this advantage by extending their front of attack from Semendria on the Danube right round to Ushitza beyond the Drina. Their object was to envelop the Serbs and seize, firstly, Valievo, their advanced base, secondly, Kraguievatz the Serbian arsenal, and, finally, Nish, to which the Serbian Court and Government had withdrawn.

The only chance the Serbs had of success was to shorten their line by withdrawing to the semicircular mountain ridge which lies south and south-east of Valievo, and even so their prospects were gloomy. Two wars had already depleted Serbia's manhood and her munitions, and her numbers were sadly inferior to the Austrians. But individually her troops were far better fighters than their opponents, and the Crown Prince, Marshal Putnik, and General Míshitch, the commander of the 1st Serbian Army, quite outclassed Potiorek in tactics, strategy, and knowledge of the terrain. By 10 November the Austrians were in Valievo, and Potiorek was inclined to rest on his laurels. For a fatal fortnight he did nothing, and even detached three of his corps to serve in the Carpathians against the Russians who were there doing Serbia the service they had done in East Prussia to the Allies on the Marne. In that interval Greek and other munitions were conveyed in spite of Bulgar and Turkish intervention to the hard-pressed Serbians; King Peter, old, blind, and deaf, came from Nish to make a stirring appeal to his troops; and when on 1-3 December Potiorek once more advanced to the ridges of Rudnik and Maljen, he encountered a re-munitioned army, skilfully posted in strong positions and pledged to death or victory. Victory was its guerdon all along the line; the Austrian left centre and centre were broken on the 5th; at night their right was shattered near Ushitza; and on the morrow the whole army was in retreat, which soon became a rout. There were 80,000 casualties before, on the 15th, the fugitives were back in their own land across the Drina, the Danube, and the Save, leaving Belgrade once more in the hands of the heroic Serbs.

Austria had, however, acquired a strange new friend in the Turk, who had thrice besieged Vienna, and with whom she had waged an intermittent warfare of the Crescent and the Cross for some four centuries; and the blood-stained hand of Turkey was stretched out to save its "natural allies"—to quote Bernhardi—at Buda-Pesth and Potsdam. There was, indeed, a bond of sympathy, for in each of the enemy capitals a ruling caste oppressed one or more subject nationalities. Prussia stood for the Junker domination of the German tribes; Austria, for Teutonic government of Czechs, Slovaks, and Poles; Hungary, for Magyar dictation to Jugo-Slavs and Rumanes; and Turkey, for the exploitation or extermination of Armenians, Greeks, and Arabs. The Young Turk, who had dispossessed Abdul Hamid in 1908, only differed from the Old in being more efficient and less of a gentleman, and in seeking his inspiration from Krupp's guns and Treitschke's philosophy instead of from the Koran. He was a Turk without the Turk's excuse, and the adventurer Enver, who inaugurated the rule of the Committee of Union and Progress by assassinating his rivals, was willing to give Germany control of the Berlin-Baghdad route in return for a free hand with the subject nationalities of the Ottoman Empire. Russia was the common obstacle to both ambitions; but, Russia finally crippled, the Balkan States would become Turco-Teutonic provinces, and the Near East a German avenue into Asia, while Egypt might be recovered for the Sultan and made a base for German penetration of Africa.

Millions of German money had already been invested in this scheme, and the Kaiser's versatile piety had assumed a Mohammedan hue in the East. He had proclaimed himself the friend of every Mohammedan under the sun, and had carefully refrained from wounding the feelings of the authors of the Armenian massacres. The defeat of his Turkish friends in the Balkan Wars had been almost as great a blow to him as to them, and he had seen in the subsequent discord of the victors a chance of crushing them all. Rumania, he thought, was tied to his chariot-wheels by its Hohenzollern king, and Greece by its Hohenzollern queen; and Bulgaria could be won through its hatred of the successful Serbs. Serbia conquered, the corridor would be complete; but Serbia could not be permanently crushed while Russia remained intact, and Turkey would be a useful ally in the Russian campaign. There were millions of Mohammedans under Russian rule, and a Turkish invasion of the Caucasus, even if it did not stimulate insurrection in Russia, would keep hundreds of thousands of Russian troops from East Prussia, Poland, or Galicia.

Apart from the vulgar bribes which affected the Young Turk politicians there were other motives to move the populace. A Jehad against the Christian might stir the honest fanatic; well-to-do Turks had invested some of their savings in two Turkish Dreadnoughts under construction in England which the British Government had commandeered; and two German warships, the Goeben and the Breslau, had arrived at the Golden Horn to impress or to encourage the Ottoman mind. Such were some of the straws which finally broke the back of sober resistance to the warlike gamble of Enver and Talaat; but the substantial argument was the chance which was offered for Turkey to get back some of what her inveterate Russian enemy had seized in the course of a century and her inveterate British friend had pocketed as the price of her protection. On 29 October a horde of Bedouins invaded the Sinai Peninsula while Turkish torpedo boats raided Odessa, and on 1 November the British ambassador departed from Constantinople. The two Central Empires had enlisted their first ally, and the war had taken another stride towards Armageddon.

CHAPTER IV

THE WAR ON AND BEYOND THE SEAS

The declaration of war by Great Britain on 4 August converted the conflict into one unlike any other that had been waged since Napoleon was sent to St. Helena in 1815; and sea-power was once more revealed to a somewhat purblind world. There had, indeed, been wars in which navies had been engaged, and Japan in 1904 had exhibited the latest model of a naval battle. But Japan only commanded the sea in Far Eastern waters; and the wars in which Great Britain herself was engaged since 1815 had displayed her command in limited spheres and at the expense of enemies who had no pretensions to be her naval rivals. But in 1914 the second navy in the world seemed by the conduct of Germany to challenge the first, and for nearly four and a half years there were hopes and fears of a titanic contest for the command of the sea. But in fact the challenge was not forthcoming, and from first to last the command remained in our hands through Germany's default. There was no Trafalgar because no one came forth to fight, and in the end the German Navy surrendered without a struggle.

But while our command of the sea was not disputed in deed by the Germans, it was disputed in word by domestic critics and denied by loquacious generals; and the exploits of German submarines, airships, and aeroplanes lent some colour to the denial and to the assertion that England had ceased to be an island. Both contentions were the outcome of inadequate knowledge and worse confusion of thought. Islands are made by the sea and not by the air; even if the Germans had secured command of the air, which they did not, that command would not have given them the advantages which accrue from the command of the sea. It might please pessimists to believe that England would be cowed into submission by air-raids, but the most inveterate scaremongers hesitated to assert that armies with their indispensable artillery and equipment could be dropped on British soil from the skies. Belgium and France were far more troubled than we by aircraft; but it was not aircraft that carried German armies to Brussels and near to the gates of Paris, and London was saved from the fate of Louvain by British command of the sea. Nor was that command abolished or even threatened by submarines, and the fear lest it was came of the mentality which denies the existence of a power on the ground that it is not perfect. Command of the sea never has been and never can be absolute. French privateers had never been more active nor British losses at sea more acute than after Trafalgar, when no French Navy ventured out of port; and the destruction of every German Dreadnought would not have affected by one iota the success of German submarines.

The command of the sea does not mean immunity from the risks of naval warfare or from loss by the capture or sinking of merchant vessels. It does not imply absolute security for British coasts, for British coasts have been raided in every great war that Britain has waged. It does not even involve the defeat or destruction of the enemy's naval forces, or it would be a simple task for any naval Power to deprive us of the command of the sea by locking its fleets in harbour, and on that theory the forts of the Dardanelles would have enabled Turkey to deny the command of the sea to the combined fleets of the world. The meaning is familiar enough to intelligent students of history. Bacon sketched it three hundred years ago when he wrote, "He that commands the sea is at great liberty and may take as much and as little of the war as he will . . . and the wealth of both Indies seems in great part but an accessory to the command of the seas." "Both Indies" have grown to-day to include the resources of nearly the whole extra-European world which the command of the sea placed at the disposal of the Entente and denied to the Central Empires; and the last great war, like those against Napoleon, Louis XIV, and Philip II, was decided by the same indispensable factor in world-power. Others might control for a time a continent; only those who command the sea can dispose of the destinies of the world.

But while an essential factor in world-power, the command of the sea is not its sum; and the war throughout its course illustrated the weakness of attack by sea against a well-defended coast. No attempt was made to land an army on German territory, and complete command of the Ægean did not avail for the capture of Gallipoli. It could not turn sea into land nor enable a navy to do an army's work, and command of the sea while a more extensive is a less intensive kind of power than command of the land. The nature of the command varies, indeed, with the solidity of the element in which it is exercised: land is more solid than water, and water than air; the command of the land is therefore more complete than command of the sea, and command of the sea than command of the air; and endless confusion arose from the use of the same word to describe three different degrees of control. Victory can be achieved on sea, conquest only on land; and nothing like victory, let alone conquest, in war has yet been won in the air. Conquest, however, while it cannot be effected, can be prevented on sea, as it was at Salamis in 1588, at Trafalgar, and Navarino; for sea-power, while conclusive for defence, is merely conducive to offence, and that is why it has ever been a means of liberty rather than of despotism. Armies are the weapons of autocracy, navies those of freedom; for peoples do not live upon water, and only armies command their homes. Command of the sea is a sufficient protection for an island-empire; to conquer others it needs a superior army, and the absence of such an army proved the defensive aims of the British Empire before the war. World domination could only be secured by the combination of a dominant army with a dominant navy, and hence the significance of the German naval programme designed at least to prevent the counteraction of one by the other.

But while a supreme navy suffices to protect an island empire, it does not suffice to defend continental states; and the importance of British sea-power was that it gave us and other oversea peoples the liberty to take as much or as little part as we chose in a war to defend states that were threatened on land. The existence of that facility did not determine the extent to which it might be used by ourselves or by allies. That would depend upon the size of the armies we raised and the labour we spent upon their equipment; and we might have restricted our expeditionary forces to the numbers we sent under Marlborough against Louis XIV or under Wellington against Napoleon. But we could not have sent any without the command of the sea; and the essence of that command is that, firstly, it prevented the enemy from using his armies to invade our shores, and, secondly, it enabled us to send whatever forces we liked to whatever sphere of operations was not commanded by the enemy's armies. Philip II had demonstrated once for all the emptiness of the invasion scare when he sent a superb military expedition, the Spanish Armada, across a sea which he did not command; and the efforts of German submarines failed to affect the transport of our own and our Allies' troops or seriously to impede their communications.

The command of the sea was, in fact, abandoned by the Germans when on 26 July 1914 their fleet was recalled from the Norwegian fiords; and the cruisers which the outbreak of war found beyond reach of German territorial waters were in turn and in time destroyed. One Dreadnought, the Goeben, and a light cruiser, the Breslau, escaped to play a chequered part in the war. Caught by its outbreak in the Mediterranean, they attempted to make the Straits, were headed off by the British, and gained Messina on 5 August. Evading the British Fleet under circumstances which were held to cast no reflection on the British commander, and with assistance which it was deemed impolitic to make public, they pursued their flight eastward, gallantly assaulted by the smaller and slower Gloucester off Cape Matapan, until they reached the Dardanelles and took the Turkish Government under their charge. Out in the Atlantic the swift Karlsruhe caused some anxiety till she was wrecked in the West Indies, and the Geier was interned at Honolulu by the United States. A few converted merchantmen also pursued a brief career as raiders: the Cap Trafalgar was disposed of in a spirited action by the converted Cunarder Carmania on 14 September off Brazil; the Kaiser Wilhelm der Grosse was sunk by the Highflyer off Cape Verde Islands on 27 August; and the Spreewald was captured in the North Atlantic by the Berwick on 12 September. For the rest, the German mercantile marine was interned in neutral ports or restricted to Baltic waters, and apart from Von Spee and the submarines the German flag disappeared from the seas.

The Germans had realized from the start a vital difference between war on sea and war on land. The land affords some protection to the weaker combatant especially on the defensive; the sea gives none. There are no trenches in the sea, but only graves. It is merciless to the vanquished, and the casualties in a beaten fleet are total losses; instead of prisoners, fugitives, and wounded, there is one vast list of drowned. Ships that are sunk do not return to the battle-line, and their loss takes long to repair. Years are required to build a Dreadnought, and years to make a seaman. Armies are easier to create and more difficult to destroy than fleets, and the sailor's fight is ever one to a finish, with little chance of escape from the dread alternative. It is a case of all or nothing; there are no water-tight compartments in sea-power, no fluctuating spheres of power, no divided areas in some of which one and in some the other combatant may be supreme. Apart from land-locked waters the sea is one and indivisible, and he who has the command, commands it everywhere. The battle at sea is a battle without a morrow for those who lose; and from the day when the Germans wisely withdrew into Kiel and Wilhelmshaven there was little chance that they would come out to fight to a finish except as a counsel of despair or until they could by mine or submarine or skilful raid reduce the disparity of force. That was the purpose of their early naval strategy; it proved ineffective owing to British skill and caution, and it became hopeless when it appeared that we could build ships much faster than the Germans could sink them or build ships themselves; and the Germans then turned from the task of destroying the British Navy to that of destroying the commerce on which we depended for subsistence, from the hope of securing the command of the sea for themselves to that of turning it into a "no man's land," a desert which no allied or neutral ship could cross.

The mine-sowing began the moment war was declared, and on 5 August the Konigin Luise was sunk in the nefarious act of sowing loose mines in the North Sea. Fixed mines for coast and harbour defence or minefields at sea are legitimate means of war, provided that warning is given of the dangerous area; loose mines are prohibited by international law, because they can make no distinction in their destruction between neutrals and belligerents, merchantmen and men-of-war. But the German flag having practically disappeared from the seas, the Germans paid little heed to the risks of other people. On 6 August a light cruiser, the Amphion, struck one of these mines and was sunk, and on

3 September a gunboat, the Speedy, met with a similar fate. A more serious loss, though only one man was killed, was that of the super-Dreadnought Audacious, which struck a mine to the north of Ireland on 27 October and sank as she was being towed into harbour; and a mine caused the loss of the Hampshire, with Lord Kitchener on board, in June 1916.

The submarine proved, however, the greater danger, and there was nothing illegal in the sinking of men-of-war or transports. On 5 September the Pathfinder, a light cruiser, was torpedoed and sunk, and on the 13th the British retaliated by sinking the German light cruiser Hela near Heligoland. The warning, however, had not been taken to heart, and on 22 September the German submarine commander, Otto Weddigen, successively sank the Aboukir, the Hogue, and the Cressy, three old but substantial cruisers on patrol duty off the Dutch coast. The Hogue and the Cressy were lost because they came up to the rescue and were protected by no screen of destroyers, and 680 officers and men were drowned. A fourth cruiser, the Hawke, was torpedoed off Aberdeen on 15 October, and on 1 January 1915 the Formidable, of 15,000 tons, was sunk off Start Point on her way to the Dardanelles, with a loss of 600 of her crew. The Germans were not, however, immune in their submarine campaign. H.M.S. Birmingham rammed and sank a German submarine on 6 August, the Badger did the like on 25 October, and U18 was sunk on 23 November; Weddigen himself was rammed, with the loss of his submarine and all on board, later on by the Dreadnought.

The British losses by mine and submarine created some discontent on the ground that our naval strategy was defensive rather than offensive; and military critics, whose notions of naval warfare were derived from the study of German text-books on the principles of war on land, continually pressed for a more active policy, and asked why our superior navy did not treat the German Fleet as the German Army treated its enemies in France and Belgium. It was forgotten that he who possesses all must always be on the defensive; there must be something tangible to attack before there can be an offensive, and there could have been no Trafalgar had Napoleon kept his fleet in harbour. The abandonment of the high seas by the German Navy precluded a naval battle, and the defensive strength of harbour defences which kept Nelson outside

Toulon had so increased as to make it vastly harder for Jellicoe to penetrate Wilhelmshaven or Kiel. Naval power, which the war proved to be more than ever effective on sea, was shown to be more than ever powerless on shore. The mine and the submarine made the sustained bombardment of land fortifications a dangerous practice, and moving batteries on shore were more than a match for ships, because they could not be sunk and could be more easily repaired or replaced. There were wild dreams of British forces landing on German coasts, and still wilder alarms about German armies descending on British shores; but the only landing effected on hostile territory during the war was at Gallipoli, and it did not encourage a similar attempt against the better defended lands held by the Germans. We had to content ourselves with the practical realization in war of our continual claim in peace that sea-power is an instrument for the defence of island states rather than one for offence against continental peoples. Only when and where those peoples wished to be defended and opened their ports to their allies, was it found possible to land a relieving force. The British armies which liberated Brussels had to travel via Boulogne and not Ostend; and the German ships which sheltered in port had to be routed out by the pressure of Allied arms on land.

The naval actions of the war were therefore of the nature of outpost raids and skirmishes rather than of battles. The first that developed any serious fighting took place in the Bight of Heligoland on 28 August. Apparently with the design of inducing the Germans to come out, a flotilla of submarines under Commodore Keyes was sent close in to Heligoland, with some destroyers and two light cruisers, the Arethusa and Fearless, behind them, and more substantial vessels out of sight in the offing. Presently there appeared a German force of destroyers and two cruisers, the Ariadne and the Strassburg; they were driven off mainly by the gallant fighting of the Arethusa; but thinking there was no further support the Germans then sent out three heavier cruisers, the Mainz, the Koln, and apparently the Yorck. The Arethusa and Fearless held their own for two or three hours until Beatty's battle-cruisers, led by the Lion, came safely through the German mine-fields and submarines to their assistance. The Lion's 13.5-inch guns soon settled the issue: the Mainz and the Köln were sunk, while no British unit was lost, and the casualties were 32 killed and 52 wounded against 300 German prisoners and double that number of other casualties. The overwhelming effect of heavier gunfire had been clearly demonstrated, and it was further illustrated on 17 October by the destruction of four German destroyers off the Dutch coast by the light cruiser Undaunted accompanied by four British destroyers; but the next exhibition of naval gun-power was to be at our expense.

Among the incidental advantages which the adhesion of Great Britain brought to the Entente was the intervention of Japan, which, apart from its alliance with us, had never forgiven Germany the part she took in depriving Japan of the fruits of her victory over China in 1894, and regarded as a standing offence the naval base which Germany had established at Tsingtau and the hold she had acquired on North Pacific islands. On 15 August Japan demanded within eight days the surrender of the lease of Tsingtau and the evacuation of Far Eastern waters by German warships. No answer was, of course, returned, but the German squadron under Von Spee wisely left Tsingtau in anticipation of its investment by the Japanese. It began on the 27th, and troops were landed on 2 September: on the 23rd a British contingent arrived from Wei-hai-wei to co-operate, and gradually the lines of investment and the heavy artillery were drawn closer. The final assault was fixed for 7 November, but the Germans forestalled it by surrender; there were 3000 prisoners out of an original garrison of 5000, and Germany's last overseas base, on which she had spent £20,000,000, passed into the enemy's hands. Australian troops had already occupied without serious opposition German New Guinea, the Bismarck archipelago, and the Gilbert and Caroline Islands, while Samoa surrendered to a New Zealand force, and the Marshall Islands to the Japanese.

Von Spee's squadron was thus left without a German naval base; but one of its vessels was to show that there was still a career for a raider, and the others were to demonstrate the paradox that neutral ports might be more useful than bases of their own, inasmuch as they could not be treated like Tsingtau. On fleeing from the Japanese menace Von Spee had steamed eastwards across the Pacific, but two of his cruisers, the Königsberg and the Emden, were detached to help the Germans in East Africa and to raid British commerce in the Indian Ocean. On 20 September the Königsberg sank H.M.S. Pegasus at Zanzibar, but failed to give much assistance in the projected attack on Mombasa, and was presently bottled up in the Rufigi River. The Emden under Captain Müller had better success. Throughout September and October she haunted the coasts of India and harried British trade, setting fire to an oil-tank at Madras, torpedoing a Russian cruiser and a French destroyer in the roadstead of Penang, and capturing in all some seventeen British merchantmen. She had, however, lost her own attendant colliers about 25 October, and a raid on the Cocos or Keeling islands on 9 November was interrupted by the arrival of H.M.S. Sydney, which had been warned by wireless, on her way from Australia. In less than two hours the Sydney's 6-in. guns had battered the Emden to pieces, and with only 18 casualties had killed or wounded 230 of the enemy. Müller became an honourable prisoner of war; he had proved himself the most skilful of German captains and the best of German gentlemen.

Meanwhile Von Spee had gained the South American coast and made himself at home in its friendly ports and islands. He had with him two sister cruisers, the Scharnhorst and the Gneisenau, each of 11,400 tons and an armament of eight 8.2-inch guns, and three smaller cruisers, the Dresden, Leipzig, and Nürnberg, each about the size of the Emden, from 3200 to 3540 tons, and carrying ten 4.1-inch guns; none of them had a speed of less than 22 knots. To protect the South Pacific trade the British Government had in August sent Admiral Cradock with a somewhat miscellaneous squadron, consisting of the Canopus, a pre-Dreadnought battleship of nearly 13,000 tons, with 6-inch armour, four 12-inch guns, and a speed of 19 knots; the Good Hope, a cruiser of 14,000 tons, with two 9.2-inch and sixteen 6-inch guns, and a speed of 22 knots; the Monmouth of 9800 tons, fourteen 6-inch guns, and the same speed as the Good Hope; the Glasgow of 4800 tons, with two 6-inch and ten 4-inch guns, and a speed of 25 knots; and the Otranto, an armed liner. Reinforcements were expected from home, and possibly from Japan; but the squadrons were not unequally matched in weight of metal, though the British were handicapped by the diversity and antiquity of their armament. The balance was, however, destroyed before the battle, because, as Cradock in the third week of October made his way north along the Pacific coast, the Canopus developed defects which necessitated her being left behind for repairs.

The squadrons fell in with one another north-west of Coronel late in the afternoon of 1 November. Cradock had turned south, presumably to join the Canopus, but Von Spee secured the inestimable advantage of the in-shore course, and as the sun set it silhouetted the British ships against the sky while the gathering gloom obscured the Germans. The fight was really between the two leading cruisers on each side, the Good Hope and the Monmouth against the Scharnhorst and the Gneisenau. The Germans got the range first, and the Good Hope's two 9.2-inch guns were soon put out of action in spite of their superior weight. At 7:50 she blew up, and the Monmouth was a wreck. The lightly-armoured Glasgow had no option but to use her superior speed and escape to warn the Canopus. This she did, and the two got safely round Cape Horn to the Falkland Isles, leaving for the time the Germans in command of the South Pacific coast. Sixteen hundred and fifty officers, midshipmen, and men lost their lives with Cradock, and none were rescued by the Germans. There was hardly a parallel in British naval history for such a defeat.

Prompt measures were taken to retrieve it. Lord Fisher had succeeded Prince Louis of Battenberg at the Admiralty on 30 October, and one of his first acts was to dispatch on 5 November a squadron under Admiral Sturdee, comprising the Invincible and Inflexible, and four lighter cruisers, the Carnarvon, Kent, Cornwall, and Bristol; the Glasgow was picked up in the South Atlantic, while the Canopus was at Port Stanley in the Falklands. The Invincible and Inflexible were the two first battle-cruisers built; each had a tonnage of 17,250, a speed of 27-28 knots, and eight 12-inch guns which could be fired as a broadside to right or left; and there would be little chance for Von Spee if he encountered such a weight of metal. Sturdee reached Port Stanley on 7 December. Von Spee, who had been refitting at Juan Fernandez, left it on 15 November, possibly fearing the Japanese approach, and made for Cape Horn and the Atlantic. His plan was to snap up the Canopus and the Glasgow, get what he could out of the Falklands, and then proceed to support the rebellion in South Africa. Early on 8 December he unsuspectingly approached Port Stanley, not discovering the presence of Sturdee's squadron until it was too late. He then made off north-eastwards with the Scharnhorst and the Gneisenau, while his lighter cruisers turned south-eastwards. The former were sunk in the afternoon by the two British battle-cruisers and the Carnarvon, while the latter succumbed in the evening to the Kent, Glasgow, and Cornwall; only the Dresden escaped, to be sunk in five minutes on 14 March 1915 at Juan Fernandez by the Kent and the Glasgow. The Invincible had no casualties, the Inflexible one man killed; the Kent had four killed and twelve wounded, and the Glasgow nine and four. About two hundred Germans were saved from drowning, but they did not include Von Spee.

Such were the effects upon human life of a disparity of weight of metal in naval action. No skill could avoid the brutal precision of mechanical and material superiority. Von Spee had it at Coronel, Sturdee at the Falklands, and there is no reason to suppose that if the persons had been exchanged, the result would have been any different. It is the romance of the past which attributes naval success mainly to superior seamanship or courage; the "little" Revenge was the super-Dreadnought of her time, and the victories of the Elizabethan sea-dogs were as surely won by superior weight of metal as those of Nelson or to-day. Von Spee and his men fought as bravely and as skilfully as Cradock and his; and the war for command of the sea went against the Germans because while the Germans were building pre-Dreadnoughts and casting 8-inch guns, we were building Dreadnoughts and casting 10 or 12-inch guns; and while they were constructing their Dreadnoughts, we were building super-Dreadnoughts with 13.5 and 15-inch guns. Success in naval warfare goes not so much to the brave as to those who think ahead in terms of mechanical force.

The last German cruisers outside harbour were now destroyed, and barely a raider remained at large, while the British went on gathering the fruits of their command of the sea by mustering in Europe the forces of the Empire and acquiring abroad the disjointed German colonies. Naval strategy was reduced to the dull but arduous task of blocking the exits from the North Sea and guarding against the furtive German raids. The battle-fleet was stationed in Scapa Flow, the cruisers off Rosyth, while little more than a patrol—backed by a squadron of pre-Dreadnoughts in the Channel—was left to watch the Straits of Dover and supplement the mine-fields. Both combatants drew advantage from the narrow front of Germany's outlook towards the sea; the exits were easier for us to close than Nelson had found the lengthy coast of France, and no German Fleet slipped across the Atlantic as Villeneuve did in 1805. On the other hand, the narrow front was easier to fortify, protect with mine-fields, and defend against attack. If there was to be a conclusive naval battle, the field would be in the North Sea, and the only hope of success for the Germans lay in the dispersion of our battle-fleet.

This was the object of the German raids on Yarmouth on 3 November, and on Scarborough, Whitby, and the Hartlepools on 16 December. The former effected nothing except sowing of some floating mines which subsequently sank British submarine and two fishing-smacks, while one of the participating cruisers, the Yorck, struck a German mine and sank on entering Wilhelmshaven. The December raid was more successful in its murderous intention of extending the schrecklichkeit practised in Belgium to civilians on British shores. British delegates had insisted at The Hague in 1907 on large rights of naval bombardment, and the Germans expanded the plea that the presence of civilians does not exempt a fortified town from bombardment into the argument that the presence of a soldier or even of war-material justifies the shelling of a crowd of civilians or a watering-place. There was a cavalry station at Scarborough, a coastguard at Whitby, and some infantry and a battery at Hartlepool; Scarborough also had a wireless installation, and Hartlepool its docks, and both were undoubtedly used for purposes of war. The truth is that war tends to pervade and absorb the whole energies of the community, and the only legitimate criticism of German methods is that they pushed to extremes of barbarity premisses which were commonly admitted and could logically lead in no other direction. The old restriction of war to a few actual combatants disappeared as manhood took to universal service, womanhood to munition-making, and whole nations to war-work, and as the reach of artillery and aircraft extended the sphere of operations hundreds of miles behind the battle-lines. Eighteen were killed at Scarborough, mostly women and children, and 70 were wounded; Whitby had 3 killed and 2 wounded, but the damage at Hartlepool was serious. Six hundred houses were damaged or destroyed, 119 persons were killed, over 300 were wounded, and the mines the Germans scattered sank three steamers with considerable loss of life. The raiders escaped by the skin of their teeth in a fog which closed down just as two British battle-cruisers appeared on the scene of their retreat. That the raid had been effected at all evoked some protest from a public unaware that such incidents have always been an inevitable accompaniment of all our naval wars; and critics declared that we had lost the command of the sea in the first great war in our history in which not an enemy landed on English soil except as a prisoner. It was the German plan to provoke such comment, a feeling of insecurity, and a demand for the scattering of our Grand Fleet along the coasts for defence in order that it might be dealt with in detail; but the design was happily defeated by the restraint of the people and the sense of better judges.

The Germans, however, were encouraged by their success to repeat the attempt once too often, and on 24 January 1915 a more ambitious effort was made by Admiral Hipper to emulate these raids, or perhaps rather to lure the British on to mine-fields north of Heligoland which he extended before he set out. He had with him three of the best German battle-cruisers, the Derfflinger, Seydlitz, and Moltke, with speeds ranging from 27 to 25 knots, tonnage from 26,000 to 22,000, and 12 or 11-inch guns; the Blücher of 15,550 tons, 24 knots, and 8.2-inch guns; six light cruisers and a torpedo flotilla. The Germans rarely if ever came out without information of their intended movement preceding them, and Beatty put to sea within an hour of their start. His flagship was the Lion, 26,350 tons, 29 knots, and eight 13.5-inch guns, and he had five other battle-cruisers, the Tiger, 28,000 tons, 28 knots, and the same armament as the Lion; the Princess Royal, a sister ship of the Lion; the New Zealand, 18,800 tons, 25 knots, and eight 12-inch guns; and the Indomitable, sister to Sturdee's Invincible and Inflexible. There were also four cruisers of the "town" class, three light cruisers, and torpedo flotillas. The fight was, however, mainly between the battle-crusiers. As soon as Hipper heard of Beatty's approach he turned south-east. Gradually he was overhauled, each of the leading British cruisers, Lion, Tiger, and Princess Royal firing salvos into the slower Blücher as they passed on to tackle the Moltke, Seydlitz, and Derfflinger. The Blücher was finally reduced to a wreck by the New Zealand and Indomitable, and then torpedoed by the Meteor; bombs from German aircraft prevented our boats from rescuing more than 120 survivors from the sinking ship. Meanwhile the Lion was damaged by a shell and had to fall behind, and an hour and twenty minutes passed before Beatty could return to the scene of action; he found that his second in command had broken off the fight out of respect for the German mine-field, which seems, however, to have been still thirty or forty miles away. The German battle-cruisers, which might apparently have been destroyed, thus got home with a severe battering which incapacitated them for action for some months. No British ship was lost, and our casualties were about a score of men.

The result was disappointing in the escape of the German cruisers, but it left no doubt about the command of the sea. It was, indeed, being daily demonstrated by the security of the Channel passage, the muster of forces from oversea, and the conquest of German colonies. These were mainly in Africa, and consisted of Togoland, the German Cameroons, German South-West Africa, and East Africa. The tide of conquest flowed in this order round Africa from north-west to south-east, and Togoland, which was also the smallest, was the first to be subdued. It was about the size of Ireland, and was hemmed in on all sides, by British sea-power on the south, Nigeria on the west, and French colonies on the north and east; and converging attacks forced the handful of German troops to unconditional surrender on 27 August, The Cameroons were larger than the German Empire in Europe, and the first attacks, being made with inadequate preparation, were repulsed in the latter days of August. On 27 September, however, by cooperation between French troops and two British warships, Duala the capital was captured and the whole coast-line was seized.

The conquest of German South-West Africa was a more serious matter, not only because the Germans were there more numerous and better organized, but because the task was complicated by the politics of the Union. It was not a Crown colony subject to the orders of the Imperial Government; troops could only move at the instance of a responsible local administration, and the back-veld Boers, led by Hertzog and De Wet, were strenuously opposed to participation in the war on the British side. Fortunately, perhaps, the Germans began hostilities by raiding the frontiers of Cape Colony, and on 18 September the British retaliated by seizing Luderitz Bay, which, like their other port, Swakopmund, the Germans had abandoned to concentrate at their inland capital, Windhoek. On the 26th there was a small British reverse at Sandfontein, which was followed by the more serious news of Maritz' rebellion in the Cape. Maritz had fought against the British in the Boer War and for the Germans against the revolted Hereros; he now held the ambiguous position of rank in the German Army and command of British forces, but came down on the German side of the fence. Botha ordered his arrest, and Maritz, with German assistance in arms and ammunition, attempted to overrun the north-west of Cape Colony. A fortnight's campaign in October ended with the dispersal of his commandos by Colonel Van Deventer.

Maritz was the stormy petrel of a far more serious disturbance. While the grant of self-government to the Transvaal and the Orange River Colony in 1908 had placated the great majority and the better-educated Boers, tradition and prejudice kept their hold upon the more conservative minority; and some like Beyers, who had once been received by the Kaiser, looked to a war with Germany to restore their ancient independence. On 24 October De Wet seized Heilbronn in the Orange State, and Beyers Rustenburg in the Transvaal. Botha's appeal to the loyal Boers met, however, with an effective response, and soon he had 30,000 men at his disposal. He acted with remarkable swiftness: on the 27th he dispersed the commandos of Beyers and Kemp, and on 7 November General Smuts announced that there were but a few scattered bands of rebels in the Transvaal. De Wet made a longer run by his elusive heels, but found the motor-transport of his enemies an insuperable bar to the repetition of his exploits of 1900-2. He had a slight success at Doornberg on 7 November, when his force amounted to 2000 men; but Botha now came south into the Orange State and completely defeated De Wet on the 11th to the east of Winburg. De Wet himself escaped and attempted a junction with Beyers who had fled south from the Transvaal. But he was gradually driven westward into the Kalahari desert and overtaken by Colonel Jordaan's motors a hundred miles west of Mafeking on 1 December, while Beyers was drowned in trying to cross the Vaal on the 8th. De Wet was once more given his life, and the other rebels were treated with a lenience which nothing but its wisdom could excuse.

The rising put off to another year the conquest of German South-West Africa. The conquest of East Africa (see Map, p. 249) was postponed for a longer period by the inherent difficulties of the task and the imported defects in its management. German

East Africa was actually and potentially by far the most valuable of German oversea possessions. Twice the size of Germany, it had a population of eight million natives and five thousand Europeans. Although tropical in its climate, high ground, and especially the slopes of Kilimanjaro, provided inhabitable land for white men, and its wealth in forests, gold and other minerals, pastoral and agricultural facilities was considerable. There were four excellent ports, and from two of them, Tanga and the capital, Dar-es-Salaam, railways ran far into the interior. On the north it was bounded by British East Africa and Uganda, on the west by the Belgian Congo State, and on the south-west by British Nyasaland and Northern Rhodesia, while on the south Portuguese Mozambique provided some means of supply and an ultimate refuge in defeat. The German forces were greatly superior to those of the British in East Africa, and the Uganda railway from Mombasa to Lake Victoria Nyanza running parallel with the frontier was a tempting object of attack. The Germans took the offensive against the British north and south-west, without achieving any great success. But only the arrival of reinforcements from India on 3 September and the failure of the Konigsberg to co-operate prevented the fall of Mombasa, and only the inadequacy of the British maps, on which the Germans had for once to rely, frustrated their attack on the Uganda railway. Karungu was also besieged on Lake Victoria Nyanza, but relieved by a couple of British vessels; the invaders of Northern Rhodesia were beaten back; and a naval force bombarded Dar-es-Salaam and destroyed the wireless installation. The arrival of a second expeditionary force from India on 1 November was the prelude to a greater reverse. Landing at Tanga on the 4th, it was met by a German force, superior in the art of bush fighting if not in numbers which hurried down from Moschi, and was compelled to re-embark with a loss of 800 casualties. During the brief span of their colonial experience the Germans had learnt as much about colonial warfare as we could teach them after centuries; for traditions are not an unmixed blessing in the art of war.

CHAPTER V

ESTABLISHING THE WESTERN FRONT

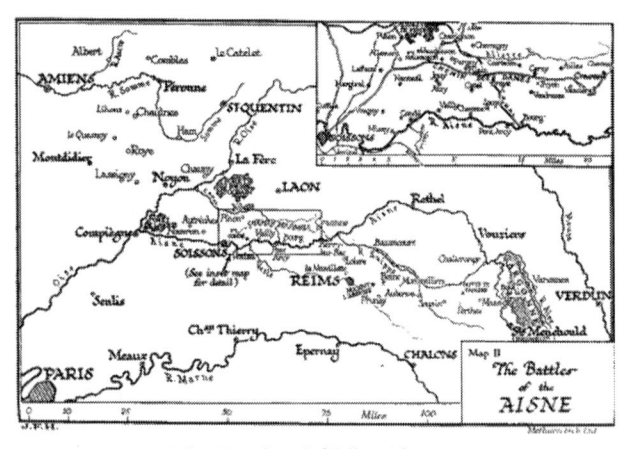

The Battles Of The Aisne

Throughout the war there was an undercurrent of criticism against the dispersion of British forces and dissipation of British energy, and the briefest history of it cannot avoid a certain amount of discursiveness. The reason, if not the justification, is the same in both cases; for happily or unhappily the British Empire is scattered all over the globe, and unless colonies were to be abandoned to enemy attacks and the natural forces of native discontents, they had to be defended in part at least by British troops. Fortunately the task required but a fraction of the military strength which Germany needed to hold Alsace-Lorraine in time of peace, and long before the end Great Britain received from her dominions fourfold the help in Europe that she had to lend them overseas. The rally to the British flag was to us one of the most inspiring, and to the Germans one of the most dispiriting, portents in the war; but it took time to bear its fruits, and meanwhile the cause of civilization had to rely upon the gallantry of French armies and the numerically weak British forces fighting on the Marne and on the Aisne.

The human eye is ever longing to pierce the veil of the future, but it was perhaps as well that men could not foresee, as the Allies drove the Germans across the lower reaches of the Aisne, how long that river would be reddened with the blood of the contending forces. They thought that the tide of invasion would recede as fast as it had advanced, and it was only as the days of German resistance lengthened into weeks, and the weeks into months of the longest battle in history, that staffs and armies and peoples began to grasp the awful potentialities of scientific progress in the art of modern war. The battle without a morrow had long been the ideal consummation for victorious strategy, but no one had yet foreseen the battle without an end and armies without flanks. That sooner or later one or other combatant would be outflanked had been the universal assumption of the strategist; but in the autumn of 1914 the combatant forces gradually extended their fronts in the effort until they rested upon the frontier of Switzerland and the sea, and the deadlock of a deadly embrace began which was not effectively broken until the wrestling of four years wore down the strength of the wrestlers and left the final decision in the hands of new-comers to the European field of battle.

The deadlock was no part of the original German plan, but German forethought during the advance to the Marne had provided entrenchments in the rear for the event of a retreat, and the natural strength of the forest of St. Gobain, the Chemin des Dames, and the Argonne as well as a study of the campaign of 1814 had suggested an obvious line of defence. It was not, however, expected by the Entente higher command which proceeded with its frontal attack on the assumption that the Germans were merely fighting rearguard actions to secure their further retirement; and it was only when the German front refused to budge that pressure spread out to the Allied left wing in an attempt to turn the German right flank, which would have stood more chance of success had it come a fortnight earlier as a first instead of a second thought. An even better alternative might have been to revert to Joffre's original plan, which had failed in August on the Saar, to thrust forward against the Crown Prince and threaten the left of the Germans and the communications of their forces in Belgium and northern France. But it is easier on paper after the event than it was in action at the time to convert an improvised defensive into a considered offensive strategy; and the Germans themselves had occasion during the autumn and the rest of the war to regret that their second thoughts had not come first.

The battle of the Aisne began, like that of the Marne, on Sunday, 13 September. The Germans' retreat had taken them north of the river except at a few bridgeheads, but the river was deep and its crossings were all commanded by fire from German batteries concealed on the slopes rising up from the northern bank. Maunoury's 6th Army attacked on the left from Compiègne and the Forêt de l'Aigle to Soissons, and several divisions were got across. From Soissons eastward for fifteen miles to Pont-Arcy the line of attack was held by the British Army; the whole of the 4th Division got across near Venizel, and most of the 5th and 3rd Divisions farther east, but the Germans succeeded in holding the bridge at Condé. The 2nd Division was also only partially successful in the region of Chavonne, but the whole of the 1st got across at Pont-Arcy and Bourg. On Monday, Maunoury pressed forward up the heights, capturing Autrèches and Nouvron, but, like the British on his right between Vregny and Vailly, he found the German positions impregnable on the plateau. Haig's First Corps was more successful farther east; Vendresse and Troyon were captured and the Chemin des Dames was almost reached. But D'Esperey's 5th French army could make little impression on the Craonne plateau; Foch's 9th was unable to force the Suippe to the east of Reims, and Langle's 4th, while it occupied Souain, was similarly held up in Champagne.

On the 15th the Germans counter-attacked. Maunoury was driven out of Nouvron and Autrèches, the British were forced back from Vregny almost to the river, and the Moroccan troops withdrew on Haig's right flank. There was a lull on the 16th, and on the 17th Maunoury recovered the quarries of Autrèches; but east of Reims the 9th Army had fallen back from the Suippe, and the Prussian Guard had captured Nogent l'Abbesse and was threatening Foch's connexion with Langle in Champagne. The 18th saw little progress on either side, except along the Oise, where Maunoury had as early as the 15th begun to outflank the German right. This success, coupled with the stalemate along the rest of the front, suggested to Joffre a change of strategy. Numerically the opposing forces were not unequal, but the Germans had all the advantages of position. To attack up carefully protected slopes with a river in the rear and its crossings commanded by the enemy's fire, promised little hope of success, and threatened disaster in case of failure and retreat. Accordingly, Joffre, taking some risks by weakening his centre, began on the 16th to lengthen and strengthen his left by forming two new armies. Castlenau gave up his command of the 2nd to Dubail in Lorraine and took over the new 7th, and a 10th was entrusted to Maud'huy, another of the professors of military history to whom the French and the Russian armies owed so much of their generalship. By the 20th Maunoury had swung his left round until it stretched at a right angle from Compiègne north to the west of Lassigny. Castelnau's 7th continued the line north through Roye to the Albert plateau; and on the 30th Maud'huy's 10th took up the tale through Arras to Lens.

But if the impact of equal forces on the Aisne flattened them out towards the west, it had the same effect in the other direction, though here it was the Germans who took the offensive in trying to penetrate Sarrail's flank on the Meuse and thus get behind the whole front of the Allies. Verdun was the nut to be cracked, but Sarrail had been extending its defences so as to put the city beyond the reach of the German howitzers and surrounding it with miles of trenches and wire-entanglements; and the Germans preferred to attempt another method than frontal attack. About the 20th four new corps, chiefly of Württemburgers, appeared in Lorraine, bringing their forces up to seven against Sarrail's three; and an attack was made on Fort Troyon on the Meuse which reduced it to a dust-heap but failed to carry the Germans across the river. A more serious onslaught was made on the 23rd against St. Mihiel, which was captured while the neighbouring forts of Paroches and the Camp des Romains were destroyed. But again the Germans were prevented from pushing their advantage, and were left with no more than a wonderful salient which looked on the map like Germany putting out its tongue at France and resisted all efforts to repress this insolence until the closing months of the war.

Having achieved but a sterile success to the south of Verdun, the Crown Prince encountered a greater failure to the west. On 3 October he attacked Sarrail's centre in the forest of the Argonne, seeking to recapture St. Menehould, the headquarters he had abandoned on 14 September. His troops were caught in La Grurie wood and so badly mauled that they temporarily lost Varennes and the main road through the Argonne to Verdun. Foiled in both these directions, the Germans revenged themselves by bombarding Reims in the centre and ruining its cathedral; "the commonest, ugliest stone," wrote a German general, "placed to mark the burial-place of a German grenadier is a more glorious and perfect monument than all the cathedrals in Europe put together." The bombardment did not help them much; Neuvillette, which they had seized two miles north of Reims, was lost again on 28 September, and the French also recovered Prunay, the German occupation of which had driven a wedge between Foch's and Langle's armies. On the other hand, Berry-au-Bac, where the great road crossed the Aisne and the French often reported progress, remained in German hands for four years longer. Both sides were now firmly entrenched, and their armies were learning that new art of trench warfare which was to tax their ingenuity, test their endurance, and drain their strength, until years later this war of positions once more gave place to a war of movement. The lines had become stabilized, and between Reims and the Alps they did not alter by half a dozen miles at any point from September 1914 until September 1918. The question of October was whether and where they would be fixed between the Aisne and the sea.

Joffre's outflanking move was promptly countered, if not indeed anticipated, by the German higher command, and in the first days of October there was a general drift of German forces towards their right and the Channel ports. Most and the best of the new levies were sent into Belgium, and the stoutest troops in the fighting line were shifted from East to West. Alsace was almost denuded; the Bavarians were moved from Lorraine towards Lille and Arras, and the Duke of Württemberg into Belgian Flanders. Von Bulow was sent to face Castelnau and Maud'huy between the Oise and the Somme, and only Von Kluck and the Crown Prince with a new general, Von Heeringen, from Alsace were left to hold the line of the Aisne. Von Moltke was superseded by Falkenhayn, and a new phase came over German strategy. The knock-out blow against France had failed, and the little British Army threatened to grow. France had been the only foe the Germans had counted in the West, but a new enemy was developing strength, and the German front was turned to meet the novel danger.

The British Army made a movement which was sympathetic with this change and symptomatic of the future course of the war. It was clearly out of place along the Aisne in trenches which could be held by French territorials and where its long communications crossed those of three French armies. It was needed in Flanders close to its bases and to the Channel ports which the Germans had now resolved to seize in the hope of cutting or straining the Anglo-French liaison and furthering their new campaign on land and sea against their gathering British foes. The idea had occurred to Sir John French before the end of September, and on the 29th he propounded it to Joffre; Joffre concurred, called up an 8th Army under D'Urbal to support and prolong the extension of the line into Flanders, and placed Foch in general charge of the operations north of Noyon. The transport began on 3 October and was admirably carried out, though some of the ultra-patriotic English newspapers did their best to help the enemy by their enterprise in evading the Censor and giving news of the movement to the public; for if business was business to the profiteer, news was news to its vendors.

For a fortnight the British were on the road and out of the fight, which was left for the most part to Castelnau's 7th and Maud'huy's 10th Armies; and strenuous fighting it was for all-important objects. There was little profit in a British out-march round the German flank in Flanders unless the links between it and the Oise could be maintained, and the Germans were as speedily reinforcing and extending their right as we were preparing to turn it. At first Castelnau seemed to be making rapid and substantial progress; he captured Noyon on 21 September, was pushing on by Lassigny to Roye, and optimistic maps in the English press depicted the German right being bent back to St. Quentin and the French outflanking it as far north-east as Le Catelet. These were not intelligent anticipations. Von Kluck had been reinforced, and a desperate battle ensued from the 25th to the 28th, in which Castelnau was driven back from Noyon and Lassigny. This counter-attack was repulsed with great losses at Quesnoy and Lihons a little farther north, but Maud'huy was not less heavily engaged north of the Somme in a several days' struggle for the Albert plateau. The line established was supposed to run through Combles and Bapaume, and it was not till long afterwards that the public realized how far it had sagged to the westwards, or what that sagging meant when the British had to fight their way up to Bapaume.

North of that watershed the fronts were fluid, if the scattered bodies of French Territorials and German cavalry could be said to constitute a front at all; and there was a strenuous race and struggle to turn the respective flanks. Neither side, it was soon apparent, would succeed in that object, and the practical question was at what point the outflanking contest would reach the coast. The German ambition was to push their right as far south as the mouth of the Seine, while the Allies hoped to thrust their left to the north until it joined the Belgian Army at Antwerp. Maud'huy had entered Arras on 30 September, and some of his Territorials pushed forward to Lille and Douai. During the first three days of October he was fighting hard on the eastern slopes of Vimy Ridge but was compelled to fall back on Arras, while the Germans occupied Lille and Douai and their cavalry penetrated as far as Bailleul, Hazebrouck, and Cassel. But the British from the Aisne were moving up towards their positions on Maud'huy's left, the Aire-La Bassée Canal being fixed as the point of their junction, and the 7th Division, with a division of cavalry, had landed at Ostend and Zeebrugge while the Naval Division was sent to assist in the defence of Antwerp. The Allied dream of a front along the Scheldt to Antwerp, barring German access to the sea, seemed on the verge of realization; but dramatic as the moment was, the tension would have been far more acute had men grasped what a difference possession of the Belgian coast was to make in the course of the war.

Success was missed by the Allies because it had been a more urgent task to break the German offensive on the Marne than to save the remnants of Belgian soil and assist the detached Belgian Army; and the whole of our available force had been sent to the vital spot. Isolation is always dubious strategy, but there were sound as well as natural motives behind the decision which led the Belgian Army after the German occupation of Brussels on 20 August to fall back north-westwards on Antwerp instead of southwards to join the Allies at Mons and Charleroi. The isolation did not involve ineffectiveness, and so far away as the Marne the Allies experienced the benefit of Belgian fighting at Antwerp. Three successive sorties alarmed the Germans for the safety of their far-flung right and its communications, and diverted reserves from their front in France to their rear in Belgium (see Map, p. 34). The first began on 24 August and drove the Germans from Malines, while 2000 British marines landed at Ostend. Then the Belgian right stretched out a hand towards the British and captured Alost, while the left struck at Cortenburg on the line between Brussels and Louvain. The communications of the capital were thus threatened on three sides, and the Germans had to recall at least three of their corps from France. It was this interference with their vital plans in France, coupled with the panic produced by the Belgian advance, which provoked the Germans into their barbarities at Louvain, Malines, and Termonde. Schrecklichkeit was to deter the contemptible Belgian Army from spoiling a mighty German success. That was the view of the German staff, and a soldiery prone as ever to pillage and rapine, needed little encouragement to extend to civilians, women, and children the violence which their leaders organized against cathedrals and cities.

Panic produces plots in all countries—in the minds of the panic-stricken, and Germans no doubt believed in the tales of civilian conspiracies which they used to justify their military crimes. Major Von Manteuffel ordered the systematic destruction of Louvain, with its ancient university and magnificent library. The Cathedral and Palais de Justice at Malines were ruined by bombardment after the Belgian troops had left it; and Termonde was burnt because a fine was not paid in time. Massacre, looting, and outrage attained a licence which only the Germans themselves had equalled during the Thirty Years' War. It and other orgies were a natural expression of German militarism; for excessive restraint in one direction provokes relaxation in others, and the tighter the bond of martial law, the less the respect for civil codes. The proverbial licence of soldiery is the reaction against their military discipline.

The second, called "the great sortie" from Antwerp, nearly coincided with the battle of the Marne. It began on 9 September: Termonde was reoccupied, but the main effort was towards Aerschot and Louvain. Aerschot was recaptured on the 9th, though the fiercest struggle took place at Weerde between Malines and Brussels. Kessel, just outside Louvain, was taken on the 10th, but German reinforcements began to arrive on the 11th, and two days later the Belgians were back in their positions on the Nethe, their retirement being marked, as before, by a fresh series of German atrocities. A third sortie induced by representations of the French higher command and by the impression that the German forces before Antwerp had been reduced, was planned for 26-27 September, and some fighting occurred at Alost and Moll. But by this time the new Germany strategy was at work, and the "side-shows" of the first phase of the war became the main objectives of the second. The French Army was fairly secure in its trenches and the way to Paris was barred. But the approach to the Channel ports was not yet closed, and Antwerp was on the way to the Belgian coast. It was a fine city to ransom; its loss might convince the Belgians that there was no hope for their independence; and historical Germans bethought themselves of Napoleon's description of Antwerp as a pistol pointed at England's heart. Its fall would be some consolation for the lack of a second Sedan, and on 28 September the siege began.

The Antwerp defences had been, like those of Liège and Namur, designed by Brialmont, and were begun in 1861. But the rapid growth of the city and the increasing range of guns made Brialmont's ring of forts, which was drawn little more than two miles from the walls, useless as a protection against bombardment, and twenty years later a wider circle of forts, which was barely completed when war broke out, was begun ten miles farther out, beyond the Rupel and the Nethe, and extending almost to Malines. One of the objects of the Belgian sorties had been to keep this ring intact and prevent the German howitzers from being brought up within range of the city. But there are only two means by which forts can be made effective defences; either their artillery must be equal in range and power to that of the attacking force, or the attacking force must be prevented by defending troops from bringing its howitzers within range. Neither of these two conditions was fulfilled. The Belgian trenches, so far as any had been dug, were close under this outer ring of forts, and the German 28-cm. howitzers had an effective range of at least a mile and a half longer than that of any guns the Belgians could mount. These howitzers had already disposed of the fortifications of Liège, Namur, and

Maubeuge, and it was only a question of days and hours when they would make a breach in the outer defences of Antwerp.

Their fire was concentrated on Forts Waelhem and Wavre, south and east of Antwerp. Both had been destroyed by 1 October, and the reservoir near the former, which supplied the city with water, was broken down, flooding the Belgian trenches north of the Nethe, beyond which they had now taken refuge. Farther to the left Termonde was seized by German infantry and the Belgians driven across the Scheldt. On the 2nd the Government resolved to leave Antwerp, but its departure and the flight of the civilians were postponed by the arrival of Mr. Churchill, First Lord of the Admiralty, and first a brigade of Royal Marines and then two naval brigades of splendid but raw and ill-armed recruits. They were at once sent out to help the Belgians to defend their trenches along the north bank of the Nethe against the German numbers and their more effective shells. On the 5th and following night both the left and centre of the defence were pierced, the Germans crossed the Nethe, and began to concentrate their howitzers on the inner line of ramparts. On the 7th the exodus from the city began by land and water, and amid heartrending scenes a quarter of a million people strove to reach the Dutch frontier or safety on the sea. The Belgian and British troops did their best to hold off the Germans while the flight proceeded and the city was subject to bombardment. It was doubtful whether any would get away, for the Germans had at last begun serious fighting up the Scheldt in order to cut off the retreat towards Zeebrugge and Ostend. In the narrow gap between the intruding Germans and the Dutch frontier some were forced across the latter and interned; others fell into the enemy's hands; and less than a third of the first Naval Brigade escaped to England. On the 9th the bombardment ceased, and on the 10th the Germans made their formal entry into a well-nigh deserted city. They had got their pistol pointed at the heart of England, but like Napoleon they learnt that it was a pistol which could only be fired by sea-power.

Most of the Belgian Army with the remnants of the British forces got away to the coast through the gap beyond the Scheldt which Von Beseler had failed to close in time; and it is impossible to say whether the gallant efforts of the Royal Marines and naval brigades did more to facilitate this escape than the postponement of the retreat, caused by their arrival, did to frustrate it. As an end in itself the expedition for the relief of Antwerp was a failure; but it was designed to subserve a larger operation, the scope of which has not yet been revealed. At the time of its dispatch there may still have been hopes for the success of Joffre's larger strategical scheme of bending back the German flank in Flanders behind the Scheldt; and obviously, if the failure of the Germans at the Marne and a successful defence of Antwerp by the Entente should induce the Dutch to intervene, the German position in the West would be completely turned. In either case "other and more powerful considerations," as the Admiralty expressed it on 17 October, prevented the "large operation" of which the expedition of the Naval Division had been merely a part, from being carried out; and the "powerful consideration" may have been the forces which Germany was massing at Aix and in Belgium to defeat the Entente strategy in Flanders.

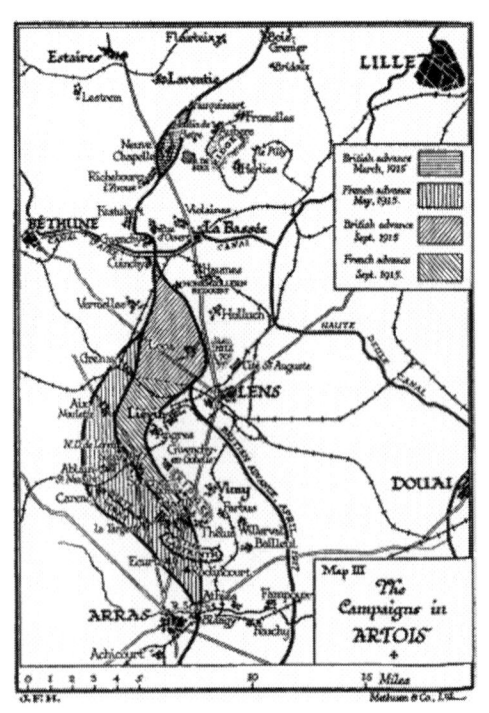

The Campaigns In Artois

The fall of Antwerp was as fatal to our scheme of controlling the Scheldt as Castlenau's and Maud'huy's successful defence between the Oise and Arras had been to the German project of reaching the mouth of the Seine; and it still remained to be seen at what point the expanding pressure upon the opposing flanks would impinge upon the coast. Neither side had yet reconciled itself to or perhaps conceived of such a stalemate to their strategy. Rawlinson's 7th Division of infantry and 3rd of cavalry had not been landed at Zeebrugge and Ostend on 6 October to defend those ports or even the Yser, and the fresh German armies advancing through Belgium were not intended to waste their strength on the ridges in front of Ypres or floods around Dixmude. The Germans hoped, if not to turn the Entente flank, at least to seize Dunkirk, Calais, and Boulogne; and Joffre and French were planning to make La Bassée, Lille, and Menin the pivot of a turning movement which should liberate Brussels, isolate Von Beseler in Antwerp, and threaten the rear of the German position along the Aisne. To render these plans feasible it was necessary that La Bassée and Lille should be held and that the indefinite German flank in Flanders should be outreached; and thus the country from Arras northwards to the coast became the ground on which the autumn campaign in the West was doomed to be decided.

Antwerp fell amid a fluid front. On 9 October Maud'huy's 10th Army was holding up in front of Arras; but his Territorials were falling back on Lille and its environment as the Belgians retreated to join Rawlinson at Ostend. French's three corps were on their way to prolong and establish Maud'huy's left, and an 8th French army under D'Urbal was designed to fling the line yet farther north. But the Germans were bent on a similar object, and their masses of cavalry, released from the front on the Aisne by its settlement into trenches, were keeping open the country and the issue. The rival armies were like two doors swinging towards one another on the same hinge; but they were not wooden or rigid, and the banging together began at the hinge near La Bassée and extended northwards to the coast in a concussion spread over several days. On 11 October Smith-Dorrien's 2nd Corps reached the La Bassée Canal between Aire and Béthune, while Gough's cavalry was clearing the German patrols out of the forest of Nieppe. On the 12th he attempted a frontal attack on La Bassée, but found the German position too strong, and determined to try to wheel round it on the north. This movement had some success; the 3rd Division drove the Germans from village to village until on the 17th Aubers and Herlies, north to north-east of La Bassée, were taken by assault. But the Germans were simultaneously and in the same way driving in the French Territorials; on the 13th they occupied Lille, and on the 19th an Irish brigade which had advanced beyond Herlies to Le Pilly was cut off and captured. So far as the 2nd Corps was concerned the doors had banged together.

Pulteney's 3rd was moving towards collision on the left. It detrained from St. Omer on the 11th, drove the Germans out of Meteren on the 13th, occupied Bailleul and Armentières and then crossed the Lys, gaining a line from Le Gheir, north of Armentières, to Bois Grenier by the 17th. An attempt to clear the right bank farther north failed against the opposition of the German front from Radinghen to Frelinghien and thence along the river. Here, too, the way was barred, but north of the Lys there was as yet no stable control. There were some French and British cavalry and some weak detachments of infantry; but Haig's 1st Corps had not yet completed its transport from the Aisne, Rawlinson's 7th Division was being expanded into a 4th Corps, and the Belgian Army was painfully making its retreat from Antwerp. On the 13th Von Beseler was in Ghent, on the 14th in Bruges, and on the 16th in Ostend. The outflanking here was being done by the Germans with uncomfortable rapidity. On the day that the Germans entered Ostend, the Belgians were driven out of the forest of Houthulst and took refuge far behind the Yser. Four French cavalry divisions recovered the forest on the 17th, but the 7th British Division which had occupied Roulers on the 13th was driven back to a line south-east of Ypres running through Zandvoorde, Gheluvelt, and Zonnebeke (see Map, p. 288).

D'Urbal's 8th French army now, however, came up to support the exhausted Belgians and assist in holding the Yser from Dixmude to the sea, where British warships were assembled to harass the German flank along the dunes; and Sir John French thought the moment had come for an offensive wheel round Menin towards the Scheldt. Haig's 1st Corps was expected shortly to fill the gap between Rawlinson's 4th and D'Urbal, and Rawlinson was instructed to advance on the 18th, seize Menin, and then await

Haig, who was to move through Ypres on to Thourout, Bruges, and Ghent. In England it was confidently expected that the Germans, who had arrived at Ostend on a Friday, would enjoy but a week-end visit to the seaside resort, and the newspapers were not more sadly optimistic or ill-informed than headquarters in France. The orders given on the 18th and 19th could only have been the outcome of complete ignorance of the strength of the German Army, which was as much underestimated by the Intelligence Department on the spot as it was later exaggerated by writers on the campaign. In reality four new German Corps were already at Brussels or Courtrai mainly from Württemberg and Bavaria, and although the presence in them of men with grey beards and boys with none gave rise to some ill-timed satisfaction in the British press, these Landsturm troops were not to be despised. Rawlinson moved on Menin on the 19th, but was stopped three miles away by the German masses coming from Courtrai, and had to entrench on a line running east of Gheluvelt. On the same day the 1st Corps detrained at St. Omer and marched towards Ypres. Instead of advancing on Thourout and beyond, it had to dig itself in on a line of defence from Rawlinson's left at Zonnebeke to Bixschoote, where the French began their own and the Belgian front along the Yser to Nieuport.

The impact of the opposing forces had flattened them out until they extended to the coast, and the point at which they reached it remained fixed for four years to a day. Instead of a brilliant strategical run round the enemy's flanks to a distant goal in his rear, there was fated to be a strenuous scrimmage all along the line. It was a democratic sort of war, depending for its decision upon the stoutness of the pack rather than on the genius of the individual. The pressure was differently distributed at different periods during those endless years; now it was Ypres, now Verdun, then the Somme and the Chemin des Dames that was selected for the special push; and in time as their man-power began to fail the Germans laid greater stress on the concrete of their lines. But the line was never really broken, and no flank was ever fully turned. It wavered at places and times now in favour of one side and now in that of the other; but the end only came when the whole was pushed back by superior weight of numbers, advancing at an average rate of less than a mile a day.

The first great trial of strength is associated in British minds with the first battle of Ypres. The French dwell rather on the equally strenuous struggle farther south round Arras under Foch. For the line of battle stretched north from the Albert plateau for a hundred miles, and we can hardly claim that the boys and the middle-aged men, at whom some were inclined to scoff, in Flanders were the pick of the German troops sent into the fray. The glory of the defence consisted rather in the resistance of better troops to superior numbers backed by a vast preponderance of artillery. The estimates of the German forces are still little more than conjectures; and the figures of a million and a half Germans to half a million French, British, and Belgians, or of fifty corps to twelve and a half, will probably be corrected when the German statistics are known. If it is further true that at the actual points of fighting the disproportion was five to one, we need no further illustration of the ills which inadequate co-ordination imposes on an Alliance, and inadequate staff-work and intelligence on any fighting force. The Allied tactics were probably not so clumsy nor the German troops so feeble as these thoughtless estimates imply.

It was not a struggle in which there was much scope for strategy on either side, because there had been no fixed data on which to base it. Each combatant had been bent on out-flanking the other before the sea was reached and success denied; but neither knew from day to day or hour to hour where his own or the enemy's line would be. It was idle to plan at headquarters the investment of places which might at the moment be well behind the lines, or the defence of others which the enemy might already have passed; and the alleged inexplicable nature of the German strategy seems to be largely due to an antedating of the establishment of a line of battle. They might have done better to concentrate on Arras with a view to breaking the Anglo-French liaison on the La Bassée Canal and isolating the British Army, than to distribute their onslaughts over a front of a hundred miles. But the problem was to outflank a wing which was still in the air, and not to break a line which was not yet formed; and even if it were in existence, subsequent experience would have justified the conviction that success was to be obtained by pressure along an extended front rather than by concentration on limited sectors like Verdun, or even the 18-mile front of the battle of the Somme. The struggle which closed the autumn campaign in the West was not, in fact, a new battle fought on a preconceived plan, but the final clash of armies seeking to outmarch each other's flanks in a battle begun on the Marne; and the popular German advertisement of a new campaign against the Channel ports and a different enemy than the French was merely a fresh coat of paint designed to cover a structure that had gone to pieces.

Apart from the effort to outflank, neither side could therefore have any definite plan, and neither was able to choose the scene of conflict. Two years later, when they withdrew to the Hindenburg lines, the Germans admitted freely enough that the earlier line had been none of their choice, and it was certainly none of ours. It was, in fact, imposed upon both the combatants by that same balance of forces which eventually also imposed upon them, against their will, the deadlock in the West. On 19 October Sir John French was still hoping that Haig could outflank the Germans at Ghent, and the presence of the Kaiser on the coast a few days later suggests that his generals still cherished the idea of an outmarch rather than a break-through. It was the British Navy that put the final check on that design, and accident played its part. Three Brazilian monitors of shallow draught but heavy armament had been purchased by the Admiralty in August: they could work inshore even along the shallow waters of the Belgian coast which precluded counter-attack by submarines, and from 18 to 28 October their guns swept the Belgian shore for six miles inland and repelled the onslaught of the German right on Nieuport. Haig's outflanking project had been rendered equally impossible by the strength of the German resistance to Rawlinson's move on Menin, and by the 21st both sides had been pinned down to a ding-dong soldiers' battle all along the front. Its chronology is as important as its localities, and it is hard to follow the course of the struggle if the narrative loses itself in the different threads of the various corps engaged. For all were fighting at the same time, and the only generalizations possible are that the struggle tended to concentrate from both wings towards the apex at Ypres and to culminate in the combat of the last day of the month.

This bird's-eye view and lack of information about the details do less than justice to the crucial battle, which Maud'huy under Foch's general direction waged against the Germans round Arras and both they and the French regard as one of the decisive incidents in the war. Clearly, if Von Buelow succeeded in breaking through towards Doullens or Béthune there was little to stop his reaching Boulogne or Abbeville, and the British Army would be first isolated and then driven into the sea. The struggle for Arras began on the 20th, after the Germans had secured an initial advantage by seizing Lens, and Von Buelow was given the Prussian Guard to achieve its capture. The climax was reached on the 24th in an attempt to take the important railway junction of Achicourt just south of the city. Arras itself was reduced almost to ruins by the German bombardment; but Maud'huy's men held good, and on the 26th were even able to take the offensive. The Germans were driven out of their most advanced positions, though they held the Vimy Ridge, and accepting defeat before Arras, transferred some of their best troops, including the Prussian Guards, farther north. Possibly this relinquishment was the worst of their tactical mistakes, but the higher commands on both sides had learnt the cost of persisting in attempts to break through, and Falkenhayn may well have thought it best to seek a weaker spot.

Maud'huy's successful resistance made it possible for Smith-Dorrien's 2nd Corps to hold a line north of the La Bassée Canal, though not the line on which he had first come up against the Germans advancing from Lille. That formed a right angle, stretching north-east from Givenchy to Herlies and then north-west to Fauquissart; but on the 22nd his right was driven out of Violaines, and the salient had to be evacuated by withdrawal to a line in front of Givenchy, Festubert, and Neuve Chapelle. On the 27th Neuve Chapelle was taken by the Germans. A gallant attack by Indian troops, who had been brought up from Marseilles to assist Smith-Dorrien's tried and depleted corps, checked their advance on the 28th and drove them back into Neuve Chapelle; and another German attack was held before Festubert. Here Sir James Willcock's Indian Corps had a hard task for the next few days, and a breach in our lines on 2 November was only repaired by a desperate charge of the Gurkhas. The winter of northern France was to have more effect on their physique than German warfare on their moral, and after a final assault on Givenchy—one of the virgin pivots of the war in the West—on 7 November, the battle in front of the 2nd Corps subsided into an artillery duel. The fighting in front of Pulteney's 3rd Corps, which carried on the line from Smith-Dorrien's left towards Ypres, was overshadowed by the struggle round that city; but it had enough to do to maintain the connexion. Its hold on the left bank of the Lys north of Armentières was strenuously disputed; on the 20th the Germans seized Le Gheir at the south-east corner of Ploegstreet Wood, but were immediately driven out. They took it again on the 29th and some trenches in the wood with no more permanent success, but managed on the 30th to take and retain St. Yves a little farther north.

This was part of the Ypres fighting, and downwards from the coast the surge of battle was also drawn into that maelstrom. The British naval guns had destroyed the attraction of the dunes, and the Germans turned towards the inland marshes along the Yser. On the 23rd they crossed it and advanced to Ramscapelle, but were driven back by the Belgians, while fourteen unsuccessful attacks were made the following night on Dixmude, farther south. A more successful attempt was made on the 24th and 25th on Schoorbakke, and the Germans advanced towards the railway embankment near Pervyse. The Belgians now bethought themselves of the expedient their forbears had found effective in the days of William the Silent and Alexander Farnese. The Yser was dammed at Nieuport, the sluices were opened above Dixmude, and slowly the river rose above its banks and spread over the meadow-flats the Germans were striving to cross. Men were drowned and guns submerged, and presently an impassable sheet of water protected the Belgians on the railway from Nieuport to Dixmude. The Germans, however, made two more efforts to pierce the Belgian line north and south of the inundation. On the 30th they seized Ramscapelle, but were expelled by the French on the 31st, and on 7 November a determined attack was made on Dixmude, now defended by Admiral Ronarc'h and his French marines. It succeeded after three days' fighting and a heavy bombardment on the 10th. But Dixmude had, as was natural in a country which had generally feared attack from France, been built on the eastern bank of the Yser; and the Germans were never able to debouch across the river (see Map, p. 288).

The capture of Dixmude coincided with the last attack on Ypres. That famous battle was but an act in the drama played along the Flanders front, and it may not have been more decisive and was perhaps less dramatic than the battle of Arras. But the act extended throughout the play, and gradually attracted more and more attention. It was a natural continuation of the outflanking struggle, and there was no interval between the British attempt to get to Ghent and the German effort to reach the Channel ports. The two ambitions here clashed in front of Ypres. Rawlinson's failure before Menin left him facing south-east, while the expulsion of the Belgians and then the French Territorials from the Houthulst forest left Haig and the French contingents facing north-east from Bixschoote to Zonnebeke; the apex of this Ypres salient was at Becelaere. D'Urbal's 8th Army from Bixschoote north to Dixmude played a subsidiary part similar to that of Pulteney's 3rd Corps farther south; but had it not been for the supports he was able to send to Haig's assistance, the Germans would assuredly have broken through.

The attack began from the apex to our right at Zillebeke on the 21st, and its momentum showed that nothing more than stubborn defence was possible. The 7th Division bore the brunt of the attack, and Haig's 1st Corps was precluded from a counter-offensive by the need of detaching supports to the south-east of Ypres, where long stretches of line were only held by cavalry, and Pulteney was being pressed in front of Ploegstreet. On the 23rd the Germans made an impetuous onslaught on Langemarck, but the pressure was relieved by a French advance on the left and their taking over the line of our 1st Division, which enabled Haig to move in support of the centre. Nevertheless the Germans drove it from Becelaere and got into Polygon Wood. At night on the 25th they struck at Kruseik, between Gheluvelt and Zandvoorde. There followed a suspicious lull, and on the 29th the reinforced Germans drove against the centre of the 1st Corps at Gheluvelt; an initial success was reversed later on in the day, but on the 30th the attack shifted towards the right at Zandvoorde, and the 1st Division was forced back a mile to Zillebeke, while the 2nd conformed and the 2nd Cavalry Division was driven from Hollebeke back to St. Eloi. The Kaiser arrived that day and the crisis on the morrow. Gheluvelt was the point selected for the blow, and the 1st Division was thrust back into the woods in front of Hooge, where headquarters were heavily shelled. The flank of the 7th Division was thus exposed, and the Royal Scots Fusiliers were wiped out. Fortunately the arrival of Moussy with part of the 9th French Corps averted further disaster, though he had to collect regimental cooks and other unarmed men to help in holding the line. Allenby's cavalry farther south was in equally desperate straits near Hollebeke, and he was only saved by the transference of Kavanagh's 7th brigade from the north of Hooge to his assistance. North of the Ypres-Menin road the German attack had not been seriously pressed, and it was from this direction that help came between 2 and 3 p.m., the hour which Sir John French once described as the most critical in the Ypres battle. The main instrument was the 2nd Worcesters, who fell upon the German advanced and exposed right, and retook Gheluvelt by a bayonet charge. This relieved the pressure on the 7th Division, and by nightfall their positions had been regained.

But the battle was not yet over. On 1 November the Germans renewed their attack on Allenby and captured Hollebeke and Messines, and then in the night Wytschaete. Luckily on that day the French 16th Corps arrived and recovered Wytschaete. The Germans themselves now needed reinforcements and time to recover, and for some days there was little fighting except an unequal artillery duel. On the 6th a German attack on Zillebeke nearly succeeded, but was eventually repulsed by a charge of the Household Cavalry. Another pause followed, but the Germans were bent on one more effort, and the Prussian Guards were brought up from Arras to make it on the 11th. They charged on the Menin road against Gheluvelt and drove the 1st Division back into the woods behind; but then they were held, and counter-attacks recovered most of the lost positions. The Germans by this time were tired of Ypres, though they continued for four days longer to struggle for Bixschoote, where Dubois and his Zouaves put up a splendid and successful defence, and a few spasmodic attempts were made at Zillebeke and elsewhere between 12 and 17 November. Then, with the arrival of further French reinforcements, the Germans desisted, and the line of battle in Flanders sank into an uneasy winter torpor. The second as well as the first thoughts of the German command for the campaign of 1914 in the West had come to nought, or to what was nearly as bad, a stalemate; and the East was calling with an urgent and distracting voice to other fields of battle.

CHAPTER VI

THE FIRST WINTER OF THE WAR

The lull which followed the battle of Ypres was not entirely due to the winter season or to the Flanders mud, for both sides had other reasons for quiescence in the West. The Germans had definitely failed in their original plan of destroying the French armies before the Russians could intervene, and they were now threatened with the ruin of their Austrian ally and the invasion of their own Silesian borders. The steam-roller, which had been moving to and fro across the Polish plains, seemed to have at last secured a solid impetus in the forward direction which might conceivably carry it to the Brandenburg Gate by Christmas. Württemburgers and Bavarians might afford to keep their eyes fixed on the Channel ports and their troops in Belgium; but the affections of Prussians were set on their homes in the East, and Hindenburg was calling for reinforcement more clamantly than the Western commanders. Defence was for many a month to be the German strategy in the West, and, in spite of the failure of their higher ambitions, they had secured a good deal worth defending. Belgium, with its great mining and other industrial resources, was theirs to relieve the strain on German labour and raw materials; from the Briey district in Lorraine they were drawing ores without which they could not long have continued the war; and the coalfields of northern France were divided between their owners and the invaders. The strain which the lack of these resources put upon the industries and shipping of Great Britain was incalculable, and the inability of the Entente to defend the French and Belgian frontiers or to expel the invader prolonged the war for at least a couple of years.

There were thus compensations for the Germans if they could merely hold what they had taken from other people; and the Entente on its side had its reasons for quiescence. French reserves, which were too late at Charleroi and Sedan, were in time at Arras and Ypres, but our own were still in the making. A dreadful toll had been taken of the heroes of Mons, and the original Expeditionary Force had been sadly depleted. It was a difficulty which time would remedy, for Great Britain was teeming with recruits in training from every quarter of the Empire. The response to its need had been almost overwhelming, and the Government was hard pressed to embody the hundreds of thousands of volunteers at home and to provide transport for those overseas. At one moment in September the War Office took the extraordinary step of checking the rush by refusing all recruits, however fit, who were less than 5 ft. 6 in. in height; and to arm and equip and train the accepted was a task which required time and a vast readjustment of industry. It was not assisted by a business community which took as its early motto "business as usual," and was mainly alarmed by the fear of unemployment. But the traditions of peace were potent in other than Government circles, and history afforded no precedent for the crisis, nor for the spirit in which it was met by the youth of the Empire, who feared less for their lives than most of their elders did for their profits.

The first source from which the regular forces could be recruited was the Territorials. They had been formed before the war on the idea that they were required merely for home defence, and no one had yet thought of the equivocation that home defence included that of India, Egypt, Belgium, and France, or offence in Mesopotamia and the Dardanelles. There was no need for the Government to rely on that quibble, for the Territorials volunteered almost in mass for foreign service, and the difficulty was to impress Lord Kitchener with the value of a force with which his absence in the East had made him unfamiliar. As it was, some of the best of the regiments, like the London Scottish, put in an appearance at Ypres, while numbers were sent to Egypt and India to release for service in Europe the regular forces there. With them came native Indian regiments, Sikhs, Gurkhas, and Bhopals, whose voluntary service provided the most touching testimonial to its character that the British Empire has ever received; for they did not govern themselves, and it is no small thing to govern others in such a way as to provoke loyalty unto death. No less moving was the response from Dominions which were thought by the ill-informed to be straining at the leash of Imperial domination. The Canadians, having the shortest route, were the first to come, and on 16 October the advance guard disembarked at Liverpool. They were followed by scores and then hundreds of thousands from Australia and New Zealand, and finally from South Africa, where for the moment the task of suppressing rebellion and dealing with German South-West Africa kept them at more immediate duties nearer home. They were all volunteers; for although Canada adopted conscription in the last year of the war, Australia rejected the proposal twice, and it was never made in South Africa; and the splendid colonial troops which covered themselves with glory in the war contained no conscripts among their numbers.

During the winter of 1914-15 Great Britain was a vast camp of men from all quarters of the Empire training for that offensive in the spring on which men's hopes were set. A saying attributed to Lord Kitchener passed from mouth to mouth, to the effect that he did not know when the war would end, but that it would begin in May. Hitherto our forces engaged had been merely an advance guard of our manpower, and it was a common anticipation that the Allied offensive would bring the war to a successful conclusion by the end of 1915. With such hopes President Poincaré cheered the French troops in their trenches at Christmas, and in January a semi-official communiqué announced that the French had broken the German offensive and could break the German defensive whenever they chose. This pleasing illusion was maintained, not so much by a censorship of the truth as by incapacity on the part of those in authority to discern it, and by a natural tendency of the wish to be father of the thought. German communiqués afforded some means of correction, but they were universally disbelieved or discounted as containing an amount of falsehood of which no ally could be guilty, although, until the last few months of the war, they were rather less misleading than our own. Nor was it only official news that was delusive. "The Times," for instance, in January put the total German "losses" down to date at two million and a quarter; and an expert historian debited Germany with a "dead loss, perhaps, of little less than three million by the beginning of

April," whereas the casualties barely reached half that figure, and of the casualties a vast percentage consisted of slight wounds which did not prevent a speedy return to the fighting-line. Medical science prolonged the war by reducing disease and restoring the sick and wounded; and the military statistician went as far astray in his prophecies of the exhaustion of Germany's man-power as the economist in his predictions of its bankruptcy and starvation by blockade.

Nevertheless the conviction that, whether we or the Germans attacked, they had double our casualties, comforted the public during the war of trenches; not merely were we holding our own while our reserves in training were mounting to millions, but all the time we were thought to be wearing down the enemy's strength, and his prudent economy in the use of men and munitions was taken as proof of his poverty in resources. His real work in those winter months was done behind the lines in factory and in barracks, and its value was tested and revealed in the coming campaign, which found the front in the West almost precisely where it was left to the autumn. Here and there a village or a line of trenches had been taken, but by different sides, and the balance was hardly worth counting. A sand-dune was captured near Nieuport, a trench in front of St. Eloi, and ten days' fighting round La Bassée, which severely tried the Indian troops, nearly led to the loss of Givenchy, but quite to the gain of a brickfield. Early in December the French took the château of Vermelles and improved their positions at Lihons and Quesnoy, but suffered in January a reverse north of Vailly. In Champagne they captured Perthes in February and made some progress in the Argonne; in the Woevre they nibbled at both sides of the St. Mihiel wedge, while in Alsace they acquired Steinbach but lost the Hartmannsweilerkopf. But against this balance of gain must be set a more subtle but comprehensive loss. The contest was not limited to the occasional bursts of fighting or to the steady endurance required for holding the trenches amid the discomfort of mud and water, bombs and shell-fire. It also took the form of incessant competition in the perfection of surface and underground defences. The Germans excelled in this art; but even if they had not, the silent development of the strength of defence would have told in the defenders' favour when the time came for attack; and it was an advantage which told all along the line and more than atoned for the local loss of a trench or position. The truth was that during a seeming stalemate the Germans made ample provision for holding their lines in the West while they prepared and dealt a staggering blow at their formidable foe in the East.

A week before the Prussian Guard made its final charge at Ypres, Belgians reported the moving of masses of German troops away to the East. We have seen that the need was urgent, for Cossacks were already across the Silesian frontier, and Hindenburg required all the help he could get for his counter-offensive. He was planning an attack from Thorn up the Vistula primarily to strike the right flank of the Russian advance through Poland on Silesia and Cracow, and secondly to menace Warsaw. The command was entrusted to Mackensen, while Ruszky withstood the Germans with his right near Plock on the Vistula, his centre behind the Bzura, and his left stretching out towards Lodz. The Germans attacked all along the line on 18 November, but Ruszky's left seemed to afford the easiest prey; it had no natural line of defence, and Hindenburg's devastation during his retreat in October made the arrival of reinforcements from Ivanov farther south unlikely. Nevertheless Mackensen's most impetuous drive was against Ruszky's centre across the causeway at Piontek; it promised a dramatic success, and nearly ended in resounding disaster. The Russian centre was broken and the left thrust back upon Lodz, where it was attacked on three sides and seemed doomed to destruction. But the wedge was not sufficiently wide; it merely created a pocket in the Russian line. The sides held fast and Ruszky began to close the mouth. For three days, 24-26 November, the Germans fought desperately to get out, and at length the remnant succeeded, owing mainly to the lateness of reinforcements sent by Rennenkampf at Ruszky's request. Troops, however, were rapidly being rushed up to Mackensen's help, and on 6 December the Russian left withdrew from Lodz, the industrial capital of Poland with half a million inhabitants. The advantage of the retirement was to straighten the Russian line in face of the determined effort which Hindenburg was bent on making to secure Warsaw as a Christmas present for the Kaiser (see Map, p. 146).

The line selected for defence ran almost due north to south from the Vistula up the Bzura and its tributary the Rawka to Rawa and thence across the Pilitza to Opocznow. The territory abandoned was well worth the security gained on this line, and for three weeks the Germans stormed against it in vain. A flank attack from the north of the Vistula was driven back by the Russians at Mlawa, and no better success attended the German frontal onslaughts at Sochaczew, where the main road to Warsaw crosses the Bzura, and at Bolimow, where another crosses the Rawka. The Germans spent their Christmas in the trenches instead of in the Polish capital, thirty-five miles away. Somewhat better fortune was experienced by the Hungarian offensive against the Russians in Galicia, which was part of Hindenburg's plan. Dmitrieff was almost in the suburbs of Cracow at the beginning of December, but his left was then threatened by the Hungarian seizure of the Dukla pass, and he had to retreat to the line of the Dunajec and the Nida with his flank drawn back to Krosno and Jaslo. Presently the Hungarians threatened also the Lupkow and Uszok passes farther east; but reinforcements arrived, Brussilov closed the passes, and Dmitrieff's left swung forward again. It did not, however, advance beyond the Biala, and the Russians spent their Christmas as far from Cracow as the Germans did theirs from Warsaw.

Winter, however, brought less respite from war on the frozen plains of Poland than on the sodden soil of Flanders. The first and second attacks upon Warsaw were followed by a third in January; there was a winter battle by the Masurian lakes in February, and a fierce struggle along the Niemen in March; and the Russian offensive across the Carpathians was only stopped by the German spring campaign. The Russians, indeed, were doomed to bear the brunt of the war in 1915, at first with success and afterwards in adversity; for the Germans had reversed the strategy with which they had begun the war. Then they had relied on the defensive in the East while they gathered up all their strength for the crushing of France. That blow having failed, they were now preparing to drive Russia out of the war, while they trusted to their line in the West to hold against any efforts to break it. The change of plan was probably a mistake, though it brought such success at the moment that volatile critics in England were persuaded that the original war on the West had been merely a blind for real designs in the East. At any rate, in the West we had cause to be thankful that the German attacks were but local, and that the serious offensive against Verdun did not come until 1916, when we were prepared to counter it on the Somme.

Meanwhile there was some excuse for the German choice. There was safety enough for the moment in France and Flanders, and events justified Germany's confidence that no Entente attack in 1915 could seriously disturb the German lines. No such grounds for complacence existed on her Eastern frontiers. East Prussia was not yet free, and graver danger threatened the Hungarian ally on which the Prussian relied only less than he did on himself. Galicia was in Russian hands, and Russian man-power was thought to be inexhaustible. The menace on both the Carpathian and the Prussian flanks could only be properly met by destroying the central position in Poland, and persistence in the attacks on Warsaw was essential to German strategy in the East. The frontal attack at the end of January which failed for the third time was followed by a flanking attack on the Niemen which also failed, and then by a drive on the southern flank in Galicia which turned the whole Russian front of 900 miles, led to a wholesale retreat, and precipitated the greatest set-back the Allies suffered in the war. Germany failed against the democracies of the West, she succeeded against a government more autocratic than her own.

During January the Russian centre in front of Warsaw had been weakened for the sake of movements against the enemy's extreme flanks, which were undertaken in response to requests from the Western Powers in order to divert German reinforcements from France and Flanders. There was a fresh advance towards the Masurian lakes in East Prussia, and far to the south Alexeiev captured a Carpathian pass at Kirlibaba. Mackensen took advantage of this dispersion to organize a strenuous attack on the Russian lines near the confluence of the Bzura and the Rawka. It began on the night of 1 February, and the Russians were on the 2nd and 3rd pressed back from their position on the heights at Borzymow and Gumin. But two railways from Warsaw ran north and south of the threatened front, and reinforcements brought up along them stopped the German advance. It would in any case have been held before the still stronger lines at Blonie which were the real defences of Warsaw on the west, and Hindenburg now gave up the frontal attack as hopeless. It was only, however, to turn to the northern flank and repeat his attempt of October to pierce the great chain of fortresses which defended Poland along the line of the Niemen and the Narew from Kovno to Novo Georgievsk.

His movement was further provoked by the Russian raid which had already advanced once more across the border to close on Tilsit, Insterburg, and Angerburg and well to the west of Lyck. Hindenburg was ever fertile in surprises on this familiar ground, and on 7 February his left, commanded by Eichhorn, drove the Russians back along the railway to Kovno, and within a week had occupied Mariampol. His right was also well across the frontier, marching on Grodno and Ossowiec. Superior forces and railway communications accounted for his success, and one Russian corps met with a disaster. But conditions on the Russian side of the frontier equalized matters. The Germans occupied Suwalki and Augustowo, and even crossed the Niemen at Drusskeniki between Olita and Grodno, while farther north they seized Tauroggen. But they were unable to cut the Kovno-Warsaw railway which ran but ten miles east of the Niemen, and Ossowiec farther south successfully stood a siege. By the middle of March Hindenburg had withdrawn his left and centre to cover the Prussian frontier. He had suffered considerably, but his right got off even less lightly.

It was here that his main strategic objective lay. The thrust against the Niemen had been simply designed to drive the Russians out of Prussia and protect the left of the German offensive to the south on the Narew and Warsaw. Since the German failure in December a Russian army had been pushing slowly down the right bank of the Vistula in front of Plock. This movement was checked in February, and the Germans hoped by an advance from Mlawa to get across the Narew south of Pultusk. The centre of the Russian defence was at Prasnysz where eight roads meet, but the defending force was weak, and on 24 February the Germans captured the town. But the extreme Russian left made a heroic stand on the ridge between Prasnysz and Ciechanow against Germans in front and on both sides of them. Their resistance produced a situation somewhat resembling that at Lodz, for a rapid concentration of Russian reinforcements swept round to the help of the flank at Ciechanow, while others attacked the German left at Krasnosielce. The Germans encircling Ciechanow found themselves encircled at Prasnysz, and as at Lodz they had to fight desperately for three days to escape. They were assisted by the rudimentary equipment of the Russian forces; rifles and ammunition were scarce, bayonets and hand-grenades were none too plentiful, and some of the privates are even said to have fought with pitchforks. By such hand-to-hand and bloody warfare the Germans were driven out of Prasnysz back towards Stegna and Chorzele and their flank attack on Warsaw foiled. Ruszky's strategy and Russian heroism had gained one of the most singular victories in the war.

At the other end of the Russian front, along the Carpathians, politics were beginning to exert a powerful influence upon strategy. South-Eastern Europe was reacting to the Serbian successes in December, and Rumania, like Italy, and with similar Latin feelings, was negotiating with the Entente about terms of intervention. On 27 January a loan of five million pounds was arranged by Great Britain, and while we provided financial inducements Russia dispatched a sympathetic force to overrun the Bukovina, a country kindred to Rumania which she might acquire by co-operation. There would be little risk in joining the war if Russian armies could debouch from the Carpathians; and the intervention of Rumania would link up the Serbians with the Russians and envelop unfortunate Hungary on three sides. But the spring was not yet, and Rumania would wait and see. Her king was a Hohenzollern, and his people were divided in their sympathies. If there were Rumanes under Magyar rule across the Transylvanian Alps, there were also Rumanes under Russian rule across the river Pruth; and the filching of Bessarabia by Russia in 1878 still rankled in the Rumanian mind. Bratianu, the Prime Minister, was a cautious statesman, quite capable of seeing that the occupation of the Bukovina by the Russians was a political demonstration rather than a proof of military capacity to burst the Carpathian barrier. But another argument was thus adduced to show the Prussians the need of victory in the East unless they wished the defence of their two existing fronts to be complicated by another in the south. Hungary was their chief economic, political, and military bastion outside their own dominions, and the subtle bond between Magyar and Prussian notions of government, which gave them a common interest in the war, was now drawn closer by the appointment of Tisza's henchman, Count Burian, as Foreign Secretary to the Hapsburg Empire. For Tisza, the Hungarian Premier, was in all but nationality a Prussian Junker, and his domination depended as much upon a Teutonic victory over the Slavs as a Teutonic victory did upon the retention of the Hungarian granary and a bulwark in the south.

The Carpathians were therefore the key to the future of the war and history of south-eastern Europe. The Russians had in the autumn established a solid control of the Galician outlets from the mountain passes, but had made no serious attempt to achieve the far more difficult task of securing command of the foothills south of the range, which alone would enable them to conquer the plains of Hungary. For a mountain pass is like a river bridgehead; one may often possess it without being able to debouch. The Austrians experienced that difficulty in their winter offensive against the Russian flank in Galicia. They made little progress against Brussilov at the Dukla and Lupkow passes, but farther east they seized most of the mountain routes, and Alexeiev was pressed back in Bukovina. Their centre under Linsingen was, however, held up by the Russians at Hill 992 near Kosziowa, and all efforts to dislodge the defenders failed. This defence saved Galicia for the time and prevented the relief of Przemysl, which otherwise would have been certain. For the Austrian right succeeded late in February in recovering Czernowitz, Kolomea, and on 3 March, Stanislau. Reinforcements, however, now reached the Russians; Stanislau was recaptured, the Austrians lost much of what they had gained, and on the 22nd Przemysl weakly surrendered. Its fame as a fortress had been enhanced by its five months' siege since October, but it did not redound to the credit of its defenders. They were superior in numbers to the besiegers, were amply provisioned, and well supplied with heavy artillery and all the munitions of war. Every sort of blunder seems to have been committed by the commander, who apparently regarded the siege as a relief from more arduous work in the field, and capitulated because the repulse of the rescuing expedition foreboded an increase of inconvenience.

The surrender liberated the besieging force for operations elsewhere, and the Russians began a serious effort to surmount the Carpathian rampart. They got well to the south of the Dukla, made substantial progress in the centre through the Rostoki pass, and by the middle of April held the crests for a continuous seventy miles; cavalry penetrated much farther down the slopes, and the Austrians prepared to evacuate the Ungvar valley. Reciprocal raids occurred elsewhere on the Eastern front: the Russians seized and burnt Memel, and the Germans retaliated by the bombardment of Libau. Despite warnings like that of "The Times" Petrograd correspondent on 13 April to the effect that the Germans had not only sent enormous reinforcements to the Carpathians, but had taken charge of the operations, there was general confidence in the West in a coming triumphant Russian offensive. Dmitrieff himself had no suspicion of what was in store until a few days before the storm broke; and a Panslav society in Petrograd passed and published abroad a resolution that in view of the victorious progress of the Russian armies across the Carpathians, the contemplated intervention of Italy in the war was belated and undesirable.

The Russian Government cannot have been ignorant of the weakness of Russian armies, not in man-power, still less in skill or courage, but in artillery and equipment; but it had no conception of the material and mechanical force which Germany was prepared to bring to the urgent task of relieving the pressure on her ally. Nor was it for nothing that Turkey had been cajoled and bribed into making war. Turkish generalship and organization were negligible quantities, but Germany could supply those defects, and Turkish bravery and man-power could be used as a valuable means of distracting Russia's attention and diverting forces from the Polish and Galician fronts. This had been the main purpose of the campaign in the Caucasus which Turkey waged in the winter. They began by seizing Tabriz in the province of Azerbaijan, which though nominally Persian had been for some time occupied partly by Russian and partly by Turkish troops; but the Russians were first across the Russo-Turkish frontier and captured Bayazid, Khorasan, and Kuprikeui. These advance-guards were, however, pushed back by the Turks, whose leader and evil genius, the half-Polish and German-educated adventurer, Enver, had conceived an ambitious design of encircling the Russian armies between Sarikamysh and Ardahan. In December the Turks succeeded in making their arduous way across the snow-clad mountains, and on 1 January they were in Ardahan. But the task would have tried the German Army itself in summer, and Enver had attempted more than he could achieve. His army corps were successively isolated and defeated in a series of engagements collectively known as the battle of Sarikamysh, and driven back across the frontier with heavy losses. Tabriz was reoccupied by the Russians, though they were not able to follow up their victory by the capture of Erzerum (see Map, p. 182).

The other diversion, which the Turks were used to create against the Entente, was in Egypt. British rule, in spite of the vast benefits it conferred, was not universally acceptable to the Egyptian people and still less to Egyptian officials; and chief among those who resented their restriction to the straight and narrow path of honest administration was the Khedive Abbas II. He threw in his lot with the Turks, and was deposed in his absence, while the shadowy Turkish suzerainty over Egypt was converted into a substantial British protectorate. Cyprus, which had been in British occupation since 1878, was annexed at the same time to the British Crown. The Turks had been deluded by the Germans with hopes of recovering their ancient control of Egypt, and they at once began their feeble efforts to realize their ambitions. In November an expedition started from Palestine to cut the Suez Canal, a main artery of the British Empire, and stir the embers of Moslem fanaticism in Egypt. It disappeared in the sands of the intervening desert. Another, better prepared with German assistance, reached the east bank of the Canal at various points on 2 February, but miserably failed to effect a crossing; its only success was its escape, which was partly explained by a sandstorm, and Egypt had rest until the winter brought the campaigning season round again (see Map, p. 352).

The British retort to Egypt and the Caucasus lay in the Persian Gulf and the Dardanelles. The Persian Gulf had long been a scene of British trade and political enterprise to which the inertia of its rulers rendered Persia susceptible; and its position as a possible Russian outlet to the sea on the flank of our communications with India had produced some rivalry for Persian favours. The advent of a third comer in the shape of the Germans, with their plans for a Germanized Turkish Empire controlling the Berlin-Baghdad route, changed the rivalry into co-operation; and an attack on the Turks at the head of the Persian Gulf was an obvious reply to the Turkish campaign in the Caucasus. It afforded an easy means of employing the native Indian army in the common cause without the long sea journey to France or the risks inflicted by northern winters upon sub-tropical races. During the first half of November detachments of the Indian army sailed up the Shat-el-Arab, the joint estuary of the Tigris and the Euphrates, defeated the Turks at Sahil on the 17th, occupied Basra on the 22nd, and cut off Kurna, which surrendered on 9 December. The local Turks were weak in numbers and equipment, and distance removed them from the stimulus of Enver's energy and German organization. It was not until April 1915 that an effective reaction to the British advance was attempted. Then the Turks and Arabs concerted a movement against the whole line stretching round from Ahwaz within the Persian frontier to Shaiba south-west of Basra. The real attack was on Shaiba, and the battle lasted from 12 to 15 April. The Turks were completely defeated, with some 6000 casualties; but the most important effect was to convert the Arabs into our allies. The advantage was pressed in June, and on the 3rd Amara was captured seventy-five miles to the north of Kurna. The way was open for an advance on Baghdad as soon as autumn made exertion possible in that torrid zone (see Map, p. 177).

Sir John Nixon's success in the Mesopotamian delta was, however, but a pin-prick in a distant part compared with the blow that was aimed at the heart of the Turkish Empire in the Dardanelles; and the merits of that famous but ill-starred enterprise, and of the strategy which inspired it, have been one of the most debated questions of the war. Soldiers and civilians, writers and talkers, and even thinkers were divided into two camps, Westerners and Easterners, those who believed that the war could only be won by frontal attack in the West, and those who discerned a way round to victory in the Near or the Farther East. Volumes might be, and no doubt will be, written on this controversy, and its implications have infinite variety. It involved questions of policy as well as strategy, and therefore raised the delicate problem of the relations between civil and military authority. The soldier only deals with armies, and in the field his voice is properly supreme; but policy may be as far above strategy as strategy is above tactics; and policy may dictate a strategy which would not commend itself on military principles. The soldier has nothing to do with the policy, but policy and diplomacy may or may not bring fresh allies into the war and fresh armies into the field; and a strategy which may be unsound on purely military grounds may be completely justified by political reasons. The diversion of a force from the main field of operations where it is needed to a more distant objective, seems suicidal to the general in command; but if, without provoking disaster on the field it has left, it has the effect of turning the enemy's flank, detaching his actual or deterring his potential allies, and inducing neutrals to intervene, it may win a war although it postpones or risks the success of a campaign.

On the other hand, it was urged that the fundamental principle of strategy is to concentrate all available forces where the enemy has concentrated his, beat him there, and thus win a victory which will carry with it the desired results in all the subsidiary spheres. Germany once beaten in the West, it was argued, there would be no need to trouble about the Balkans or the amateur strategy which looked to Laibach or Aleppo as the vital spot in the situation. This principle was erected into a dogma, and dogma is a dangerous impediment to the art of war. War is an art, and therefore consists in the adaptation of varying means to conditions which are not constant. Strategy is not, apart from its mechanical adjuncts, a science in which properties are fixed, axioms can be assumed, and the results of experiments foretold; the combination of two armies and a commander-in-chief does not produce the same uniform result as the combination of two parts of hydrogen and one of oxygen; and formulae are as irrational in war as in any other human art. Dogmas deduced from the experience of some wars are inapplicable to others; and the science of wars between France and Germany becomes mere imposture when it seeks to dictate dogma to wars in which the British Empire is involved. The particular dogma about concentration had three defects: it left the initiative to the enemy, thus surrendering the advantage, secured by the command of the sea, of being able to strike in other directions; it assumed that the enemy could be beaten on that front without disturbance on his flanks or in his rear; and it abandoned the Near and the Farther East to any schemes on which the Germans might choose to employ their own or their allies' subsidiary forces.

No one, on the other hand, imagined that the Western front could be denuded of the armies required to maintain it. The question was really how to use the considerable margin of force between what was essential for defence and what was needed for a successful offensive. Should it be employed for frontal attack in the West, or flank attack in the East? Caution counselled one course, adventure suggested the other. Surplus force intended for an offensive on the West would be available, if need arose, for defence; it would not, if it were a thousand miles away, and our needs in the spring of 1918 seemed to supply an effective answer to arguments drawn from our later successes in the Balkans and in Syria. The antithesis is, however, largely a false one, due to the exigencies of popular debate and the habit of treating war as an abstract science independent of changing but actual conditions. No one denies that a diversion of our main effort from France to Laibach in the winter of 1917 would have been fatal to us in the spring of 1918, but it is not clear that the thousands of troops we lost at Loos and the French in Champagne in the autumn of 1915 might not better have been employed in saving Serbia or forcing the Dardanelles.

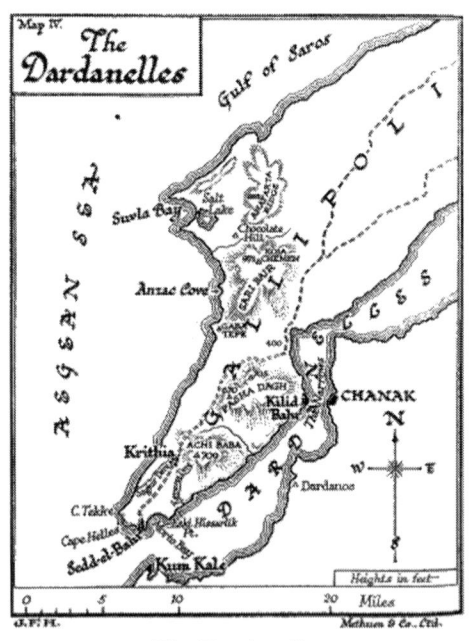

The Dardanelles

There was much to be said for the policy, and even the strategy, which led to the Dardanelles expedition. Flanks had disappeared on the Western front; the lines extended from the Alps to the sea, and it was natural that, commanding the sea, we should seek to turn them farther afield. We had asked Russia to relieve the pressure on our Western front by using her military force in Prussia and Galicia; and it was reasonable enough for Russia to ask us to reciprocate and relieve the Turkish pressure on her flank in the Caucasus by a naval attack on Turkey. The German Fleet lay snug in port beyond the reach of naval power: could not our supremacy on the sea find an offensive function somewhere else? There was, moreover, our own position in Egypt to be defended; no one proposed evacuation, and the best defence of Egypt was a blow at the Dardanelles in the direction of Turkey's capital. It was, in fact, no more a dissipation of forces to send troops to force the Dardanelles than to send them to hold the Suez Canal, and from the point of view of policy, which was even more important, the effect of the expedition might be a concentration of power or Powers against the Central Empires. Serbia had successfully held the gate of the Balkans against Austria: Rumania's intervention would extend the lines of possible attack, Greece inclined in the same direction, and the forcing of the Dardanelles would assuredly have deterred Bulgaria from hostile intervention, and almost certainly have decided her to join a common Balkan move against the Teutons and the Turks. To the war on the Eastern and Western fronts, which was already a German nightmare, would be added one on an almost undefended Southern frontier. Austria could not long resist if Italy also intervened, and the collapse of the Hapsburg Empire would open up an advance against Germany from the south which would circumvent the Rhine and the Oder and turn the gigantic bastion she had constructed in France and Belgium into a house of cards. Well might the Dardanelles expedition be hailed in the press as a stroke of strategical genius and associated with Mr. Churchill's imagination. Easy also is it to understand the concentrated fear and force which the Germans put into Mackensen's coming drive in Galicia.

There is, indeed, less material for censure in the policy of the Dardanelles expedition than in the Allies' decision to couple with it a military offensive on the Western front and to divorce the naval and military efforts in the Aegean. Divided counsels produced divided efforts. Mr. Churchill, backed up, we are led to infer, by Mr. Lloyd George, secured his naval expedition; but he failed, until it was too late, to secure its military complement because the troops were earmarked for costly and premature attacks on the German lines in France. Deprived of this assistance, the naval expedition seems to have relied on the hope of Greek cooperation to the extent of two army corps, which Venizelos was only prevented from dispatching by the vigour of the Prussian Queen of Greece and by the veto of the King. Possibly there was precipitation, for the naval attack did not await the arrival of the military forces, which were before long on the way, extorted, it would seem, by impetuous pressure from a reluctant and unconvinced authority.

For this purely naval attack on the defences of the Dardanelles there is little to be said; for no argument of advantage from success can justify an attempt which is fore-doomed to failure, and history demonstrated beyond a doubt the strength of modern forts against the modern battleship. Nor was it in the Dardanelles a test between an ordinary sea attack and a normal land defence. The strength of the position attacked was trebled by the forts on both sides of the channel and by its twist at the Narrows, which enabled the land batteries to concentrate fire on the attacking fleet from in front as well as on both flanks. There was no room to manoeuvre in a channel less than a mile in width, and even when the mine-fields had been swept, the Turks could send fresh mines down the constant stream, and discharge torpedoes from hidden tubes along both shores. Against such formidable defences even the guns of the Queen Elizabeth were an inadequate attack, and forts that were said to be silenced repeatedly renewed their bombardment.

The first stage of the attack began on 19 February; it consisted in demolishing by concentric fire the outpost fortifications at Kum Kale and Cape Helles. This proved comparatively simple, and after a week of bad weather the mine-sweepers were able to clear the channel for four miles. It was a different matter when the real defences in the Narrows were attacked early in March. The chief bombardment was from outside in the Gulf of Saros, where it was hoped that the guns of the Queen Elizabeth and her consorts would by indirect fire dispose of Chanak and the other forts. None of them were, however, silenced with the possible exception of Dardanos, and Turkish howitzers, cunningly concealed in the scrub along the shore, provided an unpleasant surrise by hitting the Queen Elizabeth. Nevertheless, it was thought that enough had been effected to justify an attempt to force the Narrows on the 18th. Three successive squadrons of British and French ships were sent up the Straits, but the Turks had only waited till the channel was full of vessels to release their floating mines and land-torpedoes. First the French Bouvet, then the Irresistible, and thirdly the Ocean were struck by mines and sunk, the Bouvet with most of her crew. Three battleships and 2000 men had been lost in an attack which did not even reach the entrance to the Narrows; and for six weeks occasional bombardments hardly concealed the fact that the frustrated naval attack was awaiting the co-operation of the army to give it some chance of success.

More progress was happily made during the winter in still more distant spheres, although the conquest of German colonies was regarded by the pure strategist as belonging to the illegitimate and divergent rather than to the legitimate and subsidiary type of military operation. Policy may, however, outweigh strategy, and the circumstance that the victor only retains as the price of peace his conquests, or part of them, made in war, extenuates if it does not justify divergent operations. They were divergent enterprises which gave us India, Canada, and the Cape of Good Hope; and assuredly the defeat of Germany on the Western front would not alone have brought German colonies under the sceptre of a League of Nations. Even from the point of view of a strategy limited to Central Europe these operations had their value; for they enlisted against the common foe forces which would certainly not have been employed had we merely stood on the defensive in the overseas Dominions, and when their work was done in distant parts these forces gravitated towards the centre with a weight which would have grown more crushing had resistance been prolonged. Only surrender by the enemy stayed Allenby's and Marshall's Oriental hosts in Asia and anticipated the arrival on the Western front of further aid from Africa. A blow at the heart may be the normal strategy, but it is not the only nor always the best means of dealing with an antagonist clad in a breastplate of steel.

The scene of the least successful of these colonial wars was still East Africa. The reverse of Tanga in November was followed by another at Jassin on 19 January, and at the end of the winter the Germans could claim that their territory was clear of our troops while several German detachments were in ours; but we had seized the island of Mafia off the mouth of the Rufigi and declared a blockade of the German East African coast. On the other side of the continent we made steady progress in reducing the vast territory of the Cameroons; but the success of the season was

Botha's conquest of German South-West Africa. The last remnants of the rebellion under Maritz and Kemp were stamped out at Upington on 3 February, and on 14 January Swakopmund was captured from the sea. Botha selected that as his base, while Smuts directed three columns farther south. The first advanced on the capital Windhoek from Luderitz Bay, the second from Warmbad near the Orange River, and the third from Kimberley. The second, under Van Deventer, had the heaviest work, but the fighting was not as a rule severe. The campaign was a triumph of forethought, strategy, and organization which left the Germans no choice but a series of retirements, culminating in the surrender of Windhoek on 12 May, and the capitulation of the entire remaining German forces at Grootfontein on 9 July.

On the sea the Germans had abandoned hope of victory. The balance of power in our favour, which had been insufficient to relieve Jellicoe of considerable anxiety, began to increase rapidly with the completion of the Queen Elizabeth class in April; and Germany turned her anticipatory gaze towards her submarines. Just as Napoleon's efforts by means of the Berlin and Milan decrees to ruin us by war on commerce came after the final collapse of his naval ambitions at Trafalgar, so Germany's submarine campaign followed upon her recognition of the hopelessness of her naval situation. On 18 February she proclaimed the waters round the British Isles a war zone in which enemy merchantmen would, and neutrals might, be sunk by submarines irrespective of the risks to non-combatants and neutrals. This was a flagrant violation of the rules of international law which safeguarded the shipping of neutrals, and only sanctioned the condemnation of contraband goods in prize courts, and the destruction of enemy vessels when they could not be taken into port and provision had been made for the safety of their crews and passengers. The German submarines were not in a position to guarantee any of these conditions; and trading on the legal maximum that no one can be required to do what is impossible, the Germans claimed immunity from these obligations.

To this the British Government replied on 1 March with a blockade which was more humane and more effective, but none the less involved an autocratic extension of belligerent rights. All oversea trade with Germany was to be as far as possible intercepted;

goods, whether contraband or not, were at least to be detained; and the right of search was to be rendered more secure by being exercised in British ports, to which neutral ships were brought, instead of on the high seas amid the danger of submarine attack. These measures inflicted no loss of life and no loss of property that was not contraband. But they made havoc with the ideas that neutrals were entitled to trade with both belligerents, and that neither belligerent could intercept commerce which did not directly serve for military purposes. It was not, for instance, a breach of neutrality to sell munitions to a belligerent, though belligerents were entitled to seize them if they could; and we ourselves bought vast quantities from the United States. America was, however, deeply attached to that "freedom of the seas" which enabled neutrals to sell, without interference, goods which were not contraband, to either belligerent; and our extension of contraband to cover food supplies gave deep offence. The difficulty arose not only from the inevitable tendency of law to disappear amid the clash of arms, but from the modern absorption of all energies, civilian as well as military, in the warlike operations of the State. The food of civilians making munitions became a vital element in the conduct of war, and the distinction between civil and military purposes was lost in the fusion of all activities for a common end.

Disquieting as was the course of military operations during the spring, the diplomatic situation caused even more anxiety; and public opinion was as impervious to the one as to the other. American protests against our action on the seas were received with ill-concealed resentment, popular newspapers adjured the Government to "stand no nonsense from the United States," President Wilson's name was hissed by British audiences, and the man in the street seemed bent on estranging the neutral on whose assistance we were in the end to rely for victory in the war. It needed all the resources of an unpopular wisdom and diplomacy to steer between the Scylla of alienating friends by our blockade and the Charybdis of being, in Mr. Asquith's words, "strangled in a network of juridical niceties." The Germans came to our aid with a colossal crime. On 7 May the passenger-ship Lusitania was torpedoed off the south coast of Ireland with the loss of 1100 souls, many of them women and children, and some of them Americans; and the news was hailed in Germany with transports of delight from ministers of religion and all but an insignificant section of the people; medals were officially struck to commemorate the deed. British lives had been lost through Russian action off the Dogger Bank in 1904 without provoking war, and the sinking of the Lusitania did not precipitate war between Germany and the United States. But it eased the friction over our blockade, and gave for the first time some general American support to the pro-Entente sentiment which had from the beginning been strong in the New England States. A moral force was created in reserve which would in time redress the military disasters which the Entente had yet to encounter.

CHAPTER VII

THE FAILURE OF THE ALLIED OFFENSIVE

Effective and timely military co-operation had been denied to the naval attack on the Dardanelles because our available forces had been mortgaged since January to an allied offensive in the West; and the gradual recognition of the fact that the naval enterprise could not succeed without the diversion of troops to that object committed the Entente to the simultaneous prosecution of two major operations which could only converge in case of success. This was but one of the factors in the spring campaign which exhibited Allied strategy at its worst. Even in the West there was inadequate co-operation, and the efforts made were both disjointed and premature. We had yet to learn that alphabet of annihilation without which the art of breaking German lines could not be mastered; and there still lingered the idea that isolated attacks on distant and narrow sectors of the front could rupture the German line and either roll it up or compel a general retreat. Possibly some such plan might have had some chance of success had the forces of the Entente been concentrated upon a single effort, and optimistic critics anticipated a breach to the north of Verdun which might close or at least threaten the neck of the German bottle between Metz and Limburg and precipitate a withdrawal from their carefully prepared positions in northern France and Belgium. But fear of a German counter-offensive threatening the Channel ports, difficulties of transport across lines of communication, and defective unity in ideas and in command condemned the Allied attacks to separate sectors of the front and spheres of operation;

even that general supervision which Foch had exercised over all the forces engaged in the October and November battles seems to have disappeared before the spring, and the French offensive began in the Woevre while the British attacked the other flank protecting Lille (see Map, p. 79).

The point selected was Neuve Chapelle, a village at the foot of the Aubers ridge which guarded La Bassée to the south-west and Lille to the north-east. The German line there formed a marked salient, and an attack on the ridge, if completely successful, would shake the security of Lille, and if but moderately successful would cut off La Bassée and straighten the line as far as Givenchy. The moral indicated by the elaborate defences constructed by the Germans during the winter had been at any rate partially learnt, and the infantry attack on the morning of 10 March was preceded by an artillery preparation which set a new standard of destruction and was designed to obliterate trenches, barbed wire, and machine-gun positions. It was effective over the greater part of the front attacked, and in the centre and on our right the Fourth and Indian Corps quickly overcame the dazed and decimated Germans and pushed beyond Neuve Chapelle to the Bois du Biez and slopes of the Aubers ridge beyond. But our left had no such fortune in the north of the village and at the neighbouring Moulin de Piétre. There, for some inexplicable reason, the defences had hardly been touched by the artillery preparation, and the 23rd Brigade in particular suffered dismally as they tore with their hands at the barbed wire and were shot down by the German machine guns. The defences unbroken by artillery were impenetrable by human bodies, and the defenders were also able to enfilade the troops which had got through farther south and were now attacking the second German line. The staff-work, too, was deplorable, and reserves were late or went astray, though it is doubtful whether anything could have retrieved the initial error which left the German defences intact, impeded the whole advance, and enabled the enemy to recover and bring up reserves before the attack was renewed on the two following days. Possibly our high-explosive had been exhausted. In any case there was nothing to do but to count and consolidate our gains. A village and a strip of territory some three miles by one had been secured, and we estimated the German casualties at 20,000, and they themselves at 12,000; our own were nearly 13,000. The chief effect was produced on the German mind by the shock of our artillery: "this," was the childish complaint of the masters of high-explosive, "is not war, it is murder." But German annoyance was poor compensation for the shrinking of our ambitions, and there was cold comfort in the failure of the German counter-attacks here and at St. Eloi farther north; for the Germans were merely out for defence in the West and we for a successful offensive, which had to be tried again.

The French with their larger forces and greater experience were perhaps somewhat more fortunate, but their local successes in the Woevre and Alsace had no more effect upon the general situation. Early in April a series of attacks, spread over five days and hampered by snowstorms, gave them the plateau of Les Éparges on the northern side of the St. Mihiel wedge and enabled them to advance towards Étain on the road from Verdun to Metz. The importance they attached to these operations is shown by their claim on 10 April that at Les Éparges the Germans in two months had had losses amounting to 30,000. Progress was also made along the southern side of the wedge between St. Mihiel and Pont-à-Mousson; but although ground was gained as a result of strenuous combat extending over several weeks, the wedge stood firm; and the effort to drive it out as a preliminary to the larger operations contemplated in Lorraine was presently abandoned. In Alsace Sondernach was taken and an advance was made during April down the Fecht towards Metzeral and Munster, and the summit of the Hartmannsweilerkopf was recovered. But the progress never really disturbed the Germans, and indeed they would probably have viewed greater success in that divergent sphere with comparative equanimity, knowing that it would waste an unfriendly country and would not threaten their main communications or position.

These operations, combined with the Russian descent of the Carpathians, were announced in "The Times" of 10 April as "the opening of the Allied offensive in the summer campaign of 1915." But the disaster which soon overtook the Russian plans had its effect upon Allied designs in the West, and induced an attempt to menace the Germans in a quarter more likely to disturb their concentration on the East than a campaign against the St. Mihiel wedge or in the mountain frontiers of Alsace. The tender spot on the West was Lille, with its concentration of railways and importance as protecting the right flank of the German front along the Aisne and the left flank of their hold on the Belgian coast. The Germans learnt, divined, or anticipated the design, and sought to parry or break the force of the projected blow by a defensive-offensive against Ypres. The attack was not their real offensive for 1915, but they developed the habit of distracting attention from their main objectives by decking out their subsidiary operations with some new devilry of ingenuity; and just as in 1918 they bombarded Paris with guns having a range of 75 miles when their real objective was the British front, so in 1915, when their main effort was against the Russians, they treated the defenders of Ypres to their first experiments in poison-gas. They had tried the effect on the humbler creation some time before, and had indicated their intentions by accusing their enemies of the practice they had themselves in mind; but it came as a ghastly surprise to the French Territorials and British and Canadian troops along the Yser on 22 April (see Map, p. 288).

The attack had clearly been planned beforehand, because the preparation of the chlorine gas, arrangement of the gas-tubes along the front, and delay for the requisite conditions wind and weather required time; and the absence of any great concentration of troops merely showed that, in view of their commitments in the East, the Germans only sought at Ypres a local and tactical success. It was a mere accident that the gas attack north-east of the city followed upon strenuous fighting for Hill 60 at the southeast re-entrant, and the choice of locality was due to the German knowledge of the facts that the French regulars had been removed from the Yser and our own heavy guns from Ypres in order to take part in offensives farther south. The attack on Hill 60 was begun by us on 17th April, and its object was to acquire a gun position which commanded the German trenches in the Hollebeke district. The struggle lasted for five days and was one of the fiercest local combats in the war; at the end of it we were still on what was left of a mound of earth.

The German offensive on the north-eastern front of Ypres was heralded by a bombardment of the city on the 20th which was designed as a barrage to cut off communications with the front along the roads which all ran through Ypres. On the evening of the 22nd the gas attack developed, and as the clouds of green vapour moved down on the French Territorials, unprovided with any sort of gas-masks and unprepared for the terrifying effects of poison en masse, they broke and fled, exposing the flank of the Canadians on their right from Langemarck to Grafenstafel. Never did troops make a more heroic debut in war under more trying conditions. Less affected by the gas than the French Territorials, the Canadians counter-attacked the German left flank, temporarily recaptured guns, and stayed the advance. The gaping breach on their left was partially filled by reinforcements from the 28th Division on the 23rd, but the Germans were across the canal at Het Sas and Lizerne, and the Canadians between St. Julien and Grafenstafel were fighting on three fronts. A second gas attack followed on the 24th, and presently St. Julien had to be abandoned. Reinforcements were, however, coming up; French regulars brilliantly recaptured Lizerne and Het Sas and secured the west bank of the canal against a German advance; and by the 29th the Canadians, who had saved the situation but had suffered heavily in the effort, were replaced by British troops. There was still desperate fighting to do for many days, and the curve of the Ypres salient had been reduced to a narrow oblong stretching from Ypres to Grafenstafel and the Polygon Wood, and little more than half in breadth what it was in length. A shortening of the line was inevitable, and it was effected with great skill and little loss on 3-4 May. But heavy bombardment continued to take a dreadful toll of life until a final gas attack on the 24th concluded the German effort. Crude respirators had been hastily supplied to our troops and the gas attack was less effective than before, but we were left with a line which ran in a curve a bare three miles from Ypres, and

> "an acre sown indeed
> With the richest royallest seed
> That the earth did e'er suck in."

But if that soil round Ypres was a tomb of British bodies, it became the grave of German hopes. The shrunken line was enough, and it remained unbroken till the war had ceased. The military gain, if any, lay with the Germans, whose casualties were far less than ours. But the moral advantage lay with us. It was not quite so clear as is commonly thought. The use of poison-gas as a weapon of war was not a German invention; it was suggested by a British chemist to Japan during the Russo-Japanese War. But chemists have nothing to do with international law or morality, and responsibility rests with Governments for their adoption of methods provided by science. Nor is there any clear moral distinction between asphyxiating shells and gas emitted from tubes. All war is torture; and, the morality of torture once admitted, the moral reasons for discrimination between particular degrees of suffering and efficiency cease to be very convincing. The moral advantage to us consisted in the heroism which our troops endured the torture. If they could unprepared withstand the gas attacks at Ypres, there was nothing of which their manhood need be afraid; while the Germans were in the humiliating position of one who, foiled in legitimate combat, had tried to take an unfair advantage and has failed. Poison-gas was an ill-bred attempt at revenge for what they called murder at Neuve Chapelle, just as they found consolation in the sinking of the Lusitania for the ignominous situation of their High Seas Fleet.

The offensive at Ypres slackened to meet the Allied attacks elsewhere, and our troops in the salient at least were not insensible to the fact that even the Germans had insufficient artillery or high-explosive to maintain an intense bombardment all along the line. Both the French and ourselves began on 9 May, and the object was to threaten the German position in front of Lens and Lille. Lens was protected by a bulge in the German front which ran round by Grenay, Aix-Noulette, Notre Dame de Lorette, Ablain, and Carency to the north-west of Arras, and then south-eastwards by La Targette, Écurie, and Roclincourt. Between this line and Lens lay the Vimy Ridge, and in front of its southwestern slopes the Germans had constructed elaborate fortifications above and underground known as the White Work and the Labyrinth. For the attack the French had made careful preparations, and their concentration of eleven hundred guns and almost limitless shells exceeded in intensity any previous experiment. They were rewarded by the comparative ease with which their initial successes were secured. Barbed wire and earthen parapets were blown to pieces before the infantry attacked and in an hour and a half coveted two and a half miles. La Targette and the White Work were captured and an entrance forced into Neuville St. Vaast. Farther north a second attack was required, and it was not until the 12th that Carency, Ablain, and the summit of Notre Dame were mastered. The line had been broken, but the fragments resolved themselves into almost impregnable strongholds; it took another fortnight before the Souchez sugar-refinery, half a mile in front of Ablain, fell, and the Labyrinth held out, while behind these defences rose the Vimy Ridge to defy for another two years all attacks upon Lens (see Maps, pp. 79, 302).

The lesson was that of Neuve Chapelle on a larger scale, and all the more impressive because of the careful preparations made for victory. The breach of narrow front was useless, because lines were no longer made of men, but of fortifications which held instead of rolling up, when broken, and seeking safety in retreat. The simultaneous British attacks near Neuve Chapelle repeated the French experience and our own in March. The first was north of Neuve Chapelle towards Fromelles, and broke down through inadequate artillery preparation; the second, made on 16 May in front of Richebourg l'Avoué towards the Bois du Biez and Rue d'Ouvert, was somewhat more successful, and Sir John French wrote encouragingly about the entire first line of the enemy's trenches having been captured on a front of 3000 yards with ten machine guns; but one brigade alone lost 45 officers and 1179 men, and La Bassée and the Aubers ridge were as forbidding as ever. It was not by victories of that compass that the Germans would be diverted from their Galician drive; and the other major operation in the Dardanelles to which the Entente had been committed gave little better cause for satisfaction.

The French had naturally refused to divert a single division from their troops on the Western front, and their contingent consisted of a detachment of some colonial troops, fusiliers marins, and the Foreign Legion. The substantial force took longer to collect, and had to be provided by Britain. Sir Ian Hamilton was placed in command, and he was given the 29th Division, the Naval Division, a Territorial Division, and the Australian and New Zealand Divisions serving in Egypt, which was now considered safe for the summer. The total amounted to three corps, or 120,000 men. The Turks were directed by the German general Liman von Sanders, and he expected the landing to be attempted near Bulair on the flat and narrow isthmus which joined the Gallipoli Peninsula to the mainland. His expectation is perhaps the best justification for Sir Ian's selection of other spots, but there were few that were practicable, and none that did not involve enormous difficulties, for Liman von Sanders' anticipation of an attack at Bulair did not preclude some effective precautions against a landing elsewhere.

The attempt began on 25 April at six different points. Some way up the outer or north-western shore of the peninsula the Australian and New Zealand Army Corps effected a landing at Gaba Tepe, later called Anzac from the initials of the force. Farther down another was made in front of the village of Krithia, and the remaining four attempts were on beaches stretching round the point of the peninsula from Tekke to Morto Bay. All prospered fairly well except at Sedd-el-Bahr, where a concentration of Turkish fire kept most of the troops from disembarking for thirty-two hours, and near Krithia, where on the 26th a counter-attack drove our forces back into their boats. Zeal carried the Anzacs nearly to the summit of the hills overlooking the Straits, and excess of it led to heavy losses in a Turkish counterattack; nor could the parties of British troops who got within a few hundred yards of Krithia on the 28th maintain their position, and the result of this first attempt was to give us possession of the extremity of the peninsula from a mile above Eski Hissarlik inside the Straits to three miles above Tekke on the Aegean, and of an exposed ridge of cliffs at Anzac. A French force had landed at Kum Kale on the Asiatic mainland, but only to destroy the Turkish batteries there (see Map, p. 107).

The coup de main had obviously failed, and the struggle for Gallipoli resolved itself into a costly attack by inferior forces on land against an almost impregnable position. Never were the difficulties of invasion by sea more strikingly demonstrated, and it was a misfortune that the generals who continued throughout the war to distract the popular mind by depicting a German invasion of England, were not all sent to study the process in the Dardanelles. In front of our narrow footholds the Turks, amounting to 200,000 men, held positions rising to over 700 feet at Achi Baba and Pasha Dagh, and defended by masses of artillery and machine and elaborate systems of trenches upon which the big guns from our ships appeared to have little effect. Two British submarines did gallant work by getting up the Straits under the mine-fields and disturbing the Turkish communications across the Sea of Marmara; but there remained land-routes on either shore, and reserves arrived more quickly on the Turkish than on the British front. From 6-8 May a second attack was made up the Saghir Dere towards Krithia and the Kereves Dere towards Achi Baba, while the Anzacs created as much diversion as possible from Gaba Tepe. But the bombardment from ships and shore-batteries failed to destroy the Turkish trenches, and an advance of a thousand yards, which failed to reach the enemy's main positions, was only achieved at the cost of casualties amounting by the end of May to more than the losses in battle during the whole Boer War. A third attack on 4 June reinforced the lesson that nothing short of an army large enough for a major operation could master the Dardanelles, and meanwhile an elusive German submarine was threatening the naval supports. The Goliath had been sunk by a Turkish torpedo boat on 12 May, and the submarine disposed of the Triumph on the 26th and the Majestic on the following day. Silently the Queen Elizabeth and her more important consorts withdrew to safer waters, and the naval attempt to force the Dardanelles was gradually transformed into a military siege of the peninsula.

The spring offensive of the Allies had gone to pieces everywhere except in the distant spheres of South Africa and Mesopotamia, while the German offensive was carrying all before it in Galicia. The first great disillusionment of the war was at hand, and its promised beginning in May looked uncommonly like a repetition of the previous August. Popular discontent focused itself on the lack of munitions, and especially of high-explosives, which "The Times" military correspondent declared on 14 May to have been a fatal bar to our success. "Some truth there was, but brewed and dashed with lies," as Dryden remarked of Titus Oates' plot. There were other bars as fatal, the lack of guns, men, and generalship; and the ultimate responsibility for the shortage rested with those experts, Allied as well as our own, who thought six Divisions an adequate British force when the war broke out. For the amount of high-explosive required depends upon the number of guns and gunners to use it and the length of line that is held; and experience of South African warfare had led generals to discount the value of heavy guns and high-explosive and to magnify that of mobility and mounted men. It was only when trenches stretching from the Alps to the sea were made impervious by German wire and concrete to assault that the need for unlimited high-explosive dawned on the minds of the higher commands. The French were able, thanks to the protection afforded by the British Navy, to divert labour from naval construction and repair to the production of munitions and even to send naval guns to the trenches. But that very fact added to the paramount claim of the navy in Great Britain for munitions; and a soldier must have been strangely blind to the debt the Empire and the Entente owed to the British Navy before he could urge his own Government to follow the French example.

The British Cabinet had begun to appreciate the need in September 1914, and on 21 April 1915 Mr. Lloyd George gave in the House of Commons the rate of our increased output as from 20 in September to 90 in November, 156 in December, 186 in January, 256 in February, and 388 in March, and added that the production of high-explosives had been placed on a footing which relieved us of all anxiety. Even an increase of 2000 per cent was doubtless inadequate to our needs, and Mr. Asquith's frequently misquoted denial that our operations had been hampered by the deficiency, showed that both Ministers had been misled by their technical advisers. But the French, who fired 300,000 shells on 9 May, were, in spite of that fact and their greater forces, not much more successful in front of Lens than we at Neuve Chapelle; and unlimited explosives did not bring us far on the road to victory until more than three years after Mr. Lloyd George had been appointed Minister of Munitions in May 1915 to revolutionize the situation which had inspired him with such confidence in April. We had more to learn in the art of war than the manufacture of munitions, and the dream that a better supply would have enabled us to beat the Germans in the spring of 1915—without any American troops at all and with a British Army about a tenth of the effective strength that was in the end required—was as idle as the German fancy that their similar superiority should have brought us to our knees in the autumn of 1914.

The delusion served, however, to shake Mr. Asquith's Government to its foundations. Lord Kitchener himself, the popular idol for whom the press had clamoured at the beginning of the war, was deposed from his shrine in ultra-patriotic hearts because he had devoted himself to the raising of armies more than to the making of munitions. But the first offensive in the press, as often happened in the field, fell short of its objective: Lord Kitchener received the Garter amid the plaudits of "Punch," and the curious spectacle was exhibited of the most excitable journal in the realm being publicly burnt on the Stock Exchange by the nation's most excitable body of citizens. Another incident supervened upon the munitions outcry; Lord Fisher resigned from the Admiralty on 15 May. He had had notorious differences with Mr. Churchill over the Dardanelles and other questions; and unable to do without either at the Admiralty, Mr. Asquith dispensed with both, and covered up the deficiency by a Coalition. The principal Unionists joined the Cabinet, and the chief Liberal Jonah was Lord Haldane, who knew a great deal about Germany and was therefore accused of being pro-German. He also knew something of science, and might conceivably have been more alive to the need of munitions than Lord Kitchener. But the nation would not have tolerated his presence at the War Office, and even resented it on the Woolsack. He left his seat to successors who did not fill his place.

Apart from this concession to popular prejudice, the Coalition was an advantage from the national though not from the Premier's personal or party point of view. He would have been wiser in his own interests to have resigned and left the responsibility to men whose supporters believed that with a little more energy and foresight the war could be won in a few months or at most a year. Few had as yet realized that the struggle was one between mighty nations which only the perseverance of peoples, and not the merits of Ministers, could decide; and the inevitable deferment of foolish hopes would sooner or later have produced a reaction in favour of the retiring Premier and his party. But it would have been accompanied by a revival of party warfare which would have undoubtedly weakened national unity and impaired the prospects of success; and all parties to the Coalition—Liberal, Unionist, and Labour—were patriotically inspired when they agreed to share a burden which the wiser among their leaders foresaw would tax their united strength.

There was need enough for unity during the summer of 1915 when the Allied offensive in the West had broken down, little progress was being made in the Dardanelles, and the Germans were driving the Russians like chaff before them. The one gleam of light was the intervention of Italy, which might distract Austrian forces from the Galician front and in any case meant some accession of strength to the Allied cause. Italy had already rendered inestimable services to the Entente by proclaiming that Germany's action was offensive in character, and therefore dispensed Italy from an obligation to support her partners in the Triple Alliance; and her neutrality during August and intervention in May disproved the gibe of the French diplomatist that she would rush to the rescue of the conqueror. The question throughout the winter was whether she would complete her breach of the Triple Alliance by attacking her former Allies. The grievance upon which diplomacy fixed was the reciprocal compensation which Austria and Italy had promised each other in case either were forced to disturb the status quo in the Balkans. Austria pleaded that her invasion of Serbia involved no permanent disturbance, because no permanent annexation was intended; to which Baron Sonnino retorted that Austria had declared, during the Turkish-Italian war, that an Italian bombardment of the Dardanelles or even the use of searchlights against the Turkish coast would constitute a breach of the agreement. In March Baron Burian accepted the principle that compensation was due to Italy, and discussion arose as to its nature and extent. The Italian Government pressed its advantage, and demanded not only the whole of Italia irredenta, that unredeemed territory peopled by Italians in the Trentino and across the Adriatic, which had been left under Hapsburg dominion after the wars of Italian liberation, but practically the whole north-eastern coasts of the Adriatic which were inhabited by a predominantly Slav population.

Austria, under German pressure, travelled far on the path of concession, but no conclusion could be reached that way. For concessions at the expense of the Jugo-Slavs would not be recognized by the Entente if it won the war; and if the Central Empires were successful, they were not likely to regard these promises extracted from them in their hour of need as more binding than other scraps of paper. The negotiations were, indeed, no more than a diplomatic method of forcing the issue and setting a standard for the concessions to be demanded from the Entente as the price of Italy's intervention. We could not afford, it was thought, to offer less than Austria, and we probably underestimated Italy's fears and difficulties. She was really bound to intervene, because if she stood out, she would lose whichever side won. There was a triangular duel for the control of the Adriatic; if the Central Empires were victorious the Adriatic would become a Teutonic lake; if the Entente succeeded, its north-eastern shores would become Jugo-Slav. Italy could only avoid that dilemma by intervention in favour of the winning side, and thus establishing a claim to share in the fruits of victory. Her ambitions were considerable: not only did she insist that control of the eastern shores of the Adriatic was essential to the safety of her own exposed and harbourless coasts, but she regarded herself as the heir of Venice, which "once did hold the gorgeous East in fee"; and she hoped to retain the Greek islands of the Dodecanese which she had seized during the Turkish War, and to acquire a foothold in Asia Minor and on the Illyrian coast along the Straits of Otranto. It would not be easy to harmonize her claims with those of Serbia who was already our ally, nor those of Greece whose adhesion was expected. But Italy's sword seemed worth the risk and the price in the spring of 1915, and the Treaty of London was concluded on 26 April which promised her most of what she desired, and produced some of the hardest tasks for the ultimate Congress of Peace.

The compact was from the first more honoured in the breach than the observance. Italy undertook to wage war by all means at her disposal in union with France, Great Britain, and Russia against the Powers at war with them. But for another year she remained at peace with Germany. War was, indeed, declared upon Austria on 22 May, but the union with the Allies was limited almost exclusively to the prosecution of Italy's territorial ambitions, and the forces employed hardly produced effects to correspond with the facts that the population of Italy was almost equal to that of France and that the bulk of the Austrian armies were involved in the struggle with Russia. Italy had, indeed, peculiar disadvantages; she was more divided in mind about the war than any of the great protagonists, and the splendid qualities of her Bersaglieri and Alpini were not shared by all her troops. Her war strength was put at a million men, and she still had to cope with Turkish forces in Tripoli which only surrendered at the end of the war as a condition of the armistice concluded between Great Britain and Turkey. She was further hampered by lack of coal and inadequate industrial equipment, and her northern frontier had been so drawn in the Alps as to give Austria every advantage of the passes both for offence and defence. To these drawbacks were added a defective strategy dictated by political idiosyncrasies. The capture of Trieste rather than the defeat of the enemy was made the great objective of the campaign. It had the advantage that it might not involve German troops in its defence, and the defect that it was a divergent operation which even if successful would have no material influence on the general course of the war. Soon, too, it became evident that Trieste was not likely to fall until Austria was defeated on other fields or fell into impotence through domestic disruption (see Map, p. 298).

The campaign began with scattered Italian offensives all along the northern frontier, designed to wrest from the Austrians their control of the Alpine heights and passes, and to secure the flank of the main attack across the Isonzo towards Trieste. Slight successes were gained at various points, and the enemy was pressed back almost to the head of Lake Garda. But no serious impression was made on his positions except along the lower reaches of the Isonzo. Here the west bank from Tolmino down to Monfalcone and the sea fell into Italian hands. Gradisca was captured on 10 June and the river was crossed at different points. On the 20th the Italians announced their firm establishment on the slopes of Monte Nero above Tolmino and Caporetto, and on 26 July a similar success on Monte San Michele and Monte dei Sei Busi farther south near Gorizia. On 4 August they were even said to be making progress on the Carso to the south-east. But all these gains were illusory. Gorizia itself remained in Austrian hands for another year, the heights east of it were not mastered until 1917, and neither Tolmino nor the Carso fell to the Italians until the war had been lost and won. There was nothing here to disturb the Austrian concentration of effort against their Russian foes or to call for German assistance to their Austrian allies. Italy did, however, on 20 August declare war upon Turkey, with which she had not yet made a definitive peace since the outbreak of hostilities in 1911; and it was even announced that she would send an expedition to the Eastern Mediterranean. This was taken to mean a descent upon Adalia in Asia Minor, where Italy desired to stake out her claims in the expectation of an early dissolution of the Turkish Empire. But the Turks showed unexpected signs of animation under German stimulants, and the "eastern Mediterranean" expedition was reduced to the nearer and more practical exploit of seizing Avlona which there were not even Turkish troops to defend. Italy was not alone to blame, for the first use the Serbs made of Italy's committal to the Entente cause was to dash across to the Adriatic coast where their rival claims conflicted.

The Gallipoli campaign therefore dragged its weary length along throughout the torrid heat of summer without an Italian diversion, serving mainly as a demonstration of practical though ineffective sympathy with our Russian allies. Another attack on Krithia, launched on 28 June, gave us control of the Saghir Dere and led to considerable Turkish losses in the counter-attacks which Enver, defying Liman's wiser advice, had ordered; and the French under Gouraud made a corresponding advance on the eastern shore of the peninsula. Gouraud received a wound which required the amputation of his leg and his retirement to France, where he later rendered more brilliant and far more effective service. On 12 July yet another effort was made to capture Krithia without substantial success; and the much-tried armies on that forbidding and barren field then sat down to await the reinforcements demanded and the new plan which was maturing for the solution of the problem.

Stagnation also set in along the Western front, and the summer campaign was marked by as little movement as the winter. An attack was made in the Argonne on 20 June more in the interests of the Crown Prince's reputation than in those of strategy; and the advance which attained the depth of a mile was reduced by counter-attacks on 14 July to 400 yards. Another at Hooge in front of Ypres on 30 July was marked by the first employment in battle of one of our new divisions recruited since the war began, and on the German side by the use of liquid fire. It was successful in making an awkward dent in our line, but again a counterattack on 9 August restored the situation. That, however, was one which suited the Germans, for they were simply out to hold their lines in the West, while behind those lines they commandeered French and Belgian labour and worked French and Belgian mines to eke out their own munitions of war and supply the needs of their campaign on the other side of Europe. Towards stopping that our checks to their local attacks in the West and offensive operations of our own did nothing. Important and sweeping French successes continued to be announced from time to time in the press, and occasionally positions were captured and retained, as at Buval near Souchez, Hébuterne, and Quenneviéres. The Germans, too, failed in their attacks on Les Éparges, while the French succeeded in capturing Metzeral in Alsace. But the great offensive in Artois had subsided into stubborn hand-to-hand fighting in the Labyrinth, which was as costly as a first-class battle without producing its results.

So spring passed into summer and the days began to wane, with the Germans reaping the fruits of their foresight and preparations in the East, while we pinned our faith to the silver lining of the clouds and looked day by day for that offensive which was to relieve our hard-pressed Allies but did not come. The truth was hidden from the public eye, and possibly with prudence; for there are times in which without illusions the weight of gloom would be intolerable. The difficulty is that illusion also dims the sense of danger and of duty; our belated provision for war was still retarded by strikes, profiteering, and perversity, and the King's example of total abstinence failed to prevent the nation from spending more on drink in war than in peace. An imperfectly educated people is slow to grasp a novel situation; and it was only by stealth and caution that it could be led along the path of preparation for the part we had to play by national service, national thrift, and national control.

CHAPTER VIII

THE DEFEAT OF RUSSIA

THE winter, spring, and summer which had passed with so little change on the other fronts, owed their lack of decisive movement not to the comforting delusion of the French official communiqué that Germany's offensive had been broken and her defensive could be broken whenever it was thought desirable, but to the fact that she had reversed her strategy, and reached the conclusion that Russia could be defeated more easily than France. Russia, indeed, had almost limitless man-power, but the war had already shown the importance of munitions, and Germany quickly learnt the lesson. Russia was ill-equipped with munitions and the industrial facilities for their manufacture; nor could the want be supplied by her allies, since, apart from their own needs, their communications with Russia were circuitous, uncertain, and inadequate. The Murmansk railway was not complete, the route to Archangel was icebound from November to May, and the single rail across Siberia was further hampered by indolence and corruption on the part of the railway workers and their staff. Russia was the most isolated of the Allies, and the attempt to open a shorter connexion by a naval attack on the Dardanelles had been frustrated. Without assistance from the West, Russia would be beaten, and without it she could not recover. There were good reasons for the policy which led Germany, during the winter and behind an unpenetrated veil of secrecy, to concentrate her energies upon the production of guns and munitions for the Eastern front.

The strategical position of Russia was no more sound than the state of her armaments. She occupied a vast salient, the southern flank of which was the Carpathians. They formed a substantial protection, since the passes afforded poor facilities for transporting the mass of artillery on which Germany relied for success in her attack. But the safety of the flank depended upon the integrity of the front, and a successful German drive in Galicia would expose the entire position of the Russian armies in Poland. The two reasons subsequently given for the dismissal of the Grand Duke Nicholas from the supreme command were, firstly, that he had in the autumn advanced too precipitately into Silesia, and secondly, that in the spring he exhausted his strength in trying to pierce the Carpathians and thus left his front on the Dunajec too weak to resist Mackensen's furious onslaught. But it is doubtful whether any strategic correctitude could have saved the Russian armies from the effects of German superior armaments. The Germans were playing for high stakes, nothing less than the destruction of Russia's offensive capacity; but they were justified in their game by the cards they held in their hand.

The attack began on 28 April with a forward move on Dmitrieff's left at Gorlice. The pressure compelled him to weaken his centre along the Biala in front of Ciezkowice. Then on 1 May Mackensen's vast volume of fire burst forth; over 700,000 shells are said to have fallen upon the Russian position, and their defences were blown out of existence. Under cover of this fire, to which the Russians could make little reply, the Biala was crossed, Ciezkowice and Gorlice were captured, and Dmitrieff's line was broken; on the 2nd his army was in full retreat to the Wisloka, twenty miles back in his rear, where no trenches had been dug, and there was little hope of checking the Germans. Nevertheless a heroic stand was here made for five days by Caucasian and other reinforcements. On the 7th Mackensen forced a crossing at Jaslo, and next day he pursued his advantage by seizing two bridgeheads across the Wistok farther on, one at Fryslak to the north and the other at Rymanow to the south. Brussilov's army along the Carpathian foothills at Dukla had to beat a precipitate retreat and lost heavily; it was nearly severed from Dmitrieff's centre. But a counterattack from Sanok in the south and a stand by the Russians at Dembica towards the north procured a slight respite, and by the i4th the bulk of the Russian armies were across the San with their right at Jaroslav, their left at Kosziowa, their centre at Przemysl, and their forces in Poland conforming to the retirement.

The latter part of the retreat had been of a more orderly character and began to follow a plan, but the plan involved a great deal more than the surrender of Galicia between the San and the Dunajec. Mackensen's force was overpowering, and the German design was not to lengthen the line by compelling a Russian retreat to the San; it only fell short of complete success because the Russian armies had not so far been isolated and destroyed, but there was still the likelihood of their being driven back until the whole of Galicia was recovered and Poland lost. For the rest of the month Mackensen's huge machine of destruction was moving forward to the second stage of its journey on the San. Its progress was delayed by Russian counter-attacks on the Austrians under Von Woyrsch in Poland and on Mackensen's other wing which was advancing from the Carpathians on to the Dniester. But by the i8th Kosziowa had fallen and the Germans had seized the line of the San from Sieniawa to Jaroslav. Przemysl had not been further fortified by the Russians since its capture; it would clearly meet the same fate as Antwerp from the German howitzers unless the Russian armies in the field could keep the German artillery at a distance. They could only delay matters until the stores and material were removed from the fortress. It was now a salient threatened with encirclement on the north and south. Russian counter-attacks at Sieniawa and Mosciska relieved the pressure for some days, but before the end of May Mackensen's howitzers were at work, and Przemysl was evacuated by the Russians on 1 June.

On the same day Stryj fell to Von Linsingen and on 7 June he forced the Dniester at Zurawno. But he had advanced too far ahead of his communications and reserves, and on the 8th Brussilov drove him back over the Dniester with severe losses. The Dniester was indeed the scene of stubborn fighting for many days, and on the 18th the Russian Government announced that the enemy had lost between 120,000 and 150,000 men in their efforts to cross it on a front of forty miles. But the Russian stand on the Dniester only left it to Mackensen's centre and left to turn the Grodek position and ensure the fall of Lemberg. By 20 June the Russian communications north of the Galician capital were severed by a battle at Rawa Ruska, and on the 22nd, after nine months' Russian occupation, it once more fell into Austrian hands. The Russians had not done much to commend their cause to the inhabitants during their stay;

the opportunity was seized for proselytizing in the interests of the Orthodox Church, and Sczeptycki the Archbishop of Lemberg, a member of the Uniate Church which had made terms with Roman Catholicism, was treated with a harshness compared with which the indignities inflicted by the Germans upon Cardinal Mercier of Malines were trivial; he was interned in a Russian monastery and deprived of all religious rites save those which were to him heretical.

The fall of Lemberg was followed by the loss of the Dniester line as far as Halicz, and all beyond it including the Bukovina, and the Russians fell back behind the Gnilia Lipa, where Ivanov prolonged a stubborn resistance. But the aims of the Germans in Galicia had been achieved with the capture of Lemberg except in so far as the remnants of the Russian armies remained intact. The city formed a formidable bastion for defence because of its ample lines of communication with the south and west, and inadequate lines to the north and east. A farther German advance across the Russian frontier in that direction would be an eccentric movement, and the front of attack was accordingly swung round from east to north, where the Russian position in Poland had been outflanked. The reconquest of Galicia produced fruits enough in the restoration of Austrian and Hungarian confidence and the repression of pro-Entente tendencies in the Balkans. But it was only a part of the most ambitious and successful campaign the Germans fought in the war. May and June were but the prelude to greater successes in July, August, and September.

The heaviest blows were to be struck in the Polish centre, but diversions had already been made on the extreme German left in the north. Libau had fallen on 9 May, and during that and the following month the German armies under Von Buelow overran the duchy of Courland as far as Windau on the coast and Shavli half-way to Riga. This movement was regarded with comparative indifference as being a divergent operation calculated at worst to do no more than distract Russian forces from more critical points. But it was in keeping with a German design considered grandiose until it nearly succeeded. The bulk of Russia's forces were concentrated in the Polish triangle of which the apex was at Warsaw, the base ran from Kovno by Brest-Litovsk to the Galician frontier, the north-western side in front of the railway from Kovno to Warsaw, and the southern in front of that from Warsaw to Lublin, Cholm, Kovel, Rovno, and Kiev. The German plan was not merely to squeeze the Russians out of the triangle by pressure on the sides and intercept as much of their forces as possible, but also to outflank the whole position by striking behind the base from the north at Vilna; and a naval attack on Riga was part of the projected operations.

The Galician drive had furnished the territorial means for the attack on the southern side of the Polish triangle; and although Ivanov was farther pushed back from the Gnilia Lipa to the Strypa and thence almost to the Sereth, this Eastern advance became irrelevant to the main strategic design, and German reinforcements were collecting mostly under Gallwitz, Scholtz, and Von Eichhorn along the Narew and the Niemen for an onslaught on the north-western side of the triangle. The Austrian Prince Leopold's forces which fronted Warsaw on the Bzura at the apex were comparatively weak, and were only intended to gather the fruits of the real fighting done by the Germans on the flanks. The Germans rode roughshod enough over Austrian susceptibilities when efficiency required it; but they atoned for the brusqueness by conceding a large share in the spectacular aspects of triumph; and just as the Austrians entered Lemberg first and not its real conqueror Mackensen, so Prince Leopold was cast for the part of the victor of Warsaw. But first of all the Galician armies had to face north to take their allotted share in the scheme by driving the Russians back across the railway between Lublin and Kovel.

Within a few days of the fall of Lemberg they had crossed the Russian frontier, turning the Vistula and advancing in two columns, one under the Archduke Joseph towards Krasnik on the road to Lublin, and the other farther east under Mackensen towards Krasnostav on the way to Cholm. The Russian army in Poland west of the Vistula had gradually to conform to the retreating line and fall back in a north-easterly direction towards the river. By 2 July the Archduke was in Krasnik, but here he was checked by the Russian position defending the railway line; on the 5th the Russians, who had been reinforced, counter-attacked, and in a battle lasting till the 9th drove the Austrians back. Similarly Mackensen found himself held up between Zamosc and Krasnostav, and for a week the struggle for the Lublin-Cholm railway resolved itself into an artillery duel. The attack was resumed on the 16th simultaneously with Von Gallwitz's movement against the other side of the triangle. The Archduke failed after ten assaults to carry the Russian position in front of him at Wilkolaz, but Mackensen was more successful at Krasnostav. He enveloped the Russian right, drove it beyond Krasnostav, and was soon within striking distance of the railway.

Meanwhile, to the north Gallwitz had forced the Russians from Prasnysz towards the Narew on the 14th, and crossed it himself on the 23rd between Pultusk and Rozhan as well as between Ostrolenka and Lomza; and by the 25th he was on the banks of the Bug, within twenty miles of the railway connecting Warsaw with Petrograd. The great line of fortresses along the Narew were now exposed to bombardment by German howitzers; the Russians in front of Warsaw withdrew from their winter defences along the Rawka and Bzura to the inner lines of Blonie; and south of Warsaw they retired from Opatow, then from Radom, and then to the great fortress of Ivangorod on the Vistula. Even that was now threatened by Mackensen's advance to the Lublin line in its rear. It was broken on the 29th, and on the 30th the Germans were in Lublin and Cholm. Warsaw was doomed, and, indeed, the Grand Duke Nicholas had as early as the 15th decided upon its evacuation. The fighting along the Lublin-Cholm line, and the strenuous resistance the Russians offered on the 26th to Gallwitz's renewed attacks on the Narew, were intended not to save Warsaw, but the armies defending and the stores within it. On 4 August the troops abandoned the Blonie lines and marched through the city, blowing up the bridges across the Vistula. Next day Prince Leopold made his triumphal entry, and the first year of the war closed on the Eastern front with an event of greater significance even than that which the Kaiser attached to it. To him the capture of Warsaw was a resounding tribute to the success of German arms: to future generations the import of the Russian departure will doubtless be the term it set to Russian rule in Poland, and it may be deemed one of the ironies of history that Hohenzollern autocracy should have been made the instrument to wreck the Russian domination. In spite of themselves the Germans assisted to achieve the common purposes of the great war of liberation.

Russian autocracy was indeed stricken to death by its own inherent maladies nearer home than Poland. Shallow democrats in the West were deploring the lack of prevision and provision exhibited by their democratic Governments, but no democracy endured a tithe of the sufferings inflicted upon Russian soldiers by the blindness, incompetence, and corruption of the bureaucratic Tsardom. Confident in the successes which the heroism of its troops had won over the discordant forces of the Hapsburg Empire and those which Germany could spare from the Western front, it had neglected to perform any of the promises it had made to conciliate the inhabitants of Poland and Galicia, and had even failed to take the commonest military precautions to safeguard its victories. Nothing had been done in Galicia to put the captured Przemysl into a state of defence, and even the bridge across the San had not been repaired to provide a direct line of supply to the front on the Dunajec. Offers of skilled labour from other countries to improve the inefficient service of Russian railways and the inept direction of industries and munition factories were ignored. The business organization of Russia had been managed mainly by Germans before the war; too much of it was left in their hands after war began, with the result that the Putilov munition works, for instance, were reduced to half-time by German control; and there was no one to take the place of those who departed. Russian generals were among the most skilful of strategists, and men like Ruszky, Alexeiev, Brussilov, and others would have been invincible had Russia's man-power been competently equipped. As it was, every sort of provision was neglected; the artillery of one army was limited to two shells a day; a whole division had on one occasion to face an attack without a rifle among them, and troops were put into trenches relying for weapons on those which fell from the hands of their dead or wounded comrades. These were the organized atrocities of autocratic bureaucracy, and it was little wonder that in time they bred in the breasts of Russian soldiers a fiercer resentment against their rulers who betrayed them than against the enemy whom they fought.

The retreat which followed the fall of Warsaw was sympathetically represented as a masterly operation, and the failure of the Germans to envelop and isolate the Russian armies as proof of the breakdown of their strategy. But all retreats in the war, with the exception of the Turks' before Allenby, were similarly described in the appropriate quarters. It was the common characteristic of the victors that they could not win decisive battles in the sense of earlier wars, and of the vanquished that they evaded the expected Sedans and Waterloos. Even the Germans with all their initial advantages of preparation and surprise could not break the Allied armies in their first offensive on the West, and the same inability dogged their still more rapid footsteps in the East. It is a consequence of the reliance of modern armies on the mechanical force of artillery to which the Germans were especially addicted; for while 16-inch howitzers could pulverise any position, they could not pursue with the speed required to encircle and capture armies in the field. Hence salients, which when viewed in the light of older conditions seemed traps which could not be eluded, were in practice evaded because, with Allenby's one exception, cavalry failed to atone for the slower movement of the more powerful arm of artillery. There was nothing therefore miraculous in the Russian escape, and the strategy of the Grand Duke was hardly so brilliant as it was represented. At the beginning of the war Alexeiev, then Ivanov's chief of staff, is said to have counselled a Russian retreat like those which lured Charles XII and Napoleon to their doom; but the temptations of Austrian weakness and German concentration on the West and the plight of France and Belgium led to the adoption of other advice and the premature invasion of Prussia, Galicia, and Hungary; and in August 1915 it was too late for a voluntary and innocuous retreat. The safety of the majority had to be bought at a heavy price in casualties, in loss of guns and material, in suffering for the troops and civilians, and in national dejection. What might have been cheerfully done by choice was despondently done by compulsion.

The evacuation of Warsaw was the first step in the withdrawal from the apex of the Polish triangle which it was hoped the resistance of the sides would enable the Russians to complete without disaster; and a large garrison with adequate guns and ammunition was left at Novo Georgievsk to impede the German advance and hamper communications with their front. The greatest menace was on the north-west along the Narew and beyond in Courland where Von Buelow was preparing to strike behind the base of the triangle. On 10 August Von Scholtz breached the line of fortresses by storming Lomza, but Kovno was a much more critical point. It was the angle of the base, and its fall would not only threaten the base running south to Brest-Litovsk and all the Russian armies west of that line, but would greatly facilitate Von Buelow's sweep round beyond it and Vilna. The bombardment began on the day that Warsaw fell. Kovno was expected to hold out at least to the end of the month, but it fell on the 17th, and the general in command was subsequently sentenced to fifteen years' hard labour for his inadequate defence and absence from his post of duty. On the following day Von Gallwitz cut the line between Kovno and Brest at Bielsk, and on the 19th Novo Georgievsk fell to the howitzers of Von Beseler, the expert of Antwerp. Ossowiec, which had stood so well against the earlier German invasions, followed on the 23rd, and Von Beseler was brought up to give the coup de grâce to Brest. Its loss was perhaps inevitable after the fall of Kovno, but it completed the destruction of the base of the triangle and involved the withdrawal of the whole Russian line beyond the Pripet marshes which would break its continuity; and there was cold comfort in the fact that Ewarts got away with most of his troops and stores and that a Russian mine, exploded two days after their departure, destroyed a thousand Germans and set a precedent for similar machinations on their part when they retreated in the West.

Fortresses now toppled down like ninepins. On the 26th Augustowo was evacuated and Bialystok captured. On the 27th Olita was abandoned and on 2 September Grodno. The Germans thus gained the whole line from Kovno to Brest, and things were going no better in the south. The fall of Lemberg had given the German right a position far to the east of their left, and Mackensen advancing from Lublin and Cholm had driven the Russians across the Bug at Wlodawa before Brest-Litovsk was taken. The marshes of Pripet were at their driest in August, and Mackensen encountered few obstacles as he pressed on from Brest to Kobrin and thence to Pinsk along the rail to Moscow. In Galicia Ivanov was pushed back to the Strypa and then the Sereth, and on the upper reaches of those rivers Brody was captured and two of the Volhynian fortresses, Dubno and Lutsk. Rovno itself was threatened, and with it the southern stretch of that lateral railway from Riga to Lemberg on which the Germans had set their hearts.

But the most ominous German advance was far to the north, where Von Buelow was profiting by the fall of Kovno, marching on Mitau and Riga, and threatening both to cut the railway between Vilna and Petrograd and confine the Russian retreat to congested and narrow lines of communication along which they could not escape. This northern advance was accompanied by a naval offensive in the Baltic, designed to seize Riga and turn the line of the Dvina on which the Russians hoped to stand in the last resort. Fortunately this part of the campaign broke down before matters had reached their worst on land. It looked like a naval operation planned, or at least attempted, by soldiers professionally incapable of grasping the elementary principles of naval or amphibious warfare. After an unsuccessful attack on the southern inlet to the Gulf of Riga on 10 August, the Germans during a thick fog on the 17th sought to land troops at Pernau in large flat-bottomed barges without having secured command of the sea; and the entire landing-force was captured or destroyed. Simultaneously the Russian Fleet engaged the Germans, who had eight destroyers and two cruisers sunk or put out of action; the only Russian vessel lost was an old gunboat. The Dvina lines were not to be turned by strategy like this, and Russia was henceforth free from naval interference until her sailors played her false.

Von Buelow was still, however, to be reckoned with, and he was the substantial danger. On 28 August he began his movement against the Dvina, which would, if successful, cut off all the Russian armies from direct communication with Petrograd. The blow was struck at Friedrichstadt, where the river is crossed by the only practicable road between Riga and Jacobstadt, but the design was to turn the whole front as far as Dvinsk; and Von Buelow held out to his troops the alluring prospect of winter quarters in Riga and a march on Petrograd in the spring. On 3 September the left bank was cleared for some miles, but all attempts to cross were frustrated. The out-march on the extreme German left had failed, and the critical point moved south towards Vilna. The danger here was serious enough, for the depletion of the Russian forces and length of their line had left a gap between Dvinsk and Vilna, and into this gap the Germans thrust a huge cavalry force which more nearly turned the Russian line than any other movement in the campaign.

The way was prepared by the great ten-days' battle of Meiszagola. The unexpectedly rapid fall of Kovno and Grodno had enabled the Germans to threaten the envelopment of Ewarts' army both on the south and the north, on the Niemen towards Mosty and Lida and farther north towards Vilna. The struggle for Vilna was decided at Meiszagola, a village about fifteen miles north-west of the old Lithuanian capital. It was captured on 12 September, and masses of German cavalry swept round from Vilkomir towards Sventsiany and crossed the Petrograd railway to outflank the retreating Russian troops. The evacuation of Vilna began on the 13th, and two days later the menace from the German cavalry became more apparent. Fresh divisions were apparently brought up from Courland with 140 guns; on the 16th they were at Vidzy and on the 17th at Vileika, nearly seventy miles due east of Vilna and in the rear of the Russians escaping thence. They were thus also close to Molodetchno on the railway along which Ewarts was falling back from Skidel, Mosty, and Lida; and control of that junction would have put two Russian armies at their mercy.

Just in time Ruszky was restored to the command of the northern group of Russian armies, and the victor of Rawa Ruska and Prasnysz was not doomed now to break his uniform record of success. The situation was not unlike that at Prasnysz, and it was relieved in a similar way by a Russian counter-offensive from Dvinsk against the flank of the German cavalry. Vidzy was recaptured on the 20th, and farther south the pressure slackened along the Vilna-Vileika railway; Smorgon was retaken by a brilliant bayonet charge on the 21st. The door had been kept from closing on Russian armies seeking to escape from the salient between Lida and Molodetchno, while the Germans were squeezed out of that which they had made to the north. They were driven out of Vileika, and gradually the lines were straightened and stabilized so as to run almost due south from Dvinsk by Postavy, Lake Narotch, and Smorgon. Other factors than Ruszky's brilliant strategy contributed to this dramatic defeat of the final German effort of the campaign to annihilate the Russian forces. The Germans had lost in men and impetus during their long advance. Superb though their organization was, lengthening lines of communication across a country ill-supplied with roads and railways, and the necessity of guarding against a hostile population told upon their armies in the fighting-line. The heaviest blow will spend itself in time against an elusive foe, and the longest arm will find the limit of its reach. The Germans had not planned a march on Moscow, but they had hoped to overrun the Russian armies and occupy the winter quarters of their choice.

These were denied them on the Dvina, and they had not secured the coveted Riga-Rovno line.

They were indeed left farther from it in the south than in the north. Their defeat east of Vilna enabled Ewarts to escape from the encirclement threatened by the advance from Kovno and Grodno; and although he had to leave Lida and was subsequently pushed behind the junction of Baranowitchi, thus surrendering to the Germans the control of the railway from Vilna to that point, it remained in Russian hands to Rovno. Mackensen was unable to advance from Pinsk, which he occupied on 16 September, to the railway at Luninetz, while Ivanov reacted successfully against the German attacks along the Kovel-Sarny line and recovered a good deal of the ground lost in the Volhynian triangle and eastern extremity of Galicia. Mackensen's army may have been weakened by calls from the north and from the south for a campaign which was already planned but not yet suspected; at any rate it was too weak to achieve its objectives, the capture of Sarny, Rovno, and Tarnopol, which would have completed the hold of the Germans on the Vilna-Kovno line and given them a base for a farther advance in the spring on Odessa and for the isolation of Rumania. On 7 September, as Mackensen's forces were moving on Rovno and the Sereth at Tarnopol and Trembowla, Ivanov counter-attacked from Rovno and Brussilov and Lechitzky on the Sereth. By the 9th the two latter had captured 17,000 prisoners and a considerable number of guns; and Ivanov followed up this success by retaking Lutsk and Dubno by the 23rd. Kovel was even threatened, but the pressure was not maintained. Sarny, Rovno, and Tarnopol were saved, but Lutsk and Dubno reverted to the Germans, and the line in the east was stabilized with the Volhynian triangle and the railway from Vilna to Rovno divided between the antagonists.

The success of Ruszky in the north and of Ivanov in the south in setting a term to the terrifying sweep of the German advance produced a temporary optimism in Russia comparable with that which followed the victory on the Marne; and in neither case did the Allies realize the extent of the advantage gained by the Germans or foresee the years that would pass before the loss could be recovered. The Grand Duke Nicholas was relieved of his command and sent to take over that in the Caucasus. He was succeeded by the Tsar himself, who was unlikely to interfere with the military measures of Alexeiev, his chief of staff; and the Duma seconded the Tsar's attempt to express the determination of the Russian peoples to withstand the Germans until victory was secured. Nevertheless, the profound effects of the Russian defeat could not be removed by any laudable efforts at keeping up appearances. It was a resounding disaster which condemned Europe to three more years of war, and Russia to a convulsion which would permanently alter the whole course of her history and position in the world. Miliukov raised in the Duma the question of responsible government, and if the debacle of 1915 was slower than Sedan in producing the downfall of the system to which it was due, it was not because the disaster was less, but because Russia was a less organized country than France, and her illiterate population reacted more slowly than the French.

The Russian Front

At the moment the best face was put on affairs; and although one correspondent was allowed to report that the heart of the Russian people had grown cold to the Allies who had watched their misfortunes without raising a finger in the shape of a serious offensive to help, public opinion was fed on the comfort in which a facile optimism is so fertile. German casualties were multiplied at will, despondent diaries of individual German officers killed or captured were given unlimited publicity, and roseate pictures were painted of the colossal drain of man-power involved in winter trench-warfare in Russia and in holding vast tracts of hostile country. It was assumed that the Germans would suffer more than the Russians, although again and again whole Russian battalions in those trenches were wiped out by German artillery and machine guns to which the Russians had not the wherewithal to reply except with fresh masses of human flesh; and little was said of the millions of Russian prisoners and civilians who were put to far more effective use in making munitions and producing food for their enemies than they ever had been for Russia or themselves, and without whose labour Germany's man-power would have been exhausted one or two years before the end of the war. It was considered a triumph that the Germans had not reached Petrograd or Moscow, but it might have been well if they had. They had, however, no such ambitions. Just as the reconquest of Galicia had been mainly designed as providing the base for a flank attack upon Russia, so the conquest of Poland was to be used as providing protection for Germany against Russian interference with her plans in the Balkans. Sofia and Constantinople opened up more alluring prospects and a path that led farther than Moscow or Petrograd; and while public opinion in England and France was dreaming of a repetition of 1812, public opinion in Germany was feasting on visions of Cairo, Baghdad, and Teheran, and the possibility of evading the British blockade through outlets to the Indian Ocean.

All eyes that could see were turned to the Dardanelles. There British troops were making the one serious counter-offensive to the German attack on Russia, and success would redeem the Russian failure and foil the hopes the Germans were building upon their victory. The immediate future of the Balkans, the Black Sea, and Asia Minor, and it might be the more distant future of Egypt and the East, hung upon the issue at Gallipoli. During July the reinforcements for which Sir Ian Hamilton had asked were gathering in Egypt and in Gallipoli; and on 6 August the new plan of attack was begun. There were to be four distinct items; a feint was to be made of landing north of Bulair, the attack on Krithia was to be renewed in order to hold the Turkish troops there and draw others in that direction, and a similar advance was planned for the Anzacs with a similar motive, but also to co-operate with the real and fresh offensive. This took the form of a landing at Suvla Bay, the extreme north-westerly point of the peninsula between Anzac and Bulair. The diversions were reasonably successful, as successful, indeed, as previous attacks had been in those localities when they were the principal efforts. The chief of them was a threefold advance north-east, east, and south-east from Anzac Cove on Sari Bair with its highest point at Koja-Chemen. Conspicuous gallantry was shown in the three days' fighting; and while, as earlier at Krithia, the summits defied the greatest valour, enough progress was made in these subsidiary attacks to justify the hope of general success if the principal effort at Suvla Bay went well (see Map, p. 107).

It began without any great mishap, and General Stopford's 9th Corps was successfully landed on the shores of Suvla Bay during the night of 6-7 August and deployed next morning in the plain without serious resistance. The surprise had been effected, but it would be useless unless the attack was pressed with energy and without delay. Yet torpor crept over the enterprise during that torrid afternoon; many of the troops were in action for the first time in their lives, and, understanding that water was obtainable from the lake close by, they had drained their water-bottles by eight o'clock in the morning. A thunderstorm mended matters a little, and Chocolate Hill was carried on the right. But all next day an inferior Turkish force, assisted by a planned or accidental conflagration of the scrub, managed by skilful use of a screen of sharpshooters to hold up our advance all along the line. Sir Ian Hamilton himself arrived that night and strove by persuasion to infuse some energy into the attack. But by the 9th it was already too late, for the Turks had had time to bring up reinforcements, and an attack on the Anafarta ridge on the 10th was repulsed. Five days later General Stopford relinquished the command of the 9th Corps, to which he had been somewhat reluctantly appointed by Lord Kitchener, and the 29th Division was brought up from Cape Helles to renew the attack on 21 August. It might have succeeded had it been originally employed in place of the inexperienced troops; but by this time there could be nothing but a frontal attack on a watchful foe, and it ended like the similar efforts in May and June. Some ground was gained, contact was established with the Anzacs, and a continuous line of six miles was secured from the north of Suvla Bay to the south of Anzac Cove. But before the Turks could be expelled from the peninsula and a passage cleared through the Dardanelles there would be a long and weary struggle, in which progress would be as slow and beset by as many obstacles as it was on the Western front. Russia was to obtain no relief that way; as a counter-offensive to the German campaign of 1915, the attack on the Dardanelles had failed; and the failure produced a deeper impression upon the Balkans than if the attempt had never been made. The way was clear for the next move of German diplomacy and war.

CHAPTER IX

THE CLIMAX OF GERMAN SUCCESS

No one's eyes had been more keenly trained on the Dardanelles operations during the spring and summer than those of Ferdinand, King and Tsar of Bulgaria. Descended from Orleanist Bourbons on the mother's side and from the house of Saxe-Coburg-Gotha on the father's, he was purely Prussian in his realpolitik, and observed no principle in his conduct save that of aggrandizement for his adopted country and himself. The treaty of Bukarest in 1913 had given them both a common and a legitimate grievance, and the great war was welcomed in Bulgaria as an opportunity for revenge. The means would be the assistance Bulgaria might render to the victor, and who that might be was a matter of indifference if he possessed the essential qualifications of victory and insensibility to the feelings of Bulgaria's neighbours and to the sanctity of scraps of paper. This was a defect in the Entente from Ferdinand's point of view. Bulgaria could with difficulty be satisfied except by Serbian sacrifices which the Entente was loath to make. The Central Empires had no scruples on that point; but Bulgaria also wanted something from Rumania, Turkey, and Greece, and Turkey was an ally, Rumania a neutral whom it was not wise to offend, and Greece had as its queen a sister of the Kaiser who was distinctly her husband's better half.

The Balkans

Serbia alone, however, had received by the Treaty of Bukarest enough territory claimed by Bulgaria to provide a sufficient inducement for Bulgaria's intervention in the war, once she was persuaded that a victory of the Central Empires would place it at their disposal. Efforts were made by the Entente during the summer to counteract this attraction by inducing Serbia to reconsider her annexations in Macedonia. But her successes in the autumn of 1914 had stiffened her attitude, and in any case she could not be expected to make that comprehensive surrender of Macedonia which the Central Empires were quite prepared to promise Bulgaria. The decisive factor in the diplomatic situation was, however, the progress of German arms and prospects of German victory; for it was only the victor who would have any favours to bestow, and the course of the war in the summer convinced the Bulgarian Government that Germany was the horse on which prudent people should put their money. On 17 July a secret treaty was concluded guaranteeing Bulgaria in return for intervention the whole of Macedonia possessed by Serbia as well as an extension of Bulgaria's frontiers at Serbia's expense farther north. Bulgaria was also allowed to extort a separate price from Turkey in the shape of a strip of land along the Maritza controlling that river and Adrianople. An even more sinister concession to Bulgarian exorbitance was that of Epirus, a district assigned to Albania in 1913 but populated by Greeks who had revolted and claimed incorporation in Greece. This Prussian complaisance was doubtless due to the fact that Venizelos, who had resigned owing to Constantine's opposition to his policy, had at the Greek general election in June secured nearly a two to one majority in the Greek Chamber. Greece could not be allowed the benefit of a Prussian queen when it chose Venizelos as Prime Minister.

The bond had been signed between the Central Empires and their Bulgarian taskmaster; but the doctrine of rebus sic stantibus was as well understood in Bulgaria as in Prussia, and the treaty would have remained a scrap of paper had Russia expelled the German invaders or Britain broken the barrier at the Dardanlles. As it was, nothing occurred in August or September to weaken Bulgaria's fidelity to the secret compact. The failure of the attack at Suvla Bay was followed by the futile routine of trench warfare; an equally barren result threatened the long-prepared attacks in Artois and Champagne; and, Russia having more than enough to do in reorganizing her shaken armies, the Central Empires were free to turn their attention southwards. Success in the Balkans was not this time to be staked on Austrian control, and Mackensen, whose armies in Galicia were nearest to the scene, was naturally selected to repeat in Serbia the triumphs of his Galician drive. The task would be all the easier because Serbia was a country small compared with Russia, and would, moreover, be distracted by the coming Bulgarian stab in the back. Her Government, conscious of this danger, had, indeed, wished to anticipate it by a frontal attack on Bulgaria; but her offensive was vetoed by the Entente. Possibly it was a case in which moral scruples unduly weighted the scales against military advantage. There was no real doubt about Bulgaria's intentions, and she would have had no grounds for complaint had Serbia attacked before Mackensen was prepared for his part in the joint assassination. The real doubt concerned the attitude of Greece. She was bound by treaty to assist Serbia in that case, and Venizelos would assuredly do his best to fulfil the bond.

But the obligation would not arise if Serbia were the aggressor, and Venizelos would be powerless. The fault of the Entente, if it was a fault, lay in the failure to act on the presumption that Constantine would prove as false to international obligation as his imperial brother-in-law when he invaded Belgium, and in the assumption that the difference between Serbian aggression and defence would involve the difference between Greece being an ally and a neutral.

The diplomatic crisis grew to a climax as Mackensen's forces reached the northern bank of the Danube, for the arrest of the German offensive in Russia was not entirely due to German difficulties or Russian valour and strategy, and by the middle of August German divisions were already being diverted from the Russian front. In the middle of September Bulgaria concluded her compact with Turkey, and on the 19th Mackensen's batteries opened their bombardment of Belgrade. On the 21st Venizelos asked the Western Allies for 150,000 troops, which were promised on the 24th, and on the 23rd Bulgaria ordered a general mobilization and Greece retorted in kind. Bulgaria proclaimed her intention to observe neutrality, and when on the 27th Serbia requested the consent of the Allies to an offensive, it was refused. Entente diplomatists at Sofia were still under the impression that Bulgarian intervention could be avoided, and a vigorous protest by the leaders of all the Opposition parties in the Sobranje against the Government's policy gave some colour to their views. But by 10 October it became known that many German officers were busy in consultation with the Bulgarian Staff; on the 3rd Russia required Bulgaria to break with the Teutonic Powers, and on the 5th herself broke off diplomatic relations. A week later the Bulgarian Army invaded Serbia and the Bulgarian Government declared war. Mackensen had crossed the Danube on the 7th and taken Belgrade on the 9th. On the 19th an imperial manifesto was issued from Petrograd denouncing Bulgaria's treason to the Slav cause and leaving the fate of the traitor to the "just punishment of God." It was assuredly not to be inflicted by the Government whose designs on Constantinople had been the principal obstacle to the success of Entente diplomacy in the Balkans. Bulgaria did, indeed, betray the Slav to the Teuton, but no Balkan State could view with equanimity the prospect of being ground to powder between the upper and nether millstone of Russia on the Danube and on the Dardanelles.

Nor was Bulgaria the only traitor responsible for the Serbian tragedy. On 5 October Venizelos announced to the Greek Chamber in no uncertain terms the intention of his ministry to draw the sword on Serbia's side if Bulgaria attacked. The following day he was summoned to the palace and told that Constantine disapproved; he resigned in the afternoon, and the Chamber compromised its future and its country's by supporting an alternative ministry under Zaimis, which proclaimed its neutrality and refused on 11 October the assistance for which Serbia asked under the terms of their alliance. Russia was willing but unable to help, and large threats and insignificant demonstrations against the Bulgarian coast were all she could contribute to the protection of the little State in whose interests she had entered the war. The burden fell on the Western Powers who had never contemplated it, and they were divided in mind. British ships wrought effective destruction upon the Bulgarian depots and communications along the Aegean coast; but bombardment there was of little use to Serbia, and the British General Staff pronounced against an expedition to Salonika. Sir Edward Carson resigned as a protest against this inaction, while Delcassé resigned in France because Briand was more adventurous. Briand carried his point, succeeded Viviani as Premier, and committed both Powers to the Salonika policy. Italy stood aloof; her antagonism to Serbia and Greece made her ever averse from an offensive against Bulgaria.

The Salonika expedition, which consisted at first of troops transferred from Gallipoli, came too late and was too weak to effect more than a part of its purpose. It would have been more effective had the Allies consented to the Serbian proposal for an attack on Bulgaria; for in that case the Serbian armies would have been aligned along the Bulgarian frontier with their right within reach from Salonika. As it was, they faced north towards Mackensen, and the Bulgarian offensive towards Uskub took the Serbians in the rear, cut their communications with Salonika down the Vardar, and eventually forced a retreat into the Albanian mountains. Serbia would in any case have been overrun, and Mackensen's conquest of its northern half would have been more rapid than it was. But the Serbian armies might have remained intact and given a good account of themselves against both their enemies in the mountain fastnesses of the south with their retreat secured to Salonika, instead of being split into two and most of them driven, to escape as best they could with frightful mortality along impossible tracks towards the Adriatic.

War and disease had reduced the Serbian armies before the campaign began to some 200,000 men, and their enemies brought at least double that number against them. The Serbians were, moreover, constrained by the counsels of the Allies to preserve what they could of their forces as a nucleus for future resistance, and thus to stand only so long as retreat remained open. Threatened on three sides by superior numbers, they were in an untenable position and had a well-nigh impossible task; and only skill, endurance, and courage brought the remnants out of the death-trap laid by collusion between the Central Empires and Bulgaria. The campaign was for the Serbians simply a series of rearguard actions encouraged at first by the delusive hope that the Allies might yet be in time. They might have been, had they been numerous enough. The French from Cape Helles came first, landed at Salonika on 5-7 October, and by the 27th had occupied the valley of the Vardar as far north as Krivolak. They also seized the commanding heights of Kara Hodjali north-east of the river, and repulsed the Bulgarian attempts to drive them off in the first week of November; while to the west they stretched out a hand towards the Serbians defending the Babuna Pass. With adequate forces they could have pushed beyond Veles to Uskub, broken the wedge which the Bulgarians had driven in between them and the Serbians, restored the line of the Vardar, and secured the Serbian retreat.

It was this Bulgarian stab in the back which made havoc of the Serbian defence. Mackensen made slow progress at first, partly because he had no wish to drive the Serbians south until the Bulgars had cut off their retreat down the Vardar. Belgrade did not fall until three weeks after the bombardment had opened; but with the intervention of the Bulgarian armies all along the bare Serbian flank, events moved with tragic rapidity. On 17 October the Salonika line was pierced at Vrania, Veles fell on the 20th, and Uskub on the 21st. By the 26th Mackensen and the Bulgarians had effected a junction in the north and cleared the Danube route into the Balkans. Nish fell on 5 November after three days' fierce fighting, and the Constantinople railway thus passed into enemy hands. In the north-west the Austrians were pressing on from Ushitza down by the

Montenegrin frontier towards Mitrovitza, threatening to crush the Serbians on the Kossovo plateau between them and the Bulgars. To save the main Serbian force and keep open a retreat through Albania, a stand had to be made at Katchanik against the Bulgars advancing north from Uskub. It was successful to that extent, and when at one moment the Serbs temporarily broke the Bulgarian front, a junction seemed possible with the French advance from Veles. But both Allies were too weak for the solid Bulgarian wedge. The Serbs had to fall back from Kossovo and the French to their entrenched camp at Kavadar. A still narrower chance intervened between the French and the Serbs who were fighting at the Babuna Pass to bar the way to Prilep and Monastir, and at one time the French flung out their left to within ten miles of the Serbian position. But their own communications were threatened all down the narrow line of the Vardar, and they were hopelessly outnumbered by the Bulgarian forces. Retreat was the common misfortune and necessity. Prilep fell on 16 November; and farther north, as the Serbians retreated into Montenegro and Albania, the Austrians occupied Novi Bazar on 20 November, and Mitrovitza and Prishtina on the 23rd. On the 28th the Germans announced that "with the flight of the scanty remnants of the Serbian army into the Albanian mountains our main operations are closed."

There was something still for the Bulgars to do. Pursuing the Serbians in retreat from the Babuna Pass they reached the Greek frontier and cut the railway between Salonika and Monastir at Kenali on 29 November, and on 5 December occupied Monastir itself. The Greek frontier was a feeble protection, and the French at Kavadar were threatened with encirclement on their left. Kavadar had to be evacuated and a retreat secured by hard fighting at Demir Kapu. Simultaneously the British holding the front towards Lake Doiran were severely attacked, and on 6-7 December had 1300 casualties and lost 8 guns. But the enemy failed to cut off the retreat, and by the 12th both the French and British forces were on Greek territory fortifying a magnificent position which stretched from the mouth of the Vardar round to the Gulf of Orphano and enclosed the Chalchidice peninsula. Strong measures had to be taken to ensure the safety of Salonika with its cosmopolitan population, and the enemy hoped for its fall in January. But there was great reluctance to attack lines which were daily growing more formidable and were held by troops that were being gradually reinforced. Bulgarian ambition was also restrained by German counsels, for even Constantine and his new and pusillanimous premier, Skouloudis, might resent the occupation of Salonika by their hereditary rivals, and the Kaiser trusted more to family and diplomatic influence at Athens than to Bulgarian valour. The Germans themselves were more intent on consolidating the Berlin-Constantinople corridor and their hold upon the Turks than on Salonika, which fell within the Austrian sphere of influence, and might thus, if taken, become an apple of discord between its captors.

Austria had to content herself with dominion along the eastern shores of the Adriatic. The conquest of Serbia had left Montenegro an unprotected oasis surrounded by enemy territory; and Italy, which alone might have defended the Black Mountain, was unable or disinclined to make the effort. Lovtchen fell on 10 January, and the Austrians occupied Cettinje three days later. The Germans announced the unconditional surrender of the country, and some sort of capitulation was made by some sort of Montenegrins. But King Nicholas escaped to Italy and thence to France, while the greater part of his army made their way south to Scutari to join the Serbians who had retreated to the Adriatic coast. An Italian force marched up from Avlona to Durazzo to protect them, and Essad Pasha, a pro-Entente Albanian who had established a principality of his own on the fall of the Prince of Wied, rendered useful assistance. Eventually about 130,000 Serbian troops were transported to safety across the Adriatic, while the Serbian Government was provided with a home at Corfu in spite of the protests of the Greek administration. Save for neutral Greece and Rumania, the Italian foothold at Avlona and ours at Gallipoli, the whole of the Balkans had passed into the enemy's hands; for Essad's rule was as brief as it was circumscribed, and the Italians withdrew from Durazzo as the Austrians advanced to the southern frontier of Albania, and menaced Greek territory far beyond the reach of protection from Salonika.

While Greece and Rumania seemed to depend for their existence upon the forbearance of the Central Empires, our foothold in Gallipoli was even more precarious, and the first use the Germans made of their corridor to Constantinople was to furnish the Turks with howitzers designed to blow our forces off the peninsula. In October Sir Charles Monro had been sent out to take over the command from Sir Ian Hamilton and report on the situation. His report, which, owing to the singular relations then existing between someone in the Government and the press, was known to selected journalists within a few hours of its reception in London, was in favour of evacuation. The Cabinet was not prepared to accept that decision without further advice, and dispatched Lord Kitchener to make a survey of the political and military situation in the Ægean on the spot. He confirmed Monro's opinion; and in spite of the damage to our reputation and the losses which it was thought such an operation would inevitably involve, orders were given for a complete withdrawal from the Gallipoli Peninsula.

Some of the forces had already been transferred to Salonika, and the evacuation was to be completed in two stages, the first at Suvla Bay and Anzac and the last at Cape Helles. Success depended upon weather suitable for embarkation and skill in organizing transport and concealing our intentions from the enemy. No one dared to hope for so complete a co-operation of these factors as that which characterized the enterprise on 18-19 December. The weather was ideal in spite of the season, an attack from Cape Helles diverted the attention of the Turks, and the whole force at Suvla Bay and Anzac was embarked during two successive nights with only a single casualty. Marvellous as this success appeared, its repetition at Cape Helles on 7-8 January was even more extraordinary, although a Turkish attack on the 7th threatened to develop into that rearguard action which had been considered almost inevitable. But it was a mere incident in trench warfare, and they were as blind to our real intentions at Cape Helles as they had been three weeks before at Suvla Bay and Anzac—unless, indeed, with true Oriental passivity, they were content to see us leave their land in peace and had no mind to seek a triumph of destruction which would inure to the benefit of their uncongenial allies.

The brilliant success of the withdrawal from the Dardanelles provided some solace for the failure of the campaign, but did nothing to relieve from responsibility those who had designed its inception and directed its earlier course; and a Commission, which was appointed in the following summer, produced on 8th March 1917 an interim report which threw a vivid but partial and biased light not only on the Dardanelles campaign, but on the governmental organization which was responsible for the failures as well as the successes of the British Empire during the greater part of the war. Both were largely the outcome of that autocracy in war with which popular sentiment and the popular press had invested Lord Kitchener. It swallowed up everything else: the Cabinet left the war to the War Council and the War Council to a triumvirate consisting of Mr. Asquith, Lord Kitchener, and Mr. Churchill; but of these the greatest was Lord Kitchener. "All-powerful, imperturbable, and reserved," said Mr. Churchill, "he dominated absolutely our counsels at this time . . . He was the sole mouthpiece of War Office opinion in the War Council . . . When he gave a decision it was invariably accepted as final." He occupied, in the words of the Report, "a position such as has probably never been held by any previous Secretary of State for War," though it cannot compare with the elder Pitt's in 1757-61. Oriental experience had not improved his qualifications for the post; secretiveness, testified the Secretary of the War Council, made him reluctant to communicate military information even to his colleagues on the Council; the General Staff sank into insignificance, and the regulations prescribing the duties of its Chief were treated as non-existent. Mr. Churchill was debarred from a similar dictatorship at the Admiralty mainly because he was not a seaman and had Lord Fisher as his professional mentor; while Mr. Asquith busied himself with keeping the peace between his two obtrusive colleagues, neither of whom expressed the considered views of the Services they represented.

Thus the Dardanelles campaign was less an active expression of policy or strategy than the passive result of conflicting influences and opinions. As early as November 1914 Mr. Churchill had suggested an attack there or elsewhere on the Turkish coast as a means of protecting Egypt, but the idea was not seriously considered until on 2 January 1915 an urgent request was received from Russia for some diversion to relieve the Turkish pressure in the Caucasus. There was a corresponding need to deter Bulgaria from casting in her lot with the Central Empires, and on 13 January the War Council resolved upon the "preparation" of a naval attack on the Dardanelles. Its members were in some doubt as to what was meant by their resolution. Lord Fisher was averse from the scheme because he preferred another sphere of action, possibly the Baltic or Zeebrugge, with which Jellicoe's mind was also occupied;

and he hoped that preparation did not involve execution. Lord Kitchener warmly supported the idea of a naval attack, but most of his colleagues assumed that the operation would automatically become amphibious and involve the army as well; at any rate this impression was clearly stamped on their' minds after the purely naval attack had failed. Lord Kitchener, however, was strongly opposed to military cooperation; a great advantage of a purely naval attack was, he thought, that it could be abandoned at any moment, and he maintained that he had no troops to spare. Meanwhile Russia enthusiastically welcomed the notion, France concurred, and Mr. Churchill had secured an uncertain amount of naval backing for an expedition, the nature of which was not defined. But Lord Fisher grew more pronounced in his opposition, and when on 28 January the War Council proceeded from preparation to execution, he accepted the decision with a reluctance that nearly drove him to resign.

No sooner, however, had the War Council decided on a purely naval expedition than it found itself involved in an amphibious enterprise. "We drifted," said the Director of Military Operations, "into the big military attack"; and on 16 February it was resolved to send out the 29th Division and to reinforce it with troops from Egypt. The naval bombardment did not begin till three days later, and therefore it was no naval failure that produced this resolution; it was rather an unconscious reversion to the Council's original idea which had been dropped out of deference to Lord Kitchener. The same influence delayed the execution of the plan of 16 February: the 29th Division was to have started on the 22nd, but on the 20th it was countermanded by Lord Kitchener. Animated discussions ensued at the War Council on the 24th and 26th, but Lord Kitchener could not overcome his anxieties on the score of home defence and the Western front, and the Council yielded to his pressure. It was not till 10 March that the ill-success of the naval attack, advices from officers on the spot, and reassurances about the situation nearer home overcame the reluctance to dispatch the 29th division and other forces under Sir Ian Hamilton. Lord Kitchener now desired haste, and complained that 14 April, the date suggested by Hamilton, would be too late for the military attack. It was not found practicable until the 25th, and according to Enver Pasha the delay enabled the Turks thoroughly to fortify the Peninsula and to equip it with over 200 Austrian Skoda guns. Enver's further statement that the navy could have got through unaided, although it agreed with Mr. Churchill's opinion, is more doubtful. Out of the sixteen vessels employed to force the Dardanelles by 23 March, seven had been sunk or otherwise put out of action.

The same hesitation that characterized the inception of the military attack marked its prosecution, and forces which might have been adequate at an earlier stage were insufficient to break down the defences which delay enabled the Turks to organize. Nevertheless the enterprise might have succeeded but for errors of judgment in its execution, notably at Suvla Bay; and success would have buried in oblivion the mistakes of the campaign and its initiation just as it has done similar miscalculations in scores of precedents in history. There were, moreover, vital causes of failure which could not be canvassed at the time or even alleged in mitigation by the Commission of Inquiry; and the publication of its report on 8 March 1917, without the evidence on which it was based or reference to these other causes, was a masterpiece of political strategy designed to concentrate the odium of failure on those who were only responsible in part and to preclude their return to political power. Of these hidden causes there were two in particular: one the possibly justifiable refusal of Greece to lend her army to the scheme when a comparatively small military force might have been sufficient, and the other the far more culpable failure of Russia to co-operate with the 100,000 troops which were to have been landed at Midia and would have either found the northern approaches to Constantinople almost undefended or have diverted enough Turkish forces from the Dardanelles to give the southern attack a reasonable prospect of success. As it was, the British Empire had to content itself with the idea that 120,000 military casualties, apart from the French and the naval losses— which might have bought the downfall of Turkey shortened the war by a year at least, and saved a greater number of lives—had the minor effect of immobilizing 300,000 Turks and facilitating the defence of Egypt and the conquest of Mesopotamia and Syria.

The failure of the larger hope was a blow to the "Easterners" who discerned in the Dardanelles the strategic key to victory in the war and expected to turn the argument against divergent operations by pointing to a converging advance from the Balkans upon the

Central Empires. But the "Westerners," who maintained that the war could be won and could only be won in France and Belgium, were not much happier at the end of 1915. The British and French commands alike had subordinated the Dardanelles and Salonika expeditions to the needs of an autumn offensive on the West; and the argument between the two schools of thought is narrowed down, so far as the autumn of 1915 is concerned, to the question whether the troops we lost in September and October at Loos and in Champagne might not have been more effectively employed at the Dardanelles or Salonika. That they were not needed for defence in the West is obvious, since the line was held in spite of their loss. They were, in fact, mortgaged to an offensive which produced less strategical effect than the casualties in the East; for without the Salonika expedition, at least, Greece would have fallen completely under German dominion, and our control of the Ægean and our communications with Egypt would have been seriously imperilled. The controversy was an idle one so far as it was conducted on abstract principles, because war is an art in which success depends upon changing conditions which dictate one sort of strategy at one time and another at another. There were times when neglect of the West would have been fatal; there were others at which neglect of the East was almost as disastrous, and the autumn of 1915 belonged to the latter rather than to the former category. Neglect of the East would, indeed, have been not merely excusable but an imperative duty, had the situation in the West been what it was in the autumn of 1914 or spring of 1918. But there was no such necessity in September 1915: troops were not then withheld from the East to defend our lines in the West against a German offensive, but to take the offensive ourselves; and illusory hopes of success were based upon the known inferiority of German numbers in France due to their concentration in Russia.

The Entente advantage in bayonets on the Western front was between three and four to two, and it also had the ampler reserves. Sir John French commanded nearly a million men and General Joffre more than double that number, while our advantage in guns and munitions was not less marked; an almost unlimited supply of shells had been accumulated during the summer, and the new Creusot howitzers outdid the monsters from Essen and Skoda. Thirty fresh miles of French front had been taken over by the British, but it was not continuous. Plumer's Second and Haig's First armies still held the line from Ypres to south of La Bassée, but D'Urbal's Tenth French army intervened between Haig and the new Third British army which stretched from Arras to the Somme. It was not, however, along the British front but in Champagne that the main attack was planned. The objective was Vouziers, and the design was to break the German communications from east to west along the Aisne and thus compel an extensive retreat from the angle of the German front on the Oise and the Somme. If the subsidiary attack on the British front also succeeded, the Germans would suffer disaster and be compelled to evacuate much of the ground they held in France (see Map, p. 67).

A desultory bombardment of the whole front had begun early in the month, and on the 23rd a more intense fire, designed to obliterate the first line of German defences, opened from La Bassée to Arras and in Champagne. On the 25th the infantry attacked in high hopes and high spirits: for months, declared Joffre in his order of the day, we had been increasing our strength and our resources while the enemy had been consuming his, and the hour had come for victory. The striking force was Langle de Cary's Fourth Army, and the front of attack ran for fifteen miles from Auberive to Massiges. The bombardment had been effective and the élan of French, and particularly Marchand's colonial troops, carried most of the German first and parts of their second line of defence, and thousands of prisoners and scores of guns fell into their hands. But victory was not in this Western warfare of the twentieth century won in a day, and the morrow of a successful attack, which used to be fatal to the defeated, was now more trying to the victors. Instead of their well-protected lines they had to lie in the open or in the blasted trenches of the enemy, and from thence to attack a second and a third line of defences not less strong than the first, but less battered by bombardment. The second French effort, made on the 29th, was less successful than the first; some more prisoners and guns were taken, and a breach was made in the second line, but it was too narrow for the cavalry to penetrate. A third French attack on 6 October secured the village and Butte de Tahure which commanded the Bazancourt-Challerange railway, the first of the lateral lines of communication which it had been the object of the campaign to break; and later in the month the French made some local progress in other parts of the front. But on 30 October German counter-attacks, which had failed elsewhere, succeeded in recapturing the Butte de Tahure and recovering the use of the railway; and while the French had advanced on a front of fifteen miles to a depth of two and a half in places, the net result of the great attack was to leave them without appreciable advantage save in the disputable respect of greater German losses and the withdrawal of some divisions from the Russian front.

The subsidiary attacks between Ypres to Arras produced the same general kind of result. They extended almost continuously all along the line, but except to the north and south of Lens do not appear to have been designed to do more than prevent the opposing troops from being sent to reinforce the defence against the main offensive. For this purpose they were perhaps needlessly aggressive, for each resulted in the capture of ground which could not be held, and the forces engaged in these local enterprises were badly needed to clinch the nearly successful major operation. Later on in the war it was found that enemy troops could be contained along the line without such numerous and expensive precautionary attacks, and possibly these were really intended not so much to contain the enemy as to test his line with the idea of finding some weak spot which might be pierced. None of them succeeded to that extent, though Bellewarde was temporarily taken in front of Ypres, Le Bridoux redoubt in front of Bois Grenier, the slopes of the Aubers ridge, and some trenches near La Bassée. The last operation, if more force had been put into it, might have secured La Bassée and done more to convert the battle of Loos into a substantial victory than could ever have been achieved by a series of local successes farther north.

That battle was the principal British effort, and it only fell short of a real victory because the reserves were not on the spot to follow up the initial success which might almost seem to have surprised the higher command. The front extended from the La Bassée Canal to the outskirts of Lens, and as in Champagne the attack on 25 September was preceded by an intense bombardment which destroyed the first German trenches and wire-entanglements. Nearly everywhere the advance was at first successful. The Hohenzollern redoubt was captured, the Lens-La Bassée road was crossed, and even Haisnes and Hulluch reached. But the greatest success was farthest south, where the village of Loos was rushed by the 15th Division and then Hill 70. Even there the Highlanders would not stop, but went on impetuously as far as the Cité St. Auguste, well outflanking Lens and past the hindmost of the German lines. This was all by 9.30 a.m., within four hours of the first attack. But there were no reserves at hand to consolidate the victory and hold up the German counter-attacks. There were plenty miles away in the rear, retained by Sir John French because along the extended line of attack from Ypres to Lens it was not known where they would most be needed; and even when the need was clear, interrupted telephones and defective staff-work caused confusion and delay. Eventually the 11th Corps fresh from England and to fighting was marched eight miles and put into the battle line without sufficient food or water. Gradually our troops were pushed back from Hill 70, across the Lens-La Bassée road, and out of the Hohenzollern redoubt. The line was restored to some extent by the Guards on the 27th, and Loos remained firmly in our hands; but a great opportunity had been lost, and the great stroke of the 15th Division had not been turned into a great advance. Lens had been almost in our grasp, and with it a lever to loosen the German hold on Lille (see Map, p. 79).

The fault was partly due to the fact that D'Urbal's simultaneous offensive south of Lens had fallen short of the Vimy Ridge and left our right flank almost in the air in front of Grenay where the two lines joined. D'Urbal's army was, like our own, greatly superior in numbers to the Germans opposite, seventeen to nine Divisions, and the French artillery preparation for the attack on 25 September was equally elaborate. Unhappily the French offensive did not begin till one o'clock, three hours after the Highlanders had swarmed over Hill 70 and into Cité St. Auguste; and when it did begin, its left, where it joined the British right, was held up in front of Souchez till the following day, and the Germans used the interval to recover from the staggering blow they had received at Loos. On the 26th the French were more successful. Souchez, most of the Givenchy Wood, La Folie farm, and Thelus were captured, and on the 28th they made some progress up the Vimy slopes. The impression of success exceeded the reality, and a historian writing some months afterwards declared that by the 29th "the Vimy Heights had been won": it required a considerable Canadian victory a year and a half later to give much substance to this claim, and most of the ground secured in September 1915, including the Givenchy Wood, La Folie, and Thelus, was found to be in German hands when the line from Lens to Arras was taken over by British troops.

Attacks and counter-attacks, particularly round the Hohenzollern redoubt, during October led to little but slaughter, and the line in the West relapsed into winter stability and stagnation where they had been a year before with changes which only a large-scale map revealed. There had been at least 120,000 French casualties and more than 50,000 British; each side claimed that the enemy's losses far exceeded its own, and there was probably little to choose. A fortnight's battle in the West cost the Allies as much as nine months in the Dardanelles, though in the former it was the French and in the latter the British who bore the brunt. The optimism of the civilians with regard to the Dardanelles was capped by the optimism of the soldiers on the Western front; and neither was in a position to throw stones at the strategy of the other. Mr. Churchill disappeared from the Admiralty in May and from the Cabinet in October, and Sir John French lost his command of the British forces in December. His ostensible cheerfulness had been useful in the early days of shock and stress; but the part had been somewhat overdone in public and underdone in private, and it was becoming clearer, though not yet sufficiently clear, that brilliant cavalry generalship was not the quality most required to control the gigantic machinery of a modern army. Nevertheless, the criticisms that were levelled against the ineptitude and mental inelasticity of the generals and the staff of the old army overshot the mark. No one ventured to bring such a charge against the staff-work of the French, and yet the French had been no more successful in Champagne than we had been in Artois. The truth was that no generalship could have given the Entente victory over the Germans in 1915. The war was constantly and correctly described as a soldiers' war or a war of nations, but the meaning of the description was not fully realized. The Entente had to deal with a mighty people, splendidly organized and equipped for war, and against that colossal force mere generalship was like a sort of legerdemain pitted against an avalanche. The only power that could cope with the Germans was that of people similarly determined and equally trained and organized, and the only way in which they could be defeated was by exhaustion. Individual skill in modern politics and war tells mainly in matters of personal rivalry; it is our aristocratic quality which breaks its head in vain against the stolid mass of democratic forces. The single people in the long run beats the single man, and the community of nations overcomes the rebel State.

So far the rebel had succeeded because he took the world by storm and by surprise. The Germans in 1915 had played a skilful game and won. They had calculated that their line in the West could be held by inferior forces against any attacks the Entente could launch against it, while they broke the strength of Russia and overran the Balkans; and their calculations proved correct. It is conceivable that they might have done better to concentrate in 1915 as in 1914 against the Western Powers, but it is more probable that here, too, they were wise in their military conceit. The offensive that had failed in 1914 when British forces were a hundred thousand without munitions to correspond, would hardly have succeeded when they had grown to a million; and neglect of the East might well have meant invasion by Russia, the collapse of Austria, Czecho-Slovak and Jugo-Slav revolts, the defeat of Turkey, and the intervention of Rumania and Bulgaria on the Entente side. More could hardly have been achieved by Germany with the resources at her disposal; but she had not won the war. She had won a respite from defeat, as she was to do again in 1916 and in 1917, and her successes enabled her to postpone the reckoning from 1916 to 1918. But it was a fatal reprieve which she only used to weave her winding-sheet; and her efforts to snatch a German peace out of the transient balance of power, which her victories had set up, involved her in that fight to a finish with civilization which made her an outcast in disgrace as well as in defeat.

CHAPTER X

THE SECOND WINTER OF THE WAR

The failure of the Entente offensives in the Dardanelles and in France had at last convinced the public of the truth of Lord Kitchener's prophecy, that the war would be long if it was to result in a German defeat. Obstinate optimists had in 1914 believed in a victory before the first Christmas, while more reasonable critics hoped for one by the end of the following year. When the second Christmas came round the date of triumph had been postponed for another year or two, and few expected that it would arrive much before the end of the three years' term Lord Kitchener had suggested, or come at all unless greater efforts were made than had hitherto been the case. The magnificent response to the call for voluntary enlistment in 1914 had confirmed the traditional English view in favour of volunteers; between two and three million men had been raised by this method, either as members of the new army or as Territorials who freely surrendered their privilege of being called upon to serve for home defence alone; and it was but slowly that the nation was constrained to abandon the voluntary principle for that system of conscription which savoured so strongly of the militarism we were out to fight. But the Russian disasters and the failure of our offensives in the spring warned the Government of the advisability of at least preparing for other measures, and an Act had been passed for a national registration on 15 August of all males between the ages of 15 and 65. The autumn confirmed the foreboding of spring, and on 5 October Lord Derby undertook on behalf of the Government a recruiting campaign by which those who had not enlisted were induced to do so on the condition that they would not be compelled to serve before those who had feebler claims to exemption.

This campaign failed to produce the comprehensive results required, and at Christmas the Government took the plunge of proposing conscription for all unmarried men under the age of forty-two who were physically fit, and whose enlistment was not precluded by the national importance of their occupation or the onerous nature of their domestic liabilities. Even this measure of conscription was found inadequate by the following spring, and in May 1916 the exemption of married men was cancelled, and a general system of conscription on the continental model was introduced. Both measures were passed by large majorities, and encountered no organized opposition in the country. A few hundreds of conscientious objectors preferred to be treated as criminals rather than contribute in any way to the shedding of blood even in the defence of their country and themselves; and only the baser among their fellow-men attributed to them any worse motive than impractical idealism. The example of the mother-country was subsequently followed, with more liberal exemptions, by New Zealand and the Dominion of Canada; but Australia, which had long enjoyed compulsory military service for home defence, and was the only country in which the issue had to be submitted to a referendum, twice rejected the extension of the principle of compulsion to service outside the borders of the Commonwealth. The Channel Islands, which also had compulsion for their own insular defence, were equally loath to expand the idea, and Ireland was for political and some logical reasons exempted from the scope of the British Act; the Home Rule Bill had been placed on the statute-book, though its operation had been suspended, and it was thought as politic to allow her as it was to allow the Dominions to make her own decision.

In other matters than conscription Great Britain was slowly and reluctantly constrained to follow the German lead until the whole country became a controlled establishment; and a series of Defence of the Realm Acts deprived Englishmen of nearly all those liberties which they had regarded for centuries as proofs of their superior wisdom, but were now found to be merely the accidents of their past insular security. Freedom of the press, of speech, and even of private correspondence was subjected to censorship, and there was not in the whole range of our indictments against foreign autocracy one charge which might not with some colour be brought against ourselves. Fear entered once more into the English mind, and fear produced its invariable results, until precedents for what was done in the twentieth century had to be sought in the worst days of the Star Chamber, Titus Oates, and Judge Jeffreys. Once more, when the panic reached its height during the spring of 1918, British subjects were deprived of liberty without due process of law and by arbitrary tribunals sitting behind closed doors; once more we reverted to the old maxim of Roman law and the everlasting plea of despots, salus populi suprema lex, and learnt to practise ourselves the precepts we scorned in others. Liberty and even law were found to be luxuries in which war made us too poor to indulge. Truth itself was made tongue-tied to authority and became the handmaid of the State. To save ourselves and the world from barbarism we had to descend to the barbarous level of our foes, and poison-gas and the killing and starvation of women and children were developed into effective methods of warfare. It was all done in the name of humanity; for to shorten the war was the humanest course, and the shortest way was that of the greatest destruction. The means of destruction were developed at a prodigious rate, and England became a vast laboratory of death. War for the time was our only industry, and all who could be spared from the actual work of killing were pressed into the task of providing the weapons, the food, and the education for those on more active service.

Germany set the pace both in efficiency and in cruelty, and her success in 1915 convinced her that she could defy the moral scruples of mankind with impunity. Nothing save verbal protests had followed the sinking of the Lusitania, and even those had led Mr. Bryan, President Wilson's Secretary of State, to resign for fear lest they might prove too strong. That crime was accordingly succeeded by others, and further American lives were lost by the torpedoing of the Arabic on 19 August, the Ancona on 7 November, and the Persia on 30 December. The unneutral conduct of Dr. Dumba, the Austro-Hungarian ambassador in the United States, did, however, precipitate a demand for his recall; and American relations grew far more strained with Austria than with her more powerful and pernicious partner. For the moment President Wilson seemed more concerned with Great Britain's disrespect for American trade than with Germany's disrespect for American lives, and put forward a claim to be regarded as the champion of neutrality which contrasted oddly with his inaction a year before when Belgian neutrality was at stake. No one, however, could boast of consistency during the war, and President Wilson atoned for his earlier tenderness towards neutral rights by fathering in the end a league of nations which would abolish neutrality altogether. No doubt, his somewhat censorious protests against the British blockade and the methods of its enforcement were primarily intended for domestic consumption, and even then their effect was severely discounted by the growing tale of German outrage; the world at large was in no mood to listen to the laments of profiteers when its ears were tingling with the story of Edith Cavell's execution. She was an English nurse in Belgium who had tended with impartiality German and Belgian wounded; but she had facilitated the escape of some of the latter, and the Germans allowed no feeling of chivalry or humanity to interfere with the barbarous logic of their martial law. On 12 October, in spite of the efforts of American diplomacy and the horror of the civilized world, she was shot by order of a German court martial confirmed by the German military governor of Belgium. There were many heroines in the war, but none achieved a surer fame, because no one's fate exhibited in a clearer light the spirit with which humanity was at grips.

It was to the credit of humanity that this single outrage produced a greater horror than the German Zeppelin campaign, which reached its height in the winter and affected a large proportion of the civilian population. It was an extension of the policy of the Scarborough raids, and while it could be justified on the ambiguous and contradictory provisions of The Hague Convention, which exposed to the risk of bombardment any locality containing soldiers, munitions, or material for war, or means for military transport, its object was mainly to terrorize the civilian population; and the Zeppelin, in particular, was an engine of war which could not discriminate between legitimate and other objects of attack. This disability also applied to the aeroplane, and there was something very childish in the persistent assumptions that Entente air-raids were not only exclusively aimed at, but invariably successful in achieving military damage—even when the

French boasted of having on 22 September dropped thirty bombs on the King of Württemburg's palace at Stuttgart—and that the Germans always projected civilian destruction and never succeeded in effecting anything else. It was part of that delirium of wartime psychology, which induces all belligerents to believe that no one but an enemy ever commits atrocities, and no one but an ally is capable of virtue.

The possibility of air-raids had long been foreseen, and as early as the first October of the war the lights of London had been dimmed. The first attempt by Zeppelins was made on Norfolk on 19 January 1915 without any loss of life or appreciable loss of property. More damage was done to property by a second raid on 14 April directed against the Tyne, and four more were made in April on various parts along the East Coast. On 10 May a woman was killed and some houses demolished at Southend, and on the 31st the Zeppelins first reached London to the great delight of the German people. The East and North-east coasts were repeatedly raided in June, and by the end of the first year of war, 89 civilians had been killed and 220 injured, while possibly half a dozen Zeppelins had suffered destruction in the various theatres of war. One was destroyed by Lieutenant Warneford's monoplane in Belgium on 7 June, but none fell victims to anti-aircraft defences in England. The raids became more serious as the nights grew darker: on 7 September 20 were killed and 86 injured in London, and on 13 October 56 were killed and 114 injured. Bad weather produced a respite in November and December, but on 31 January 1916 the north Midlands had 67 killed and 117 injured, and in March and April similar casualties attended raids on the Lowlands of Scotland and the East Coast from Yorkshire to Kent. France suffered as well as England, but the Germans took a peculiar pleasure in the English raids, because they thought Zeppelins were the only means of bringing home to the English people the realities of war.

Air-raids were, however, one of the horrors of war rather than a means of achieving victory, and the military importance of aircraft never attained proportions corresponding to the space the subject occupied in the public press and the popular mind. They did not affect the duration of the war by a single day, and throughout the winter of 1915-16 it seemed to increase in horror without any other sort of progression on land or water. There was no naval action because Germany kept her fleet in harbour, and relied upon mines and submarines to wear down not so much the naval strength as the economic resources of the Allies. Occasionally a cruiser or smaller vessel was lost, and one pre-Dreadnought battleship, the Edward VII. But German successes were mostly scored against merchant vessels and similar craft; and our activities in the Balkans, coupled with the facilities afforded by the Aegean to submarines, made the Eastern Mediterranean a favourite scene for their operations. By the end of 1915 over a thousand vessels, Allied and neutral, of one sort or another, had been put out of action by mines and submarines; but the fact that few of them had any fighting value concealed the importance of their economic loss from the eyes of the public if not of the Government itself. A more legitimate and romantic form of depredation was the cruise of the Moewe, a disguised auxiliary cruiser, which succeeded in January and February 1916 in capturing fifteen British merchantmen in the Atlantic, and returned safe to Kiel with prisoners and booty. The absence of German commerce made British retaliation impossible except in the Baltic, where our submarines had some remarkable successes until Sweden closed the entrance by mining her territorial waters. She was within her rights in doing so, but the effect of her action was to give German commerce in the Baltic a security which was lacking to the commerce of the world outside, because Holland and Denmark shrank from following Sweden's example. Mr. Balfour pointed out the unfriendly nature of Sweden's action, but Russia was particularly averse from adding Sweden to her enemies at that juncture, and remonstrances were in vain.

On land the most active spheres of operation were in winter naturally in the tropical or sub-tropical regions. The East African campaign still hung fire owing to various causes, principally perhaps because of doubts and possibly disputes whether it belonged primarily to the sphere of purely British, Indian, or South African activity, and could best be fought with the different kinds of troops those various Governments had at their disposal. The earlier operations had been undertaken mainly by troops from India, and for a year longer there was little but border fighting until in March 1916 General Smuts arrived with South African forces to begin the serious work of conquest. The principal work of the winter was the reduction of the Cameroons. Considerable progress had been made by June in overrunning this vast territory, half as large again as the German Empire in Europe: the French had occupied Lome from the south, while the British, after some checks on the Nigerian frontier, had advanced to Ngaundere. The rainy season then set in, and operations were suspended until October. The Germans had transferred their capital to Yaunde, which was made the objective of converging attacks by British, French, and Belgian columns from north, east, and south. The British reached it on 1 January 1916, but the movements had been admirably timed, and the French came three days later. Only isolated posts in distant localities remained, and the last of them fell on 18 February.

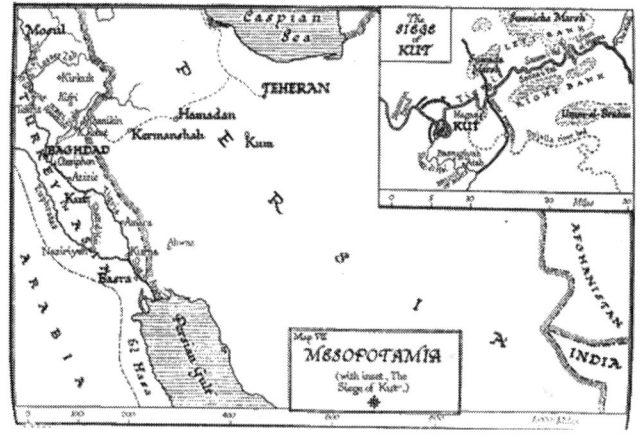

Mesopotamia

From Egypt the Turks had been diverted, since their defeat in February 1915, by the attack on the Dardanelles; but the German advance in the Balkans had synchronized with attempts to disturb us on the western borders of Egypt by German and Turkish intrigues with the Senussi federation of Moslem tribes, and in Tripoli, which the Italians had never succeeded in completely subjugating. Trouble began to threaten in November 1915, and the frontier post at Sollum was withdrawn to Mersa Matruh, the terminus of a railway line from Alexandria. The Arab attacks began on 13 December and increased in strength until the middle of January 1916; but with their inferior equipment and means of communication they had little chance of success and were easily beaten off with considerable losses, which led to dissension among the Arab forces and then to their dissipation. They were finally defeated at Agagia on 26 February, and Sollum was regained on 14 March. There was no further trouble on the western frontier of Egypt, and a repercussion of the Senussi discontent far south in Darfur was satisfactorily suppressed by a detachment of the Egyptian Army which occupied El Fasher on 22 May. East of the Suez Canal there were only raids in which we were generally successful, except for the loss of Katia on 23 April; in retaliation El Arish was destroyed by bombardment from British monitors on 18 May.

In Egypt we stood and were still to stand for another year upon the defensive; but farther east in Mesopotamia we were slipping into an adventurous and chequered offensive which grew insensibly after the manner of the Dardanelles campaign. Our original operations at the head of the Persian Gulf had, indeed, unlike the attack on Gallipoli, been defensive in their purpose; but the distinction between the two easily disappears in military operations, and the Germans were only more logical militarists than other people when they openly avowed that offence was the best means of defence. British dominion in India and in Egypt had grown upon that principle, and it grew in much the same way in Mesopotamia. The security of our control of the Persian Gulf required, we discovered, the occupation of Basra; the defence of Basra demanded an advance to Kurna, and from Kurna we had proceeded in June to Amara. There we realized that our left flank might be turned at Nasiriyeh, and having got both Amara and Nasiriyeh, one on the Tigris and the other at the junction of the Euphrates with the Shatt-el-Hai (which links the Euphrates with the Tigris at Kut), we concluded that our position would be improved if, by seizing Kut, we could bar a Turkish advance down either the Tigris or the Shatt-el-Hai. The logic was sound enough for those who had the means to enforce it; and in spite of the torrid heat, the river route and our gun-boats enabled us to master Nasiriyeh on 25 July. Early in August began the advance up the Tigris from Amara to Kut, whither the Turks had retired. They had been well taught by their German instructors, and their position astride the river was well entrenched. But Townshend's attack was skilfully planned; feinting on the Turkish right on 27 September, he outflanked and drove in their left on the 28th, and at the end of a long day disposed of the Turkish reinforcements and entered Kut on the 29th.

The campaigning season was only about to begin; the Turks had decamped in disorganization towards Baghdad; and the temptation to follow proved irresistible. When so much had been done with such ease, it seemed to be flying in the face of Providence not to make a dash for Baghdad and seize the end of that railway-route on which the Germans were beginning to work with such energy from the other direction in the Balkans. If it led from Berlin to Baghdad, might it not also lead from Baghdad to Berlin? There was assuredly a touch of fantastic imagination in the transformation which first came over and then overcame our strategy in the East, and we found that the transition from defence to offence was slight compared with the change from a sound to a speculative offensive. Kut might be essential to the defence of the delta, but if Baghdad was needed for the protection of Kut, there was no limit east of the Bosporus to which the line and the logic of defence might not be pushed. The argument might have been sound, had it reposed on a firmer foundation of force. But the impetus and the organization which had carried us to Kut would be spent before we reached Baghdad; and arrangements for transport, commissariat, and medical aid, which might have served for the lesser needs and the shorter lines of communication, broke down in utter confusion under the demands of the larger ambition which they had not been planned to fulfil. We had but 13,000 bayonets, two-thirds of whom were Indian troops, while the Turks could call up reserves many times that number; and our men were worn with ten months' incessant campaigning under a tropical sun. General Townshend protested against the adventure, but was overruled by Sir John Nixon and the Commander-in-chief in India.

Within a week from the fall of Kut the advance on Baghdad began, and at Azizie half-way between the two, the Turks were routed again as they had been at Kut. By 12 November, Townshend was in front of Ctesiphon, about twenty-four miles from Baghdad. Here the Turks were strongly entrenched. Their right was protected by the Mahmudiyeh Canal which ran from the Tigris to the Euphrates, and their main position consisted of two strongly fortified lines on the eastern bank of the Tigris. Townshend's attack on the 22nd resembled his attack on Kut, and after hard fighting the first line was carried. But the second was the real Turkish defence, and our wearied and smaller forces could not cope with the continuous stream of Turkish reinforcements. The Turks lost heavily in their counterattacks on the 23rd, but they could afford to do so, while we could only succeed by a speedy and inexpensive victory which the strength of the Turkish position and reinforcements forbade. The gamble had failed, and the only thing to do was to cut the loss and retreat as well as we could. No proper provision had been made for such an eventuality, and the horrors of that retirement reflected grave discredit on those responsible for the campaign. Hard pressed by the pursuing Turks, our diminished force was back at Kut on 3 December, where in a few days it was surrounded by the enemy now under the command of the German Marshal von der Goltz.

The Germans had not been idle on the flanks of this bid for Baghdad, and their intrigues in Persia led to a revolt of the gendarmerie, which was officered by Swedes, and to the seizure by the pro-German insurgents of Kum, Hamadan, and other towns in central Persia. Fortunately this move was countered by prompt action on the part of Russia. Teheran was occupied by Russian forces by the end of November, Kum and Hamadan by 11 December, and a pro-Entente Government was established. The German route through Persia towards Afghanistan was blocked for the time; but pro-German forces at Kermanshah impeded a Russian march to the relief of Kut, where a fresh Turkish division from Gallipoli arrived on 23 December and a vigorous effort was made to carry the place by assault. It failed, and the Turks sat down to a blockade, while farther south they constructed formidable obstacles to the advance of the relieving forces coming up the river. Their position was selected with considerable skill at Sanna-i-Yat on a narrow strip of land between the Suweicha marshes and the river, while between it and Kut there was established the strongly-fortified Es Sinn line. The depth of these defences was nearly twenty-five miles, and the task of carrying the successive lines would tax anything but a relieving force far greater than that which was attempting it.

Sir John Nixon had been succeeded by Sir Percy Lake, but the advancing force was under the immediate command of General Aylmer. On 21 January he failed to carry the first of the lines at

Umm-el-Hanna, although it was announced in Parliament that British forces had reached the last position at Es Sinn; and it was not till 7-8 March that Aylmer made a bold attempt at once to turn the Sanna-i-Yat defences and relieve Kut by a surprise attack on the right bank of the river. Everything depended once more upon initial success, for length of communications and lack of supplies made continuous pressure impossible; and the Turks were ready and their defences strong. Aylmer was no more fortunate at Es Sinn than Townshend at Ctesiphon, and the command was taken by General Gorringe. He reverted on 5 April to the lines on the left bank at Umm-el-Hanna. They were carried, and twelve hours later the further line at Felahiyeh. Keary's Lahore division had been equally successful on the right bank; but a flood caused by the melting snows on the Armenian hills interposed to bar the way to the relief of Kut. A final attempt was made on the 23rd across the water-logged land in front of Sanna-i-Yat; but advance was impossible along the narrow causeway which alone gave foothold for the troops, and on the 29th Townshend's force in Kut, consisting of 2000 British and 6000 Indian troops, surrendered after a siege of nearly five months.

After Gallipoli, Mesopotamia. Until March 1918 our reverses in these two "side-shows" were counted our worst disasters in the war, and to the electorally-heated imagination of Mr. Lloyd George they appeared even later as the sum and substance of British achievement before he became Prime Minister. In the case of Kut the responsibility rested mainly with the Indian Government, to which also was due our brilliant recovery in the East when Lord Chelmsford, Sir Charles Monro, and Sir Stanley Maude—all appointed in 1916—had time to retrieve the mistakes of their predecessors in the Viceroyalty, Command-in-chief of the Indian Army, and command of the Mesopotamian forces. Meanwhile, it was fortunate for the prestige of the Entente in the East that Russia's collapse in Europe appeared to have no effect upon the vigour of her action in the middle East. The Grand Duke Nicholas, who had been transferred to the command in the Caucasus, found an admirable chief of staff in General Yudenitch, and between them they brought off a stroke against Turkey which was more sensational than the Turks' success at Kut and Gallipoli.

Erzerum was reckoned the strongest fortress in the Turkish Empire, but amid the distractions of the Dardanelles and Mesopotamian campaigns it had escaped proper attention from the Turks and their German experts, and the Grand Duke profited by the fact that Turkish troops, relieved from the pressure at Gallipoli, were sent to Kut and not to the Caucasus. Moreover, the ordinary line of communication with Erzerum by the sea and Trebizond had been cut by the Russian destruction of Turkish shipping, and transport by land was almost as difficult as it was between the head of the Persian Gulf and Kut. The Russian communications were better, but theirs was an adventurous enterprise across mountain passes under the arctic conditions of midwinter; and few people had any inkling of its inception when Yudenitch began to move on 11 January. By the 16th he was at Kuprikeui where the road crosses the Araxes, and in a two days' battle he broke the Turkish army, driving its remnants south towards Mush and clearing the way to Erzerum. Time was required to bring up the heavy guns, but early in February the forts on Deve Boyun were under bombardment, and another Russian army advancing from the north down the valley of the Kara Su defeated a Turkish division and captured Kara Gubek on the 12th and Tafta on the 14th. From the south the Russians were also crossing the Palantuken Dagh, and the fate of Erzerum was sealed. Its evacuation was completed early on the 16th, and a few hours later the Cossacks rode into the city. To the south the Russian left entered Mush and Bitlis, gaining the northern shores of Lake Van, while their right slowly pushed along the Black Sea coast in the direction of Trebizond. In Persia, too, the Russians occupied Kermanshah and descended the pass to Khanikin and the Mesopotamian plain; but it was an adventurous body of cavalry rather than a substantial military force which joined hands with the British on the Tigris some weeks after the fall of Kut. The Russians had to some extent redeemed their failure in Europe, but others they had not been able to save.

The Caucasus

In Europe their defence was materially assisted by the British and French attacks in Artois and Champagne and by the needs of Mackensen's offensive in the Balkans. To both areas troops were diverted from the German front in Russia, and the centre was especially denuded. No advantage was, however, taken of this weakness, partly because of Russia's general debility and partly because what efforts she could afford were required for the defence of the Dvina and for the sympathetic activity of Ivanov in Galicia, which was the nearest approach Russia could make to intervention in the Balkans. The German attack on the line of the Dvina was not merely intended to fend off a Russian attack in the centre; it had also the positive aim of securing Riga and comfortable winter quarters for the German army in the north. Riga, however, was not an easy nut to crack; its flank was defended by the sea, immediately south of it were marshes across which only causeways ran, and to the east stretched the formidable obstacle of the Dvina. Roads and rails for the most part crossed it at Dvinsk, and the southern approaches to Dvinsk itself lay through land and water as intricately mixed as in the Masurian mazes of East Prussia. But on Dvinsk the German attack was concentrated, and after a preliminary failure on 25 September a week's bombardment and assault began on 3

October. The siege guns which had been so fatal at Kovno and elsewhere were brought up against a minor fortress and failed. Ruszky was in command, and he took care to keep the howitzers out of range of the city by an arc of far-flung trenches which the numerous scattered lakes saved from outflanking. Illukst was at one time taken by the Germans but found of little value for the larger purpose; and German prisoners complained that Dvinsk, which they failed to take, had cost them more than all the greater fortresses they had captured. In the third week of October Hindenburg transferred his efforts back to Riga, where he met with little better success. He got as far as Olai on the direct route from Mitau, and even secured a foothold on Dahlen Island in the river south-east of Riga; but these successes profited him no more than the capture of Illukst. On 7 November the Russians recaptured Olai, and on the 10th, with the help of their fleet, drove back the Germans, who had advanced along the coast, beyond Shlock and Kemmern and Kish, extending their lines to Ragassem and Kalnzem. In the same month a similar Russian counter-offensive recaptured Illutsk and pushed the Germans farther away from Dvinsk (see Map, p. 274).

Far to the south below the Pripet marshes which divided the Russian front into two, the Germans and the Russians under Brussilov engaged in thrust and counter-thrust along the Styr which caused Czartorysk to change hands again and again, and earned for these operations the nickname of "the Poliesian quadrille"; and the fluctuations on the Strypa were equally indecisive. But the situation in the Balkans suggested the need for something less ambiguous nearer the Rumanian frontier if Rumanian neutrality was to be preserved; and the objective selected for Ivanov's new offensive was Czernowitz the capital of the Bukovina. The attack began on 24 December, and the struggle lasted for over three weeks. Containing battles were fought along the Strypa and the Styr, and Czartorysk passed once more into Russian hands and Kolki was added to their gains. But the main object was not attained. The Russians seized the heights between Toporoutz and Raranzce and threw some shells into Czernowitz, but they failed to capture the crucial point at Uscieczko on the Dniester. Mackensen and five divisions had, however, to be diverted from the Balkans, and Russia's offensive in the Bukovina helped to conceal her designs on Erzerum. Rumania was saved from descending on the wrong side of the fence; but her natural reluctance to abandon her perch prohibited that Russian attack on Bulgaria through Rumanian territory which might otherwise have been made, but would probably have failed and would in any case have come too late to relieve the Serbian disaster.

The winter of 1915-16 thus passed with little to relieve the gloom. Erzerum had balanced Kut, and the Cameroons had ceased to be a German land. But these were trifles compared to the gigantic clash of arms in Europe, and here the Germans had done more than in their first year's fighting. Russia had been dealt a far more staggering blow than France in 1914, and Serbia and Montenegro had fared worse than Belgium, while in both East and West our counter-offensives had been ineffectual. The Germans naturally thought they had won the war; they had merely reached the climax of their success, and that climax did not constitute a victory. The Allies' heads were "bloody but unbowed," and they were still the masters of their fate. The sea was theirs and all that therein lay; some of them were only in process of mobilizing their resources; and the moral factor in war which, like the mills of God grinds slowly but grinds exceeding small, required patience for its full development. Meanwhile the German military machine had done no more than establish a balance of power which was to be tilted in one direction by the Russian Revolution and then in the other by American intervention.

CHAPTER XI

THE SECOND GERMAN OFFENSIVE IN THE WEST

It was a commonplace of the old diplomacy that the most effective way to deceive a rival diplomatist was to tell him the truth, and similar conditions enabled the Germans to delude the British public if not the British Government, so general was the conviction that the Germans would not or could not say anything that was not false. This simple-minded attitude towards our enemies made it easy for them to combine virtue with efficiency, and German statesmen were at times singularly candid in the estimates they published of the situation. One of these truthful pictures was drawn by the German Chancellor in December 1915 when he pointed out that it was not in Germany's thoughts or interests to seek further conquests for her arms: the more territory they conquered, the thinner would be their lines and the greater the difficulty of maintaining them. But patriotic imagination detected behind this apparent frankness a design to conquer Egypt and India, or at least to dominate the Persian Gulf, and averted attention from the probability that it implied a desire to substitute a solid decision in the West for territorial speculation in the East. Nothing, indeed, was more certain than that Germany, having temporarily freed herself and her allies from danger in the East, would recall her attention to these enemies in the West by whose defeat alone could she hope to win the war; and before the end of 1915 there were rumours of the transport of German guns and troops from the East to the Western front.

It was also reasonably certain that the new offensive would not follow the lines of the old, and that, whatever form it took, it would not be a repetition of the attempt to outmarch the Allied left and crush a British force which had grown from a hundred thousand to over a million bayonets. Time was also to show that no subsequent German offensive could hope to achieve the kind of success that had been missed on the Marne. The German ambition had in 1914 been to annihilate the French and British armies and dictate a victorious peace. In 1916 such a triumph was out of the question. In spite of her victories, Germany had been reduced to the defensive, and her future offensives were merely means to prolong her defence, to anticipate and frustrate the attacks of her enemies, and wring an advantageous peace out of the defeat of their attempts to drive her from the territorial conquests she had made. The height of her expectations was to show that her fronts were impregnable East and West, and that the Allies could not compel, but could only purchase German evacuation of the occupied ground by accepting the surrender of such tracts and other terms as Germany chose to concede. She was really in the position she pretended to have been before the war broke out of having to attack in order to maintain what she held; and if she began, it would not be for the purpose of breaking and enveloping the Allied armies, but to preclude their offensive and improve and strengthen her own position. She was, in fact, beleaguered, her attacks were really sallies, and her hope was to keep the besiegers at such a distance that they could make no impression upon the heart of her economic and military situation.

The battles of Verdun therefore bear no resemblance to the Western campaign of 1914 or the Eastern campaign of 1915. They were limited to a narrow area, and involved but a fraction of the German forces, while the bulk even of those in the West was distributed along the other sectors of the front. They were fought partly to deprive the French of what the Germans regarded as a "sally-port" into Germany, and partly to anticipate in detail that general pressure on all fronts which the Germans dreaded as the Allied strategy for 1916. At last, they feared, there was really co-ordination in the Entente, and there might be such a synchronizing of its offensives that Germany, in spite of her interior lines, would be unable to transfer the weight of her forces from one threatened point to another. Her strategy in the spring was to forestall this comprehensive danger. By an attack on Verdun in February the French and the British might be provoked into a premature movement before their allies were ready; Italy's threatened advance might be paralysed by a thrust at its flank in May; and both Western dangers might thus be parried before Russia was ready to move once more in the summer. The excellence of Germany's transport organization would enable her, in spite of her numerical inferiority, to bring adequate if not superior forces to repel attacks which depended for success upon their being simultaneous.

It was, however, incumbent on Germany to prevent her defensive offensives from combining the major costs of an offensive with the minor advantages produced by a defence; and economy in the waste of man-power was becoming urgent. Hence her attacks must be on a more limited front than those of the Allies in September, and resistance must be overcome rather by artillery than by infantry charges. The guns were to do at Verdun what they had achieved on the Dunajec, but there is little to show that the Germans expected to repeat in France their drives of the year before in Galicia and in Poland. The Entente lines in France were stronger and less thinly held than the longer lines in the East, and while they might be pushed back from a salient like Verdun, it was not imagined that they could be broken and rolled up as they might have been in 1914. Eighteen months of war had set limits to German ambition which were admitted in counsel and conversation though not allowed to appear in print; and the strategy of 1916 was not one which the Germans would have chosen had their choice been free, but the best they could devise under the conditions imposed upon them by their situation. It was not until Russia had completely collapsed that they recovered for the moment in the spring of 1918 that freedom from fear on the Eastern front which enabled them to resume the action with which they started the war and put all their strength into a final and real offensive in the West.

While throughout the winter the Allies were congratulating themselves upon the inferiority of German shelling in the West and innocently vaunting a superior expenditure of ammunition, which made no more impression on the German lines than the enemy's shelling did on ours, the Germans were reserving their fire and accumulating shells for more effective use; and in addition to their artillery, they had recovered the advantage in respect of aircraft. Hitherto we had done better than the Germans in the fighting, as distinguished from the raiding, in the air, not so much because our machines were better and certainly not because they were more numerous, but because in the air youthful ingenuity and daring had its chance unfettered by the restraining and depressing hand of regimental mediocrity; and where machine-made discipline was at a discount, youth and enterprise were at a premium. This general rule was subject to exceptions caused by the ding-dong race of scientific invention, and for the moment the Germans had in their Fokker an aeroplane of decisive superiority. They began to appear in increasing numbers above and behind our lines, and to secure some of those advantages in reconnaisance which transferred to aircraft in this war the functions performed in earlier wars by cavalry. The Germans were able to concentrate at Verdun with their minds easier about the rest of their front when their aircraft could detect any signs of an approaching offensive elsewhere.

They also succeeded in concealing their own intentions; for while there were premonitory symptoms which had given some French officers an inkling of what was coming, adequate preparations had not been made for the storm at Verdun, and attention had been distracted by German feints at other points of the line. These attacks were made on both the British and French sectors. The taking and retaking of Hartmannsweilerkopf went on with a frequency that was all the more confusing because each side only published its successes. On 28 January the Germans made a successful attack on the French near Frise on the Somme and pushed back their lines towards Braye on a two-mile front; but they were less fortunate in their simultaneous effort against Carnoy, where the British had just taken over that part of the front previously held by the 10th French Army and extending thence to the north of Arras. Probably the Germans imagined that this extension had weakened our lines at Ypres; and on 8 February they began a bombardment which developed into a fierce struggle for Hooge and The Bluff on the Ypres-Commines Canal. The ground lost was mostly recovered by counter-attacks on 2 and 27 March and 3 April, but it could not all be held against further German attacks later in the month. Similarly some gains on the Vimy Ridge in the middle of May were lost again on the 21st, and early in June the Germans thrust us back behind Hooge. But these attacks and others along the front were merely feints designed to conceal the German preparations against

Verdun, and to prevent the Allied forces from concentrating on its defence after the plan had been revealed.

Verdun was selected for attack because its proximity to the German frontier made it dangerous in the hands of the enemy, and also made it easier for the Germans to concentrate on its attack the masses of artillery with which they proposed to do the fighting, while its salience hampered the French lines of communication. There were three lines of defence. The outermost ran in an arc nine miles from Verdun round in front of Malancourt, Béthincourt, Forges, Brabant, Ornes, Fromezey, and Fresnes; the second was some three miles nearer in, and the third ran by Bras, Douaumont, Vaux, and Eix. The danger consisted in the facts that the outer lines were thinly held by Territorials and the inner lines had not been properly fortified; for the French, unequalled in the élan of attack, never developed that patient and meticulous preparation for defence which stood the Germans in good stead, and always found it easier to visualize attacks than to materialize defences. Verdun, having survived the epidemic so fatal to fortresses in 1914, was treated as immune from serious danger in 1916. If, therefore, the Germans could batter to pieces the first position, the rest might easily fall, and they came dangerously near to fulfilling their hopes of reaching Verdun in four days.

At seven o'clock on the morning of Monday, 21 February, there burst forth on the centre of the front a heavier bombardment than any before experienced. The French defences were obliterated, and five hours later the Germans walked into possession. A counter-attack checked their progress in the afternoon, and the flanks of the French centre held out at Brabant and Herbebois throughout that day and the next. But the depression in the centre created a salient on either side, and the French could only fight desperate rearguard actions while the line was straightened out; by Wednesday morning they were back on a line running due east from Samogneux. But the German pressure on the centre was renewed and the French were pressed back to Beaumont and the Bois des Fosses. Ornes on the east and Samogneux on the west had to be abandoned, and on the 24th the Germans were threatening the centre of the last of the French lines of defence at Louvemont and Hill 347. Only a desperate rally enabled the French to keep their front intact while their left was withdrawn from Champneuville and Talou hill to

Vacherauville and the Poivre hill, and their right from Bezonvaux and the Bois des Caurières to the Douaumont plateau. On the 25th the Germans launched what they thought was their final attack in the battle for Verdun, and before nightfall the news was telegraphed to Berlin that Fort Douaumont, the key of the last line of defence, had fallen.

It was a natural but unrealized anticipation. Eighteen German divisions were pitted against the worn and weary remnants of the original French defenders, and the Brandenburgers had captured the fort. But its ruins were merely a detail in the Douaumont position. To the east the French held the redoubt and to the west the village of Douaumont; and instead of carrying the plateau the Germans had been checked on its summit. Their other main attack had fared even worse on the Poivre hill to the west; and although Louvemont and Hill 347 had been carried in the centre, the fifth day of the battle closed with the Germans behind instead of beyond the real defences of the city they had hoped to reach in four. On that day, too, Pétain arrived to take over the command, and he was followed by reinforcements. On the morrow a furious counter-attack drove the Germans out of the greater part of Fort Douaumont and back to the northern edge of the plateau, and the crisis of the first surprise had passed. The battle continued, but the fact that it spread eastwards round to Eix and Manheulles showed that the concentrated thrust at the centre had failed; and the shortening of the French curve round by Fromezey, Étain, Buzy, and Fresnes to a straight line running from Vaux to Les Éparges strengthened rather than weakened the defence.

The Germans now shifted their ground of attack from the east to the west of the Meuse, and on 2 March a four days' bombardment began of the Malancourt-Forges line. They sought to conceal their change of plan by renewing the struggle for Douaumont, but on 6 March they drove the French from Forges and Regnéville back to their real defences on the ridge behind, of which the Mort Homme (Hill 295) was the crest, and Hills 304 and 265 its western and eastern supports. Their first attack was on the eastern sector of this front, and by nightfall they had gained Hill 265 and penetrated into the Bois des Corbeaux which stretched between it and Mort Homme. The struggle continued throughout the 7th and 8th, but on the 9th-11th the Germans varied it by reverting to the east bank of the Meuse and making a costly but unsuccessful attempt to outflank Douaumont by capturing Vaux, Damloup, Eix, and Manheulles. This diversion did not slacken the pressure on the west bank of the Meuse, and the French were forced back from the Bois des Corbeaux to the Bois de Cumières; on 14 March the Germans made a great bid for Mort Homme, and Berlin announced its capture. But they had only taken its north-eastern slopes, and on the 17th they sought a fresh approach from the west by means of a converging attack from Avocourt and Malancourt on Hill 304. The bombardment lasted until the 20th, when the Germans forced their way through Avocourt wood. They were driven back by a counter-attack on the 29th, but Malancourt fell on the 31st, and the French further withdrew from Haucourt. On 2 April the Germans also succeeded in driving an awkward wedge into the Bois de la Caillette between Vaux and Douaumont, but Mangin thrust it back on the following day.

There was yet another struggle for Mort Homme. On 7 April the French had evacuated their salient at Béthincourt and re-formed their front on a straight line running just north of Mort Homme. On the 9th the Germans, having failed in their local attacks, attempted a general movement against the whole front west of the Meuse. The battle raged for three days, and at one time the Germans penetrated into Cumières; but they were driven back by the French artillery, and the general assault, in spite of its carnage, produced no greater gain for the Germans than a ravine on the edge of the Poivre hill. From that date the first battle of Verdun died away amid local efforts along the lines east and west of the Meuse. But the Germans were still obstinately wedded to their scheme of exhausting France before the time came for a general Allied offensive; and they felt that they could not cut their losses and acquiesce in the blow to their prestige and to the credit of the Crown Prince. A respite, however was needed for the reorganization of the command and the re-formation of the armies shattered in the fruitless attacks and it was not until 3 May that the Germans were ready to begin the second battle of Verdun.

This time it opened on the west bank of the Meuse, and Mort Homme was as before the obstacle and the objective. After two days' bombardment the Germans gained some trenches north of Hill 304, and on the 7th they attacked it on three sides and compelled the French to abandon the crest. This reduced Mort Homme to a difficult salient, and after a few days' lull the Germans gained the summit on 21 May by an expenditure of man-power out of all proportion to the value of the result. By the 24th they had secured what was left of Cumières at a similar cost, and the French line ran straight from Avocourt in front of Esnes and Chattancourt to the Meuse. On the east bank the onslaught was no less furious, and on 7 May the Germans drove the French out of Douaumont fort and down the road towards Fleury. Mangin recovered the greater part of Douaumont on the 22nd, but German reinforcements took it again on the 24th, and on the 25th pushed on by Haudromont wood and Thiaumont farm, outflanking Vaux on the west. Further progress was made in the following days, and on 1 June the fall of Damloup uncovered the eastern flank of the Vaux position. The fort itself made a marvellous resistance under Major Raynal, and held out till the 6th.

There was a lull for four days, but on the 11th the struggle recommenced with the Germans only four miles from Verdun. It raged chiefly on the slopes of Froideterre and round the village of Fleury close by, and the climax came on the 23rd. On that day the Germans got into Fleury and were driven out; on the 24th they were in again, but on the 30th the French recovered Thiaumont and neutralized the German advantage. On the morrow the Western front was aflame with the battle of the Somme. Verdun had done its work and taken its wages. The struggle flickered on; Fleury changed hands again in July and August, and so did Thiaumont. But the attack had lost its vital importance and the decisive scene had shifted to the west where the Germans and not the French were on the defensive. Pétain and then Nivelle, who succeeded him in April, had held the fort till the appointed time; and their heroic troops had made their name and that of Verdun a possession for ever. Falkenhayn, who had taken Moltke's place as chief of the German Staff and was responsible for the German strategy at Verdun, was removed to another sphere of activity; but the Germans themselves were right when they attributed failure less to their own defects than to the valour of their foes. These, they exclaimed, were not the French they had met at Sedan in 1870. They were not. Then, they were the soldiers of an Emperor who went to war with the cry "to Berlin" on their lips. Now, they were the soldiers of a democratic

Republic fighting for home and freedom, a fragment of the eternal soul of France.

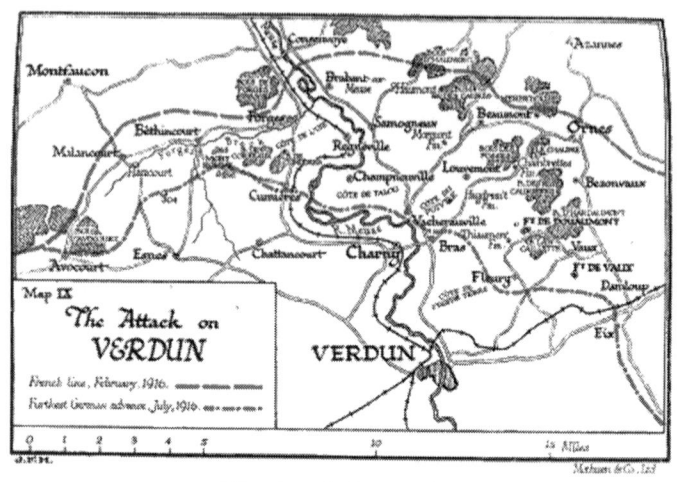

The Attack On Verdun

The central act of the German offensive thus closed with defeat at Verdun; there were two others, one fought in the Alps and the other on the sea. The Italian campaigns were never more than subsidiary operations in the war, for it was not until 27 August 1916 that Italy declared war on Germany, and the number of German divisions on the Italian front was never more than six. Even to Austria Russia was the dangerous foe, and Italian strategy threatened at worst no more than the temporary loss of Trieste, a trifle compared with that of Galicia. For the difficulties of the terrain, jealousy between Italians and Jugo-Slavs, and Italy's lack of the industrial means for equipping a sufficiently formidable army, put it beyond her power to threaten any vital spot in the Hapsburg dominions. Italy, moreover, had not entered the war with the same motives or same unanimity as the other Powers, and her army at the front was not the same embodiment of national strength and spirit. The Austrian offensive in May was therefore due rather to the temptations held out by the weakness of the Italian flank than to any urgent necessity of defence against the projected Italian advance. Nevertheless the Italian plains were always seductive, and it would obviously be convenient to dispose of the Italian threat before Austria had again to face the serious menace of Russian invasion; and an attack on the Asiago plateau was Austria's natural contribution to the general German plan of anticipating in detail the combined Entente offensive (see Map, p. 298).

The first year of the Austro-Italian war had seen no real impression made on Austria's mountain defences, and even in the valley of the Isonzo Gorizia still forbade an Italian advance on Trieste. The Italian line was the worst possible for defence, and it depended for its security upon the fact that the bulk of the Austrian forces were involved in Russia and in the Balkans. The front was on the Isonzo, but a flank of over 200 miles invited a thrust down one of the various passes towards Venice which, if successful, would cause the whole front to collapse like a pack of cards; and marvellous though the feats of Italian valour and mechanical ingenuity had been in the mountain fighting throughout the winter, they had not wrested the passes from Austria's hands. The attack was preceded by a bombardment which began on 14 May, and the scene selected lay on a line drawn from Trent to Venice through the Sette Communi, Posina, and Pasubio. The flanks held fairly firm, but the centre gave way, and on the 20th-24th the line was withdrawn on the left to Posina and Pasubio. Things were no better in the Sette Communi on the right, but west of Pasubio the Italians stopped the Austrian advance in the pass of Buole on 30 May. On the same day, however, they had to evacuate Arsiero and Asiago, south of the Sette Communi. But by now Cadorna had got his reinforcements, and on 3 June he announced that the Austrian offensive was checked. The attack was, however, renewed on the 13th, and the Austrians advanced to within four miles of Valstagna and the railway running down the Brenta valley to Padua. They got no farther, and before the end of June Cadorna began his counter-offensive. By that time the thoughts of the Austrians and most of their troops were elsewhere; and just as the German campaign at Verdun was ruined by the Entente offensive on the Somme, the Austrian advance from the Trentino was stopped by the Russian attack in the East. In the first week of June Brussilov had gone through the Austrian lines like brown paper at Lutsk and Dubno.

The third German offensive was on the sea, but no operation in the war remains more obscure with regard to its motives, conduct, and importance than the battle of Jutland; a century passed before Nelson's tactics at Trafalgar were made clear, and a long period may have to elapse before there is any solution of the problems surrounding the great naval battle of modern times. The British admiral in command has expressed his considered opinion that the meeting of the German and British fleets on 30 May was an accident; but assuredly it was not by accident that the whole naval forces of Germany were on that day outside their accustomed harbours, and they could not have been brought into action against their own consent. There was some motive in that unusual appearance, and the motives of strategy are to be found in the conditions of policy. That Germany needed a victory in 1916 is obvious from her persistence, despite the gravest losses, in the Verdun campaign; but if she needed one over France, she needed one yet more sorely over Britain; and if it was worth while losing one or two hundred thousand men at Verdun, it was worth while taking considerable risks at sea on the chance of frustrating British participation in the coming offensive on the Somme.

Deliverance from the nightmare of a combined Entente offensive was but a part of the fruits which would follow from a German victory at sea. It would probably decide the issue of the war at a single blow. Germany had, of course, known all along that the Entente depended absolutely for success upon Great Britain's command of the sea; but it was not easy to shake that command, and so long as there seemed a prospect of winning the war by other means, the frightful risks of a naval battle would be avoided. By the spring of 1916 those other means were receding beyond the region of hope or possibility. Russia was repairing her arms; Great Britain was making stupendous preparations; France had withstood the shock of Verdun; and the hopes which Germany built on discontent in Ireland, her intrigues with Irish prisoners of war, and the escapades of Sir Roger Casement, crumbled after the insurrection which broke out in Dublin in April. The autumn promised a sere and yellow leaf to the German High Command. Nor did this darkened European vista exhaust the clouds on the horizon. After the torpedoing of the Sussex on 24 March President Wilson had extorted from the German Government a pledge not to sink without warning merchant vessels found inside or outside the war zone which the Germans had proclaimed in February, and had refused to accept the condition they sought to attach to the pledge, that he would require corresponding pledges from Great Britain to observe the "freedom of the seas." Tirpitz had been dismissed to give verisimilitude to Germany's new virtue; but she had no intention of keeping her pledge any longer than was convenient, or abandoning any reasonable prospect of bringing us to our knees by a submarine campaign, and she knew that its effective extension would provoke American intervention. Such intervention would, however, be negligible if in the meantime Britain's Fleet had been crippled and her control of the sea undermined.

A successful naval battle might therefore not only impair British participation but preclude that of the United States. Otherwise the two together would dissipate any lingering German hopes of victory; and the imminence of the danger counselled the taking of risks which had hitherto been eschewed. But the results of a naval defeat are not risked if they are likely to prove fatal, unless there is some chance of success; and Germany had some grounds for hope under both these heads. A fleet which flees is little better than no fleet at all, and for two years Germany had put up with British command of the seas. The destruction of her battle-fleet would no doubt depress her people, but it would not seriously interfere with her submarine campaign, and on land the war would go on as it had done. Still, the existence of the German Fleet was a factor in the moral of the German people; and the Government would not have risked it without some hopes of at least a partial success. The hopes depended partly on the skill of the new commander, Von Scheer, and partly on his too-well justified belief that the Germans possessed better shells, better armour, better searchlights, and more accurate range-tests than the British Navy. The guns were also ranged for elevation up to 30 deg., whereas the British elevation was only 15 or 20; and the difference was fatal to some of our battle-cruisers. The conclusion seems to have been that an adventure was worth while, and that if the weather conditions were wisely selected, it was feasible to fight a naval battle on the principle of limited liability, breaking it off if and when the losses incurred exceeded the value of the results obtained. Clearly, for instance, if the German battle-fleet could engage the British battle-cruisers without itself being engaged by the British battle-fleet, the event might justify moderate expectations.

On the morning of 31 May the German High Seas Fleet set out on its "northern enterprise." What the German Government meant by that phrase has never been revealed. It has been inferred that a concentration of naval and military force against Russia was planned to anticipate Brussilov's coming offensive, but there were no signs of that movement on land, and the Germans had enough to do with Verdun and their lines elsewhere in France without committing themselves to another adventure in Russia; while the idea of a raid on the shipping between England and Norway seems an inadequate explanation of the force sent out. On the other hand, if the design was to cripple the British Navy, the opportune moment had been lost, for the adverse balance against the German Fleet had been enormously increased since the war broke out. In the autumn of 1914 occasional breakdowns in the machinery of British super-Dreadnoughts, accidents like the torpedoing of the Audacious, and the inadequacy of dock-accommodation had made uneasy the minds of men who dwelt upon these contingencies and made no allowance for similar mishaps to the enemy. But even they were reassured when in April 1915 British construction far outstripped any German possibilities; and as time went on the race grew ever more unequal. It is true that France ceased to partake in the competition, leaving this silent struggle of the workshop and the dockyard to Great Britain; and the chance of a battle in the Baltic had to be abandoned because no Allied battleships could be relied upon to reinforce the North Sea Fleet. But Britain's margin was ample enough, and at the battle of Jutland her weight of metal was as two to one. The Germans, however, had advantages of their own, particularly in a delaying fuse which caused their shells to explode after penetrating the enemy's armour instead of before. Their capital ships were also better armoured, and rarely sank when struck by shells or torpedoes. This was also true of the British battleships, and none were sunk on either side except the old German Pommern; but the British battle-cruisers fared badly. The German marksmanship was also better during the earlier stages of the battle, though inferior later on; and they had in Von Scheer an admiral of conspicuous ability.

The accident of the battle arose from the fact that the British Fleet was simultaneously on 31 May engaged in one of its periodical sweeps through the North Sea. It had already turned back towards its northern bases when at 2.20 p.m. enemy vessels were signalled to the east. Beatty, who had under his orders the four "Cats," Queen Mary, Princess Royal, Lion, and Tiger, together with two other battle-cruisers, the Indefatigable and New Zealand, and the four biggest and newest battleships, Barham, Warspite, Valiant, and Malaya (the Queen Elizabeth herself was undergoing repairs at Rosyth), at once turned back south-eastwards to cut off the enemy from his retreat along the Jutland coast. The enemy vessels were Hipper's cruisers, and they also turned south to fall back on their battle-fleet, at whose proximity Beatty can only have guessed. At 3.48 the action began with Hipper's battle-cruisers, Derfflinger, Lutzow, Moltke, Seydlitz, and Van der Thann; none of them carried heavier than 12-in. guns, while Beatty's "Cats" had 13.5-inch and his Queen Elizabeths 15-inch guns. A light-cruiser attack against our line was crumpled up by corresponding vessels, but the bigger German ships escaped fatal damage from our heavier fire (it took hours to dispose of the enemy at the Falklands), and by 4.42 they were in sight of their battle-fleet.

Beatty's business was now to turn and draw the Germans northwards into Jellicoe's jaws, but the turning in face of the German battle-fleet was a critical manoeuvre. Beatty's battleships were north-west on his starboard quarter, and as his battle-cruisers turned they masked the Queen Elizabeths' fire while exposing themselves to the concentrated attention of the German Fleet. A high-angle shell fell on the thinly protected deck of the Queen Mary; she blew up and sank in a few seconds. Another fell down the ammunition shaft of the Indefatigable with the same appalling result. Beatty was not deflected from his course; possibly no other could have been taken. The rest of his cruisers got round without mishap, and the brunt of the fighting now passed to Evan-Thomas's Queen Elizabeths, who stalled off the whole German Fleet as both forces steamed north in Jellicoe's direction. It was probably during this stage that most of the damage was done to the German Fleet. The Lutzow and the Pommern were sunk; the battleship Konig was so battered that her forecastle was only 6½ feet above water when she struggled into port; and the Seydlitz and the Derfflinger were in little better case.

At 5.56 Beatty sighted Jellicoe's battleships at five miles' distance on his port bow. His task was now to cross the front of the German line, head it off east and southwards, and afford Jellicoe room for deployment between Beatty himself and Evan-Thomas. For reasons of tactics and prudence Jellicoe deployed on his port wing, i.e., towards the east, This took him away from the Germans, but tended to cut them off from their base. The deployment was skilfully executed, though Admiral Hood and his battle-cruiser the Invincible, while taking position in front of Beatty, suffered the fate of the Queen Mary and Indefatigable; and the British Fleet soon formed a single line curving round east and south-eastwards like a net into which the Germans were being drawn. The crisis had arrived, and German naval power seemed on the verge of extinction. But the weather came to assist Von Scheer's tactical skill. He turned with less misfortune than had attended Beatty's similar manoeuvre two hours earlier, and set himself to fight a magnificent rearguard action and extricate his fleet as best he could. Fortunately for him the visibility grew steadily worse, and with it the range of fire diminished. This deprived Jellicoe of the advantage of his heavier guns, and indeed reduced the range of gun-fire to that of torpedoes. Here Von Scheer discovered his chance, and it was upon torpedo attacks that he relied for the defence of his fleet. Jellicoe, with his superior speed, could have closed had he deemed it wise. But he thought of what hung on the fate of the fleet he commanded, and shrank from exposing his battleships to the risk of torpedo destruction. His dilemma was acute: gun-fire was very effective at 18,000 yards, the torpedo began to be so at 10,000. Our cue was to fight between the two; but low visibility hid the German ships outside torpedo range, while within it fifty lucky German torpedoes might have sent every British Dreadnought to the bottom and decided the war in Germany's favour. On the other hand, we might have sunk every German ship and conceivably ended the war in 1917. War is an experimental science; but this experiment was never made, and no one can say what the result would have been if it had. Beatty wished to make it, Jellicoe refrained.

So the fight went on, the mist hiding the Germans at longer range and their torpedo attacks deterring us from a closer encounter. At 7.5 Jellicoe attempted to close on the Germans by turning three points to starboard. Von Scheer replied with a torpedo attack, and to avoid it some of our ships turned four, and some of them six, points to port. Seizing the opportunity, Von Scheer made off to the west, helped by the mist and by his own smoke screen; and shortly the Germans were lost to sight. Night closed in with the British Fleet between the Germans and their base at Wilhelmshaven hoping to complete their work on a glorious First of June. Jellicoe and Beatty agreed that to continue the battle in darkness amid torpedo-craft and submarines was impossible, and Von Scheer had other designs in view. It was a night of excursions and alarms with many destroyer actions. When dawn broke the Germans were not to be seen. Cut off from direct access to Wilhelmshaven, Von Scheer had turned from south-west round to north and then east, and had got his ships one by one past the rear of the British line into harbour. His escape is the mystery of the battle: throughout the night his starboard ships were continually barging into vessels on our port, but no news of these encounters reached the commander-in-chief. Till nearly noon Jellicoe watched for a fleet that never appeared, and then made his way back to his base, a victor baulked of the ostensible fruits of his victory. The disappointment was made worse by the ineptitude of the Admiralty and the ignorance of the press, which emphasized our losses without explaining the significance of our success. Besides the three battle-cruisers we lost three armoured cruisers, Defence, Black Prince, and Warrior of 13,000 or more tons apiece, and eight destroyers, while the super-Dreadnought Marlborough was badly holed and the Warspite was put out of action. The German looses in destroyers may have been equal or greater, but in cruisers they were considerably less. The Government was foolish enough to deny the loss of the Lutzow and admit it a few days later. But our own estimates were not conspicuous for their accuracy; and the German official account published on 16 June and long regarded as "a tissue of careful falsifications," was admitted after the armistice to have been substantially correct.

The public in both countries were indeed egregiously wrong in their judgment because they were completely ignorant of naval warfare, and measured success at sea by mathematical equations just as they measured progress on land by miles. It was only the navies engaged that knew the truth, and they had inadequate means of making their knowledge known. British sailors were loath to admit even among themselves the defects in their vessels, gunnery, and leadership which the battle revealed; but they made less a secret of Von Scheer's skill. He had with a smaller force inflicted greater damage on his enemy, and he had snatched his fleet from the jaws of destruction. He was no doubt favoured by the weather, and he turned to the best advantage his facilities of defence; for the enemy in retreat can use his torpedoes with greater effect than his pursuer, can tempt him into minefields and submarine traps, and conceal himself by smoke-screens. German Dreadnoughts had, moreover, been built for defence in home waters and not for keeping the seas. Space, which was used to strengthen their armour, had in our capital ships to serve the needs of offence, speed, and comfort; and subsequent inspection at Scapa Flow showed that the German High Seas Fleet was not designed to provide its crews with living room for more than seventy-two hours without recourse to port.

But all these advantages and Von Scheer's skill could not reverse the verdict in that trial of strength, and our qualms about the battle of Jutland were a just nemesis on our inveterate habit of judging by material tests. The decisive factor in war is not the material but the moral effect; and while the German Fleet was not destroyed at the battle of Jutland, its moral was hopelessly shattered. Few of the German sailors who had been in a naval battle had hitherto returned to tell the tale, and those who went out in the High Seas Fleet on 31 May had been taught to believe in its invincibility. But, said a German officer, "the way we were utterly crushed from the moment your battle fleet came into action took the heart out of them. Another hour of daylight would have finished it," while only three men in Jellicoe's main battle fleet were wounded. Der Tag had come with a vengeance, and from that day every attempt to take out the German Fleet to battle produced a mutiny or the threat of one.

The third enemy offensive had come to greater grief than the other two; and the battle of Jutland had justified the earlier German strategy which kept the German Fleet safe in harbour while it kept our own in British waters and faint hearts on tenterhooks. Germany's naval power had now gone with the moral of its crews, though the ghost of it haunted for two and a half years longer the timid minds of our materialists on shore, and retained on this side of the Channel hundreds of thousands of troops needed for offence or defence in France and Flanders. The German Fleet had never, however, been a predominant factor in the war, and it was with a different proposition that the Entente had to deal when at last its turn came to take the offensive and make a real attempt to break the German lines.

CHAPTER XII

THE ALLIED COUNTER-OFFENSIVE

In spite of the disasters she had suffered in 1915 and of her winter campaigns in Galicia and the Caucasus, Russia was the first of the Allies to take the offensive in 1916. She was, indeed, engaged in attacking at some point or other along her vast and various fronts from December till April. In February she again attempted to seize the important bridgehead across the Dniester at Usciesko and carried it on 22 March. Four days before that she had initiated another offensive on the shores of Lake Narotch, and in April she was pressing on Trebizond. The Lake Narotch operation was possibly designed to frustrate a German attack on Riga, and it was only that preventive success that was achieved. It is true that the first and second German lines were carried after artillery preparation by the Russian infantry. But the scanty Russian artillery behaved like a travelling circus; having done its business, it packed up and removed to seek another opening. The Germans discovered the move, blasted the Russian trenches, and on 28-29 April recovered more than they had lost. The campaign in Armenia was more successful, and on 18 April Trebizond passed securely into Russian hands, giving her a shorter route across the Black Sea and a better base for future operations in Asia Minor (see Maps, pp. 146, 182).

These, however, were minor operations compared with the offensive for which Brussilov was preparing in May as the Russian contribution to the combined attack on the Central Empires. It was not timed to take place until the end of June. But the Austrian pressure on Italy from the Trentino seems to have forced an acceleration which the German attack on Verdun failed to extort from the Western Allies; and on 3 June a bombardment began on the whole of the Russian front from the Pripet marshes southwards to the Rumanian border. Ivanov had been recalled to headquarters and the line was under Brussilov, with four generals—Kaledin, Sakharoff, Scherbachev, and Lechitsky—to command his various army-groups. Opposed to them were four Austrian generals and the German Bothmer, who held the front from Zalocze on the upper Sereth to the Dniester. From Kolki northwards the Pripet swamps made progress difficult, and Bothmer offered a stubborn resistance on the Strypa. But in the Volhynian triangle and the Bukovina the attack achieved a surprising success. The infantry advance began on the 4th and by noon the Austrian front was completely broken. In two days the Russians advanced more than twenty miles, and on the 6th they entered Lutsk, the Archduke Joseph Ferdinand's headquarters, capturing enormous booty and many thousands of prisoners. On both sides the breach was widened; to the north Rojitche and to the south Dubno both fell on the 8th, and the Volhynian triangle passed completely into Russian hands. Their triumph continued for another week: their salient was deepened by a further advance to Zaturtsky and Svidniki, within twenty-five miles of Kovel, and broadened by the fall of Kolki to the north and Demidovka and Kozin to the south. In less than a fortnight Kaledin and Sakharoff had covered fifty miles and taken 70,000 prisoners.

Scherbachev was less successful against Bothmer in front of Tarnopol; but his left wing carried Buczacz, farther south, and crossed the Strypa, while beyond the Dniester Lechitsky outdid Kaledin's success at Lutsk. Forcing the passage of the Dniester near Okna on that same 4th of June, he broke the Austrian front and drove one half of it west to Horodenka and the other half southeast towards Czernowitz. The latter portion was now an isolated and disorganized fragment of the Austrian army which could do nothing but escape across the Pruth and the Carpathians leaving Lechitsky to overrun the Bukovina. On the 17th the Russians entered Czernowitz, its capital, and six days later they reached Kimpolung, its most southerly town. Other columns swept west to Sniatyn and Kuty, and by the 23rd the whole of the province had been conquered. The Austrians were in no position to impose a pause upon the frontier of Galicia, and Kolomea fell on the 29th.

Tlumacz followed on the 30th and Bothmer's right was seriously threatened. Gathering some German reinforcements he counter-attacked on 2 July, recovered Tlumacz, and checked Lechitsky's right, though his left continued its advance along the Carpathian foothills and captured Delatyn on 8 July, thus cutting the railway to Marmaros Sziget. The Dniester and the Pruth were now flooded with July rains, and a month elapsed before Lechitsky could resume his march.

Other causes had checked the Russians farther north. Brussilov's offensive may have been merely a vast reconnaissance in force, but its astonishing success had stirred the Germans to prompt action. Ewarts was beginning an attack on the important junction of Baranovitchi north of the Pripet marshes, and presently the line of battle spread down the Shchara and along the Oginski canal. If he succeeded like Brussilov, Brest-Litovsk might be caught between two fires with dire results to the whole German front in Russia and future in the Balkans. It was a peril to which the German prospects at Verdun and forebodings on the Somme were secondary considerations; and both the Western allies profited from Brussilov's campaign. One German corps was hurried from Verdun to Kovel in six days, and others followed at a less exhausting speed. Austrians also came from the Tyrol and the Balkans, and Ludendorff was sent to restore confidence in the command. Kovel was the southern key to Brest-Litovsk; the northern flank could look after itself since Ewarts was making little progress, and Bothmer had barred the way for the time to the other essential points at Lemberg and Stanislau. But Kovel was in serious danger, for the Russians had penetrated to Lokatchi due south of that fortress; and it was for its defence that Ludendorff organized the Austrian counter-offensive in the latter half of June.

Kovel was saved. The Russian line was pressed back from Lokatchi to Zaturtsky, from Svidniki to Rojitche, and behind the Stokhod. But the counter-offensive was spent by the end of the month, and early in July the Russians resumed their advance. North of the Pripet Ewarts was no more successful than he had been in June; German divisions were made of sterner stuff than the Austrian, and Hindenburg knew well enough what was at stake. After heavy losses the Russian attack died away without appreciable gain of ground, and north of the Pripet at least the enemy line was secure. Nor, even south of it, was Brussilov able to do much more than straighten his own, bringing it forward to the point reached by his salient in front of Lutsk. This, however, involved some danger to Lemberg and effected the fall of Stanislau farther south. The chief obstacle was Bothmer in the centre, on whose stubborn resistance the Germans prided themselves although most of his troops were Austrian; and he occupied most of the Russian attention for the rest of the campaign. But the most striking advance was made in the north of Brussilov's command, where summer had dried the low-lying ground south of the Pripet marshes. Here General Lesch, whose Third Russian Army had been brought down from north of the Pripet, broke the Austrian line on the Styr between Kolki and Rafalovka on 4-5 July, and in four days reached the Stokhod. He even crossed it at points, but failed to carry it in its entirety so as to threaten the northern defences of Kovel.

The main offensive was launched in Galicia, doubtless with a view to its reaction upon the attitude of Rumania; and here Bothmer was menaced by Sakharoff in the north and Lechitsky in the south. To disconcert the northern attack the Germans had planned a counter-offensive on the 18th, but Sakharoff got his blow in first three days before. Forcing the Austrians across the Styr in front of Dubno, he advanced along its tributary the Lipa, captured Mikhailovka and Bludov, and then swinging south occupied Berestechko and threatened Brody on the 20th. It was entered after a week's fighting on the 28th. Thence he struck south towards the railway from Krasne to Tarnopol which supplied Bothmer's left, while Bothmer's right was being simultaneously threatened by Lechitsky now that the floods on the Dniester had subsided. On 7 August he recaptured Tlumacz and reached the Dniester near Nijniow; on the 10th he forced his way into Stanislau, while Scherbachev attacked on the north bank of the Dniester. Almost outflanked on the north by Sakharoff and on the south by Scherbachev and Lechitsky, Bothmer had at length to retreat to the Zlota Lipa with his right in front of Halicz, his centre at Brzezany, and his left at Zborov. He was vigorously attacked by Scherbachev, and his right was pushed back on both banks of the Dniester as far as Halicz until it stood upon the Narajovka. But the centre stood firm against Scherbachev's great effort of the 29th, though Potutory was taken and Brzezany reduced to a salient; and the fighting of September and October failed to modify the position anywhere except far south in the Carpathians, where Lechitsky secured Mount Kapul and the Jablonitza and Kirlibaba passes, and advanced as far west as Huta.

This movement was in sympathy with the Rumanian declaration of war on 27 August, and spoilt the Russian chances of a successful concentration against Bothmer. Russia was not sufficiently furnished with munitions or trained men to provide for two great efforts on that front, and her summer campaign had failed of complete success largely because of the services it rendered to her allies. No fewer than sixteen divisions were withdrawn, between June and September, by the Germans from the Western front and one from the Balkans to meet Brussilov's offensive, and they included some of the best of the Prussian Guards. Austria diverted seven divisions from Italy, and even the Turks sent two. The offensive had cost the Central Empires something like a million casualties, many of them Czecho-Slovak and Jugo-Slav prisoners, who deserted willingly enough and in time did valiant service in strange lands to the cause of the Entente and of their own national independence. But the value of Russia's last great effort in the war was not limited to the front on which it was made. It was an excellent, though almost solitary, example of the advantages of co-ordinated strategy between the Allies, and what progress was made on the Somme, in Italy, and in Macedonia in 1916 was partly due to Russian valour on other fronts.

The British Empire, however, had eyes in the summer of that year for little except its own offensive in the West. It was mainly a British affair, for the German attack on Verdun had succeeded to the extent of making impossible both an independent French offensive and an equivalent French contribution to the joint campaign on the Somme. Like other realities of the war, this fact was hidden from the public, and hopes ran high. The failures of the autumn were recognized as due to their being premature and made on narrow fronts. We had learnt our lesson; there was a new general in command; in guns and munitions we had outstripped the Germans; our men were no longer raw recruits, and we had millions of them; and, unlike Germany, we had no alternative front to exact its toll like the Russian. The one doubt that was harboured rather than expressed related to leadership. Lord Kitchener had lost his life in the Hampshire, sunk by a mine off the west coast of the Orkneys, on 6 June. But Sir William Robertson, his chief of Staff, had acquired a great repute as an organizer, and the question was whether the officers in the field would exhibit qualities of intellect comparable with his administrative capacity or with the valour of their men.

Apart from the urgent need of relieving the pressure on Verdun, a British offensive was due as a contribution to the common task; and the front on which it would be made did not offer a great variety of choice. Whatever attractions other localities may have held out yielded to the Somme, where the French and British lines met by Maricourt, and an advance side by side was the nearest approach the Allies had yet made to unity of command or even of design. The combined effort was to be concentrated on a single front of twenty-five miles from Gommecourt, half-way between Albert and Arras, to Fay, five miles above Chaulnes. If it achieved the success that was hoped, it would roll up the German line north towards the Belgian coast and render untenable in the south and east the great salient of the German front. The retreat which the Germans effected to the Hindenburg lines in the spring of 1917 was the least that was expected from the summer offensive of the year before. But Germans are seldom idle, and for months they had been silently and unobserved preparing to counter the vast storm of explosives about to break on their trenches. That wire-entanglements however extensive, and trenches however intricate, could be obliterated had been proved, and the Germans were ready with their prophylactic on the ground that was chosen for attack. The rolling downs of the Bapaume ridge offered natural attractions to an army sick of the water-logged flats of Flanders, but they also afforded the Germans depth and scope for their vast underground chambers which no artillery could destroy; and these defences more than any other single cause defeated the British thrust at Gommecourt and Serre.

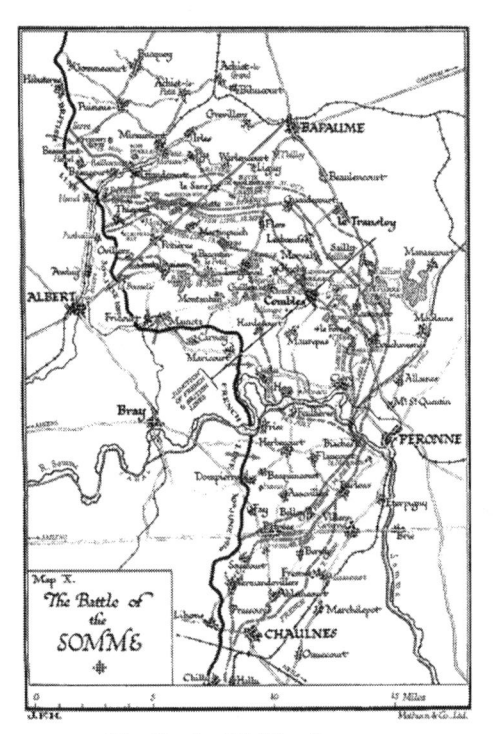

The Battle Of The Somme

This was officially described as a subsidiary operation, yet upon the assistance it rendered to the main attack farther south depended the whole nature and course of the campaign. Had that thrust eastward towards Bapaume been successful, the Germans facing the Somme would have been taken in the rear, and the painful and costly climb up the slopes to Bapaume, which lasted throughout the summer and autumn, would have been achieved in a couple of days. Places like Pozières, well towards the goal, were indeed given as our objectives for the first day of the battle of the Somme. It began on 1 July. Since the middle of June there had been an intermittent bombardment of the German lines which grew in intensity and extent from the 24th. The attack had been entrusted to the British Fourth Army, under Sir Henry Rawlinson and the French Sixth under Fayolle. It was expected by the Germans between Albert and Arras, though not along the Somme, and their artillery preparation took off some of the edge of our attack. The troops advanced with the utmost dash and determination, and detachments got far ahead of the line into Pendant copse, Thiepval, the Schwaben redoubt, and even the outskirts of Grandcourt. But few of them got back when they found that the line as a whole had held, and the losses of these troops in the fire to the left and the right and in front of them made up the bulk of the British casualties on that day.

Farther south they fared better. The outskirts of La Boisselle and Fricourt were reached; Mametz was taken, and also Montauban by the most striking advance of the day. On our right the French, whose attack had been planned by Foch, had the advantage of a surprise. North of the Somme they reached the edge of Hardecourt and Curlu; south of it they captured Dompierre, Becquincourt, Bussu, and Fay, and with these villages 6000 prisoners. The advance was greatest the farthest it was removed from where the Germans had prepared their resistance; complete success south of the Somme dwindled away to complete failure at Serre. That northern attack was not renewed, but from Ovillers south and eastwards the advantage was stubbornly pressed on the 2nd. Fricourt fell and its surrounding defences, while the French took Frise, Curlu, and Herbecourt. It was clear, however, that the German line had not, and could not be broken in the sense which the public at least attached to the word. A first or even a second and third line of trenches might be taken, but there was an indefinite series behind, and the progress was so slow that anything like a thrust right through the German defences and rout of the German forces was out of the question. It was not until the 5th that La Boiselle in the first German line was mastered, and farther east the initial success of the British was checked by a line of woods which required weeks to clear. On the 7th we took Contalmaison, but were driven out of most of it by a counter-attack. It finally fell on the 10th, but Ovillers held out till the 16th. The woods to the right offered a no less stubborn resistance. Bernafay wood was, indeed, gained on the 4th, but the German flanks in Mametz wood to the west and Trônes wood to the east were only driven in at the cost of five days' ferocious fighting from the 8th to the 13th. The French encountered similar opposition north of the Somme, but south of it they were more fortunate. On the 4th and 5th they extended their gains on their right by the capture of most of Estrées and Belloy, and after disposing of German counter-attacks leapt forward on the 9th past Flaucourt to Biaches, a mile from Péronne.

On 14 July the second stage of the battle of the Somme began with an attack before dawn. It was the national fête-day of France, but the attack was made on the British front from Contalmaison to Trônes wood. The objectives were the wood and two villages of Bazentin, High wood (the Bois des Foureaux), Longueval, and Delville wood, while Trônes wood still remained to be completely cleared. The day was one of the most successful in the four and a half months' battle, and the dash of the British troops carried them as far as all their objectives. Bazentin-le-Grand and le Petit and the wood were taken; aided by an unwonted cavalry charge which raised delusive hopes of breaking through, a great advance was made to High wood; and the Germans were driven out of most of Longueval and the Delville wood. But it was more difficult to retain these conquests; the advanced positions were exposed to enfilading German fire, and counter-attacks drove us back at various points and made the retention of others a matter of desperate conflict for weeks. High wood had to be completely evacuated; for Delville wood the South Africans, and the troops which relieved them on the 20th, had to struggle for thirteen days, and it was not wholly cleared for another month. Much of what was credited to the 14th of July had to be retaken in detailed fighting spread over many days.

On the 16th, however, the fall of Ovillers prepared the way for an attack on Pozières, which was finally captured with the help of the Australians on the 26th, and the taking of Waterlot farm on our right opened up an advance on Guillemont. Much of High wood was recovered on the 20th. On that day the French pushed east of Hardecourt and seized a section of the Combles-Clery railway, while farther south they secured the German defences from Barleux to Vermandovillers. On the 27th the last German outpost in Longueval was taken, and on 4 August the Australians began their advance from Pozières to Mouquet farm and the windmill which commanded the summit of the Bapaume ridge. The ground was contested inch by inch, and it took many weary days to win. Villages and woods all along the front were only captured by fragments, and most of the fragments were lost again more than once before they finally passed into our hands. Well into September there were bits of Delville wood and High wood still in German possession, and a concerted attack of 18 August was a failure except for the seizure of Leipzig redoubt. On the 12th, however, and again on the 16th, the French improved their position north of the Somme and got close to Maurepas, of which they completed the capture on the 24th.

September was a better month for both the Allies. There was a general attack on the 3rd, when Guillemont, which had been disputed for six weeks, was carried at length, and the French rushed Le Forest, Cléry, and the German lines up to the outskirts of Combles. Two days later the British got into Leuze wood between Guillemont and Combles, and captured Falfemont farm to the south, while a new French army extended the line of battle below Chaulnes and took Chilly and Soyécourt; on the 6th they pushed their advance both north and south of the Somme, taking above the river L'Hôpital farm and Anderlu and Marrières woods, and below it parts of Vermandovillers and Berny. The German counter-attacks were unusually unsuccessful, and on 9 September Ginchy was carried by the Irish regiments which had helped to take Guillemont. It looked as though the Allies were at least getting into their stride, or the wasting struggle was beginning to tell on the German reserves and resistance. Over two months had been spent in securing objectives marked down for the first day or two of the battle; but with the fall of Guillemont the last fragment of the German second position had fallen into our hands, their third was more or less improvised, we had a new weapon in reserve, and were half-way from our original lines to Bapaume. Farther afield Rumania had declared war, and Brussilov was still drawing German troops from West to East.

The third stage of the battle therefore opened with hopes which even the experience of the second had not been able to quench. Gough's Fifth Army had since early in July been formed as an independent command to the left of Rawlinson's Fourth, and its right comprised the 1st Canadian Corps which was to attack Courcelette. The other points of the German third line of defence were Martinpuich, Flers, Lesboeufs, and Morval. Martinpuich was the objective of a Scottish division of the New Army, Flers that of the New Zealanders, Lesboeufs and Morval those of the Guards and another division of the old Regulars. Behind the British lines were collected twenty-four "Tanks," which were to precede them in the attack and prove by this first experiment their value as a weapon of war. On the 14th a brigade of Gough's army stormed the Hohenzollern trench and a redoubt called by the Germans a wunderwerk; apart from this success, the attack diverted German attention from the real offensive, which began on the 15th with an intense bombardment. The Tanks spread terror and devastation among the German lines and the results of the day for once exceeded all expectations. Courcelette fell to the Canadians, Martinpuich to the Scots, Flers to the New Zealanders. High wood was at last enveloped in this advance, and Delville wood passed by the division of the New Army which pushed from Ginchy towards Lesboeufs. That effort on our right was, however, hampered by the Germans in the Quadrilateral and Bouleaux wood to the east of Ginchy, and the Guards were unable to carry out the most important tactical part of the day's work by carrying Lesboeufs and Morval.

The French had no such accumulation of gains on the 15th, but they conquered a larger area between the 13th and 18th. They began on the 13th with the bold capture of Bouchavesnes right across the great road from Péronne to Bapaume, and supplemented it by taking Le Priez farm on the flank of Combles. On the 17th they completed their work in Berny and Vermandovillers south of the Somme, and on the 18th added Deniécourt. On that day the British at last mastered the Quadrilateral east of Ginchy, and thus prepared for the great success which attended the next general attack on the 25th. It was the best day of the whole campaign. Lesboeufs and Morval fell on the north of Combles, while the French took Rancourt on the south-east, and away to the west Gough's army made the surprising seizure of Thiepval. Further fruits were gathered on the morrow; Gueudecourt, which had been taken but abandoned on the 25th, was recovered; the French who had then failed against Frégicourt now took it; and Combles was the prize of their joint success. Then the weather broke; and the Germans, who had already begun to prepare their Hindenburg lines far away in their rear, were enabled to cling to the Bapaume salient until they had taken all the precautions for an orderly and inexpensive retreat.

The rest of the Somme campaign was an affair of local details until Gough's Fifth Army intervened on a larger scale. Eaucourt l'Abbaye was taken on 1 October, lost on the 2nd, and retaken on the 3rd. Le Sars was captured on the 7th, the Stuff and Regina redoubts, between it and Thiepval, on the 21st; and progress was made north towards the Butte de Warlencourt and north-east towards Le Transloy. The French captured Sailly and Saillisel to the east of Morval and pushed far into the St. Pierre Vaast wood and towards Moislains, while south of the Somme they took Ablaincourt, Le Pressoir, Fresnes, Villers-Carbonnel, and Barleux, and seized the west bank of the river opposite Eterpigny above Péronne. On 9 November the weather improved, and though the October rains had made transport almost impossible across the mangled soil of the battlefield on the Somme, the conditions were not so bad north of Thiepval, where our advance had been stayed on 1 July. The situation at Beaumont-Hamel was also changed for the better by the fact that the German stronghold was now a pronounced salient enfiladed by our fire from the captured Hohenzollern, Schwaben, Stuff, and Regina redoubts. But that advantage was less felt farther north at Serre, and there the left wing of our attack on 13 November was no more successful than it had been on 1 July. Better fortune attended our effort between Serre and Beaumont-Hamel, but the farthest advance of the day was that of a New Army division on the extreme right of the attacking line. St. Pierre Divion fell almost at once, and our troops advanced on the southern heights of the Ancre to the Hansa trench half-way to Grandcourt.

The task of the centre was to take the fortress of Beaumont-Hamel, including the forked ravine to the south which required a prolonged and desperate struggle. The work was done by Highland Territorials before the early November sunset; and meanwhile the Naval Division on their right drove the Germans out of their first two lines on the northern bank of the Ancre towards Beaucourt. One battalion penetrated almost to the village, but was held up in a perilous position owing to the resistance of a strong German redoubt on its flank and almost in its rear. It stood its ground throughout the day, and at night the surrender of the German redoubt to a couple of tanks opened the way for a general attack on Beaucourt on the 14th. It was stormed by the battalion which had been waiting outside it since the previous morning. German counter-attacks on the 15th were repulsed, and on the 17th a further advance was made to the Bois d'Hollande north of Grandcourt, while Canadians from the Regina trench established themselves near its western outskirts. Another avenue towards Bapaume had been opened up, but winter postponed any further advance, and the Somme campaign had come to an end.

It had proved a sort of inverted Verdun, and the comfort we had derived from that successful defence was now extracted by the Germans from their defence of Bapaume. The parallel was not exact, because while the German gains at Verdun narrowed down to a point, ours on the Somme expanded in a circle. Yet the arguments were substantially the same: the French at Verdun were willing to sell any number of acres for armies, and the Germans professed an equal content on the Somme. Each side contended in turn that the offensive was the more costly form of warfare, and then repudiated the contention when it came to attack itself; and there was not a great deal to choose between them so far as logic was concerned. It is also clear that the Germans would have been at least as successful at Verdun as we were on the Somme but for the relief afforded by counter-offensives elsewhere, and that we should have profited no more from the Somme than the Germans did from Verdun had our Somme campaign been interrupted by German offensives on other fronts. Nor was there much to choose in the way of casualties: our estimate of the German losses as approximating 600,000 was a reasonable guess, but our own casualties were well over 400,000. The French losses were lighter, but the two together cannot have been less than the German. The Germans on the Somme, like the French at Verdun, withdrew divisions to refit before they were hopelessly broken; but what was considered wisdom in the French was reckoned weakness in the Germans and the Prussian Guards, whose return to Berlin, concealed in furniture-vans to hide their pitiable plight, was graphically described in the English press by an imaginative American journalist, were really sent as a contribution to that immense effort in the East by which, in spite of the Somme campaign, Germany first closed the gaps in the crumbling Austrian front and then overran Rumania.

There was thus a good deal of justice in the German comparison between Verdun and the Somme. The fallacy lay in the facts that our offensive was not brought to a stand by a German counter-attack but by the advent of winter, that the moves elsewhere in the West were the French ripostes at Verdun in

October and December and not German counter-offensives, and that their campaign in Rumania, in spite of its painful success, had no effect upon the vital situation in the West. That episode was against us, but the tendencies were in our favour; our losses might equal the German, but equal attrition would leave us paramount in the end, barring collapse on the part of a principal ally. It was the fundamental situation which led to the German proposals for peace at Christmas, and the superficial impression which provoked the simultaneous fall of the Asquith Government.

So, too, there was something superficial and unjust in the lay criticism of Sir Douglas Haig's generalship. "Tactics of the Stone Age," was Mr. Lloyd George's later comment, which should not have been made in public at the expense of a general for whose retention in the command he was himself responsible. Even Foch controlled the group of French armies which co-operated with us on the Somme without producing results of a different character; and it is idle to compare the achievements of the generalissimo of 1918 with those of the British commander on the Somme in 1916. Haig controlled the British forces in France and Flanders, but he had no jurisdiction beyond a mere fragment of the thousands of miles of front on which the war was waged. Neither he nor any other Entente general therefore enjoyed the strategical opportunities of a Falkenhayn, Hindenburg, or Ludendorff, who could direct their blows east or west as they pleased; and responsibility for the strategical conduct of the war rested not with the Entente generals but with the heterogeneous Governments which employed them. Each commander had to work in his own compartment and could not escape its limitations. Nor was the diversity merely one of military commands; there was also the Navy, upon which the whole Allied strategy hung, to be considered; and not only in the Entente, but in each of its several Governments there was, and there could be, no such unity of direction as was possible in the militarist Central Empires.

There was also something naive in the popular clamour for a general as a Deus ex machina. For, in spite of apparent exceptions, the tendency of the transition from heroic to democratic ages is to transfer both in war and in politics the decisive influence from the individual to the mass, from the protagonist to the private; and modern warfare, with its complexity and its science, has become mainly a matter of mechanics. Its hero is the mob, and its generals fight far away in the rear of the line of battle; even the telescope has given place to the telephone. Individual valour counts for little compared with accurate range-tests and spotting by waves of sound. Man has mastered nature only to become more dependent upon his servants, and the vast machinery which the modern general controls envelops him in its toils. He reaches his goal in a motor, and the race is won by the best machine. Generalship was but one of a vast number of factors which gave us control of the Bapaume Ridge but also prevented the Somme campaign from saving Rumania or spoiling the German defence against Russia.

The battle of the Somme did not, however, quite exhaust the Entente offensive for 1916. As it died down amid the autumn rains, the French struck back at Verdun on 24 October. Here Nivelle, who had taken over the command from Pétain in April, entrusted the attack to Mangin. The Germans were not taken by surprise, but they were unprepared for the strength of the blow, and from Fleury to Fort Douaumont positions which had taken the Germans months to win were recovered within a few hours. On the right the struggle was more protracted, but on 2 November Fort Vaux and on the 3rd the villages of Vaux and Damloup were regained. A greater success followed on 15 December. The attack extended from Vacherauville on the Meuse to Bezonvaux on the east, and all along the line the French won their objectives. Besides Vacherauville they retook Poivre hill, Haudromont wood, and Louvemont on the left, captured Chambrettes farm and Cauriéres wood in the centre, and seized Hardaumont wood and Bezonvaux on their right. Towards the north-east the Germans had almost been thrust back to the line from which they started in February, though to the north they still retained some ground, and the French counter-offensive did not extend to the west of the Meuse. It was a characteristic exaggeration of the press to represent these gains as a complete reconquest of all that the Germans had won in the spring; but enough had been done to give the Germans unpleasant anticipations for 1917 and to counsel them to draw in their horns in the material sense of retreat from their threatened position on the Somme and in the metaphorical sense of seeking peace (see Map, p. 194).

Italy, too, had been making her contribution to the Allied offensive during these months. Brussilov's onslaught in June had trod on the tail on* the Austrian invasion from the Trentino, and it was patriotic pride which led an Italian journal to describe Cadorna's recovery as the quickest and greatest reaction of the war. Italy's allies at least were not surprised when during the latter half of June her armies regained the ground evacuated by the Austrians in a skilful retreat, including Posina, Monte Cimone, Arsiero, Asiago, and the whole of the Sette Communi. Having thus protected his flank, Cadorna reverted to his frontal attack along the Isonzo and on the Carso. The Austrians still held nearly the whole of the east bank of the river and Oslavia and Podgora on the west bank in front of Gorizia. Gorizia itself was protected by two mountain strongholds, Sabatino to the north and San Michele to the south. Early in August Cadorna had completed his transfer of guns and troops from the Trentino front, and on the 4th he feinted an attack across the Isonzo at Monfalcone. On the 6th a heavy bombardment battered the whole front from Mount Sabatino to Mount San Michele; both the key-positions were taken by assault in a battle which lasted two days, and on the 9th Gorizia fell. During the next few days the advance was pushed across the Doberdo plateau, south of Gorizia, and beyond the Vallone on to the western end of the forbidding and formidable Carso. By the 15th the Italian line ran from Tivoli, north-east of Gorizia, down the river Vertoibizza, across the Vippacco and along the Carso east of Nad Logem, Opacchiasella, and Villanova. No such victory had yet been won by unaided Italian troops against their hereditary foes, and it did much to stimulate Italian confidence and enthusiasm for the war. Some further progress on the Carso was made during the autumn, and great Italian victories were announced in September, October, and November; but the Italians were never within measurable distance of capturing the key of the Carso at the Hermada, and Trieste was a very distant prospect until other causes had brought about the collapse of the Hapsburg Empire. When at the end of August Italy at last declared war on Germany, the course of the war remained unaffected, and greater store was set on the simultaneous intervention of the kindred Latin people of Rumanias (see Map, p. 298).

CHAPTER XIII

THE BALKANS AND POLITICAL REACTIONS

The combined offensive of the Allies in 1916 was not limited to the Russian, French, and Italian fronts, and there is a diplomatic story that when the battle of the Somme seemed unlikely to produce the fruits expected from it, pressure was put by one or more Western Powers upon Rumania to intervene. The story was denied in the interests of those Powers, and an alternative tale was told of a sinister plot, engineered by the Russian Prime Minister, Stuermer, by which Rumania was lured into the war in order that her defeat might pave the way for her partition between the Hapsburg and Russian Empires, Wallachia going to the one and Moldavia to the other. Both explanations were relics of the suspicion engendered by the diplomacy of the old regime rather than serious contributions to historical truth; and, while the conduct of the masters and tyros of political strategy was not calculated to render these fables incredible, there were other circumstances more intimately connected with Rumania to account for her action. After all, neither side was in August 1916 in a position to dictate to neutrals; and the Rumanian Army counted for too much in the delicate balance for any belligerent Power to invite its hostility by undue pressure. The decision was Rumania's own, and it was not unnatural. She had been on the eve of intervention more than a year before, but German successes in 1915 had constrained her to caution. By August 1916 it was clear that the Central Empires could hope for no more than a negotiated peace, and Rumania had claims which would only enter into the negotiation if she took part in the war.

Natural affinities left no doubt as to the side she would choose. Her old king Carol, who had died on 10 October 1914, was a Hohenzollern, though of the elder and Catholic line; but his successor was bred a Rumanian and a constitutional monarch. There was also a pro-German and anti-democratic party, led by Carp and Marghiloman and supported by the landlords, which harped upon Rumania's grievances against Russia and placed Bessarabia in the scales against Transylvania. But the Rumanes across the Pruth were few compared with the four millions across the Carpathians, and the hardships they shared with the Russians at the hands of the Tsardom irked them less than those injuries which the Magyars knew so well how to inflict on subject nationalities under the cloak of equal rights and liberties. The claims which Rumania might hope to enforce against a defeated Hapsburg Empire would increase her population by more than 50 per cent and make her territorially compact, while the gains she could get from Russia would be less extensive and less homogeneous, and would leave her with still more straggling frontiers. The cause was fairly clear; the occasion was provided by the failure of the Germans at Verdun, the success of Brussilov, the apparent likelihood of Turkey's collapse before the Russian advance in Asia Minor, and the promise of an Entente offensive from Salonika.

Turkey, indeed, had exhausted the credit she had won at Gallipoli and Kut. She had not been able to convert the capture of Kut into an advance down the Tigris; and on 19-20 May Gorringe had taken the key to the Es Sinn position and cleared the south bank by an advance towards the Shatt-el-Hai which would a month earlier have effected Townshend's relief. Summer, indeed, procured a respite from British attacks, but not from Russian progress in Asia Minor. On 15 July Yudenitch captured Baiburt, and Erzinghian on the 25th (see Map, p. 182). A counter-offensive, which led to the temporary loss of Bitlis and Mush, was nullified by a Russian thrust at Rayat on 25 August, and Bitlis and Mush were recovered. Asia Minor seemed to be slipping from Turkey's grasp, and her hold on Arabia was still more precarious. The Arabs had never been patient subjects of the Sultan, and the progressive vagaries of Young Turk infidels shocked the fidelity of the orthodox people of Mecca. On

9 June its Grand Sherif proclaimed Arab independence, occupied Jeddah, took Yambo, laid siege to Medina, cut the Hedjaz railway, and was joined by tribes farther south who captured Kandifah. An ineffectual Turkish effort to cope with this rebellion postponed another projected attack on Egypt, and when it was made in August it was crushed at Romani on the 3rd and 4th and the Turkish retreat was turned into a rout.

Greece remained the most dubious factor in the Balkan situation. There was no doubt where her interests lay, for the only two allies of the Central Empires were Turkey and Bulgaria, one the ancient tyrant, and the other the modern rival, of the Greeks. But Greece was divided in mind between her faith in a brilliant future and her fear of German success. Her king, with his Prussian queen and marshal's baton, was interested in the success of the German Army and of the principle of royal autocracy; and his wishes made him doubt the prospects of her foes. Apart from the Court and official influence, he was given a hold on his people by the fame which had been fathered on him in the Balkan Wars of 1912-13 and the fable that he was another Constantine the Great. So far his doubts seemed to have more justification than the faith of Venizelos; and Greece had in return for her security put up with an unconstitutional government and the shame of her broken Serbian treaty. But the strain which Constantine put upon the patience of his people reached the breaking-point in 1916. In May, acting under his orders, Greek troops admitted the Bulgars into Forts Rupel and Dragotin, the keys of the Struma Valley. Popular protests were made at Salonika, where Constantine's writ did not run; and the Entente retorted with a pacific blockade in June. But in spite of a shuffle of ministers, the Court held on its pro-German way and did whatever it could, by secret communications with Berlin and facilities for German submarines, to hamper the Entente preparations for an offensive from Salonika.

Early in August Sarrail, who was now commander-in-chief, ordered a French attack on Doiran, and Doldjeli was taken. Probably this was no more than a feint, for the real design was farther west, where the Serbians under Prince Alexander were looking forward to Monastir. Their offensive was anticipated by the Bulgars, who after some pourparlers with Rumania, were induced or constrained by their German masters to attack on the 17th. In the west Florina and Banitza were seized on Greek territory, and on the east the whole of new Greece, including Seres, Kavalla, and Demirhissar, as far as the Struma; the Greek garrisons surrendered and were sent to Germany as the Kaiser's guests (see Map, p. 151).

This was the last straw for the better part of Greece. Venizelos addressed a mass meeting of protest at Athens on the 27th, and on the 30th a revolution broke out at Salonika under Colonel Zimbrakakis, the Venizelist deputy for Seres. Regiments were enrolled for service against Bulgaria, and one of them set out for the front on 22 September. On the 24th a similar movement swept over Crete; Mytilene, Samos, and Chios and smaller Greek islands followed suit; and Venizelos left Athens to form with Admiral Condouriotes and General Danglis a provisional government of insurgent Greece at Salonika. It was grudgingly recognized by the Entente and at once declared war on Bulgaria. The mainland, south-west of Salonika, however, remained under Constantine's control, and added to its hostility to the Entente a murderous vendetta against the Venizelists. The militarist party engaged in the curious campaign of forming leagues of reservists to oppose a war which would involve their call to the colours, and a succession of embarrassed phantoms was established in office to enable the king to evade the demands of the Allies. They increased in severity from the surrender of the fleet to that of the army's batteries and then to its disbandment; but they were backed by inadequate force and bungling diplomacy. On 1 December detachments of Allied troops, landed at the Piraeus, were driven back with bloodshed, and well into the new year the King continued to defy the Entente and push Greece deeper into anarchy. On its side the Entente wished to avoid a civil war, which would be almost worse than united enmity, because it would preclude a naval blockade; but the principal cause of its blunders was its own divided counsels. France and Great Britain were stoutly Venizelist; but the Tsar had personal reasons for dreading revolutions, particularly one against his cousin, and Italy had no liking for that greater Greece which was represented by Venizelos, might become a rival in the eastern Mediterranean, and would certainly reclaim the Dodecanese from its Italian masters.

The Rumanian Campaign

Amid these scenes of Hellenic turmoil Sarrail strove to prosecute his offensive in aid of Rumania. The die had been cast by the northern kingdom on 27 August, and on the 28th Rumanian troops poured over the Carpathian passes into Transylvania. This direction of Rumanian strategy was severely criticized because it did not suit our Balkan plans. Bulgaria was the foe we had in view, and Rumania, it was said, should have launched her armies across the Danube in an effort to cut the corridor and join hands with Sarrail. The criticism was unjust for other reasons than the fact that in the treaty signed on 16 August it was stipulated that the principal aim of Rumanian action should be in the direction of Buda-Pesth. Sarrail's objective was Monastir, an eccentric route to Sofia or the Danube, and the British troops along the Struma were not cast for the part of an advance towards Rumania. Bulgaria, moreover, was not yet Rumania's enemy, and had shown signs of remaining neutral. Nor is a strategical motive ever an adequate reason for making war; there must be a political justification, and the grounds for Rumania's intervention was the injury suffered by the Rumanian population in Hungary and Transylvania. She had no quarrel with Bulgaria on the score of national rights; indeed, it was rather she who ruled over Bulgars in the Dobrudja, and a Rumanian war could only be defended in principle as a crusade to redeem the Rumania irredenta north of the Carpathians. Even had it been her business to pull the chestnuts out of the fire for the Entente, it might be urged that she did her part in opening the door for a Russian attack on Bulgaria. In 1915 the Russian reason for non-fulfilment of the threats of punishment for Bulgarian treason to the Slav cause had been the obstacle of Rumanian territory. That was now removed; and a Russian advance through the Dobrudja would not only have saved Rumania from Mackensen's envelopment, but have given effect to Russia's menace against Bulgaria, facilitated Sarrail's operations, cut the corridor, and isolated Turkey. Of all the strategic failures in the war none was more tragic than this which was imposed upon Russia, partly by her internal weakness and partly by her divergent ambitions in Asia Minor. The Rumanian advance across the Carpathians would have been sound enough strategically as well as politically, had it been properly supported by her huge but unreliable neighbour.

The Central Empires were preparing but unprepared, and the Rumanian attack prospered brilliantly at first. Apart from the political object, there was the strategic purpose of improving Rumania's defences. Her own frontier—over 700 miles in length—was even worse than Italy's because of its circular configuration; the enemy, with the interior lines, military railways, and easier approaches to the passes, could strike from the centre at any one or more of a dozen alternative points and could shift his attack from one to another flank in a fraction of the time it would take Rumania to transport her forces to meet it. She had no lateral lines for her northern frontier, and of the vertical lines only two went up to the passes. If, however, she could reach the Maros, she would not only straighten her line and shorten it by half, but deprive her enemies of their railway and other strategic advantages. On that line she might hope to resist the Teutonic counter-offensive and protect her territory, which would have been left defenceless if her armies had gone south to invade Bulgaria. For a fortnight all went well; the enemy troops in Transylvania were few, inferior, and unreliable, and one Czech battalion went over to the invaders. By 10 September Kronstadt and Orsova had been taken, Hermannstadt evacuated, and Hatszeg was in danger; at points the Rumanians had advanced some fifty miles, and the Maros line seemed almost in their grasp.

The appearance was delusive. Germany declared war on 28 August, Turkey on the 30th, and Bulgaria on 1 September. But the real danger did not come from Bulgaria, and it would have been at least as serious if Rumania had invited attack by declaring war on Bulgaria herself, and thus exceeding the requirements of the treaty of 16 August. It came from Germany, and was as little foreseen by Rumania's critics as by her Government. That Germany should have divisions to spare for another Balkan campaign after Verdun, and while the battle of the Somme and Brussilov's offensive were at their height, amazed the Entente Powers, and was, indeed, quite inconsistent with the versions of those campaigns to which they had given currency. Yet it was true: besides an Alpine corps of Bavarians, Germany sent no fewer than eight divisions to the Carpathians, and put Von Falkenhayn at their head. She also sent a lavish supply of guns, munitions, and aeroplanes to which Rumania had not the wherewithal to reply. The promised Russian supplies fell short, eaten up perhaps by Brussilov's requirements, and partly, it was said, surreptitiously withheld in the interest of Stuermer's treacherous design of a separate peace with Germany at Rumania's expense. The first blow was struck by Mackensen, whose rapid concentration of the German forces south of the Danube had not been disturbed by the promised offensive from Salonika. The treaty had fixed it for 20 August, but Sarrail's plans were betrayed by two of his officers and conveyed through a Spanish diplomatist to the enemy; possibly this was the cause of the Bulgar attack on the 17th, and Sarrail did not move until 7 September. He did, however, detain the three Bulgarian armies on the Salonika front, and Mackensen only had the help of the fourth, which had all along watched the Rumanian frontier.

On 1 September his forces invaded the Dobrudja and seized Dobritch, Balchik, and Kavarna on the coast. On the 5th they captured Turtukai on the Danube with an infantry division and a hundred guns. Silistria farther down the river was thereupon evacuated, and on the 16th Mackensen stood on the line Rasova-Kobadinu-Tuzla, a dozen miles from the important railway running from Bukarest across the Tchernavoda bridge to Constanza; Tchernavoda was the only bridge across the Danube in the Balkans, and Constanza was

Rumania's only Black Sea port. Here the stipulated Russian three divisions, composed partly of Serbs who had escaped into Rumania in 1915 and of Jugo-Slavs taken prisoners by the Russians from the Austrian forces, came to Rumania's assistance; and Mackensen was not only held, but driven back some fifteen miles. Falkenhayn, north of the Carpathians, disposed of greater strength, and during the latter half of September the Rumanians were steadily driven out of their conquests. A great feat of the Bavarian Alpine Corps was the capture on the 26th of the Roterturm Pass in the rear of the First Rumanian Army; elsewhere the retreat was carried out with skill, valour, and comparatively slight losses, and Falkenhayn found it no easy task to break the Carpathian barrier despite the advantages he possessed in every kind of equipment and in the experience of his men. But for the paralysis which overcame the Russian effort in the Carpathians he would have had the tables turned upon him, for no advance would have been possible against the Rumanian frontier had his flank been seriously threatened by the Russians from Jablonitza to the Borgo. Indeed, with a little more energy on the part of the Russian Government the Central Empires might have encountered in Transylvania a greater disaster than had yet befallen them. The Russian excuse was that their liabilities to Rumania involved an awkward extension of their front, yet it was Russia which had put most pressure on Rumania to intervene; and no account was taken of the huge extension of the Teutonic front achieved by that intervention, nor of the fate which Russia might have suffered if Falkenhayn and Mackensen had concentrated in the north the forces they led against Rumania. The relief which Russia secured thereby almost seems to support the sinister view of Stuermer's policy.

It was not until 10 October that the northern Rumanian armies were forced back to the Moldavian border; and all Falkenhayn's efforts to debouch from the central passes towards Bukarest were defeated by Rumanian valour. Nor was he more successful against Moldavia, and November arrived with its promise of snow to block the mountain-routes before he had advanced more than four miles into Rumanian territory. Mackensen, too, was held up in the Dobrudja, and a month's inactivity was only relieved by rival raids across the Danube. But by 20 October he had received reinforcements in the shape of two Turkish divisions and one

German. The Russo-Rumanian line was broken, and on the 21st the railway between Constanza and Tchernavoda. Constanza was abandoned on the 22nd, its stores of oil and wheat being burned, and on the 25th a span of the great bridge at Tchernavoda was blown up by the retreating Rumanians, while the Russians hastily withdrew thirty-five miles to Babadagh. Here on 1 November Sakharov arrived to take the command with several new divisions, for Alexeiev did his best to redeem the failings of his Government, and a counter-offensive was begun. On the 9th Sakharov recaptured Hirsova, and by the 15th he had advanced to within seven miles of Mackensen's lines defending the Constanza railway. But he was too late, for the Rumanian defence which had held north and south in the central zone was crumbling fast in the western salient.

Having failed along the direct route to Bukarest, Falkenhayn now concentrated his efforts on the passes west of the Törzburg; but he had little success in October. Two columns which crossed the mountains east of the Roterturm Pass and made for Salatrucul were flung back with heavy losses on the 18th, and Falkenhayn transferred his main attack to the Vulcan Pass still farther west. But he kept up his pressure from the Roterturm down the Aluta valley in order to detain there the Rumanian reinforcements which the extension of Lechitsky's line into Moldavia had released for service in the West; and in the first week of November his troops were threatening Rymnik. But south of the Vulcan they had come to grief at Targul Jiu, where on 27 October General Dragalina, with inferior numbers and artillery, won the most brilliant success of the campaign. Unfortunately he died of his wounds on 9 November, and with fresh reinforcements and guns the Germans under Falkenhayn's eyes resumed their advance on the 10th. Their progress was stubbornly contested, but on the 21st they entered Craiova on the main Rumanian railway, thus cutting off the western part of Rumania from the capital and isolating the army defending Orsova and Turnu Severin. Presently it was surrounded, but for nearly three weeks of gallant effort and romantic adventure it eluded its fate and only surrendered at Caracalu on 7 December after the fall of Bukarest.

Craiova was bad enough, but almost worse was to follow; for on 23 November Mackensen succeeded in forcing the passage of the Danube beween Samovit and Sistovo, and by the 27th he effected a junction with Falkenhayn's armies which had swung east and were now across the Aluta advancing on Bukarest. The Rumanians' flanks were thus both turned by the crossing of the mountain passes and of the Danube, and they had no option but a rapid retreat to a line where those flanks held firm. That line did not cover the capital, and its elaborate forts would have been merely a trap for the Rumanian army. Nevertheless, a brave and skilful attempt was made to save it by a manoeuvre battle, and hopes were entertained in allied countries that Rumania was about to repeat the success of the Marne. The success could only come later when Averescu had flanks as secure as Joffre's. Still a wedge was for the moment driven between Mackensen and Falkenhayn's centre, and the movement might have succeeded had the reserves been up to time. Bukarest fell on the 5th, and for the rest of the year the Germans continued their progress eastwards until the Russo-Rumanian forces were able to stand on a line formed by the Danube, the Sereth, and the Putna ascending to the Oitos Pass. Sakharov had been forced to withdraw from the Dobrudja, and all that was left of Rumania was its Moldavian province, less than one-third of the kingdom, with its capital near the Russian frontier at Jassy.

Sarrail's campaign in the south provided inadequate compensation. The part assigned to the British contingents under General Milne, which had taken over the front from the Vardar eastwards past Doiran and down the Struma to the sea, was the somewhat thankless one of pinning the Bulgars to that sector and preventing them from reinforcing the threatened line in the west. The various British attacks on villages east of the Struma, such as Nevolien, Jenikoi, Prosenik, and Barakli-Djuma, were thus merely raids, and the ground gained was soon evacuated for tactical or sanitary reasons. The serious offensive was towards Monastir, and the lion's part was played by the Serbian army with assistance from the French and a moderate Russian contingent; Italians from Avlona also fought occasionally. The Bulgarian offensive from Monastir in August had penetrated far into Greek territory, patrols even reaching Kailar, and it threatened, indeed, to turn Sarrail's left wing by an advance to the shores of the Gulf of Salonika when Sarrail began his attack on 7 September. The first serious fighting took place to the west of Lake Ostrovo, where on the 14th the Serbians captured Ekshisu. On the 20th they stormed Mount Kaymakchalan and recovered a footing on Serbian territory, while the French and Russians drove the Bulgars out of Florina. On the 29th, after furious Bulgarian counter-attacks, the Serbian general Mishitch descended the mountains towards the bend of the Tcherna river, and turning the left flank of the Bulgar-Germanic army forced it back to the lines at Kenali beyond the Greek frontier. These had been selected by Mackensen and strongly fortified, and a frontal attack by the French and Russians on 14 October broke down (see Map, p. 151).

Better success attended the Serbian efforts to turn the enemy flank. By 5 October they had secured the crossing of the Tcherna at Brod, and slowly they pushed across it. Bad weather delayed them for a month, but by 15 November Mishitch had mastered the river bend from Iven to Bukri; and, thus outflanked on their left, the enemy yielded to the Franco-Russian attacks on Kenali and retreated to the Bistritza, four miles from Monastir. On the 16th and 17th the Serbians again attacked on the mountains in the Tcherna bend, carried the Bulgar positions, and by the 19th had reached Dobromir and Makovo whence they threatened the line of retreat from Monastir to Prilep. On that day the Germans and Bulgars moved out of and the Allies into Monastir. Their position was further improved before the end of the year, and it is said that had Mishitch been allowed the use of reserves, Prilep would also have fallen and Monastir been spared the annoying bombardment which it suffered at intervals for nearly two years. For its capture marked the limit of Entente success in that sphere until the closing months of the war. The campaign had not been fruitless, for Greece had been saved as a brand from the burning, and presently did her part in the Allied cause. But the Balkan corridor had been expanded by the Rumanian disaster into a solid block, and revolution in Russia soon put an end to all threats from the north. The hopes that were built on Salonika were destined to remain in abeyance until events in September 1918 justified the faith of those who refused to abandon the Balkans.

The Rumanian disaster was, however, a severe trial to the confidence and the patience of public opinion. Some critics held that the war had been lost in that campaign; but it was a worthier sentiment than pessimism that gave edge to popular feeling against the Government. Official optimism had not concealed the indecisiveness of the Somme, and few had the vision to discern the deferred dividends which accrued as a bonus to other ministers in the spring. But disappointment with the achievements on the Somme was not so bitter as resentment at the failure in Rumania. Was friendship with the Entente doomed always to be fatal to little peoples? One more trusting nation had gone the way of Belgium, Serbia, and Montenegro, and the blow to our self-respect was keenly felt. The public had little knowledge of the real responsibility, but where knowledge is rare suspicion is rife; and a vicarious victim is always required when the actual culprit is out of reach. Englishmen could exact no responsibility for whatever befell in the war except from their own responsible Government; and few paused to reflect that if Russia could not protect her immediate neighbour, England and France could not save a State from which they were completely cut off both by land and sea. Nor was it open for those who knew the facts to make public comment on the conduct of an ally, and compulsory silence on the part of truth made all the more audible the malicious tongue of slander. Belgium may have been our affair, but the Balkans were that of Russia; and not the wildest of Jingoes before the war had dreamt of British forces protecting Rumania. It was indeed the very distance of the danger that induced and enabled us to indulge in recrimination against the Government; for when eighteen months later a greater and far more preventable disaster threatened us nearer home, public sense rose superior to the temptation and temper of 1916, and instead of attacking ministers the nation bent its undivided and uncomplaining energies to the task of supporting and helping them out of their dilemma.

In the autumn of the Rumanian reverse there was no peril so imminent in the West as to impose unity upon public opinion, the press, or aspiring politicians. The advance on the Somme had been slow, but it was the Germans who were in retreat; the German Navy had been demoralized at Jutland; and Germany's only retaliation had been the judicial murder of Captain Fryatt on 27 July on a charge of having defended himself against a submarine. Nine-tenths of Germany's last and greatest colony had been overrun, and German forces oversea reduced to hiding in unhealthy swamps in a corner of East Africa; while across the Sinai desert and up the banks of the Tigris were creeping those railways which were to lead to the conquest of Syria and Mesopotamia. Two German raids in the dark on the Channel flotilla and the recrudescence of German submarine activity had, indeed, provoked some criticism of the Admiralty, and the substitution of Jellicoe for Sir Henry Jackson as First Sea Lord had been already decided. But the menace of the Zeppelins, which had earlier stirred indignation in breasts unmoved by dangers at the front, had been met when on 2 and 23 September, 1 October, and 27 November successive raiders were destroyed with all their crews by incendiary bullets from aeroplanes; and the Zeppelin had ceased to worry the public mind. The aircraft policy of the Government had been vindicated by a judicial committee in the summer, and the German mechanical superiority in the air which was foreshadowed by the advent of the Fokker had not survived the subsequent improvements in British construction; while the exploits of Captain Ball put those of every German airman into the shade.

Impatience and pinpricks were, indeed, the causes of popular irritation, rather than any such crisis as those of the autumn of 1914 or the spring of 1918. Such irritants are, however, apt to provoke more resentment and provide more scope for recrimination than the stunning blows of national disaster; and in the autumn of 1916 the people felt less need of restraint than in the more perilous moments of the war. The discontent was not due to any particular causes, nor was it confined to any particular country. It was a malaise produced by the fact that the war was lasting longer and costing more than people had expected, and by popular reluctance to believe that Britons could not have beaten the Germans sooner but for the feebleness of their leaders. The public needed a stimulant other than that which mere prudence could provide; and catchpenny journals, having hunted in vain for a dictator, found at least a victim in the Cabinet of twenty-three. It was not an ideal body for prompt decision, and its chief seemed almost as slow at times to take action that was necessary as he was to commit the irretrievable blunders urged on him by his journalistic mentors, who thought the wisdom of a step immaterial provided it was taken at once. He had other qualities which disqualified him for popular favour in a time of popular passion. He was not emotional, and did not respond to the varying moods of the hour with the versatility demanded by the experts in daily sensation. He belonged to an older school of politicians who suffered, like our armies in the field, from the newer and possibly more scientific methods of their foes. He was scrupulous in his observance of accepted rules of conduct, and the charge which was pressed against him most was that of excessive loyalty. He did not intrigue against his colleagues for newspaper support, nor publicly criticize his Government's commanders in the field. He put what success his Cabinet achieved to its common credit, and took the chief responsibility for its failures himself. He was staid in adversity but slow in advertisement, and he did not figure in the cinema.

Mr. Lloyd George was the antithesis of his former leader, a Celt of the Celts, with all their amazing emotion, versatility, and intuition. There is a true story, which has even found its way into French literature, of how the Welshmen were stirred to defeat an all-conquering New Zealand football team by the strains of the "Land of my Fathers." That was the sort of tonic the British public found in Mr. Lloyd George, and it would not have been so much to their taste at a less emotional time. He was the very embodiment of an emotion that was not overburdened with scruples, and of an impulse which hardly troubled to think. He imported the temperament and the methods of the religious revivalist into the practice of politics, and he enlisted strange allies when he found a vehicle for his patriotic fervour in the language of the prize-ring. He prided himself on his aptitude for political strategy, and professed a sympathy with the mind of the man in the street which was keener even than that of Lord Northcliffe. His views were always short-sighted, and he had the most superficial knowledge of the deeper problems of war and politics. Before the war broke out he had complained that we were building Dreadnoughts against a phantom; in August 1914 he estimated our daily expenditure of three-quarters of a million as a diminishing figure; in the following April he was as much in the dark as Mr. Asquith himself about munitions, and denied that conscription would assist our success in the war. According to one of his colleagues, he was the only member of his Cabinet who favoured British participation in the Pacifist Conference of Stockholm; in the November before the great German offensive in the West he quoted with approval a plea for concentration at Laibach; and the views he expressed on the Salonika expedition varied with the fortunes of war and the fluctuations of popular favour. His remark after the armistice that we had achieved nothing in the time of his predecessor except two defeats at the hands of the Turks, was an epitome of his own intellectual limitations; and the intensity of his convictions was discounted by the infirmity of his principles.

There were, however, substantial reasons for the supplanting of Mr. Asquith by Mr. Lloyd George. Political failings like these and lapses like the Marconi scandal might well be forgiven the man who could get on with the war, or at least persuade the people of its progress. The man in the street really believed that after the change of government the war would soon be won, and subscribed with enthusiasm to a "victory" loan calculated to finance a triumph in eight months. Cooler observers discerned a solid advantage in a Prime Minister who could minister at once to the public demands in the rival spheres of speech and action, who could appease with words the popular clamour for the moon and yet be guided by others into the mundane paths of practical common sense. There was at the moment an abnormal dislocation between public opinion and actual possibilities. The harsh amalgam of democratic politics and war seemed to demand an adaptable Premier; he was ex-officio and par excellence the pivotal man, and circumstances required a liberal amount of lubrication and elasticity to ease the friction and avert a fracture.

The genesis of the movement which led to the Cabinet crisis of the first week in December remains obscure, and the transference of power was effected within the camarilla itself without so much as a reference to the House of Commons and still less to the electorate. The old system of Cabinet Government and collective responsibility disappeared, and while ministers multiplied until they numbered ninety, there was little connexion or cohesion between the endless departments. They were all subject, however, to the control of the new War Cabinet, which soon consisted, like the old War Committee, of seven members. The old body of twenty-three was reduced to less than a third its size for the purposes of supreme direction and deliberation, and increased to twice its numbers for those of departmental execution. The higher functions were still reserved for the much-abused politicians; three of them had been members of the old War Committee, and all of them, with the exception of General Smuts who was recruited in June, had been members of the old Cabinet. So-called business men were, however, admitted to departmental duties, though the most striking successes were achieved by two ministers of academic training, Mr. H. A. L. Fisher, President of the Board of Education, and Mr. R. E. Prothero, President of the Board of Agriculture. Both Navy and Army were entrusted to civilians for political reasons, though one retired in July 1917, when the submarine campaign had reached its zenith, and the other as a result of the German offensive in March 1918. Deliberation had been the foible of the Asquith regime; the characteristic of his successor's was the speed of its versatility. The War Cabinet's agenda resembled nothing so much as a railway time-table with ten minutes allowed on an average for the decision of each supremely important question reserved for its discussion; and departmental changes recurred with a rapidity which was reminiscent of French governments in times of peace.

These bureaucratic revolutions were, however, faithful reflections of the restlessness which overcame peoples in all belligerent countries as the war lengthened and produced its logical trend towards anarchy; for civilization cannot resist an unlimited strain put on it by its negation, and there were symptoms of social dissolution throughout the world in the later stages of the war. In Germany they were suppressed for the time by a powerful government and delusions fostered by the success of the Rumanian campaign; and the nation was stirred to a levée-en-masse for national service, supplemented by labour or slave raids in the occupied territories. But even in Germany the Chancellor spoke of the need of peace, and was tottering to his fall. A greater ruin was creeping towards the Russian Government, and in France a series of stormy secret sessions in the Chamber left M. Briand with the task of reconstructing his Government and reorganizing the high command. Joffre was succeeded by Nivelle, and Briand himself was driven from office four months later. In Austria a more violent fate overtook the Premier, Count Sturgkh, who was murdered on 27 October, and his successor Koerber was compelled to resign on 13 December. Three weeks earlier the old Emperor Francis Joseph, who had ascended the throne in the midst of the revolutions of 1848, passed away in time to escape the greater desolation which threatened his empire. His successor and great-nephew Charles could give no better security to his ministries. Koerber was followed by Spitzmueller, and he, after a few days by Clam-Martinitz, a

Bohemian noble. Tisza's henchman Count Burian gave way as Foreign Minister to the anti-Magyar Czernin, though Tisza himself maintained his despotic sway in Hungary until his murder in 1918.

This holocaust of European reputations did not extend across the Atlantic to the neutral United States, where President Wilson, who had only been chosen by a minority vote owing to the split between Taft and Roosevelt in 1912, secured re-election by a narrow majority in a straight fight with Mr. Hughes, the Republican candidate. Discerning critics rejoiced at the issue of the contest; for apart from the merits of the candidates, nothing could have been worse than a practical interregnum during the coming crisis in the history of the United States and of the world. Yet an interregnum there would have been, if Mr. Wilson had been defeated; for he would still by the American Constitution have remained in office till March, and as the head of a vanquished party he would have had no moral authority to deal with the German pleas for peace or their unrestricted campaign of submarine war. The peace manoeuvre began with a letter which the Kaiser wrote to his Chancellor at the end of October; it was made public by the latter's speech in the Reichstag on 12 December. The Allies were simply invited in the interests of humanity to discuss terms at a conference with their conquering but magnanimous foe. On the 18th President Wilson addressed an independent inquiry about their aims to both groups of belligerents. The Allies replied to Germany on the 30th and to President Wilson on 10 January, intimating that there could be no peace without the reparation, restitution, and guarantees which Germany was as yet determined to refuse.

The attitude of the Allies astonished no one but the Germans. On 11 January their Government issued a note to neutrals, and on the 12th the Kaiser a proclamation to his people. Mr. Balfour also discussed the situation in a persuasive dispatch to the United States. But the most illuminating comment was made in private and came from humbler quarters. A party of interned German officers in the Engadine were eagerly awaiting the news of the Allied reply to the German offer. When it arrived they could not conceal their amazement and chagrin; some of them even burst into tears, and one remarked jetzt ist alles verloren. While the Government of Great Britain was being dismissed for having accomplished nothing in the war, intelligent Germans were bemoaning that all was lost.

CHAPTER XIV

THE TURN OF THE TIDE

The German presentiment of disaster was justified by events in the spring of 1917, and the new British Government seemed to have come in on a flowing tide. In spite of the gloomy picture of the situation which Mr. Lloyd George had drawn for his chief in December, confidence in a speedy victory animated the appeal of his ministry for further financial support; and in most of the spheres of war the first quarter of 1917 saw the reaping of harvests sown by other hands. The deferred dividends on the Somme campaign were paid, and the Germans fell back from hundreds of square miles of French territory. Mesopotamia was conquered as the result of the patient labours of Sir Charles Monro and the brilliant strategy of Sir Stanley Maude, who had been appointed in August 1916. The meagre German holding in East Africa was further reduced; and even distressful Rumania put a stop to the German advance.

Security for the Rumanian forces could not, however, be found short of the Sereth, which would give them a straight line with the Russian frontier protected by the impassable delta of the Danube on their left, and a flank in the Carpathians on their right; and from the fall of Bukarest to the end of December Averescu the Rumanian commander, and Presan his chief of staff, retreated to this line fighting rearguard battles on the way. The most stubborn of these was a four days' conflict at Rimnic Sarat in the centre on 22-26 December, after which Mackensen entered the town on the 27th. Sakharov conformed to this retreat in the Dobrudja; on 4 January Macin, the last place east and south of the Danube, was evacuated, and on the 5th Braila on the opposite bank south of the Sereth and Danube confluence. On the 23rd the Bulgarians, taking advantage of the unprecedented frost, crossed the marshes at Tulcea, but were annihilated by the Rumanians on the northern bank, and remained content for the rest with the defensive. The same wintry conditions put an end to fighting at the other extremity of the line in the Carpathian passes, but in the centre Mackensen seized Focsani on the 8th and occupied the bank of the Sereth. That line had originally been fortified against the Russians, and it faced in the wrong direction; but the position was strong, and when on the 19th Mackensen sought to force it he was repulsed in a costly encounter. Russian reinforcements which might have saved Wallachia came in time to protect Moldavia; and the war-worn Rumanian army was retired to refit, the defence of the Sereth being left to the Russians. The Germans made the most of their booty in Wallachia, which suffered the fate of Belgium and of Serbia; though the stores of grain had been burnt and the Rumanian oil-wells put out of action for many months. In one respect Rumania was less fortunate than the other little nations: in his fanatical hatred of Russia, Carp rejoiced in her ally's defeat—albeit that country was his own—and Marghiloman remained in Bukarest to curry favour with its conquerors, and ultimately to become for a brief and discreditable period the Premier whom the Germans imposed on Rumania after the Treaty of Bukarest. Meanwhile the patriotic parties rallied round the ministry at Jassy and formed a Coalition Government.

The defence of Rumania now seemed to occupy all the energy Russia could spare from her domestic preoccupations. In January there was a sound strategical effort to divert German attention from the south by a counter-offensive from Riga, and an advance of some four miles was made to Kalnzem. But the Germans soon recovered most of the ground; and elsewhere the front was quiescent. There was no repetition of the great blow at Erzerum of January 1916, and in Persia Baratov's small but adventurous force was driven back by the Turks from Khanikin to Hamadan, and the resistance to Turco-Teutonic invasion and intrigue was left more and more to British effort. Co-operation seemed impossible to synchronize in the East; one partner retreated whenever the other advanced. While therefore the Russians halted in Asia Minor and withdrew in Persia, Sir Stanley Maude was gathering his forces for a spring on Baghdad. Gorringe had already in May 1916 advanced some way up the right bank of the Tigris towards Kut; but summer forbade active operations, and Maude had been duly impressed by the force which previous experiences in Mesopotamia had given to the adage about more haste and less speed. The autumn was spent in careful study and preparation, which would preclude a repetition of the retreat from Ctesiphon and the fall of Kut (see Map, p. 177).

By 12 December he was ready to attack. The Turks still held the Sanna-i-Yat positions on the left bank of the Tigris, but on the right they had been pushed back to a line running across the angle from the Tigris at Magasis towards its southern tributary the Shatt-el-Hai. The Turks under their German taskmasters had not been idle, and this angle, as well as the extension of the Turkish line along the Shatt-el-Hai and their secondary defences on the right bank of the Tigris above Kut, had been well protected by trenches and wire entanglements. The breaking down of these obstacles required stubborn fighting as well as skilful tactics, but the only alternative was to penetrate the Sanna-i-Yat positions and they had proved impregnable in the spring. A serious attempt had, however, to be made at Sanna-i-Yat in order to detain there a serious Turkish force; and while Marshall pushed his way through on the right bank, Cobbe was kept hammering on the left. On the 13th crossings of the Shatt-el-Hai were effected at Atab and Basrugiyeh some eight miles from Kut, and Marshall advanced on both banks to Kalah-Hadji-Fahan. On the 18th he reached a point on the Tigris just below Kut in the Khadairi bend. Rain and floods then impeded our advance for a month, but the Khadairi bend was gradually cleared of the Turks, and most of their positions in the angle of the Tigris and Shatt-el-Hai were taken. On 10 February Marshall pushed on beyond the Shatt-el-Hai, reached the right bank of the Tigris above the Shumran bend, and by the 16th forced the Turks in the Dahra bend across the river.

The Turks had now been driven off the right bank below, in front of, and far above Kut, but they held the left bank as far down as Sanna-i-Yat, and Maude's task was to find a way across. He chose the Shumran bend, but diverted the attention of the Turks by thrusting at Sanna-i-Yat from 17 to 22 February. On the 22nd he also made feints to cross at Magasis and Kut, but on the 23rd the real attack was made at Shumran. Troops were ferried across and a bridge built before evening, and on the 24th the Turks were driven back on to their lines of communication between Baghdad and Kut. Meanwhile Cobbe had forced six enemy lines at Sanna-i-Yat and then found the remainder deserted. The Turks were in full retreat towards Baghdad, and Cobbe entered Kut unopposed. The pursuit was taken up by Marshall, who reached Azizieh in four days. There he halted till 5 March to prepare for his final advance. On the 6th he passed deserted trenches at Ctesiphon, and on the 7th reached the Diala. For two days the Turks disputed the passage, but a force, transported to the right bank of the Tigris, enfiladed their position on the Diala and captured their trenches at Shawa Khan on the 9th. Our forces on both sides of the river entered Baghdad on the 11th, thus concluding a model campaign which reflected glory alike on the British and Indian troops engaged and on their commanders, and raised British prestige in the East higher than it had been before the fall of Kut.

The work of our armies in Egypt was less sensational, but it was making solid progress and laying firm foundations during the autumn of 1916. The Grand Sherif of Mecca was proclaimed king of the Hedjaz, and he was a thorn in the side of the Turks. Their defeat at Romani had been followed by the steady construction of a railway eastward across the desert from Kantara, and on 20 December El Arish was captured, while on the 23rd the Turks who had fled south-east to Magdhaba were there surrounded and forced to surrender. The success was repeated at Rafa on the Palestine frontier a fortnight later, and presently the whole Sinai peninsula was cleared of the enemy forces (see Map, p. 352). Early in February a final blow was struck on the western frontiers of Egypt at the Senussi, and Egypt was converted from an enemy objective into a fruitful basis of operations against the Turkish Empire. Whatever might be said for frontal attacks in the west of Europe, ways round were proved to be the shortest in the East, and the failure of the direct blow at Turkey's heart in the Dardanelles was redeemed by success along the circuitous routes through Egypt and Mesopotamia.

Among the other forgotten achievements of the first two and a half years of the war was the completion, chiefly by British arms, of the establishment in the African continent of Entente and mainly

British supremacy. For even before the Turks had been driven from the frontiers of Egypt the Germans had been expelled from all the important parts of East Africa. The progress had been slow and not very creditable to our earlier efforts, which failed through an underestimate of the German strength, and particularly of the skill and resource of the German commander Von Lettow-Vorbeck. But it was sound as well as inevitable strategy to make sure of what we had by suppressing rebellion in the South African Union and then securing its frontiers by the conquest of its German neighbour before proceeding to concentrate forces for an offensive against an isolated German stronghold which could not threaten any essential interest nor affect the main struggle for victory in the war. The case against divergent operations was strongest of all against the East African campaign; and it would have been criminal folly for the sake of amour propre or imperial expansion to diminish our safeguards against a German victory in the West, or weaken the defence of our threatened communications with Egypt and India. Von Lettow-Vorbeck had forces enough to hold his own, but he never even attempted the conquest of British East Africa or the Belgian Congo, and the most nervous anticipation could not picture him as a serious danger to other dominions.

The Conquest Of East Africa

He was therefore left very much to himself until the South African Union, having set its own house in order and secured its frontiers by expelling German rule from the southern part of the continent, was able to lend its military power and its generalship to the task of reducing the Germans in East Africa. It was formidable enough, not so much from the opposition of man as because of the obstacles nature placed in the way. A tropical climate, torrential rains which played havoc with transport, the tzetze-fly which slew beasts of burden in hundreds of thousands, impenetrable forests, impassable swamps, immense mountain masses, and an area almost as large as Central Europe, provided a problem as vast as that of the great Boer War, and more difficult of solution but for the fact that Von Lettow-Vorbeck's forces could not be compared with those of our past antagonists and present allies. Still they were far more dangerous than any we had encountered in our normal wars against native races; for they had been trained by German officers, experts with machine guns and the other scientific equipment of civilized conflict; and three ships at least had eluded the blockade and relieved Von Lettow-Vorbeck's most pressing need of munitions; and he had selected his coloured troops from the hardiest and most bellicose of the native tribes. With their help he had kept the German colony intact until 1916, and even held at Taveta an angle of British East Africa.

Smith-Dorrien had been selected for the command in the autumn of 1915, but ill-health prevented him from taking it up, and in February 1916 General Smuts arrived at Mombasa to conduct the campaign. Experience had made us shy of enforced landings from the sea; and rejecting the idea of seizing as bases Tanga or Dar-es-Salaam, which would have given him shorter lines of communication with the Cape, Smuts adopted the more circuitous route by the railway from Mombasa, with the design of forcing the gap below Kilimanjaro and driving the Germans southwards, while British and Belgian subsidiary forces impinged upon the enemy's flank from the Lakes, the Congo State, and Nyasa in the west. His advance began on 5 March and Taveta was occupied on the 10th. A frontal attack on the pass between Kilimanjaro and the Pare mountains savoured rather of British than Boer methods, and Smuts preferred to send Van Deventer round the north of Kilimanjaro to turn the German position from Longido and cut off their escape. Van Deventer was successful, and at Moschi blocked the Germans' retreat westwards; they managed, however, to slip away south-eastwards by Lake Jipe, but the Kilimanjaro massif had been cleared, and Smuts established his headquarters at Moschi. His force was now arranged in three divisions, the first under Hoskins, the second under Van Deventer, and the third under Brits; the first consisted of British and Indian troops, the two others of South African. The plan was to strike with the second division from Moschi towards Kondoa Irangi and thence at the German central railway, while the first and third cleared the Pare and Usambara mountains and the coast, and then marched on Handeni and threatened the central railway on a parallel line to Van Deventer's attack. Van Deventer's second division marched with almost incredible speed. He started from Aruscha on 1 April, and by the 19th had driven the Germans from Kondoa Irangi, more than a hundred miles away. In May and June the other divisions cleared the Pave and Usambara mountains, reached Handeni and Kangata, and with naval assistance occupied Tanga, Pangani, Sadani Bay, and Bagamoyo in July and August almost without opposition. Von Lettow-Vorbeck had transferred the bulk of his troops south and then westwards up the central railway to bar Van Deventer's progress; and in the process he had been forced to abandon the north-eastern quarter of the colony. No small part of the northwestern province of Ruanda had been lost as well: the Belgians had occupied Kigali and the British had driven the Germans from their shore of Lake Victoria Nyanza.

The rapidity and divergence of these attacks, which were admirably timed, distracted Von Lettow-Vorbeck's strategy, and in spite of his interior lines he was unable to offer successful resistance. No sooner did he send troops to bar Smuts' advance from Kangata into the Nguru hills than Van Deventer struck west, south, and south-east from Kondoa Irangi. To the west he took Singida, thus getting behind the Germans on Lake Tanganyika; to the south and south-east he got astride the central railway by 14 July and pushed down it eastwards to Kilossa, which he reached on 22 August. He was now almost due south the Nguru hills, whence Smuts, attacking from the north, had driven the Germans before the middle of August. This converging advance made Mrogoro the only line of retreat, and Smuts planned a complicated outflanking movement to intercept it. They escaped by a track unknown to our forces on the 26th, and prepared to stand south of the central railway in the Ulunguru hills. Smuts was too quick for them, but they repelled a badly-timed attack at Kissaki on 6 September. Their retreat had, however, made the coast untenable: on 3 September the capital Dar-es-Salaam surrendered, and all the remaining ports before the end of the month. Van Deventer, too, had pressed south to the Ruaha on the 10th, the Belgians occupied Tabora on the 19th, and General Northey, advancing from Nyasa in the south-west, had reached Iringa before the end of August, while some Portuguese troops crossed the Rovuma river, the frontier between German East Africa and Mozambique, and made a pretence of marching north. By the end of September the great German colony had been conquered save for the unhealthy south-eastern corner, where only the Mahenge plateau provided a decent habitation for white troops.

The campaign had, however, tried the health and endurance of our forces, and three months' respite was now taken for recuperation and reinforcement before the final task of eradicating the Germans from the remnants of their territory. The great difficulty was that, apart from the Mahenge plateau, they were not rooted to any spot, and their elusiveness was illustrated by the fact that the Tabora garrison evaded the encircling forces and joined Von Lettow-Vorbeck at Mahenge. The campaign reopened on 1 January 1917, and consisted of a converging attack on Mahenge by Hoskins from Kilwa on the coast, by Northey from Lupembe, by Van Deventer from Iringa, and by Beves and subsidiary forces from north of the Rufigi. Smuts was summoned on the 29th to England to take part in the imperial conference, and Hoskins succeeded to the chief command. Unprecedented rains impeded our operations; progress became slow, and remained so after Van Deventer replaced Hoskins at the end of May. Not till October was Mahenge occupied by the Belgians. On 26 November half of the German forces under Von Lettow-Vorbeck's lieutenant Tafel were forced to surrender between Mahenge and the Rovuma; but Von Lettow himself escaped across the frontier with sufficient troops to terrorize the Portuguese and maintain himself in their territory until the end of the war.

The victor in the East African campaign came in 1917 to a Europe where victory seemed also on the way, for the early spring saw the only German retreat of moment until the war was near its end. The battles of the previous September had convinced the Germans that their line upon the Somme was barely tenable, and they had employed the winter pause to perfect the shorter and better line upon which they had begun to work at Michaelmas. Possibly it was to frustrate these preparations that Haig reopened his campaign so early as he did. On 11 January, the day on which the Allies answered President Wilson's note, British troops began to nibble at the point of the salient on the Ancre which had been created by the battle of the Somme. It was a modest sort of offensive; for it was no part of the Allies' combined plan of operations, which had been settled in conference during November, to launch a first-class attack across the devastated battlefield of the Somme. That wasted area was as effective a barrier as a chain of Alps to military pressure, and the Germans were thus left free to withdraw from their salient without much risk of disaster. They did not contemplate any serious stand, and until the Allies were ready to strike at the flanks of their position the Germans could afford to retreat at a pace which was not seriously hustled by our advance. They showed as much promptitude, foresight, and skill in retirement as they had done in their advance; they suffered few casualties and had no appreciable loss in guns or prisoners.

The details of the movement were therefore of little moment, and owed the attention they attracted to the habit of measuring progress in war by miles marked on a map. It was the end of January before the preliminary operation of clearing the Beaumont-Hamel spur was completed, and the apparently substantial advance began with the fall of Grandcourt on 7 February. A more ambitious attack on Miraumont from the south of the Ancre was somewhat disconcerted on the 17th by a German bombardment of our troops as they assembled, although the night was dark and misty; for even in France the Germans found spies to work for them, and a number of executions for treachery failed to prevent knowledge of our plans from occasionally reaching the enemy. A week later the German retreat extended, and Warlencourt, Pys, Miraumont, and Serre were evacuated. Again the Germans stopped for a time to breathe, and it was not till 10 March that Irles, a bare mile from

Miraumont, was abandoned. By that time the Germans had only rearguards and patrols left either north or south of the Somme, and when on the 17th a general Allied advance was ordered it encountered little resistance. The area of the German withdrawal had spread over a front of a hundred miles from Arras in the north to Soissons in the south. On that day British troops occupied Bapaume, while the French, whose line we had taken over as far as the river Avre, proceeded to liberate scores of villages between it and the Aisne. On that day, too, by one of the apparent illogicalities of French politics, M. Briand's Cabinet, which had held office for the unusual period of eighteen months, resigned.

The German tide rolled sullenly and slowly back for another fortnight. Péronne, Nesle, and Chaulnes fell on the 18th, Chauny and Ham on the 19th, and on the 20th French cavalry were within five miles of St. Quentin. By the end of March the British line ran from a mile in front of Arras to the Havrincourt wood, some seven miles from Cambrai, and thence southwards to Savy, less than two miles from St. Quentin. Thence the French line ran to Moy on the Sambre canal, behind La Fère, which the Germans had flooded, and through the lower forest of St. Gobain to the plateau north-east of Soissons. The German resistance had gradually stiffened, and there was a good deal of local fighting in the first week of April while the Allies were testing the strength of the positions behind which the Germans had taken shelter. We called them the Hindenburg lines, and believed that the Germans had so named them to give them a nominal invincibility which they did not possess in fact. In Germany they were known as the Siegfried lines, a name which properly only applied to the sector between Cambrai and La Fère which was also protected by the St. Quentin canal. That was the front of the new German position; its flanks rested on the Vimy Ridge to the north, and on the St. Gobain forest and the Chemin des Dames to the south. It was a better and shorter line than that which the battles of 1914 had left to the combatants without much choice on either side, and the Germans were right enough in claiming that the Hindenburg lines were selected by themselves. Their retreat thereto was not, however, a matter of choice except in so far as they preferred it to the disaster which would otherwise have overtaken them in their more exposed positions. As a retreat the movement could hardly have been more successfully carried out; but the military distinction was marred by moral disgrace. For destruction was pushed to the venomous length of maiming for years the orchards of the peasantry in the abandoned territory. The crime may have been no more than a characteristic expression of militarist malevolence and stupidity; but it may also have been calculated to bar the path to peace by agreement and to force on the German people the choice, as a Junker expressed it later, between victory and hell.

The success of the German withdrawal discounted our spring offensive, not because any attack was designed on the Somme, but because the Hindenburg lines and the desert before them gave that part of the German front a security which enabled the German higher command to divert reserves from its defence to that of the threatened wings. Here preparations had been begun by both the French and the British before the German retreat, and it had barely reached its limit when on Easter Monday, 9 April, Haig attacked along the Vimy Ridge and in front of Arras. Since 21 March a steady bombardment had been destroying the German wire defences and harassing their back areas, and in the first days of April it rose to the pitch which portended an attack in force. Since the battle of Loos in September 1915 our front had sagged a little, and points like the Double Crassier had been recovered by the Germans. So, too, the French capture of the Vimy heights, which had been announced in May that year, proved something of a fairy tale, and in April 1917 our line ran barely east of Souchez, Neuville, and the Labyrinth. It was held by Allenby's Third Army, which joined Gough's Fifth just south of Arras, and by Horne's First, which extended Allenby's left from Lens northwards to La Bassée. The Germans had three lines of defences for their advanced positions, and then behind them the famous switch line which hinged upon the Siegfried line at Quéant and ran northwards to Drocourt, whence quarries and slag-heaps linked it on to Lens (see Maps, pp. 79, 302). This line had not been finished at the beginning of April, and hopes were no doubt entertained that complete success in the battle of Arras, reinforced by Nivelle's contemplated offensive on the Chemin des Dames, would break these incomplete defences and thus turn the whole of the Hindenburg lines.

At dawn on Easter Monday the British guns broke out with a bombardment which marked another stage in the growing intensity of artillery fire, and obliterated the first and then the second German line of trenches along a front of some twelve miles. To the north the Canadians under Sir Julian Byng carried the crest of the Vimy Ridge, and by nine o'clock had mastered it all except at a couple of points. Farther south troops that were mainly Scottish captured Le Folie farm, Blangy, and Tilloy-lez-Mofflaines, while a fortress known as the Harp, and more formidable than any on the Somme, was seized by a number of Tanks. The greatest advance of the day was made due east of Arras, where the second and third German lines were taken and Feuchy, Athies, and Fampoux were captured. On the morrow the Canadians completed their hold on the Vimy Ridge, and Farbus was taken just below it. On the 11th the important position of Monchy, which outflanked the end of the Siegfried line, was carried after a fierce struggle; and on the 12th and the following days the salient we had created was widened north and south of Monchy. The capture of Wancourt and Heninel broke off another fragment of the Siegfried line, while to the north our advance spread up to the gates of Lens; the villages of Bailleul, Willerval, Vimy, Givenchy-en-Gohelle, Angres, and Lievin, with the Double Crassier and several of the suburbs of Lens, fell into our hands. The Germans appeared to have nothing left but the unfinished Drocourt-Quéant switch line between them and a real disaster.

The battle of Arras was the most successful the British had fought on the Western front since the Germans had stabilized their defences. Our bombardment was heavier than the enemy's, and was far more effective against his wire entanglements and trenches than it had ever been before; and the new method of locating hostile batteries by tests of sound enabled our gunners to put many of them out of action. Nor throughout the war was there a finer achievement than the Canadian capture of the Vimy Ridge or the British five-mile advance in a few hours to Fampoux. The German losses in men and guns also exceeded any that the British had yet inflicted in a similar period; in the first three days of the battle some 12,000 prisoners and 150 guns were taken. The battle did not succeed in converting the war from one of positions into one of movement; but if the Vimy position could be so completely demolished in two or three days, there seemed little prospect of permanence for any German stronghold in France, and a few repetitions of the battle of Arras bade fair to make an end of the Hindenburg lines and of the German occupation of French territory. April along the Western front in 1917 wore a fair promise of spring.

Nor was it without its hopes in other spheres. Maude's conquest of Baghdad produced other fruits in the East, including a welcome change in the situation in Persia. The fall of Kut in the April before had enabled the Turks to turn against the Russians and drive Baratov's adventurous force back from Khanikin into the mountains and even east of Hamadan; but Maude's advance cut the Turks off from their base at Baghdad and threatened their line of retreat to Mosul. The Turks were in a trap: Baratov resumed his advance from the north-east, while Maude pushed up from the south-west: Khanikin was the trap-door, and Halil, the Turkish commander, made skilful efforts to keep it open. A strong screen of rearguards held up the Russians at the Piatak pass, while other troops reinforced from Mosul barred Maude's advance at Deli Abbas and on the Jebel Hamrin range. By the end of March the bulk of Halil's forces were through, and Maude had to content himself with linking up with the Russians at Kizil Robat and driving the Turks from the Diala after their troops in Persia had escaped. Their junction with those from Mosul enabled Halil to resume the offensive, but his counter-attack was repulsed on 11-12 April, and Maude proceeded to extend his defences far to the north and west of Baghdad. Feluja on the Euphrates had already been occupied in March, and the Turks driven up the river to Ramadie; and on 23 April Maude completed his advance up the Tigris by the capture of Samara, where the section of the railway running north from Baghdad came to an end. Hundreds of miles separated it from the other railhead at Nisibin, and with his front pushed out on the rivers to eighty miles from Baghdad, and with the Russians in touch with his right and holding the route into Persia, Maude might well rest for the summer content with the security of his conquests. He had done single-handed what had been planned for a joint Anglo-Russian campaign, with Russia taking the lion's share (see Map, p. 177*).

In the spring of that year it looked, indeed, as though the British Empire alone was making any headway against the enemy Powers. Even on the cosmopolitan Salonika front offensive action was left to British troops, and at no time during the war did any but troops of the British Empire partake in the defence of its dominions and protectorates. These were all safe enough by the middle of April 1917, and those that were within reach of the enemy were being used as bases for attack upon his forces. Maude, with his army based upon India had now blocked the southern route into Persia, and Sir Archibald Murray was advancing into Palestine. The capture of Rafa on the frontier was followed on 28 February by that of Khan Yunus, five miles within the Turkish border, and the Turks under their German general Kressenstein withdrew to Gaza. There, on 26 March, they were attacked by Sir Charles Dobell, of Cameroon fame, with three infantry and two mounted divisions, including a number of Anzacs. The design was to surround and capture the Turkish forces in Gaza, and the only chance of success lay in the suddenness of the blow and its surprise. For Dobell's base was distant, his men had to drink water brought from Egypt, and in spite of the railway he had not at the front stores, equipment, or troops for a lengthy struggle, while the Turks could bring up superior reinforcements. A sea fog robbed him of two hours' precious time; and although the Wady Ghuzze and other defences of Gaza were taken and a force of Anzacs actually got behind Gaza and were fighting in its northern outskirts at sunset, night fell with the task unfinished and the British divisions out of touch on their various fronts. A retirement was accordingly ordered, and on the morrow Kressenstein counter-attacked. He was driven back with considerable losses, and although Dobell had failed to take Gaza he had reached the Wady Ghuzze and secured the means of bringing his railhead right up to the front of battle. With a few weeks' respite for reinforcement and reorganization, April might yet see the British well on the way to Jerusalem; for Arras was not intended to stand alone, and in every sphere of war the Allies had planned a simultaneous offensive (*see Map, p. 352*).

But if hope was bright in the East, it was pallid compared with the certainty of ultimate triumph which blazed from the West across the Atlantic; for on the 5th of that April of promise the great Republic, with a man-power, wealth, and potential force far exceeding those of any other of Germany's foes, entered the war against her and made her defeat unavoidable save by the suicide of her European antagonists. It was not a sudden decision, for a people with such varied spiritual homes as the American, spread over so vast a territory, and looking some eastward across the Atlantic and others westward across the Pacific, but all far removed from European politics and cherishing an inherited aloofness from the Old World and a rooted antipathy to imperialisms of every sort, could not easily see with one eye or achieve unanimity in favour of a vast adventure to break with their past and unite their fortunes with those of the Old World they had left behind. We were accustomed to fighting in Europe against overweening power; the United States had taken their stand on a splendid isolation. Their first president had warned them against entangling alliances, and their fifth had erected into the Monroe Doctrine the principle of abstention from European quarrels. For a century that principle had been the polestar of American foreign policy; no other people had such a wrench to make from their moorings before they could enter the war, and no other people can understand what it cost the Americans to cut themselves adrift from their haven of democratic pacifism in order to fight for the freedom of another world.

But Fate was too strong for schismatic tradition, and the two worlds had merged into one. The shrinking of space and expansion of mind was abolishing East and West, and the two hemispheres had become one exchange and mart of commodities and ideas. They could not continue to revolve on diverse political axes, and neither was safe without the other's concurrence. To the German cry of weltmacht must sooner or later respond the American cry of weltrecht; for the war was a civil war of mankind, and upon its issue would hang the future of human government. Intervention was inevitable, not so much because the Kaiser had said he would stand no nonsense from America as because, if America was to stand no nonsense from him after victory, she would have to turn the New World into an armed camp like the Old and run the same race to ruin. The old peace and isolation were in any case gone, and the choice was between war for the time, with the prospect of permanent peace on the one hand, and peace for the time, with the permanent prospect of war on the other. There was no other way, and Germany forced the American people to realize their dilemma.

President Wilson had seen it earlier than the majority of his fellow-countrymen; but for a statesman a vision of the truth is an insufficient ground for acting upon it. He is bound, indeed, not to act upon it until he can carry with him the State he governs; otherwise he ceases to be a statesman and sinks or rises into the missionary. The zealot is ever ready to break his weapon upon the obstacle he wishes to remove, but the statesman who destroys national unity in his zeal for war does not help to win it; and American intervention was both useless and impossible until the President could act with his people behind him. Nor, as official head of the State, could he play the irresponsible part of an advocate; if he believed war to be inevitable in his country's interests, it was for him to convince the people not by argument, but by his conduct of American affairs. Idealism entered more largely into his policy than that of most statesmen, but it was bound to American mentality and national interests; for ideals which do not affect national interests do not appeal to the majority in any nation, and the lawlessness which trampled on Belgian neutrality made less impression across the Atlantic than that which destroyed American lives and property.

A subsidiary cause of delay in American intervention was the absorption of the United States in the presidential contest of 1916, but President Wilson's re-election in November gave him a freer hand than was possessed by any other democratic statesman. No American president is ever elected for a third term of office, and Mr. Wilson had no need to keep his eye on his prospects for 1920. He must, indeed, secure the assent of Congress before war could be declared, but in both Houses his party had secured a majority in November. The decisive step was not, however, taken by President Wilson, but by the German Government, and America was as much forced into war in 1917 as we were in 1914; and in both cases it was their view of military necessity which drove the Germans into political suicide. They could not, they thought in 1914, cope with Russia until they had first beaten France, and they could not beat France in time unless they trampled a way through Belgium. So in the early days of 1917, not foreseeing the fortune which the Russian revolution was to bring them, they saw no prospect of victory save through the ruin of England by means of their submarines. The Eastern and Western fronts were too strong for a successful offensive against either, the military situation was growing desperate, and their offers of peace had been scorned; the war went on in their despite, and their real offensive for 1917 was the submarine campaign. It was adopted because there was no opening on land and no hope of success in a naval battle; and its adoption justified those who held that the remedy was worse than the disease and that unrestricted submarine warfare would bring the United States into the war before it drove Great Britain out.

As late as 22 January, President Wilson, while depicting the sort of peace which would commend itself to the American people, disavowed any intention of helping to secure it by force of arms. But on the 31st Germany revoked her promise given on 4 May 1916 that vessels other than warships would not be sunk without warning, and announced her resolve forthwith to wage submarine war without any restriction. Later on Herr Bethmann-Hollweg stated that the promise had only been given because Germany's preparations were incomplete, and was revoked as soon as they were ready. The President's answer was prompt: on 3 February the German ambassador was given his passports and Mr. Gerard was recalled from Berlin. But the invitation to other neutrals to follow the President's lead was declined on this side of the Atlantic. Switzerland, without any seaboard, was not concerned with submarine warfare, and other neutrals were too much under the influence of German blandishments or terror to risk war in defence of their rights; they preferred to abandon their sailings to British ports.

At first the President contemplated no more than an armed neutrality, and proposed to equip all American mercantile vessels for self-defence. But the sinking of American ships and loss of American lives began to rouse popular anger; sailings stopped at the ports, the railways became congested with goods seeking outlet, and the remotest inland districts felt the effects of the German campaign. In March, too, the Russian revolution removed a stumbling-block to co-operation with the Entente, for American public opinion had always been sensitive to the iniquity of the old regime in Russia. At length the President summoned a special session of Congress, and on 2 April recommended a declaration of war. It was adopted in the Senate on the 4th by 82 votes to 6, and by the House of Representatives on the 5th by 373 to 50. Of the ultimate issue of the war there could now be no doubt. Time would be needed for the United States to mobilize its resources and train its armies, and the extent to which they might be required would depend upon the course of events in Europe. But the Americans were not a people to turn back having put their hand to the plough, and with their forces fully deployed they would alone be more than a match for the German Empire. Victory might be delayed, but its advent was assured, and the first fortnight of April saw the hopes of the Allies rise higher than since the war began.

CHAPTER XV

HOPE DEFERRED

Among the events which gave so brilliant a promise to the spring of 1917, not the least was the revolution in Russia. From the first, indeed, there was anxiety about the effect which so great a change in the midst of war would have upon the military efficiency of our ally. But that had suffered under the old regime, and the failure to capture Lemberg in the summer of 1916, distracted as the Central Empires were by the Somme and Italian campaigns, followed by the more discreditable failure to protect Rumania in the autumn, raised serious doubts of the competence of the imperial bureaucracy. Its honesty also fell under grave suspicion. Sazonov, the Foreign Minister, had been dismissed in August, and Stuermer became Prime Minister. A fierce indictment of his conduct by Miliukov in the Duma led to his retirement in November, and an honest Conservative, Trepov, succeeded. But Stuermer retained his power at Court as Imperial Chamberlain, and a renegade from the Liberal party, Protopopov, was introduced into the Ministry and exercised therein a growing and sinister influence. Winter saw the Russian Government turning its back on its Liberal professions, proroguing the Duma, prohibiting the meetings of town councils and Zemstvos, provoking a revolution in order to suppress it and re-establish the old despotism on its ruins, and apparently casting wistful glances back at its old alliance with the German champions of autocracy. The Tsar himself was a firm friend of the Entente, but the same could not be said of the Tsaritsa nor of the reactionary and disreputable influences to which she extended her patronage. If therefore there were risks to the Entente cause in a Russian revolution, there were also perils in its postponement; and it might well be thought that a Liberal Russia would be bound more closely and logically to the Western Powers than autocracy ever could be. A revolution would at least clarify the issue between the combatants and give a more solid basis of political principle to the Entente.

The overture was a strange and squalid tragedy. Noxious weeds grew in the shadow of the Oriental despotism of the Russian Court, and for years the Government had been at the mercy of a religious impostor and libertine called Rasputin. The trouble, remarked a Russian General, was not that Rasputin was a wizard, but that the Court laboured under the superstitions of a Russian peasant; and Rasputin, who had some mesmeric power, used it to gratify his avarice, immorality, and taste for intrigue at the expense of Russian politics and society. At last, on 29 December, he was doomed by a conclave of Grand Dukes, Princes, and politicians who informed the police of what had been done. The deed was enthusiastically celebrated next evening by the audience at the Imperial Theatre singing the national anthem; but the body was buried at Tsarkoe Selo in a silver coffin, while the Metropolitan said mass, the Tsar and Protopopov acted as pall-bearers, and the Tsaritsa as one of the chief mourners. The last days of the old regime in France, with their Cagliostro and the Diamond Necklace, produced nothing so redolent of corruption or so suggestive of impending dissolution.

Rasputin was a symptom, not a cause, and the dark forces in Russia were not eradicated by his removal. Rather they were roused to further action, and on 8 January Trepov gave place to Prince Golitzin, a mere agent of obstruction, while Protopopov proceeded with his measures to provoke disorder. The Duma was prorogued and machine guns made in England were diverted from the front to dominate the capital. The Russian revolution was, in fact, as much forced upon the Russian people as war was forced upon ourselves and America. Le peuple, wrote Sully three centuries ago, ne se soulève jamais par envie d'attaquer, mais par impatience de souffrir; and in Russia even hunger and Protopopov barely provoked the people to action. The revolution occurred not so much because they rose, as because the bureaucracy fell, and it was not so much a change from one government to another as a general cessation of all government through comprehensive inaction. The Petrograd mob did not storm a Bastille like that of Paris in 1789; it merely paraded the streets and declined to disperse or work, and the act of revolution was simply the refusal of the soldiers to fire. It was not the new wine of liberty, but the opium of lethargy that possessed the popular mind, and relaxation loosened all the fibres of the Russian State. Action came later with the Bolshevik reconstruction, but for the time dissolution was the order of the day—a dissolution that was due less to the activity of destroyers than to the decay of the body politic; and the over-government of Russia by bureaucracy and police precipitated a violent reaction towards no government at all.

The Russian revolution was not therefore planned, and its origin and progress can hardly be seen in acts. The Rasputin affair was a vendetta of society which revealed its moral disintegration, but more than two months passed before the Government collapsed. The first disorder took the form of the looting of bakers' shops on 8 March by disappointed food-queues, but a more ominous and comprehensive symptom was the abstention from work. Characteristically it was not an organized strike; the idle throng seemed to have no definite objects, and the question was not whether it would achieve them, but whether the soldiers would obey orders and fire upon the mob. On the 9th the chief newspapers ceased to appear; on the 10th the trams stopped running; on the 11th a company of the Pavlovsk regiment mutinied when told to fire, and the President of the Duma, Rodzianko, telegraphed to the Tsar that anarchy reigned in the capital, the Government was paralysed, and the transport, food, and fuel supplies were utterly disorganized. Golitzin thereupon again prorogued the Duma; but, like the French National Assembly in 1789, it refused to disperse, and declared itself the sole repository of constitutional authority. On the 12th Household troops improved upon the example of the Pavlovsk regiment, and shot their more unpopular officers when ordered to fire on the people. Other regiments sent to suppress the mutiny joined it and seized the arsenal. Then the fortress of SS. Peter and Paul surrendered, and the police were hunted down. The Duma now appointed an executive committee of its members to act as a provisional government, while, outside, an unauthorized committee of soldiers and workmen was created, for the original Duma had been purged by imperial rescript and represented chiefly the upper and middle classes. On the 13th news came that Moscow had accepted the revolution, and it was clear that the Army would offer no resistance, although the Tsar had appointed Ivanov commander-in-chief in order to suppress the insurrection. Ruszky and Brussilov signified their adhesion to the popular cause, and Ivanov failed to reach the capital. The Tsar followed him, but was stopped at Pskov on the 14th. There on the 15th—the modern Ides of March—the modern Russian Tsar or Caesar was constrained to abdicate.

On that day the Duma Coalition Ministry was announced; the Premier was Prince Lvov, Miliukov took charge of Foreign Affairs, Gutchkov of War and the Marine, and Kerensky, a Socialist, of Justice. Ministers were in favour of a regency, but the Soviet—a Russian word which originally meant no more than Council—of Soldiers' and Workmen's Delegates demanded a republic. Kerensky, however, persuaded it to support the Provisional Government by an enormous majority and the revolution appeared to have produced a government. But even in orderly countries enormous majorities secured in moments of emotion are apt to be evanescent, and the Provisional Government had an uneasy lease of life for just two months. The Duma had not made the revolution, and the middle classes for which it stood were weak in numbers and prestige. The vast mass of the Russian people consisted of peasants who were illiterate and unorganized, and cared for little but the land. The urban proletariat, not having been educated by the Government, had partially educated itself in the abstract socialism of Karl Marx, Lavrov, and Tolstoy. The Extremists followed Marx and were called Social Democrats; but they had themselves split into two sections, the Bolsheviks or Maximalists and the Mensheviks or Minimalists; the former wanted a dictatorship of the proletariat, a complete inversion of the Tsardom consisting in the substitution of the tyranny of the bottom for the tyranny of the top, while the Mensheviks were willing to recognize the claims of other classes than the proletariat. More moderate, though still socialists, were the followers of Lavrov, who called themselves Social Revolutionaries and found a leader in Kerensky. The middle classes and intelligentsia formed the bulk of the Cadet party led by Miliukov and were predominant in the Duma and the Provisional Government. In the Soviet power gradually passed farther and farther to the left, from Social Revolutionaries to Mensheviks and from Mensheviks to Bolsheviks under the leadership of Lenin, whose return from exile in Switzerland was facilitated for its own purposes by the German Government.

All parties in the Soviet were, however, agreed in their anxiety for peace, the destruction of imperialism and bureaucracy, and the reconstruction of Russia on a socialistic basis; and they concurred with the peasants in their demand for the extirpation of landlordism. The emancipation of the serfs by Alexander II in 1861 had done little more than substitute economic for legal slavery; for the emancipated peasants were only given as proprietors the refuse of the land they had tilled as serfs, and for it they had to pay tribute calculated upon the value of their labour when applied to the richer soil of their lords. Freedom therefore meant unavoidable penury, but the demand of the peasants was not so much to evade their dues to the State as to secure the richer land which would enable them to meet their obligations. It was here that they sought their indemnities and their annexations, not in the acquisition of foreign territory hundreds of miles beyond their ken. Of Belgium and Serbia they knew nothing, and all they knew of the war was that it meant ghastly losses, fighting with pitchforks against poison gas and machine guns for them, and for their masters the fruits of victory. What domestic progress Russia had made in the past had been the outcome of her defeats; success in war had always been followed by reaction. Constantinople—Tsargrad as it was called by the Russians—had no charms for the proletariat. They wanted peace, some of them because national wars divided the forces of international Socialism and postponed the war of classes, but most in order that they might consolidate their revolution and garner its ripe and refreshing fruit. They did not, however, desire a separate peace with the enemy, and Austria's offer of 15 April was declined, because a separate peace would be disadvantageous to them. What they wanted was a general peace which would give each nation what it possessed before and each proletariat a good deal more; and the design took form in the Congress of Stockholm in June.

Meanwhile discipline disappeared in Russia, and even in her armies the Soviet insisted that there should be no death-penalty, and that military orders, except on the field of battle, should proceed from a democratic committee. They knew that Russian autocracy had rested on bayonets and only fell with the failure of that support: whosoever controlled the Army would be master of Russia, and with a correct instinct the Bolsheviks set to work to convert the soldiers and seamen. It was easy work preaching peace, plenty, and indolence to the peasants at the front; and the relaxation which reduced the production of Russian industries by 40 per cent diminished still more the efficiency of the Russian Army. The Provisional Government struggled in vain against the disintegration, but its efforts were frustrated by the Congress of Soviets which began to sit in April, fell more and more under Lenin's influence, and resisted on principle all measures to retain or re-establish authority. On 13 May, Gutchkov, the Minister for War, resigned, and Miliukov followed. On the 16th the Provisional Government was succeeded by another Coalition more socialist in its complexion. Lvov remained its nominal head, but Tchernov, a social revolutionary, and two Mensheviks became Ministers, and Kerensky took Gutchkov's place at the Ministry of War. He did his best by his fervour and eloquence to reanimate the army, for he believed that only the success of Russian arms could guarantee the orderly progress of the revolution. But Alexeiev retired in June, the Congress of Soviets resolved that the Duma should be disbanded, and the view was sedulously propagated that it was wrong to fight fellow Socialists in the German Army and that the approaching Stockholm Conference would compel the bourgeois and imperialist governments to make peace without any further bloodshed.

Still Kerensky achieved some success with his impassioned appeals, and Brussilov, who had become commander-in-chief, reported that the army was recovering its moral. The Government determined to gamble on the chance of a successful offensive. It had, indeed, no other means of checking the growth of disorder, and an attack on the front was not entirely hopeless. Both the Germans and Austrians had depleted their Eastern forces to provide against dangers elsewhere, and there were still sound elements like the Cossacks in the Russian Army. It was skimmed for the purpose of all the cream of its regiments, and the scene of action was laid where Brussilov's advance had pressed farthest forward in 1916. Lemberg was to be outflanked on the south by a movement from a line reaching from Zborow across the Dniester to the foothills of the Carpathians. Three armies were employed, Erdelli's Eleventh to the north, then Tcheremisov's Seventh reaching to the Dniester, and south of it Kornilov's Eighth. Kerensky orated in khaki, and

Gutchkov served as an officer in the field. The artillery preparation began on 29 June, and on 1 July the troops advanced from their trenches. For a time they carried all before them, and revolutionary Russia bade fair to repeat the success of Brussilov's offensive in 1916. Tcheremisov's Seventh Army took Koniuchy on the 1st and Potutory on the 2nd, and captured 18,000 prisoners. Erdelli's Eleventh was more successful in attracting the bulk of the enemy reserves than in making progress; but the diversion gave Kornilov's Eighth a chance of which it made brilliant use. It attacked on the 8th and took half a dozen villages south of the Dniester, driving the Austrians back across its tributaries, the Lukwa and the Lomnica. On the 10th Halicz fell before a combined advance of Tcheremisov north and Kornilov south of the Dniester, and on the morrow Kalusz was captured well on the way to Lemberg's vital connexions at Stryj. Then the weather broke and the strength of the Russian armies turned into water. There were no reserves with the spirit of those who fell in this rapid advance, and Erdelli had failed to inspire the Eleventh Army with Kornilov's dash. On the 16th Lenin brought off his Bolshevik insurrection at Petrograd, but more fatal was the infection which spread through Erdelli's troops. It was on them that the weight of the German counter-attack fell on the 19th, and they simply wilted before it. There was no great force in the German blow, which was merely designed to relieve the pressure of Kornilov's advance; but Russian troops refused to fight, and ran away trampling underfoot and killing officers who strove to stem the rout. By the 20th German patrols were in Tarnopol, which the Russians had held since August 1914, and in a fortnight they were across the Russian frontier as far south as the borders of Bukovina (see Map, p. 146). The Seventh and Eighth Armies had to conform to this retreat, but they offered some stubborn resistance and were brought off in good order. Czernowitz fell on 3 August, and the only solid obstacle to the enemy advance in the East was the little Rumanian Army which had looked to this summer for its revenge on the invader and the recovery of its capital and Wallachia.

The Rumanian Army had during the winter been refitted and equipped with a considerable store of munitions, and its offensive was planned to follow closely on the heels of the Russian in Galicia, But the Russians were out of Tarnopol before, in the last week of July, Averescu began his advance from south of the

Oitoz Pass towards Kezdi Vasarhely; and the Russian Fourth Army under Scherbachev, which was to co-operate on Averescu's right, was deeply infected with revolutionary disorder. Nevertheless Averescu broke the enemy front, took 2000 prisoners on the first day, and on 28 July was ten miles ahead of his original line. Then Mackensen counter-attacked farther south at Focsani, while Scherbachev's regiments began to desert and the Russians in the Bukovina were being steadily driven back. On 6 and 7 August Mackensen forced the Russo-Rumanian line back from the Putna to the Susitza, taking over 3000 prisoners in three days and also pushing on towards Okna and Marasesti. In three days more the number of prisoners increased to 7000, the key to the defence of the Moldavian mountains was threatened at Adjudul, and the Court prepared to leave Jassy and take refuge in Russian territory. On the 14th Rumanian troops replaced the Russians in front of Okna in the Trotus valley and counterattacked with vigour. But the decisive battle was fought farther south, where Mackensen, advancing from Focsani, was seeking to cross the Sereth in the direction of Marasesti and Tecuciu. It was the most heroic of Rumania's struggles. Deprived of all but a fragment of her territory and her manhood, and abandoned by the only ally within reach, she had to face perhaps the ablest of German generals and over a dozen fresh divisions thrown into the battle; and almost hourly during the three days' fighting a fresh detachment of Russians deserted. Yet Rumania triumphed at the battle of Marasesti, and by the 19th the crisis had passed. The attack then shifted to Okna, where the Second Rumanian Army emulated the achievements of the First at Marasesti. Sporadic fighting went on into September, but Rumania had defended herself and saved South Russia for the time. On the 18th the Germans even withdrew from Husiatyn, an Austrian town on the Galician frontier: they had already abandoned the south for a safer adventure against the unaided Russians at Riga (see Map, p. 229).

The Baltic Campaigns

This northern campaign resembled autumn manoeuvres, and was mainly intended to test the value of the new tactics which Germany proposed to use next spring against a more serious foe. It was more realistic to experiment upon Russians than among themselves, and Von Hutier was selected to make the demonstration. The advance began in the last days of August, and on 1 September Von Hutier forced the passage of the Dvina at Uexküll, eighteen miles above Riga, which the Russians abandoned on the following day. Friedrichstadt fell next, and the Russians retired from Jacobstadt on the 21st. The Germans were now across the Dvina on a front of seventy miles, and pushed on towards Wenden, meeting with occasional resistance. But their next experiment was at the expense of the Russian Navy, which was even more demoralized than the Army, and had murdered its officers wholesale. On 12 October the Germans landed a force on the island of Oesel, and within a week had overrun that and the other islands at the mouth of the Gulf of Riga. On the 21st they crossed to the mainland, disembarking a force at Verder opposite Moen Island. There was little to hinder a march on Petrograd, had there been any sufficient inducement. But

Petrograd in the hands of the Bolsheviks was worth more to the Germans than in their own; for a German occupation of the capital would have sterilized its miasmic influence over the rest of Russia, and the Germans had only advanced so far in order to get into touch with Finland and establish pro-German governments among the little nationalities of the Baltic littoral. They had, moreover, to economize their shrinking manpower, and their reserves were being called off from all the Eastern fronts to more urgent tasks elsewhere, leaving Russia to stew in its own disintegration.

Disaster had done nothing to check the distraction of Russian domestic politics. The Cadets had most of them resigned in July owing to the Government's complaisance towards the Ukrainian demand for independence; and Kerensky succeeded Lvov as Premier on the 22nd, while Kornilov took Brussilov's place as commander-in-chief on 1 August. But while Kerensky shed his right wing, he gained no support from the left. The Bolsheviks would not forgive him his offensive in July, nor the success with which he had suppressed the Leninite rising; and a great conference at Moscow on 25 August representing every shade of Russian disorganization produced some agreement on formulas but none on action. Early in September Kerensky came to the conclusion that a dictatorship was the only cure, and gave Kornilov the impression that the latter should fill the part. Another Bolshevik insurrection was brewing in Petrograd, and on the 7th Kornilov prepared to crush it, sending Krymov forward to Gatchina within twenty miles of the capital. Kerensky now took fright at the bugbear of a military restoration, denounced Kornilov as a traitor, and threw himself on the support of the Soviets. The cry that the revolution was in danger ruined Kornilov's chances; his surrender was arranged by Alexeiev's mediation, while Krymov committed suicide.

Such were Russian politics during the week in which the Germans overran the Dvina. A republic was proclaimed on the 15th, and the government entrusted to a council of five with Kerensky at its head. It lived no longer than its numerous predecessors in the revolution. Kerensky was rash enough to renew his breach with the Bolsheviks who had helped him to ruin Kornilov, and in November they rent the man of words. Trotzky organized the blow. There was little that was Russian about this Jew, whose real name was Leo Braunstein, although he was born in Odessa; but he possessed some practical capacity. Having secured election as president of the Petrograd Soviet, he had created a military revolutionary committee and a body of Red Guards, and on 5 November summoned the Petrograd garrison to place itself under its direction. Kerensky sought to defend his Government, but most of his forces went over to the Bolsheviks, and on the 7th he fled from the city. He attempted to return at the head of some dubious troops, but they were scattered by the Red Guards at Tsarskoe Selo on the 13th and Kerensky disappeared. What there was left of government in Russia passed into the hands of a self-constituted council of People's Commissioners with Lenin as its president and Trotzky its Foreign Minister; and on the 21st the council found a commander-in-chief in one Ensign Krilenko. His business was to offer an armistice to the Germans as a preliminary to suing for peace.

Russia had gone out of the war much faster than America came in. Early in May a flotilla of destroyers joined the British Fleet, and on 26 June the first division landed in France. But it needed six months' training, and a year would pass before the weight of American reinforcements would make much material difference to the Western front. That year was bound to try the Western Allies to the utmost, and the interval between the disappearance of Russia and the arrival of the United States as an effective combatant, gave the Germans the chance of reversing the decision which they felt had gone against them before the end of 1916. They regarded the Russian revolution as a miracle wrought in their favour; but it was only by degrees that they realized the extent of their apparent good fortune and proceeded both to use and to abuse it. From the first, however, the revolution changed for the worse the situation on every front, and enemy troops, released from fear of Russia, began to appear in the West, on the Isonzo, in Mesopotamia, in Palestine, and in the Balkans. The middle of treacherous April saw the tide checked that had been flowing so strongly since the year began.

The disappointment was not, however, entirely due to the gradual elimination of Russia, for that misfortune did not fall with much weight on the Western front until many months had passed, and depression there had its causes nearer home. Commenting on the British success at the battle of Arras, an Italian journal optimistically asked its readers what would be the plight of the Central Empires when real military Powers got to work, since so much had been achieved by the semi-civilians of the British Empire. Hopes also ran high in France. Nivelle, the new commander-in-chief, had conceived an ambitious plan of crushing the Germans on a front of fifty miles between the plateau north-east of Soissons and the river Suippe in Champagne; and this offensive, coupled with the British pressure in front of Arras, was to clear the Germans out of the greater part of occupied France. Nivelle proposed to repeat on a vastly extended scale his triumphs of the previous autumn at Verdun, and he made no secret to his Government of his confidence that Laon would fall as a result of the first day's fighting. Neither Haig nor Pétain had much faith in the possibility of the plan, but Nivelle had persuaded Ribot's Ministry, which had succeeded Briand's in March, and French expectations were raised to a giddy height. There were three main objectives: to clear the Chemin des Dames, to master the Moronvillers massif and other heights north and east of Reims, and to thrust between these two great bastions along the road to Laon. Each was an objective greater than that achieved in the battle of Arras, and all were attempted at once (*see Map, p. 67*).

The artillery preparation began on 6 April and the infantry attack on Monday the 16th, a week after that on the Vimy Ridge. The battle was not easy to follow, because the French were very reserved about their reverses, and the maps gave an erroneous impression of the line from which the attack started and that on which it ended. The French were commonly thought to be holding both banks of the Aisne all the way from Soissons to Berry-au-Bac, whereas in reality they had never recovered from their retreat in January 1915 to the south bank between Missy and Chavotine. Nor, except at Troyon, were they near the Chemin des Dames; and not only had the river to be crossed, but the formidable slopes, which the Germans had beeen meticulously fortifying for two and a half years, to be surmounted. The results of the first day's onslaught fell lamentably short of the extravagant anticipations. The banks of the Aisne were cleared, some progress was made up the slopes, and from Troyon, where the original line was nearly on the ridge, an advance was made along it. But on the whole the Germans maintained their grip on the Chemin des Dames. Nor was fortune much kinder in the gap between it and the heights east of Reims. The French Tanks, here first employed, were disappointing, and Loivre was the only gain. The 17th was spent in beating off counter-attacks west of Reims, while the French offensive spread east to Moronvillers. Here the same tale had to be told; gallantry carried various points of importance, but a month's fighting failed to give the French complete control of their first day's objectives. West of Reims on the 18th and following days Nanteuil, Vailly, Laffaux, Aizy, Jouy, Ostel, and Bray were captured by Mangin, but they were all below the Chemin des Dames, and April came to an end with the road to Laon as impassable as ever. Fresh attempts were made in May; Craonne was taken on the 4th, and the California plateau to the north of it and Chevreux in the plain to the east were seized on the 6th and held against counter-attacks, while east of Reims Auberive had fallen, and by the 20th the whole summit of the Moronvillers massif was said to have been secured.

The impression that the Chemin des Dames had been conquered was not removed until it really was gained by Pétain five months later; but there was contrast enough between the promises and the achievement to produce the deepest depression in France. On 28 April Pétain was appointed chief of staff and on 15 May commander-in-chief in succession to Nivelle, while Foch became chief of staff. Little was wisely revealed abroad of French despondency or the effect of the disappointment on the moral of the army. But French journals began to clamour for unity of command of all the forces in France under a French generalissimo, pour épargner du sang Français, as one of them expressed it; and prudence constrained the higher command to revert to those limited objectives which Nivelle had abandoned. Joffre was sent to the United States to place the situation before the sister-republic; and but for American intervention France would have been nearer a peace of compromise in May 1917 than at any previous date in the war. The second battle of the Aisne gave rise to that miasma of défaitisme, associated with the names of Bolo and Caillaux, which enfeebled the spirit and effort of France until they were revived by Clémenceau's vigorous stimulants.

Haig was also laid under an obligation to relieve the pressure and gloom by prolonging his Arras offensive and seeking to extract more from his victory than it would yield; and the second phase of that battle was fought under a shadow and under constraint. But if it resulted in serious losses, it brought some additions to our gains of ground. On 23 April Gavrelle and Guémappe were captured after desperate fighting; and on the 28th an advance was made at Arleux and Oppy. On 3 May the Canadians took Fresnoy, and the Australians trenches at Bullecourt, but the Germans kept up a series of stubborn counter-attacks, especially at Fresnoy, Roeulx, and Bullecourt, and Fresnoy was lost on the 8th. On the 14th we completed our capture of Roeulx, and on the 17th that of Bullecourt. The fighting died down, towards the end of May, and the scene was shifted farther north in June to the Messines-Wytschaete Ridge. During the month of the battle of Arras we had taken over 20,000 prisoners, and the French claimed more on the Aisne. We had also bitten into the Hindenburg "line." But that line had not been broken, mainly because it was not a line, having instead of none a breadth of several miles; and, apart from the important Vimy Ridge, the German position had not been greatly shaken. The warfare was one of attrition, and the true test was that of wastage, which can only be used when the losses on both sides are exactly known. There was evidence that the Germans were feeling the strain, but so was the Entente, and the influx of troops from the Eastern front, which began in April and was felt in the Arras battle, would more than compensate for the excess (if any) in German losses. It was also clear by this time that the Germans had gained another great advantage. They might lose the war, but they would lose it in France, and the Fatherland would not suffer the destruction and desolation which it had inflicted on all its foes except the British Empire and the United States. The Germans were wisely bent on fighting to a finish where Hindenburg had fixed his lines; they were beaten there, but snatched immunity from ruin for German soil out of their defeat. Nivelle's failure in April 1917 combined with the Russian collapse to preclude an Entente repetition of the German invasion of August 1914; and Lord Curzon's mental vision of Gurkhas encamping in Berlin was destined to remain a dream.

The breakdown of Russia and of the French campaign paralysed other offensives than those on the Western front, and a sympathetic inertia spread to the Balkans. At the end of February Sarrail had told his commanders that he intended attacking all along the line at Salonika in the first week of April as his contribution to the comprehensive Allied advance. But local operations in March, which succeeded in linking up the Italians east of Avlona with Sarrail's left, did not lead up to the expected climax. The offensive was postponed until 24 April, and then it was only British troops that were sent into serious action. The desired economy of French blood was effected by a French commander-in-chief at the cost of general failure. A frontal attack by General Milne's forces was ordered on the central position at Doiran; considerable losses were incurred, and gains were secured that made no essential difference to the situation. West of the Vardar and in front of Monastir no advance was attempted; but on 8 May Milne was told to repeat his effort, which had similar results to those of his first; and Sarrail was presently superseded by Franchet d'Esperey.

Nevertheless the Russian revolution had one beneficial effect upon the Balkan situation. It removed one of the two influences which had protected Constantine and enabled him to counterwork Entente policy and strategy in the Near East. The other was neutralized by connivance in Italy's proclamation of a protectorate over Albania on 3 June; and with this compensation she was induced to remove her ban on Venizelos and to risk that greater Greece, which with a free hand that statesman bade fair to achieve. France was whole-hearted in supporting him. The chief islands had one by one rallied to his cause in the spring, and by the end of May he had 60,000 troops at his disposal. On 11 June M. Jonnart arrived at Athens as plenipotentiary for the Entente to insist on Constantine's abdication. Troops were moved down into Thessaly; the Isthmus of Corinth was seized, and warships anchored off the Piraeus. Constantine had no choice, and under compulsion nominated his second son Alexander as his successor. On the 13th he left Athens for Lugano, and on the 21st Venizelos arrived from Salonika and formed a government. The German agents were expelled, and the Greek people were reconciled to the violence of the proceedings by the substantial consolation of the raising of the blockade. Less happy was the effect of the Russian revolution in Asia Minor. All idea of an advance from Trebizond and Erzingian came to an end, and the projected campaign which was to have given the Russians Mosul while Maude advanced to Baghdad was abandoned. On 30 April the Turks announced that the enemy had evacuated Mush. In May they left the Dialah, and in July retreated from Khanikin into Persia, leaving the British right wing in the air. Gradually they abandoned Persia to the principle of self-determination and to the Turks, and Armenia to fresh experiments in massacre. Even on the Salonika front Sarrail suffered from the retiring habits of his Russian troops, and at Gaza Murray felt the force of Turkish divisions released from Russian fronts. There were at least six divisions to oppose him when he renewed his attack after three weeks' interval on 17th April. His communications had been greatly improved and the railway brought up to Deir-el-Belah, but so too had the Turkish defences, and there was little to say for a frontal attack by inferior forces without the chance of surprise. The political demand for an Egyptian contribution to the combined Allied offensive seems, however, to have been inexorable, and Sir Charles Dobell was committed to an enterprise not unlike our attacks in Gallipoli. Some initial success was won on the 17th, and the ground gained was prepared on the 18th for a final effort on the following day. Samson Ridge near the coast was taken, but Ali Muntar defied all our efforts, and counter-attacks deprived us of much of the ground that was won. Seven thousand men had been lost, and Turkish reinforcements were still arriving. Gaza could not be taken by frontal attack without greatly superior forces; and the British had to look for success to another general and a different strategy, and to postpone from Easter to Christmas their Christian celebrations in Jerusalem. The brightness of dawn in the East was clouded, and the flowers of hope that bloomed in the spring drooped in the Syrian summer and in the furnace of war in the West.

CHAPTER XVI

THE BALANCE OF POWER

THE breakdown of the strategical offensive of the Entente in the spring of 1917 was almost complete. Russia had gone her own way to military insignificance, France had failed in her far-reaching design of crushing the German front on the Aisne, Haig's victory at the battle of Arras secured merely a tactical advantage, the offensive from Salonika never started, and that from Egypt was held up at the gates of Palestine. In the absence of a combined General Staff for the Entente, it required months of individual thought and interchange of views to elaborate any alternative scheme and to readjust national forces for its execution; and the campaigning season would assuredly close before effect could be given to a fresh plan of campaign. The new Governments in England and France showed no greater foresight than the old, and had made no further progress towards a single strategical mind. Indeed, for the rest of 1917 divergence seemed to grow, and there was no such combined operation as the Somme campaign of 1916. Activity travelled away from the point of liaison, and each ally concentrated its attention more and more on its own particular front. Italy as usual had eyes only for Trieste and Albania, France turned from the Somme and the Oise to the Aisne and Verdun, and England's effort came north towards the Belgian coast. This divergence resulted from the changed view of the military situation imposed upon the Entente by Nivelle's failure. He had believed that the time had come for ambitious objectives; Haig had demurred and clung to the idea of operations limited in their scope like that of the Somme; and Pétain accepted that view when he succeeded Nivelle. There might, of course, have been limited offensives on the upper Somme and the

Oise where the two armies joined; but it was here that the Siegfried line most firmly barred the way, and when towards the end of the year a new tactic had been evolved to surmount that barrier, it was applied prematurely and without French co-operation. The unity of the Entente did not extend to community of ideas or simultaneous experiment; and novelties which might have been overwhelming if tried in unison all along the line only achieved a partial success when adopted by one of the Allies on a limited front.

Given, however, the impossibility of another combined strategical plan for 1917, there were urgent motives and sound reasons for the extension of Haig's offensive northwards from Arras to the coast. If it were successful beyond expectation, it would achieve all that Nivelle had hoped to do by a frontal attack, and would compel a general German retreat by turning the enemy's flank as Joffre had tried to turn it in October 1914. But short of such extravagant anticipations it might materially help to win the war by defeating the real German offensive for 1917. That was not a campaign on land at all, but on sea by means of the submarine, and the chief basis of operations was the Belgian coast. Submarines emerged from other lairs, but the German command of the Belgian coast shortened their distance from their objectives by hundreds of miles and correspondingly lengthened their range of operations. Bruges was their headquarters; situated inland, but connected by canal with Zeebrugge and Ostend, it afforded a base immune from any attack save those of aircraft, and Bruges was the real objective of our Flanders campaign. Incidentally, too, the Belgian coast provided harbours whence light German surface craft made occasional raids on British coasts, commerce, and communications, and also for those aeroplane attacks which became a serious nuisance as the year wore on. Apart from these considerations the German hold on Flanders was the bastion of their whole position west of the Meuse; and, but for the natural feelings of Paris, a more strenuous attempt might well have been made earlier in the war to deprive the enemy of its advantages. Obviously in the summer of 1917, if the two Allies were to be left to their own devices, there was none which suited us better than the Flanders campaign, and the official American commentator opined that it held out more fruitful prospects than the battle of the Somme. The drawback was that campaigning in Flanders depended upon the weather: a rainy season turned its flats into seas of mud, and the third quarter of 1917 was one of the wettest on record.

A preliminary obstacle to be overcome was the Messines-Wytschaete Ridge which dominated Ypres and the whole of the line from which an offensive in Flanders could start. Preparations to deal with it had been in progress since early in the year, and heavy guns had also been mounted on our positions near Nieuport. The plan indeed had been in Haig's mind since November 1916, and even earlier than that Sir Herbert Plumer had been training the Second Army for its task; it had had no serious fighting since the second battle of Ypres in April 1916, the battle of the Somme having been fought by the Fourth and Fifth, and that of Arras by the First and Third. The victory, however, was to be largely a triumph of engineering science. For nearly a year and a half tunnelling had been in progress under the ridge, and at dawn on 7 June nineteen huge mines were exploded beneath the enemy's lines in the greatest artificial eruption that had ever shattered the earth's crust. Ten days' surface bombardment had already obliterated much of the German defences, and it says something for the German moral that any resistance was offered at all when our troops advanced over the ruins of the soil. Messines was cleared by New Zealanders by 7 a.m., Wytschaete fell by noon before Ulstermen and Irish Nationalists fighting side by side, and Welshmen captured Oosttaverne a few hours later. The battle could not have have been better staged to exhibit the co-operation of the British Empire and of mechanical science and human valour. A few days later Australians pushed on to Gapaard and La Potterie in the direction of Warneton, and the Germans withdrew from all their positions in the salient. The danger to Ypres which had threatened for over two years and a half and had cost so much in British blood, had at last been exorcised, and from being an almost forlorn hope of defence the Ypres salient became the base of a promising advance (see Map, p. 288).

Yet the operation hardly equalled in positive achievement its spectacular advertisement. Months, if not years, of meticulous preparation in a sector that had not been seriously disturbed by fighting since 1915 had produced an advance of from two to three miles on a front of less than ten. It was a tactical victory of the most limited character; and the strategical value of the ridge was greatly exaggerated. It had never enabled the Germans to master the Ypres salient, and as the autumn showed, its conquest made no serious gap in the strength of the German defences. Neither on the Belgian coast nor on the Lys which protected Lille did the German line budge one inch in three months' strenuous fighting; and the salient created by that campaign between the coast and the Lys melted like wax in the furnace of the German offensive ten months later. Plumer's success might, however, have led to better things but for the untoward circumstances which hampered the Flanders campaign from the start. One of these was its initial delay; seven weeks elapsed before the conquest of the ridge was followed up, and the causes are still obscure. Probably they were political. Belgium, notwithstanding her passion for liberation, cannot have desired the rest of her soil to be restored in the condition of the Wytschaete ridge—a horror of desolation unfit for man or even for nature's growths; and there seemed little prospect of driving the Germans out except by a succession of ruinous tactical victories. Germany, moreover, was playing up to the Stockholm Conference and suggesting restoration without the accompaniment of ruin; and it was clear that if the Entente was to liberate Belgium, it must be done by other methods and at a lesser cost than the total destruction of her soil.

Preparations for other than limited tactical gains were made during June and July. The Third Army under Byng, who had succeeded Allenby, was put in charge of the whole British line from Arras southwards, and Rawlinson's Fourth and Gough's Fifth Armies were brought up to the coast and Ypres respectively, while a French army under Anthoine was located between Gough's and the Belgians on the Yser. The Germans were alarmed by Rawlinson's appearance on the coast, and anticipated a possible attack in that sector by delivering a defensive blow on 10 July against the bridgehead we held north-east of the Yser between Nieuport and the coast. We were apparently not prepared: two battalions were wiped out, part of the bridgehead was lost, and Rawlinson's Fourth Army remained a more or less passive spectator of the subsequent campaign. Its own chance of making a thrust had gone, and it waited in vain for the thrust elsewhere to turn the gate the Germans had barred between the Yser floods and the sea.

This reverse did not tend to expedite the campaign, and when it was finally launched on 31 July the weather interposed a third and fatal impediment. The first attack was successful enough. The French under Anthoine took Het Saas, Steenstrat, and Bixschoote; on their right Gough's Fifth seized Pilckem, St. Julien, Frezenberg, Verlorenhoek, Westhoek, and Hooge, the banks of the Steenbeck and the woods on the Menin road; and below that blood-stained highway Plumer's Second took Klein Zillebeke, Hollebeke, and Basse Ville on the Lys. It was, however, Von Arnim's plan to hold his front lines lightly and rely upon counter-attacks, and before the end of the day we had lost St. Julien, the north-east bank of the Steenbeck, and Westhoek. The key of the German position on the Menin road also remained in Von Arnim's hands, and no means had been found of dealing with his new and effective "pill-boxes." These were concrete huts with walls three feet thick, so sunk in the ground that their existence, or at least their importance, had escaped observation. They were too solid for Tanks to charge or for field guns to batter, and too small for accurate shelling by heavy artillery. Yet, crammed with machine guns and skilfully écheloned in the fighting zone, they presented a fatal bar to the rapid advance on which the success of our plan of campaign depended. Even so, it was not Von Arnim's skill and resource that finally ruined our prospects. Before night fell on the 31st the rain descended in torrents. For four days it continued, and even when it ceased it was followed by darkness worthier of November than of August. The field of battle was turned into a maze of lakes and bogs with endless shell-holes filled and hidden by the muddy water. The bombardment had broken the banks and dammed the streams, and rivers, instead of flowing, overflowed. Tanks became useless, and for men and animals there was as much risk of being drowned as shot.

The Germans were not immune from the weather; their counter-attacks were impeded, and their low-lying pillboxes were often traps for death by drowning. But enforced stagnation inevitably helps the defence, especially when time is the essence of success for the attack. Troops were pouring back from the Russian front; winter was coming to postpone until the spring any hopes of a drier soil, and the land lay low in Belgium all the way beyond the puny ridge of Passchendaele. It would have been wiser to accept the facts of the situation; but bull-dog tenacity has its defects, and that national totem is more remarkable for its persistence than for its discernment. On 3 August we regained St. Julien, on the 10th Westhoek, and on the 16th resumed the general movement. It made little appreciable progress on the right or in the centre, but on the left the French advanced from the Yser canal towards the Martjevaart, and our men took Wijdendrift and Langemarck. For the rest of the month it rained, and it was not till 20 September that the conditions were considered good enough for an attempt on the limited objectives to which our ambition was now reduced. It achieved better success than on 16 August, and the advance made along both sides of the Menin road was through difficult woods; but it nowhere exceeded a mile, the fighting was fearfully costly, and Veldhoek and Zevencote were the only two hamlets gained. On the 26th Haig struck again with similar results: Zonnebeke was captured, the woods cleared up to the outskirts of Reutel, and another advance made on the Menin road.

Fierce German counter-attacks were repulsed during the next few days, and on 4 October our offensive was resumed. Once more the weather played us false, but without the usual effect, and substantial progress was made all along the front. Part of Poelcapelle was taken, Grafenstafel fell into our hands, at Broodeseinde the Australians got a footing on the Passchendaele ridge, Reutel was captured, and Polderhoek château, the hinge of the German position, was stormed—only to be lost and retaken more than once before it was finally left in German possession. The next attack was designed to broaden our salient to the north between the Yser and the Houthulst Forest. It was fixed for 9 October, and rain fell as usual on the 7th and 8th. But once more it failed to stop our advance. The French and the British left between them captured St. Janshoek, Mangelaare, Veldhoek, Koekuit, and the remains ol Poelcapelle, and the Canadians made a further advance on the Passchendaele ridge by way of Nieuemolen and Keerselaarhoek. Another attack on 12 October was countermanded because of the rain, but the painful progress was resumed on 22-26 October. On the 27th the Belgians and French pushed on as far as the Blankaart Lake and the Houthulst Forest, taking Luyghem, Merckem, Kippe, and Aschoop, and on the 30th the Canadians forced their way into the outskirts of Passchendaele. Its capture was completed on 6 November and supplemented in the following days by an advance a few hundred yards along the road towards Staden.

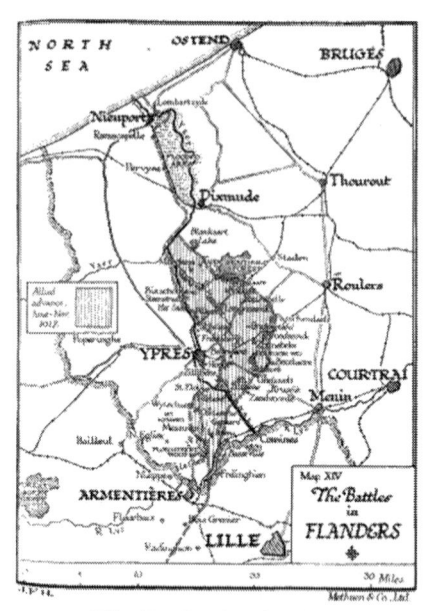

The Battles In Flanders

At last the agony came to an end. The campaign was a monument of endurance on the part of the troops engaged, and of obstinacy on the part of their commanders. The misrepresentation of the results achieved in the published communiqués provoked remonstrances from officers in the field, and apparent indifference to the losses involved roused the anger of the Australians—and other troops—against their generals. Among his own men Sir Hubert Gough lost more repute in the Flanders campaign than he did in his later retreat from St. Quentin. It was the costliest of all British advances, and cut the sorriest figure in respect of its strategical results. We had advanced somewhat less than five miles in over three months, and had gained a ridge about fifty feet higher than our original line at Ypres. The strategical gains were negligible, and as an incident in the war of attrition, the campaign cost us far more than it did the Germans. They could hardly have desired a better prelude to their coming offensive on the West than this wastage of first-class British troops. Aided by the weather, Von Arnim had succeeded in his design of yielding the minimum of ground for the maximum of British losses, and the Flanders campaign was to us what Verdun had been to the Germans.

There was a more satisfactory proportion of gains to losses in the more limited operations which characterized Pétain's substitution for Nivelle as French commander-in-chief. After Nivelle's comprehensive disappointment on the Chemin des Dames and Moronvillers heights in April, Pétain restricted the field of his attacks and took ample time to prepare them. It was not until August that the first was launched, and for a sphere of action Pétain reverted once more to Verdun. The victories of October and December 1916 were commonly represented as having recovered all that the Germans had won in the spring of that year; in fact they were confined to the right bank of the Meuse. No attempt had been made to wrest from the enemy his gains to the left of the river; and his line ran in August 1917 precisely where it had run twelve months before, a German gain at the Col de Pommerieux on 28 June having been recovered by the French on 17 July. Pétain was, however, a past-master in the art of limited offensives; his aims were less ambitious than those which Nivelle or even Haig had set before themselves, but he achieved them with scientific precision and without the devastating losses which had attended the larger and less successful projects. The terrain he selected was less affected by the vagaries of the weather, and either he was better served by his meteorological experts or was singularly favoured by fortune. His main object was not the tactical gains he secured, but the restoration of the confidence of French soldiers in their offensive capacity which had been severely shaken in April. During June and July they had been mainly engaged in repelling German attacks on the Chemin des Dames, though Gouraud, who succeeded Anthoine in the Champagne command, secured some valuable local gains on the Moronvillers heights.

The attack at Verdun was entrusted to Guillaumat, and his bombardment began on 17 August. The Germans anticipated an offensive on the left bank of the Meuse, but not the extension which Guillaumat had planned on the right bank as well. The weather was as fair at Verdun as it was foul in Flanders, and while Haig's men floundered in seas of mud, the worst against which Pétain's had to contend was clouds of dust. Their artillery had destroyed the German defences on Mort Homme, and when the infantry advanced on the 20th they carried it, the Avocourt wood, the Bois de Cumières, and the Bois des Corbeaux, in a few hours with little loss. Simultaneously on the right bank of the river they captured Talou Hill, Champneuville, Mormont farm, and part of the Bois des Fosses. On the following day the Cote de l'Oie and Regnéville fell on the left bank, and Samogneux on the right. On the 24th the French took Camard wood and Hill 304 and advanced to the south bank of the Forges brook, which remained their line until the American attack in October 1918, while further progress was made east of the Meuse on the 25th until the outskirts of Beaumont were reached. A fortnight later another slight advance was made between Beaumont and Ornes, and on both banks of the Meuse the line was at length restored to almost its position before the great German offensive of 21 February 1916. But Brabant-sur-Meuse, Haumont, Beaumont, and Ornes remained in German hands, and no attempt had been made to recover the line the French had then held on the road to Étain (see Map, p. 194). Verdun might now have been thought quite secure but for the fact that equal success on the Chemin des Dames in October did not save it from the Germans seven months later.

This second of Pétain's limited offensives was carried out by Maistre and led to a more extended German retirement. But the attack was only on a four miles' front eastward from Laffaux in the angle made by the German retreat in the spring between the Forest of St. Gobain and the Chemin des Dames (see Map, p. 67). It was preceded by a week's intense bombardment which, as at Verdun, destroyed the German defences; and although it was made in fog and rain the high ground did not suffer like Flanders from the effects, and the French attack was immediately and completely successful. Allemant, Vaudesson, Malmaison, and Chavignon, with 8000 prisoners, were taken on 23 October, and by the 27th the French had captured Pinon, Pargny, and Filain, and pressed through the Pinon forest to the banks of the Ailette and the Oise and Aisne canal. This advance turned the line which the Germans still held on the Chemin des Dames, and they found it untenable. On 2 November they withdrew down the slopes to the north bank of the Ailette, and the French occupied without resistance Courteçon, Cerny, Allies, and Chevreux, which they had vainly with thousands of casualties endeavoured to seize in April and May. The Chemin des Dames was now really won, and the contrast was pointed between the two methods and their success. Pétain's more limited offensive secured the greater strategical gains. But the French rather forgot the ease with which they finally won the Chemin des Dames in the losses their earlier efforts had cost them, and were to lose it once more because they thought it impregnable.

In spite of experience the Entente was slow in learning not to underestimate the military resourcefulness of the Germans, and Pétain's victories, coupled with the failure of the Germans to react, provoked a jubilation which was not justified. To the German Higher Command the loss of a few square miles at Verdun and the Chemin des Dames was a mere matter of detail compared with the ambitious strategy it now had in mind. Situated as the Germans were between two fronts, they were quicker to grasp the significance of events in the East than were Western Powers; and the collapse of Russia had already inspired Ludendorff with the idea and hopes of a final and victorious offensive on the West in the spring of 1918. It must come soon, or the advent of American armies would make it too late. Even the French and British forces were serious enough, and an obvious preliminary would be to weaken the enemy line in France by a diversion. The Germans knew enough about Italy to be confident that a staggering blow would not be difficult to deal, and that if it were dealt it would compel France and Great Britain to go to the rescue of their distressful ally. Italy had all along been inviting some such blow by her concentration on Trieste, a divergent quest after booty which led away from the enemy's vital parts; for the Adriatic was already closed to the Central Empires by the French and British fleets, and the fall of Trieste, however gratifying it might be to Irredentists—though Trieste had never belonged to Italy or Italian rulers—would have no appreciable effect upon the issue of the war. That quest, moreover, left the Italian flank, upon which its front entirely depended, exposed at Caporetto. It was not, indeed, probable that the Italians would have advanced very far had they set their faces towards Vienna; but if their front had faced in that direction, they would not have provoked the disastrous collapse of their whole campaign in the last week of October 1917. Hitherto Russia had prevented the Central Empires from seizing the opportunity which Italy offered; but the triumph of Bolshevism removed that protection and also supplied the Germans with political means for advancing their military ends. Not a few Italian troops had succumbed to propaganda, and when the crisis came they imitated Russian examples in a way which provoked Cadorna—in a censored message—to speak of their "naked treason."

The valour which other Italian troops had shown during the summer and their success on the Bainsizza plateau had not prepared Italy or her Allies for so great a reversal of fortune in the autumn. The attempt after the fall of Gorizia in August 1916 to force a way to Trieste had been checked by the formidable bastion of Mount Hermada, and in May 1917 Cadorna turned to the other great obstacle to his eastward advance, the Selva di Ternova with its peaks M. San Gabriele and M. San Daniele, which dominated the valley of the Vippacco and the railway to Trieste running along it. But these peaks could not be taken by a frontal attack, and an effort was made to outflank them from the north by seizing the Bainsizza plateau and the Chiapovano valley behind it. A week from 14 May was spent in the preliminary operation of extending the Italian hold over the east bank of the Isonzo above and below Plava, and in seizing the westerly edge of the Bainsizza plateau with its two peaks, M. Kuk and M. Vodice. This advance over difficult country required great endurance and valour, but it fell short of anticipations, and on the 23rd Cadorna struck another blow in the direction of the Hermada. Hudi Log, Jamiano, Flondar, and San Giovanni were captured, and for a moment a footing was gained in Kostanjevica and on the lower slopes of Hermada; but an Austrian counter-attack on 5 June recovered Flondar and drove the Italians off the Hermada.

It was clear that Italy unaided could not achieve even the limited objective of Trieste on which she had set her heart, and in July Cadorna appealed for help to Great Britain and France. The former sent and the latter promised some batteries of artillery, but no infantry could be spared in view of our commitment to the Flanders campaign and of French caution after the failure on the Chemin des Dames; and in August Cadorna resumed his attack alone. It was dictated by political rather than military motives; for there was discontent in Italy which the most rigorous censorship could not conceal, and the reference in the Pope's peace note of August to "useless slaughter" evoked serious echoes in a public mind which found inadequate compensation for the meagre and costly results of the Italian campaign in its splendid advertisement by the Italian Government. Italy needed a victory, and Cadorna achieved enough to keep up the illusion of triumphant progress. The bombardment began on 18 August and the infantry attack on the 19th over an extended front of thirty miles from Lom to the north of the Bainsizza plateau to the Hermada and the shores of the Adriatic. Most of the Bainsizza plateau was overrun, Monte Santo at its southern extremity was captured, and the Italians recovered a footing on the Hermada. A terrific and bloody battle was waged early in September for the key-position at M. San Gabriele, but heavy Austrian reinforcements from Russia prevented the Italians from mastering the crest. On the 5th they were again driven back from the Hermada and San Giovanni, while away in the north they failed to take the heights of Lom. This held up their further advance across the Bainsizza plateau, and its eastern half, containing peaks a thousand feet higher than any the Italians had conquered, remained in Austrian hands. No real progress had been made, the partial occupation of the Bainsizza plateau proved useless, the losses had been tremendous, and at the end of September Cadorna reported that his main operations were at an end. Eleven of the sixteen British batteries were recalled, the French were countermanded, and the ball was left at Ludendorff's feet.

He had begun his preparations in August when Otto von Buelow was transferred from the West to the Italian front and given an army composed of six German and seven Austrian divisions. The control of the campaign was taken over by the German Higher Command, and the troops had been trained in the new tactics which were tried by Von Hutier at Riga in the first week in September and were to be used to more serious purpose at Caporetto in October and on the Western front in 1918. Time was of the essence of Ludendorff's strategy; he could not afford, with the American peril in prospect, to prolong the war by fighting in trenches and merely defending the Hindenburg lines. Nor could he even afford that deliberate method of progress favoured by Haig and Pétain, which consisted in rapid advances on limited fronts to limited objectives, or in snail-like movements over wider areas. The strategy which by intense bombardment drove the enemy back a mile or two at the cost of so devastating the ground as to make one's own advance impossible for weeks, could not achieve a decision within the time at Ludendorff's disposal. Some means must be found of reviving the war of movement and repeating in a more decisive form the German march of August 1914. The bombardment of devastation must therefore be sacrificed in the interests of the pursuing troops, and its place be taken by gas shells; and the enemy line must be broken by the superiority of picked battalions and greater concentration of machine guns and other portable weapons. The line once broken, the advantage must be followed up by a series of fresh divisions passing through and beyond the others like successive waves, maintaining the continuity of the flowing tide. The Eastern front was used as a training ground for these new tactics, which served Ludendorff better than any advance into Russia could have done; and they came as a complete surprise at Caporetto.

That was not, indeed, particularly good terrain for the experiment, and in order to hoodwink the Italians more effectively Von Buelow did not select for his attack any sector indicated by the principal Austrian lines of communication. But these defects of Alpine country were counterbalanced by the weak moral of the troops opposed to him. One symptom of Italian instability had been outbreaks during the summer at Turin in which soldiers had fraternized with the rioters, and the mutinous regiments were sent as a penance to that sector of the front which Von Buelow was well-informed enough to select for his offensive. But the nervousness was general: Italians had never yet met German troops in battle, save perhaps in small encounters with diminutive units in Macedonia, and some consternation was created when, about the middle of October, it was ascertained that there were German divisions on the Italian front; and presently popular imagination magnified Von Buelow's thirteen divisions into the combined weight of the Central Empires, with Mackensen at its head as a bogey-man. That was at least a more acceptable explanation than the real one of the disaster which overtook the Italian Army. But it is impossible to gauge with any exactness the extent or effect of German intrigue and Bolshevist propaganda upon the Italian situation. Bolshevist envoys had been received with open arms at Turin, and Orlando, then Minister of the Interior, had refrained on principle from hampering their activities. More singular was the coincidence of Von Buelow's offensive with a Parliamentary crisis which precipitated the fall of the Boselli Ministry.

The German attack began on 24 October amid rain and snow, which never deterred the Germans, and on this occasion even assisted them by increasing the element of surprise. The infected front of the Second Army between Zaga and Auzza broke with such celerity that by dawn of the 25th Von Buelow's men had crossed the Isonzo, scaled Mount Matajur, 5000 feet high, and were pouring across the Italian frontier; and the gains of twenty-nine months were lost in as many hours. Elsewhere Italian troops fought with splendid determination, and the garrison of M. Nero held out for days and died to a man, while their comrades at Caporetto greeted the enemy with white flags, and reserves withheld their assistance. Gallantry to the left and right availed nothing against poltroonery in the centre: the Bainsizza plateau was lost, and the Third Army on the Carso was in dire peril of being cut off from its retreat. Nothing but retreat, and perhaps not even that, was open to the other armies, with the Second in the centre fleeing like a rabble and Von Buelow threatening the left and right in the rear. On the 27th Cividale, on the 28th Gorizia, and on the 29th Udine, twelve miles within the Italian frontier, fell, and Von Buelow had taken 100,000 prisoners and 700 guns. The Third Army escaped by the skin of its teeth, the excellence of its discipline, and the sacrifice of its rearguards and 500 guns at the crossing of the Tagliamento at Latisana on 1 November. Then the rain came down, and no believer in Jupiter Pluvius as a German god could maintain that that river had been turned into a roaring torrent in the interests of the German pursuit.

The Tagliamento could, however, be easily turned from the north, and the Italian retreat continued across the Livenza and the Piave where Cadorna stood on 10 November. The Adige farther south was considered by many to be Italy's real strategic frontier, but the abandonment of the Piave would surrender Venice to the enemy, and Venice was Italy's one naval base in the northern Adriatic. It must be retained, or the Italian Fleet would have to withdraw to Brindisi and leave the Adriatic and Italy's eastern coast open to incursion from Pola. But if the Piave was to be held, the German threat to turn it by a descent from the Alps down either side of the Brenta valley must be defeated; and it was here that the

Caporetto campaign was fought to a standstill in November and December. Fortunately Ludendorff had not been prepared for the magnitude of his own success, and Von Buelow's thirteen divisions had not been cast for the part of destroying the Italian armies. Their object had been twofold, firstly to compel France and Great Britain to weaken their front by sending aid to Italy, and secondly, to secure plunder in the shape of guns, munitions, and corn-growing territory. The Kaiser boasted that his armies had been set up for some time by this Italian success, and Italy's two Allies had no choice but to send divisions to her assistance, the French under Fayolle and the British under Plumer. With that the Germans were content, and although the Austrians continued their efforts to force the Piave and turn its flank down the Brenta valley, Von Buelow's six German divisions took little part in the fighting and were soon with their general sent back to the Western front.

No light task remained for the shattered Italian armies, for the Austrians had been greatly reinvigorated by their success, and continual reinforcements were arriving from the Russian front. Italy had never been a match unaided for her hereditary foes, and the prospect of British and French assistance was needed to stem the torrent of invasion descending from the mountains. The Italians fought well, and politically the nation pulled itself together; but one by one the Austrians captured in November the heights between the Piave and the Brenta which protected the Venetian plain, and it was not until 4 December that the French and British were able to relieve the pressure by taking up their respective quarters on the two cardinal positions of M. Grappa and the Montello. Even so the Austrian advance continued, while a bridgehead was secured across the Piave at Zenson. After a four days' battle on 11-15 December the Austrians reached the limits of their invasion at M. Asolone and M. Tomba on the east, and M. Melago on the west, of the Brenta valley; and before the end of the year the Italians were recovering slopes on M. Asolone and the French those of M. Tomba, while the bridgehead at Zenson was destroyed. Fighting went on well into 1918 without much material change in the situation until Austria was called upon to take her part in the final enemy onslaught in June. Nevertheless the Central Empires had achieved the most brilliant of their strategical triumphs. At slight cost to themselves they had bitten deep into Italian territory, taken a quarter of a million prisoners, 1800 guns, and vast quantities of munitions and stores, and had imposed a greatly increased strain upon the Allies who alone stood between them and victory on that Western front which Ludendorff had selected for the final test of war.

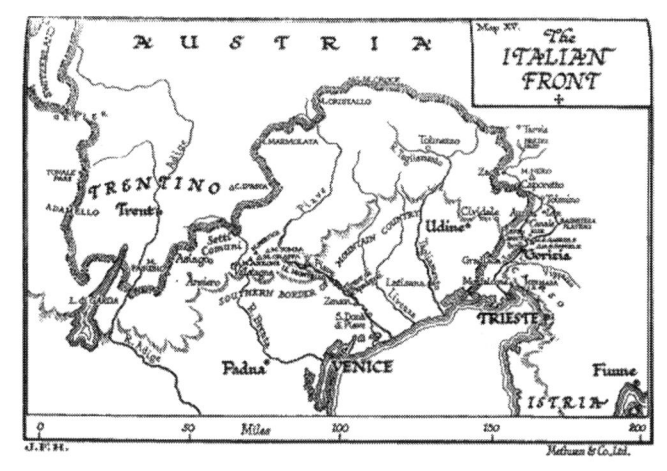

The Italian Front

CHAPTER XVII

THE EVE OF THE FINAL STRUGGLE

Two gleams of light, one of them quickly dimmed and the other distant, relieved the gloom of the last winter of the war. As the Flanders offensive subsided in the mud, Haig was preparing another blow by a different hand in a drier land; and he, too, was working to find an escape from trench-warfare on lines not unlike those of Ludendorff. Both were dissatisfied with the obstacles which intense bombardment, used for initial success, placed in the way of its prosecution; but by one of the ironies of the war, while Ludendorff now relied on the superiority of his human material, Haig looked for success to the greater ingenuity of mechanical contrivance expressed in Tanks. They were under a cloud in Flanders because they could not advance upon mud and water; but on higher ground their improved efficiency and numbers might be used to some effect. The plan adopted contemplated a narrow front but an ambitious objective. It was to break the Hindenburg lines at their nodal point in front of Cambrai. If successful it would disorganize the whole German scheme of defence in the West, and would in any case tend to divert the Germans from their Italian campaign. The objective was not Cambrai itself, but to break through the Hindenburg lines as far as Bourlon and beyond, and then to take them in reverse from Bourlon westwards and northwards to the Sensée and the Scarpe. In other words, it appeared to be an experiment in tactics which might with good fortune develop into a strategical means of achieving from the south of Douai and Lille what the Flanders campaign had failed to secure to the north of them. The German line was thin, and, had it been made of the stuff of the Italian line at Caporetto, Haig might have repeated Ludendorff's unexpected success. There was a third and more sinister explanation of the battle of Cambrai, that it was a practical attempt to answer the gibes in which the Prime Minister had indulged at the tactics of the British Army.

The task was entrusted to the Third Army which had seen little fighting since the battle of Arras died down in the spring, and had been under Sir Julian Byng since Allenby's transference to Egypt. The attack began on 20 November; there was no preliminary bombardment to cut up the ground over which the Tanks, infantry, and cavalry were to advance, and a single gun gave the signal for the start amid a favouring fog and behind a supplementary barrage of smoke which hid the advance from the German guns. The Tanks broke through the wire entanglements and destroyed the nests of machine guns, while the infantry marched forward in their track. By nightfall they had made at points greater progress than on any previous day in the war. Havrincourt, Graincourt, and Anneux— four and a half miles from the morning's front—fell on the left; Ribecourt, Marcoing, Neuf wood, Noyelles, and Masnières in the centre; and La Vacquerie, Bonavis, and Lateau wood on the right. The flies in the ointment of success were a check in front of Flesquières and a serious lack of foresight on the Scheldt canal, where the single bridge was broken at Masnières and the cavalry were held up on a front of several miles. But for the former, Byng might have mastered the vital Bourlon position, and but for the latter have crossed the canal in force, broken the last of the German lines, and taken Rumilly, Crèvecoeur, and possibly Cambrai. For the Germans had been completely surprised and needed two days to bring up any adequate reinforcements. The advance continued at a slower pace on the 21st. Flesquières was taken and then Cantaing and Fontaine-Notre-Dame; but the bid for Bourlon developed into a costly, stubborn, and indecisive struggle for five days while the Germans were being steadily reinforced.

On the right Byng pushed out to Banteux, but the end of our advance on the 29th left us with a rectangular block of territory loosely attached to our original front. The German lines had been breached, but once more it was shown that lines of concrete and wire fortifications do not roll up like lines of mere human material without an amount of pressure which our forces did not permit of applying. The new Government had been at least as deaf as the old to Haig's demands for men, though the use that had been made of reserves in Flanders justified some caution and economy in the supply; and for the success of his major operation Haig had to rely on troops which were too few and had been imperfectly trained. Meanwhile Von Marwitz, the German commander, admitting the British victory, announced his intention of wiping it out, and gathered sixteen fresh divisions to effect his purpose on the 30th. There was ample warning all along the front, but we had not grasped the significance of Von Hutier's tactics at Riga or Von Buelow's at Caporetto, nor had our commanders dreamt that the Germans without our Tanks could follow the example we had just set ourselves and attack without a warning bombardment. Their method was as unexpected as our own, and where it was applied against our right it was almost as successful. From Bonavis south to Vendhuille all our gains were lost, and within an hour and a half the Germans had pierced the line we had held since April and captured Gonnelieu, Villers-Guislain, and Gouzeaucourt. Gouzeaucourt was retaken later in the day, and at Bourlon, where the new tactics were not employed, the gallantry of our troops retained the position. More ground was also recovered next day on our right, and the German counterattack seemed to have been exhausted. But it had left us with an untenable front, and on 4-7 December Haig withdrew from Bourlon and Marcoing to the Flesquières ridge. Out of sixty square miles and fourteen villages captured we retained but sixteen and three respectively, while the Germans had secured seven square miles and two villages held by us before the battle began. The fact that our gains included a seven-mile stretch of the Siegfried line made no appreciable difference to the future course of the war; and we even failed to learn the lesson of our failure. The innate British conservatism, which was counteracted in politics by a democratic suffrage, retained its unchecked supremacy in the British Army; and the German tactics which had robbed us of our gains at Cambrai came no less as a surprise to rob us four months later of things that were much more serious.

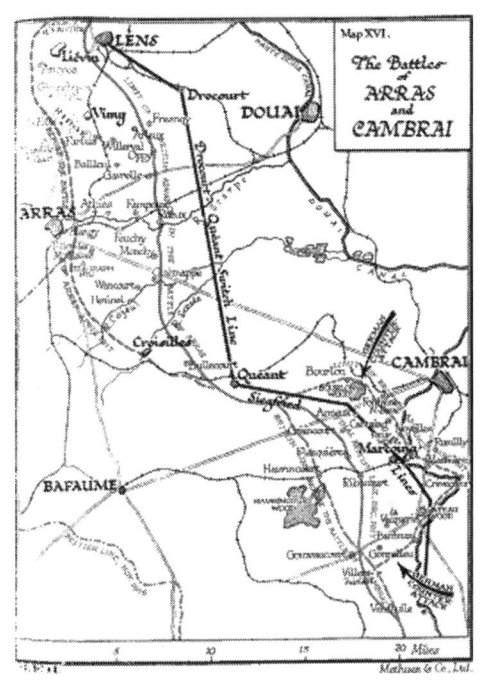

The Battles Of Arras And Cambrai

The light of Byng's success soon died away and left the gloom to be illumined by a far-off flicker in the East. Even here the effects of the Russian collapse dogged or rather prevented our steps and barred our advance from Baghdad; and without Russian co-operation Maude had to think rather of safeguarding his conquests against Falkenhayn's projects from Aleppo than of striking farther from his narrow base into the almost limitless enemy country. On 29 September he pushed forward his defences on the Euphrates by seizing Ramadie and encircling and compelling the surrender of the entire Turkish force. In October he occupied the positions abandoned by the Russians up to the Persian frontier, and early in November drove the Turks out of Tekrit towards Mosul. After destroying the Turkish base we retired; there was now no enemy either on the Tigris or the Euphrates within a hundred miles of Baghdad, and Maude's work had been rounded off. He died suddenly of cholera on the 18th, leaving a reputation second to none in the British Army. His successor, Sir William Marshall, carried on his work by forcing the Turks east of the Tigris back into the Jebel Hamrin mountains in December and then in March 1918, driving them up the Euphrates out of Hit and Khan Baghdadie to within 250 miles of Aleppo. In May he turned to the Tigris, retook Tekrit, expelled the Turks from Jebel Hamrin, Kifri, and Kirkuk, and forced them back across the Lesser Zab to within 90 miles of Mosul. But by that time the public had little attention to spare for Mesopotamia, the Turks had recovered the whole of the Russian conquests in Asia Minor, and had occupied the Caucasus right across to the Caspian Sea. Marshall's efforts had to be diverted north-east to bar the enemy's way through Persia towards India; and the advance on Aleppo was left to the army of Egypt (see Maps, pp. 177, 352).

Allenby succeeded to its command in June 1917, and had the summer in which to prepare his plans. Frontal attacks on Gaza had failed with too serious losses in March and April for their repetition to be risked, especially in view of the care which had since been taken to add to the Turkish forces and to the strength of their defences; and Allenby discovered the key of the Turkish position at Beersheba, nearly thirty miles south-east of Gaza. It was captured on 31 October with the efficient help of the Imperial Camel Corps, and on 2 November the enemy was distracted by a second blow on our extreme left which resulted in the taking of Sheikh Hasan and the outflanking of Gaza between it and the sea. The whole line between Beersheba and Gaza had, however, been elaborately fortified, and it required a week's strenuous fighting to reduce it. Then on 6-7 November our left advanced once more upon Gaza only to find it practically undefended; and by nightfall on the 7th Allenby had pushed ten miles along the coast beyond Gaza. The advance was now rapid in this direction. On the 9th we occupied Ascalon; on the 14th the Turks were driven from the junction where the branch line to Jerusalem joins the main line running down the coastal plain, and the Holy City was cut off from rail-communication with the Turkish base; and on the 16th Jaffa was captured. Allenby then swung round towards the east to threaten Jerusalem from the north, while his right wing pushed up beyond Hebron along the hills of Judæa. He wished to avoid battle near the city, and the Turks made a determined stand to the north-west of it on the Nebi Samwil ridge. By 9 December their resistance was overcome, and Jerusalem was threatened from the north-west by our left and from the south-east by our right. It surrendered on that day, and Allenby made a quiet official entrance on the 11th. He had succeeded where Richard Coeur-de-Lion had failed; Jerusalem, which for 730 years had been in Mohammedan hands, under first the Saracens and then the Turks, passed under Christian control; and there seemed better ground in the twentieth than in the sixteenth century for the Elizabethan's exalted question to his compatriots, "Are we not set upon Mount Zion to give light to all the world?"

The light was somewhat slow to penetrate elsewhere. Even in Palestine it took Allenby months to substantiate his position. By the end of December he had pushed across the El Auja north of Jaffa and taken Ramah, Beitunia, and Bireh, nine miles north of Jerusalem; but Jericho did not fall until 21 February, and little impression was made during the spring upon Mount Ephraim, where the Turks barred the road to Shechem, or on their positions east of the Jordan, although the Turks were increasingly harassed by Arab raids upon the railway leading to Maan and the Hedjaz. Es Salt was captured on 1 May, but succumbed to counter-attacks in which some British guns were captured. The heat of summer put an end to active operations, while the Turkish recovery at the expense of Russia and the German victories in Europe counselled caution, and helped to postpone till the autumn the full fruition of Allenby's strategy. He and Maude had nevertheless made our Eastern campaign the brightest pages in the sombre history of the war in 1917, and the fall of Baghdad and Jerusalem contributed not a little to the collapse of Turkey, which hastened that of the Central Empires. They were not divergent operations because they converged towards the centre, and weakness at the extremities affected the heart of the Turkish Empire. Germany would not have succumbed when she did but for the fate which had overtaken her allies elsewhere than on the Western front. But it was a far cry from these contributory operations to that policy of concentrating on "the vital junction of Muslimieh" which commended itself to excitable critics, and would have left our Western front at the mercy of the most formidable onslaught it ever had to face.

We needed all the comfort we could extract from our Eastern campaigns; for, with a gigantic German offensive threatening the West in 1918, we could be none too sure that we had dealt satisfactorily with the only serious offensive the Germans had undertaken against us in 1917. That had been their unlimited submarine warfare, which had reached its greatest fury in April, when 25 per cent of the vessels leaving British ports failed to return, but continued through, out the year to sap our strength like an open ulcer. The general public knew little of the truth, and was not competent to measure the value of such facts as were placed before it. The Germans' claim to have sunk 9 ½ million tons in the first year of unrestricted warfare was regarded as preposterous, but Sir Eric Geddes himself assessed the British loss at 6 millions.[3] Mr. Lloyd George revealed the fact that we had sunk five German submarines on 17 November, but not the fact that our total bag for December barely exceeded that figure; and on the 13th the First Lord of the Admiralty corrected the optimism of the Premier's figure by declaring that the Germans were building submarines faster than they lost them, while we were losing shipping faster than we built it. He was somewhat more cheerful in his estimate of the situation on 1 February 1918, but on 5 March had to deplore a falling-off in our construction, partly at any rate due to the depletion of man-power in that industry. Some consolation was found in the fact that the proportion of our losses to our total shipping did not greatly exceed that in the last ten years of the Napoleonic wars; but the comparison was illusory, because we were far more dependent upon oversea supplies in 1917 than in 1812, though so far as food was concerned the dependence was greatly relieved in 1918 by the efforts of the Board of Agriculture. A source of greater pride, if not of satisfaction, was the fact that our domestic shortage was due less to the sinking of our ships by German submarines, than to their diversion to the service of our Allies. Not only had the British Navy to defend all the coasts of the Entente by bottling up the German High Seas Fleet, but our mercantile marine had to provide for most of the Allies' transport and provisioning; whereas in the Napoleonic wars we had for long no allies to maintain and could concentrate upon our own requirements. The unparalleled strain of the war was due to the unparalleled extent to which the

---

3   The total British loss in the war was 7,731,212 tons. France came next with 900,000 tons.

British Empire placed its resources at the disposal of less fortunate countries; and fortunately for Powers, which later on complained of American interference, the United States seemed bent in 1918 on bettering our example.

Other incidents of naval warfare than the German submarine campaign added to the public discomposure. On 17 October two German cruisers sank two British destroyers and nine convoyed Norwegian merchant ships between the Shetlands and the Norwegian coast; on 12 December somewhere in the North Sea four German destroyers sank five neutral vessels, four British armed trawlers, and also one of the two British destroyers accompanying them, the other being disabled, while two British trawlers and two neutral vessels were also sunk off the Tyne; and on the 23rd, three British destroyers were mined or torpedoed off the Dutch coast. On the 26th it was announced that Sir Rosslyn Wemyss had succeeded Jellicoe as First Sea Lord, and other changes were made at the Admiralty. But the unpleasant incidents continued. On 14 January 1918 Yarmouth was, after a long immunity from such attacks, once more bombarded by enemy destroyers; on 15 February a British trawler and seven drifters were sunk by similar means in the Straits of Dover; and on the 24th the safe return was announced of the German raider Wolf after a cruise in which she had sunk eleven vessels in the Indian and Pacific Oceans. The extension of submarine warfare to the sinking of hospital ships was more shocking as an exhibition of barbarity than alarming as a proof of naval efficiency, and may even have been designed as a desperate measure to commit Germany beyond recall to the alternative of victory or irredeemable ruin. As an outrage against international morality it was only exceeded by the torpedoing on 6 June of a Dutch vessel on which British delegates were to have gone to The Hague to discuss with Germans the mutual amelioration of the lot of prisoners of war.

Side by side with this brutality at sea there developed a similar offensive in the air. The Zeppelin menace had been almost exorcised in the autumn of 1916 by the effectiveness of explosive bullets fired from aeroplanes which ignited the gas-bags. But on 28 November a solitary aeroplane dropped six bombs on London in full daylight, and thus gave ample warning of what might follow. No adequate steps were, however, taken to meet the danger until in the spring and summer of 1917 it was brought home in a more emphatic form. On 25 May German aeroplanes which had been diverted from their London objective by atmospheric conditions, caused 250 casualties and nearly inflicted serious military damage at Folkestone; and on 13 June the Germans effected their most successful raid by appearing over London shortly before noon and killing 157 and wounding 432 men, women, and children. The object was avowed in the German press by one of the leaders of the expedition to be the demoralization of the civilian population. Its success was due to the lack of counter-preparations; and when the experiment was repeated on 7 July four of the raiders were brought down and the casualties were reduced to 59 killed and 193 injured. After August the daylight aeroplane raids were discontinued, but only to be resumed in moonlight, and on 4 September 11 persons were killed and 62 injured in a London raid at night. These became almost nightly affairs at the end of the month; and while no single aeroplane raid at night caused anything like the loss of life inflicted on 13 June or 7 July, they were sufficiently distracting, though it pleased the patriotic press to pretend that only immigrant aliens, East-End Jews, or at least the poorest of native Britons, sought safety in flight from the risks they involved.

The raids were repeated at irregular intervals, owing to atmospheric conditions, throughout the winter until Whitsunday 19 May, when 44 were killed and 179 injured. Generally they occurred when the moon was nearly full, but on 6 December there was one when it was in its last quarter and on 18 December another when it was only four days old, and on 7 March 20 were killed and 55 injured in a raid on a moonless night. On 19 October these aeroplane raids were varied by a raid on a moonless night by Zeppelins which shut off their engines and drifted across London with a north-west wind, dropping only three bombs but killing 27 and injuring 53 persons. Six of the raiders failed to get home, and this was the last of the Zeppelin so far as London was concerned, though Zeppelin raids were made as late as 12 and 13 March on the north-east coast. Reprisals were adopted as a policy by the British Government in the autumn of 1917, and great store was set upon them in some quarters. But in spite of the vigour with which they were carried out along the Rhine, there is no reason to suppose that our aeroplane raids achieved any greater military effect than that which we had always denied to German raids on England. They certainly did not succeed in curing the Germans of their raiding propensities. That was effected by our improvements in defence, notably in our antiaircraft bullets and "aprons" suspended from balloons; and after Whitsunday, 1918, the Germans concentrated on the French, although they had shown fewer qualms about reprisals. Nor did our supremacy in the air produce the effects which many anticipated on the field of battle. Italian superiority with that arm was of little use at Caporetto, and our superiority did not materially further our advance in Flanders in the autumn of 1917 or retard the German offensive at St. Quentin in the spring of 1918. Aircraft were indispensable as eyes for an army, and to a lesser extent for a navy; but as an independent force they were as limited in their effectiveness as is artillery or cavalry without the fundamental infantry.

The obvious stalemate which marked the situation during the first half of the fourth year of the war imposed upon the belligerents a reconsideration of the political and military means of bringing it to an end. Dissatisfaction was naturally more apparent in Germany during the spring and summer and in Entente countries during the autumn of 1917; and in July the Reichstag passed its famous resolution against annexations and indemnities. Its idea of peace was that Germany should forgo annexations, and the Entente its claims to indemnities; but the chief anxiety of the Reichstag was to make capital for the cause of constitutional reform out of the dissatisfaction with Germany's military situation, and that was immediately improved by the collapse of the last Russian offensive. Bethmann-Hollweg fell for failing to control the Reichstag, but his successor Michaelis was a mere Prussian bureaucrat who only accepted the Reichstag resolution "as he understood it," and the fate of Russia soon made it clear that his understanding of "no annexations and no indemnities" did not preclude the "liberation" of large parts of Russia and their subjection to German influence, nor the insistence upon "guarantees" which would reduce Belgium and Serbia to a similar plight. The Vatican followed the German lead with a peace note in August which revealed no clear distinction between its and the German point of view; and in October, amid subdued celebrations of the fourth *entenary of Luther's Ninety-Five Theses, Count Hertling succeeded Michaelis as Imperial

Chancellor and became the first Roman Catholic minister-president of Prussia since the Reformation.

There was, indeed, a fundamental unity in this apparently discordant combination between the Protestant and the Ultramontane; for the Hohenzollern State and the Roman Catholic Church were both systems organized on that principle of autocracy which was more and more coming out as the underlying issue of the war, and it coincided with the fitness of things that the answer to the Vatican note was returned by the President of the United States. There was, in fact, no basis of accommodation, and any desire for it in Germany disappeared with the temporary improvement in her military prospects. When the failure of our campaign in Flanders was coupled with the Italian disaster at Caporetto and the Bolshevik revolution in Russia, the Reichstag resolution was spurned, constitutional reform was smothered, and the Junkers under Ludendorff's able leadership girded themselves for a final quest of peace by victory with illimitable annexations and indemnities. The Kaiser foreshadowed the coming offensive in the West by proclaiming that the only way to peace was one hewn through the ranks of those who would not make it.

In spite of this brave show, the Entente exhibited a truer confidence by expressing its dissatisfaction not in the form of seeking a compromise with the enemy, but in criticism of the conduct of the war. There had, indeed, been some political hesitation at the time of the Stockholm Conference in the summer when the Russian revolutionists invited socialists of all countries to consider a peace without annexations or indemnities. Even Mr. Lloyd George was subsequently said by his Labour colleague in the Cabinet to have contemplated British participation; and there were legitimate grounds for anxiety lest the officially countenanced if not inspired presence of German socialists at Stockholm might not give them a political advantage over unrepresented Entente countries. But the danger passed away as gleams of returning prosperity in the autumn revealed once more the true mentality of the German Government and exposed the insincerity of its pacific professions; and precipitate pacifism only revealed itself in Great Britain in a cautiously worded but dangerously doubting letter by Lord Lansdowne, published in the "Daily Telegraph" on 29 November. Once more President Wilson expressed, in his message of 4 December, the real mind of

Germany's most sober and serious enemies. He branded German autocracy as "a thing without conscience or honour or capacity for covenanted peace," and declared that peace could only come "when the German people have spokesmen whose word we can believe, and when those spokesmen are ready in the name of their people to accept the common judgment of the nations as to what shall henceforth be the bases of law and of covenant for the life of the world." Our conception of those bases was elaborated in a memorandum adopted by the Labour party later in the month which was substantially accepted by Mr. Lloyd George, after consultation with Mr. Asquith, Viscount Grey, and representatives of the Dominions, on 5 January 1918; and then three days later President Wilson defined the famous Fourteen Points which ultimately became the basis of the peace.

There was more heartburning over the conduct of the war. In France, M. Ribot's Government fell in September and was reconstituted under M. Painlevé. It succumbed in November to the effects of Caporetto, and France, like Italy, had to find a new Prime Minister. Her choice fell upon M. Clémenceau, a vigorous veteran of seventy-six. His supreme quality was an audacity from which friends as well as foes occasionally suffered, and his great service was the war he waged upon the half-hearted and the double-minded of his compatriots. England escaped a change of Ministry, but not without misgivings or the sacrifice of subordinates on account of a situation for which Ministers were equally if not more to blame. There were sweeping changes at the Admiralty, and the mutterings of a Press campaign against Sir William Robertson and Sir Douglas Haig, for which the Prime Minister had given some ground, if not the signal, by his reference to the tactics of the Stone Age. The ultimate cause of his embarrassment lay in the extravagant anticipations he had encouraged of the results to follow from his own accession to power. He had attributed the responsibility for earlier failures to end the war to his predecessors, and on his own line of argument he was himself responsible for the ill-success of 1917. In both cases the reasoning was absurd, and individual Ministers counted for little in the titanic conflict of forces. Mr. Lloyd George suffered from the Russian revolution, but he had a windfall in American intervention; the "Victory Loan" of January would not have saved the Entente from grave financial difficulties had it not been for American assistance; and the war seemed at least as far from an end after a year of the new administration as it seemed when Mr. Lloyd George came in on a promise of speedy success.

Nor was his preparation for the coming crisis marked by greater foresight than the measures of his predecessors. That it was coming in the spring was sufficiently obvious in the autumn; intelligent outsiders predicted in November that there would be a great German offensive in the West, and even drew attention to the unmistakable design of the Germans to weaken our front in France by the Italian diversion. Yet no serious steps were taken to strengthen that front in time. The Prime Minister announced in December that the Russian collapse and Italian defeat imposed fresh obligations on Great Britain, but his legislative proposals for increasing our man-power were postponed till the following session and were quite inadequate in their scope. Meanwhile the British front which was doomed to attack was being weakened by being extended from St. Quentin to Barisis in order to shorten and therefore strengthen the French front which was not the German objective. Steps were, indeed, taken to establish an Allied military council at Versailles; but the unity was more apparent than real, and the council had no authority over the individual governments or their staffs, and each continued to feel responsible and anxious mainly, if not exclusively, for its own particular front. Matters did not improve in the early months of 1918. In January Sir Henry Wilson, our military representative at Versailles, reported his opinion that the impending German offensive would be launched against the British front between St. Quentin and Cambrai. He failed to persuade his French colleagues, and if he convinced his own Government, it failed to act upon his advice. Possibly it felt bound to abide by the collective view, if any was expressed, by the Versailles Council; in that case the collective Council proved less sagacious than the British representative, and on 16 February it was announced that Sir William Robertson had resigned.

Meanwhile, American preparations were being delayed by an exceptional winter and by the inherent and enormous difficulty of converting a vast community inured to peace to the organized purposes of war. In spite of invidious comparisons by superpatriots between British sloth and Transatlantic promptitude,

America took four times as many months as the British had taken weeks to put a hundred thousand men into the firing-line; and the Germans were transferring divisions very much faster from the Eastern to the Western front. The Bolsheviks had relieved them of all anxiety on that score. Immediately after their coup d'etat on 7 November they had issued an invitation to all belligerents to negotiate for peace. The Germans naturally accepted, and on 29 November Count Hertling announced in the Reichstag their readiness to treat. On 3 December Krilenko obtained the surrender at Mohilev of the Russian General Staff, and Dukhonin, his predecessor, was barbarously murdered, though Kornilov escaped. On the 5th an armistice was signed to last till the 17th, and on the 15th a truce for another month. Cossack rebellions under Kaledin and Kornilov broke out on the Don and under Dutoff in the Urals; and Scherbachev collected a mixed anti-Bolshevik force on the borders of the Ukraine. But peace negotiations began between the Germans and Bolsheviks at Brest-Litovsk on the 22nd. The plausible German Foreign Secretary, Von Kühlmann, presided, and Austria was represented by Count Czernin. On the 25th, which was Christmas Day for the Germans but not by the unreformed Russian calendar, Von Kühlmann announced Germany's adhesion to the Russian programme of no annexations and no indemnities on condition that the Entente accepted the same principle; and an adjournment was made until 4 January to wait for its reply.

Before it was received Germany declared that Poland, Lithuania, Courland, and parts of Esthonia and Livonia—i.e. the conquered provinces of Russia—had already expressed their "self-determination" in favour of separation from Russia and protection by Germany; and on 2 January Trotzky indignantly denounced these "hypocritical peace proposals." On the 10th, however, he consented to reopen the discussions at Brest without reference to the Entente, and to recognize the independent status of the Ukraine. He was not yet prepared to accept the German terms, and after the forcible suppression of the Constituent Assembly, which had been elected in the autumn and endeavoured to meet at Petrograd on 18 January, he accused the Germans of demanding "a most monstrous annexation." He was still relying on the result of Bolshevik propaganda in Germany, and the strikes which broke out at the end of the month and the prohibition of the Vorwärts showed that it was not without effect. But their suppression by the Government deprived him of his only weapon, and on 10 February he announced that, while the Bolsheviks refused to sign an unjust peace, the state of war was ended between Germany and Russia. This chaotic suggestion did not commend itself to the Germans, and they took prompt measures to bring Trotzky to a less ambiguous frame of mind. On the 18th they occupied Dvinsk and Lutsk, and before the end of the month they were in Hapsal, Dorpat, Reval, Pskov, and Minsk, and within striking distance of Petrograd (see Map, p. 274). On the 24th the Bolsheviks intimated their willingness to accept the new German terms, far more severe than their original proposals, which included the abandonment of the whole of the Baltic Provinces, Poland, Lithuania, and the Ukraine, and the surrender of Armenia and the Caucasus to the Turks. Peace was signed on these conditions on 2 March, and confirmed by a majority of more than two to one at a congress of Soviets at Moscow on the 14th.

Shameful as this surrender was, the Bolsheviks found some compensation in the domestic triumphs of their party and their creed. Cossack resistance succumbed to their arms and propaganda. Alexeiev, who had succeeded Kaledin in the command of the Cossack forces, was defeated on 13 February; Kaledin committed suicide; and Bolshevik authority spread to the Black Sea, the Caucasus, and all across Siberia. Germany hastened to make a German peace with Finland and the Ukraine, which attempted to sow as many seeds of discord as was possible; but the bourgeois parties with whom they treated had but a slender hold on the countries they professed to represent, and Finland and the Ukraine were soon involved in civil wars in which their Governments were only able to make headway against the Bolshevik Red Guards by the help of German troops. The anarchy suited the Germans except in so far as it detained German forces from the West and impeded those supplies they sought from the Ukraine and farther afield; and by the middle of March they were in Odessa and pushing their outposts and their intrigues towards the Caucasus, the Caspian, and Central Asia. The most pitiable situation was that of Rumania, threatened as she was by the Bolsheviks on account of her monarchy and social order, and by the Central Empires on account of her alliance with the Entente. Completely cut off from those allies, she was compelled in March to sign the humiliating Treaty of Bukarest, which surrendered the Dobrudja, the Carpathian passes, and her supplies of corn and oil to the enemy, while leaving Mackensen in control of her capital and the greater part of the kingdom.

There have been few disasters in modern history comparable with the fall of Russia, and none which shows more vividly that the strength of a State depends not upon the vastness of its territory, the size of its armies, or the skill of its diplomacy, but upon the moral, the education, and contentment of its people. Of all the causes of German success in the war and of suffering to the world at large and little nations in particular, none was more potent than the blindness of Russian governments which had refused in the past to set their house in order, and by reform in time to prepare their people for the storm. Russia herself suffered most, but all her allies felt in different degrees the effects of her collapse, and in the spring of 1918 it was to put the general cause of civilization to its severest test upon the Western front. The perilous situation in which the Entente stood in March was due to other reasons than the conduct of the British War Cabinet, but there was a grim irony in its somewhat novel publication of an official advertisement and report of its preparations for victory on the eve of the greatest defeat encountered by British arms during the war.

CHAPTER XVIII

THE LAST GERMAN OFFENSIVE

More than two years before the war concluded a junior officer from the front remarked that he could not say when, but knew where, it would end, and that was not far from our existing lines in France and Flanders. As time wore on and the limitations of strategy under modern conditions grew clearer, the war assumed more and more the aspect of a single battle varying in its intensity from season to season and place to place, but constant in its continuity and in its absorption of the principal forces of the main belligerents. The unity of control culminating in unity of command which marked the closing stages of the war was therefore not so much a brilliant improvisation on the part of any general or statesman as the inevitable lesult of the history of the war; and the misfortunes of the Entente did more than its foresight to bring that consummation to pass. In the main it was due to the gradual weakening and then the collapse of Russia, which first involved the ruin of Serbia and Rumania and the wrecking of our Balkan plans, and finally dissolved the Eastern front. There could have been no unity of command had Russia remained our predominant military partner; and even in the West it never comprised the Italian Army, which retained its independence of action or inaction until the end of the war. But in 1918 the Italian front sank into a subordination almost as marked as the Russian, and the war that counted grew to a climax where it had started between the Alps and the Belgian coast. There were concentrated the French and British armies which Germany must beat before she could win peace; and there came in the American hosts which turned the scale against her.

With or without unity of command, the two million American troops which ultimately crossed the Atlantic would have given us the victory; and the view that the war was won by unity of command is as superficial as the view that the battle of St. Quentin was lost by the lack of it. That battle was lost because the Versailles Council, acting on the advice of its French rather than its British members, misjudged the direction of the coming German offensive and misplaced the reserves at its disposal. Unless, which may be the case, Foch was at variance with his French colleagues on this point, his appointment as generalissimo at any earlier stage would not have affected the results of these mistakes. Unity of command might, indeed, have led to an even more extensive weakening of the threatened British front in order to make absolutely secure that French front which the French were convinced was the German objective, and a demand was made for a further British extension beyond Barisis, but was successfully resisted at the Versailles Council before the unity of command had been established. That does not absolve the British Cabinet from its complicity in the blunder. It was equally responsible to the British people for British lives whether it was acting on its own initiative or on the mistaken advice of an ally; and there were also sins of omission of its own. Not only had it been advised by Sir Henry Wilson that the German offensive would come on the British front, but it had been warned that if it came where it was anticipated, that front, thin as it was, could not be expected to hold unless reinforcements, for which repeated requests were made, were dispatched. Remonstrances fell on deaf ears, although there were nearly 300,000 troops available in England. Mr. Lloyd George afterwards called them first-class troops, and congratulated himself and the country on the fact that they were transported to France within a fortnight after the damage had been done. For this, the most culpable Cabinet failure in the war, others besides the Cabinet were to blame; and it must be ascribed ultimately to the national sins of intellectual sloth and ignorance. Those hundreds of thousands of troops, shown to be superfluous in England by their subsequent dispatch to France, were kept at home because persons in authority believed they were needed to do the work of the British Navy and defend our shores against a German invasion. Throughout the war loquacious generals, who were not employed at the front, harped at home on that alarm, supremely ignorant of and indifferent to the unbroken experience of the world and the teaching of naval history, that military invasion across an uncommanded sea is an utter impossibility. But there was no one to teach the War Cabinet this elementary truth, and least of all could it be taught by the eminent lawyer and the able railway director whom Mr. Lloyd George successively appointed to the Admiralty to represent the ripest naval wisdom of mankind. It remained for the nation to pay the cost.

The great attack was launched at dawn on Thursday, 21 March, precisely against that sector of the British front indicated by Sir Henry Wilson two months before; and Gough's Fifth Army, which held it lightly with fourteen divisions against forty, was doomed to defeat by the failure of both the British and the French Governments to provide adequate reserves which existed in abundance both in England and in the rear of the French line, and by the fact that Haig was more anxious about his shallow front in Flanders and Pétain about his in Champagne than either was about the Somme. Generally speaking, the British front grew thinner from north to south until between the Somme and the Oise Gough had less than a bayonet a yard; and Ludendorff knew it. He also made skilful use of the advantage which the possession of the interior lines gave him in the St. Quentin-St. Gobain salient. He could mass his troops in that angle without revealing which side he meant to attack, and thus neutralize that observation which superiority in aircraft gave his antagonists. It was not so much that he brought up his forces at night and concealed them in woods, which are leafless in March, as that the bodily eye of the airmen failed to discern his intentions. He had other incidental advantages: that laborious spade-work which characterized the German Army was not a distinguishing feature of either the British or the French; and both the trenches we took over south of St. Quentin and our own to the north of it left a good deal to be desired in their defensive strength, while the great bridgehead under construction to protect the Somme south of Péronne had not been completed. The Allied advance had been slow, but since 1916 a confident conviction possessed the Allied armies that they would only move in a forward direction. Ludendorff was also able to withdraw his six divisions and many Austrian batteries from the Italian front, assured that no Italian offensive need be feared; and his tactics came as a surprise in spite of the practical warnings given at Caporetto and Cambrai. They were based not so much upon superiority of numbers as upon superiority of the selected troops to the average of the forces opposed; and success depended less upon the weight than upon the sharpness of the weapon used for the blow. Hindenburg liked a hammer; Ludendorff chose an axe with which to cleave the enemy front. When it was cleft, inferior metal might be used to widen the gap between the French and British armies and drive the latter to the coast while the former was being crushed.

The German offensive was facilitated by the abnormally dry season, which reduced the strength of the water-defences of the British right, and a dense fog favoured the attack on our forward positions. The Germans got their infantry across the Oise canal north of La Fère without being noticed, and many of our outposts were surrounded before it was known that the attack had begun, although a brief bombardment by gas and other shells had drenched our line and areas miles behind it all along the front (see Map, p. 338). The forward zone resisted heroically, but by noon the Germans were through it west of La Fère and were in our battle-zone north of St. Quentin at Ronssoy. Between these two extremes of Gough's front they reached in the afternoon Maissemy, north of St. Quentin, and the line Essigny-Benay south of it. Farther north less progress had been made against Byng's Third Army, but the Germans had reached St. Leger in their effort to thrust a wedge between Arras and Cambrai, and many villages had been captured. The prospect was gloomy for the morrow, since, although the Germans had already used sixty-four divisions they were prepared to throw in fresh ones each succeeding day, and it would be several days before reinforcements could reach the Somme either from our reserves in Flanders or the French reserves in Champagne.

The Germans made comparatively little headway on the 22nd against the Third Army; but Gough's last reserves were thrown in without stopping the German advance on our right, and the meagre French division which Fayolle was able to send across the Oise could not dam the torrent. At night the enemy had penetrated our third defensive position, and Gough ordered a retreat to the unfinished bridgehead on the Somme. Byng's right had to conform to this movement, which did not stop east of the Somme; for on the 23rd the Germans had crossed the river south-east of

Ham, more than a dozen miles from their starting-point, and the Péronne bridgehead had to be abandoned. Even on the west bank Gough's right was thus endangered, and his left was threatened by a German attempt to break a gap north of Péronne between his army and Byng's Third. This effort on the Somme, where it runs due west from Péronne to Amiens, now became the chief and most promising objective of the German strategy. The link between our two armies was extremely fragile, and misunderstandings arose between the two staffs. Fortunately the worst disaster was averted by Byng's timely withdrawal from Monchy, which disconcerted and postponed the German attack on Arras.

On Sunday the 24th the task of the British was threefold—to stem with French assistance the German advance on our right between the Somme and the Oise, to hold the line of the river from Ham northwards to Péronne, and to repel the German thrust between the Third and Fifth Armies north of the river bend. They were partially successful in the first two tasks, but north of the Somme the Germans got into Combles and the Third Army had to make a big retreat, surrendering Bapaume and nearly all the painful gains of the 1916 Somme campaign. The Germans renewed the attack with great energy on the 25th, and the British were unable to hold them up on their improvised lines. Before night they were ordered to take their stand on the old Ancre defences. This movement exposed the left flank of Gough's forces on the Somme; his front had also been driven in by German attacks across the river, while his right had been forced back beyond Guiscard, Noyon, and Nesle. Fissures began to appear on the broken front; there was something very like a gap between the French and British near Roye, and another between Byng's Fourth and Fifth Corps across the Ancre, besides that between his and Gough's armies. Byng was the first to re-establish his line, partly because reinforcements from the north reached him first. Early on the 26th the Germans had broken through our old line between Beaumont-Hamel and Hébuterne and taken Colincamps, where they had not been since 1914; but in the afternoon they were driven out again, and the recovery was permanent. Here at least the German advance had reached its limit, and there was some significance in the fact that here on that afternoon the British whippet Tanks first appeared in battle.

Gough was not so happy. He had begun to collect a miscellaneous force, like that which stopped the final German thrust at Ypres on 31 October 1914, consisting of all sorts of combatant and non-combatant details, to check the German rush on the Somme; but threats on his left, right, and front compelled him to retreat to a line running south from Bray and behind that held by the French before the battle of the Somme. Still the Germans advanced towards Montdidier, seeking to break through between Gough's right and the French, who had been driven off south-west of Roye. But the worst of the danger was north on the Somme, where Byng's orders were misunderstood and his extreme right, instead of holding the line Albert-Bray to protect Gough's left, fell back five miles to Sailly-le-Sec. The result was that on the 27th the Germans were able to cross the Somme behind Gough's left at Chipilly and compel his retreat to a line running from Bouzencourt S.E. to Rosières. There Gough's centre stoutly maintained itself during the day; but to the south the Germans drove the French out of Lassigny and Montdidier and seemed in a fair way to break the liaison between the Allies, while north of the Somme the Germans had got into Albert and Aveluy wood.

Nevertheless the clouds were beginning to lighten. The violence of the German attack was exhausting to the attackers; their communications now lay across the devastated area, and rain soon came to clog their movements. Their front of attack was, moreover, being steadily narrowed from fifty to twenty miles. The French had forced the Germans to leave the Oise after Noyon, and while their advance continued it did so with a lengthening flank no longer protected by the river. Unless Von Hutier to the south or Von Buelow to the north could break these containing and solidifying barriers, the front of the German attack would be reduced to a hopeless point before it got to Amiens. The attempt was naturally made against Arras by Von Buelow's comparatively unwearied army, and on the 28th he resumed his frustrated attack of the 23rd. This time the Germans had no fog to help them, and their troops assembling for the attack were decimated by our artillery. Nowhere did they succeed in piercing the battle zone, and a second attack in the afternoon fared no better. This was the decisive failure of the German offensive, and north of the Somme our front was now secure. South of it the Germans made some further progress on that day. The Rosières salient had to be abandoned to the Germans pushing south of it across the Somme, and a retreat made to the angle of the Luce and Avre rivers. Fayolle also was driven back to the Avre, but by counter-attacks north and south of Montdidier he prevented the enemy from debouching from that city.

The situation continued grave and the fighting severe for the next few days, but retreat and pursuit had merged into a battle on a line with take as well as give. The French front was extended up to the Luce and an extemporized Fourth Army replaced the weary remnants of the Fifth. More important was the appointment of Foch as commander-in-chief on the 25th after a conference at Doullens between Haig and Pétain, Lord Milner and Clémenceau, though it cannot have had much effect upon the operations which checked the German advance by the end of March. On 4 April Von Hutier made a final attempt to reach Amiens, and drove the Allies out of the angle of the Luce and Avre and from the west bank of the latter back to a line running west of Castel, Mailly-Raineval, Sauvillers, Cantigny, and Mesnil St. Georges. But farther the Germans could not advance either north or south of the Somme, though away to the east the French had to evacuate the sharp salient between the Oise from La Fère to Chauny and the St. Gobain forest, and to fall back behind the Aillette. The first act in the great German offensive had failed in its strategical object of breaking the Allied line, but it had achieved incomparably more than any Allied offensive in the war; and the only advances to compare with it were the German invasion of France and Belgium in 1914 and of Russia in 1915. The Germans claimed by 4 April 90,000 prisoners and 1300 guns, and the Fifth Army had been practically destroyed. It was the most formidable offensive in the history of the world, and four times as many divisions were launched against the British in March 1918 as against the French at Verdun in 1916.

But it did not exhaust the German effort. There were other acts to follow, and the second opened on 9 April, immediately after the curtain had been rung down on the first. No second offensive could, however, approach in magnitude the original plan. The Germans excelled in forethought and in methodical preparation for which ample time was needed. They had had it in the winter, and had staked their hopes upon the success of their throw in March. Now they had to improvise, and their second thoughts were second best. There were, indeed, signs of indecision in Ludendorff's later moves. Possibly he regarded the Flanders offensive in April and the attack on the Chemin des Dames in May as diversions merely intended to draw reserves away from the Amiens front and facilitate a resumption of his original design with better chance of success. Certainly those offensives were begun with limited forces, and probably succeeded beyond his expectations. But the attack on the Amiens front was never seriously resumed in spite of the success of Ludendorff's diversions; and the remainder of the campaign, so far as German initiative was concerned, resolved itself after April into an effort to repeat with more success against the French Army offensives which had failed to dispose of the British. There can hardly have been much hope in Ludendorff's mind of decisive victory in a strategy which after April left the British front almost immune from attack, while American reinforcements were pouring in at the rate of hundreds of thousands a month. But the responsibility of continuing the war under such conditions and deluding the German people with false confidence was so serious that no admission is likely to be forthcoming yet awhile of the real intentions and thoughts of the German General Staff during the summer of 1918. The truth no doubt is that Ludendorff had only a choice between a confession of failure which was bound to ruin the Government and the class he represented, and a desperate effort to make what he could out of the military situation; and he preferred gambling, so long as he had anything with which to play, to an immediate confession of bankruptcy.

For a time he had the luck which lures the gambler on, and the scene of his second act was skilfully chosen. Before 21 March Haig had kept his line better manned north than south of Arras, and the reasons which made him anxious for the defence of his northern sector counselled Ludendorff to attack it when the defeat of the Fifth Army had compelled the British commander to divert ten divisions from the north and supply their place with the weary survivors of the battle of St. Quentin. He had little room to spare between his front and the sea, and a break-through, far less extensive than that which had been effected in March, would give the Germans the coast of the Straits of Dover, enable them to bombard the Kentish shore, hamper the port of London, and perhaps reach it with long-range guns like those with which they had occasionally bombarded

Paris since 23 March. These annoyances would have been serious; but the British public paid itself a very bad compliment when it seemed to assume that the distant bombardment of London would have an effect upon the war disproportionate to that of Paris; and the notion that an impetus which carried the Germans to Calais would transport them across the Channel was merely another illustration of the comprehensive popular ignorance of the meaning of sea-power. Nieuport or Dunkirk might have taken the place of Bruges as a submarine base without greatly enhancing the success of that campaign; and Haig chose rightly when, having to weaken his northern front, he risked a sector north instead of south of La Bassée and the Vimy Ridge. Defeat to the north of those points, even though it cost us the coast as far as Calais, would not entail retreat from the Artois hills between Arras and Gris Nez or threaten our liaison with the French which had been Ludendorff's first objective. The material comments on the value of his second thoughts were that the Germans might have had the Channel ports for the asking in 1914 but did not think them worth it, and that in April 1918 Ludendorff employed but nine divisions in his initial effort to break through. Probably his real ambition was merely to shorten his line and, in view of the possible resumption of his offensive in front of Amiens, to provide against a British counter-attack on the sensitive German position along the Belgian coast.

Anticipating some such attack, Haig had deemed it wise to relieve the two Portuguese divisions which held part of the front between the Lys and La Bassée of their arduous responsibility; but he could only replace them by weary British divisions, and the change had only been half effected when, on 9 April, Ludendorff s attack began after the usual bombardment with gas and high-explosive on the 8th. The Portuguese broke fairly soon, the British flanks on either side were turned, and the whole centre had gone in a few hours. By night the Germans had captured Fleurbaix, Laventie, Neuve Chapelle, Richebourg, and Lacouture, and were on the Lys from Bac St. Maur almost as far as Lestrem. But the key-position at Givenchy was splendidly held by the 55th Division, which set a permanent limit to the German success and prevented it from obtaining anything like the dimensions of the March offensive. It continued, however, to develop on the north. On the 10th Bois Grenier fell, Armentières was evacuated, and the Germans poured across the Lys, taking Estaires, Steenwerck, and Ploegstreet and threatening the Messines ridge. That, too, followed on the 11th, while farther south the Germans secured Neuf Berquin and Lestrem. On the 12th they got into Merris and Merville and advanced to the La Bassée canal, threatening to cross it and outflank Béthune on the north-west. Here, however, they were held up in front of Robecq, between the canal and the forest of Nieppe, and turned to exploit their advantage farther north. Their advance here was slower, but by the 16th they had mastered Wytschaete, Wulverghem, Neuve Eglise, Bailleul, and Meteren, and were facing the line of hills running from Mt. Kemmel to the Mt. des Cats.

British and French reinforcements were now arriving in considerable numbers, and Ludendorff would have been prudent to rest on his laurels. He had made a pronounced bulge in our line, had diverted forces from other sectors of the defence, and compelled us to evacuate our dearly-purchased gains of the Flanders campaign in the preceding autumn. On the other hand, he had lengthened instead of shortening his own line, he had achieved no strategical object, and his troops were left in a salient which invited attack. Unless he could win the heights from Mt. Kemmel to Mt. des Cats, which commanded the country to the coast, he would be in a worse situation for defence than he was before. He was thus driven to prolong the effort, pour fresh divisions into the battle, and convert a diversion into a major operation. Doubtless popular visions of the Channel ports and the bombardment of London reinforced the sounder military reasons for persistence. There were three obvious lines of attack—on the Belgian front north of Ypres, on the Kemmel range, now held partly by French troops, and on Béthune. The first was defeated on the 17th by a brilliant Belgian resistance, and the third was repulsed on the 18th before Hinges and at Givenchy; but the second was longer delayed and more stubbornly pushed.

The effort began with an intense bombardment on the 25th, and a few hours later the Germans had captured the village and hill of Kemmel; our forces were driven back to a line running in front of Dickebusch lake, La Clytte, the Scherpenberg, and Locre. Mt. Kemmel had been regarded as the key to the position, and it looked as though the range would fall. But Kemmel was an isolated height, and the Germans were beaten in the valleys which separated it from the Scherpenberg. Their attacks reached a climax on the 29th, and after some partial success were everywhere defeated. Local fighting continued spasmodically till late in May, but it was clear that Ludendorff's second offensive had come to an end like his first. Its extension had also ruined the chance of successfully resuming the attack in front of Amiens. On 23 April the Germans attacked just south of the Somme and captured Villers-Bretonneux, but it was promptly retaken on the following day; and in the struggle along that line in May we advanced as well as improved our position. The Germans had fought their last offensive against the British front and had failed; and when after a four weeks' pause they resumed their attacks, they were directed against the French.

During the interval the British public had time to reflect upon the disaster and its effects. They were brought home by a new military service Bill extending the liability to all men under fifty-one and bringing Ireland within its scope. Panic had as much to do with these proposals as forethought. The raising of the military age was calculated to weaken our industrial more than to strengthen our military power; and the extension to Ireland handed that country over to Sinn Fein and necessitated the diversion thither of large British forces, which might otherwise have been sent to the front, without producing a single Irish conscript. The proposal was, indeed, so foolish that its authors made no attempt to carry it out. Wiser was the speedy dispatch to France of 300,000 superfluous troops who had been kept in England by nothing better than an ignorant fear of invasion. But it was the amazing rapidity with which the United States responded to Mr. Lloyd George's anxious appeals that saved the Government from the effects of its own blunders and reduced its military service Act to a measure for the infliction of gratuitous hardship. In April nearly 120,000 American troops landed in Europe, over 220,000 in May, and 275,000 in June. On 2 July President Wilson announced that over a million had sailed; that number was doubled before the summer ended, and in July General Smuts was anticipating the possible presence in France of an American army as large as the British and French combined.

The need for so colossal a force did not arise, but in April the position of his Government as well as the military situation agitated the Prime Minister and gave wildness to his words as well as to his actions. Apart from the casualties, we had lost 1000 guns, 4000 machine guns, 200,000 rifles, 70,000 tons of ammunition, and 250 million rounds of small ammunition, and 200 tanks. Circumstances wore a different complexion from the roseate hues of the early months of 1917, and Mr. Lloyd George could not escape the kind of blame he had heaped upon his predecessors. He sought to evade it in his speech at the reassembling of Parliament on the 9th by shifting the responsibility for the disaster partly on to M. Clémenceau as the principal author of the unfortunate extension of the British line, and partly on to the commander of the Fifth Army. The latter at least could not reply, and the unfairness of the attack provoked much ill-feeling in the army and elsewhere; it found expression in a letter from Major-General Maurice, lately Director of Military Operations, which was published on 7 May and challenged the accuracy of ministerial statements. His charges were so serious that the Government at once proposed a judicial inquiry. Mr. Asquith committed the tactical error of moving instead for a parliamentary committee. The Government naturally treated his motion as a vote of censure, and escaped all investigation on the ostensible plea that it preferred a different method from that proposed by Mr. Asquith. The House of Commons by 293 to 106 votes expressed its apparent satisfaction with that "ex parte statement from the Prime Minister himself" which "The Times"—then his strongest supporter in the Press—had the day before said could not dispose of a charge which "unless and until it is impartially investigated and disproved, will profoundly shake the public confidence in every statement made from the Treasury Bench." It was not, however, with the honour of ministers that the House was mainly concerned. Members were in that mood, which occurs at times in every nation's history, in which questions of morals seem irrelevant or unimportant; and what they wanted was not the truth but a plausible excuse for shirking inquiry and refusing to add a political to the military crisis. Conscious of their own responsibility for the Government, they were impatient of any discussion which might reveal unpleasant facts to their constituents or military information to the enemy.

It is difficult also not to trace a political motive, if not in the attacks on Zeebrugge and Ostend, at least in the contrast between the enormous publicity they received and the silence which shrouded the more normal but not less important or heroic work of the British Navy. The plans, indeed, had been prepared and sanctioned by Jellicoe before he left office some months earlier; but many plans have long to wait the ministerial word, and the naval operations of 23 April were as timely for political as for military reasons. The military objective was to block the submarine and destroyer exits from Zeebrugge and Ostend, both of which were connected by canals with Bruges; and an operation of that kind against the elaborately fortified Belgian coast required favourable weather conditions as well us the highest courage. The plan at Ostend was simply to sink ships in the waterway; at Zeebrugge there were also to be diversions in the form of a landing on the protecting mole and the blowing up of the viaduct which connected it with the shore. Success was only possible if mist and smoke-clouds added to the concealment of night, and those conditions depended upon the wind. They seemed favourable on the night of 22-23 April, but a quarter of an hour before the Vindictive reached the mole, a south-west breeze dispersed the smoke-clouds and precipitated a torrent of shell-fire from the German batteries. In spite of it the landing party got on to the mole and systematically destroyed its works, while a submarine loaded with explosives was run under the viaduct and exploded. Meanwhile, the blocking ships were sunk at the mouth of the canal, and the survivors of their crews were picked up and got away in the Vindictive and her consorts. At Ostend the blocking ships had to sink outside the centre of the waterway; but the effort was repeated with better success by the Vindictive on the night of 9-10 May. Even Count Reventlow described these affairs as "damned plucky," but added that they were nothing more. The further attacks on the Belgian coast which were commonly expected did not come, and the operations had no appreciable effect upon the land campaign. But they hampered the German submarine campaign to some extent; and if they demonstrated once more that sea-power is limited to the sea, they also showed that on the sea German power had become a negligible quantity. That fact was, indeed, being proved in a more effective though less heroic fashion, by the safe transport of hundreds of thousands of American troops across the Atlantic; but possibly public opinion needed the more spectacular demonstration, and it certainly showed that the spirit of British seamen was unaffected by the tremors of politicians.

Politicians appeared, indeed, to be more nervous after the crisis had passed than they were before it arose, although their alarms did not greatly affect the incurable sang-froid of the British public; and the way in which the middle-aged shouldered the unnecessary burdens imposed upon them by the improvidence of their Government, was as exemplary as the eagerness with which youth had volunteered early in the war. Their acceptance of the new obligations had its value in stimulating America to dispatch her hundreds of thousands of troops more fit for active service; and few, if any, of the elderly English recruits saw any fighting. Ludendorff's plans had already gone astray when he failed in March and April to break the liaison between the French and British armies; and his subsequent operations were ineffective attempts to prepare the ground for a final offensive which he was never allowed to begin. It would have been doomed to miscarry in any case, for his preliminaries exhausted the forces intended for the final effort, and the battles in Flanders had enhanced the failure of his original design. He took four weeks to prepare for a second subsidiary operation, and hoped to achieve a better success against the French than he had against the British. He had the advantage of taking them unawares, and on the eve of his offensive a French journal proclaimed that it would be another blow at the British front because the Germans knew that the French line was impregnable. Popular opinion in France had attributed German success at St. Quentin and in Flanders to British incompetence or cowardice, and British troops had even been hissed in the streets of Paris. The attack on the Chemin des Dames was to modify this opinion, although some tactless Frenchmen announced that reserves sent up to the British sector, which alone stood its ground, were going "au secours des Anglais."

Ludendorff's object was to widen his front towards Paris, for the lure of the capital had already diverted him from his original plan of breaking the liaison between the French and British armies in front of Amiens. That Paris was his objective in May, and not the diversion of troops from the critical junction with a view to resuming that attack, seems clear from the fact that his next blow in June was struck between Montdidier and Noyon. The Chemin des Dames would have been impregnable if properly held, but Ludendorff s information was not at fault, and the possession of the interior lines gave him the same advantage as in March of striking either right against the British or left against the French. He struck early on 27 May and achieved the most rapid advance of the war on the Western front. The line from Soissons to Reims was held by only eight divisions, four French and four British—one of these in reserve—and in a few hours the French had lost all their gains since October 1914 and were back again behind the Aisne. The British divisions, although they had been sent there to recruit after their hard work in March and April, made a better fight, and maintained themselves in their second positions all the day. But the French retreat had uncovered the British left flank, and in the evening they had to withdraw to the Aisne. By that time the French were nearer the Vesle than the Aisne, and on the 28th they were driven well south of the latter river. On the 29th the Germans broadened their front by taking Soissons, and on the 30th the apex of the salient they had made had reached the Marne between Château-Thierry and Dormans. For three days they had advanced at the rate of ten miles a day, capturing some 40,000 prisoners and 400 guns. From that date the pace slackened. The Germans did not attempt to cross the Marne, but endeavoured to widen their salient by pushing east behind Reims and west across the Soissons-Château-Thierry road. They had little success in the former direction, but in the latter they gradually pressed back the French to an irregular line which ran from Fontenoy on the Aisne southwards along the Savières river across the Ourcq, and then turned eastwards down the Clignon and reached the Marne below Château-Thierry. American troops, who had on the 27th marked their advent into battle by capturing and holding Cantigny, a critical point on the Montdidier front, now took up an equally crucial position south-west of Château-Therry and drove the Germans back on 4-5 June, while on the 6th British troops recaptured Bligny south-west of Reims.

The French themselves defeated on the 5th a German attempt to cross the Oise at Lagache south of Noyon, which was intended to link up the German offensive on the Aisne with their next attack farther west. This was launched on the 9th between Montdidier and Noyon, and its purpose was to push southwards and envelop the French defences and forces in the forests of Compiègne and

Villers-Cotterets which had stopped the German westward advance on Paris between the Aisne and the Marne. It was a dangerous threat, but this time Foch was prepared. The attack was, indeed, a matter of common anticipation, and its adoption suggested that Ludendorff was getting to the end of his expedients. The Americans at Cantigny set a western, and the French success at Lagache an eastern limit to its front; and thus confined it advanced no more than six miles in four days. The French left stood firm and a brilliant counter-attack by Mangin on the German right flank between Rubescourt and St. Maur on the 11th determined its failure, although Foch was compelled to evacuate the salient which the German advance had created in the French line east of the Oise between Ribecourt and Mt. de Choisy. Hoping that this attack had diverted French forces from the defence of the forest of Villers-Cotterets, the Germans then renewed their push along the Aisne, but were promptly checked; and no better success attended their effort on the 18th to encircle Reims still farther east.

For the moment German trust in success had to repose upon the secondary efforts of her Austrian ally on the Piave, although no German troops could now be spared to give much substance to the expectation. That front had been quiescent since the winter, but a good deal had been done to strengthen it, and the Italians were doubtless well advised to stand behind their lines rather than risk an offensive until Austria was practically hors de combat. Austria herself had little stomach for the fight. Her domestic situation was deplorable; parliamentary government had been suspended; and nearly half the population of the Empire was in veiled or open revolt. Hundreds of thousands of Czecho-Slovaks and Jugo-Slavs had joined the enemy, and some were stiffening the Piave front. But German demands were inexorable, and it was hoped that German tactics would supply the place of German troops. There were two battles in the offensive which began on 15 June, one in the mountains, the object of which was to turn the whole Italian front on the Piave, and the other a frontal attack across that river between the Montello, the pivot of the mountain and river fronts, and the sea. The first was the more promising, but achieved the less success. That front was partly held by French and British troops, and the insignificant advance which the Austrians made on the 15th was stopped on the following day. The attack on the Piave was at first more fortunate; a good deal of the Montello was taken, a serious impression was made on the Italian right wing at San Donà di Piave, and fourteen new bridges and nearly 100,000 Austrian troops were thrown across the river. Fortune came to the rescue of the Italians, and torrents of rain flooded the Piave and broke ten of the Austrian bridges. On the 18th the counter-attack began, and by a brilliant dash of soldiers and sailors the Austrian left was turned on the 21st. On the 22nd a general retreat across the river was ordered; it was skilfully carried out, and the Austrians escaped with singularly slight losses considering their precarious position. Their offensive had been an utter failure, but Diaz did not think it prudent to follow up his success with an advance across the river.

The Austrian misadventure was a meagre morsel with which to fill the gap between the latest German offensives and the crowning mercy for which the German public had been led to look; and as the precious summer weeks flew by uneasiness must have filled any German minds that were capable of discerning the realities of the situation. But the wish is father to most men's thoughts, and unpleasant facts which were not concealed by the censor were sedulously ignored or explained away. "Foch's reserves" became a jesting synonym on German lips for something which did not exist, and it was the daily exercise of journalistic wisdom to show that American armies which could not swim or fly would be prevented by German submarines from crossing the Atlantic. Ludendorff was not so blind, and had he been a patriotic statesman instead of a Junker general he would have sought to make terms while he might do so with advantage. But it is the nemesis of militarism that it never can make a peace which is tolerable to its enemies, and Ludendorff had no choice but to persist with an offensive which had become a desperate gamble. His efforts since the end of May had profited him little; he had used up most of the divisions intended for a final resumption of his attack on the Franco-British liaison; and after more than a month's delay he could only launch his last bolt against an eccentric and subsidiary objective. Foiled in front of Amiens and Paris, he turned to Reims; but there was nothing in the previous history of the war on the Western front to suggest that, even were his last offensive as successful as his first, it would bring him within measurable distance of the victory he needed. The Marne might be crossed and the railway to Nancy and

Verdun cut, as they had been in 1914, but the further advance for which he could hope from his attack on Reims would bring him no nearer to Paris, to breaking the Entente connexion, or to damming that fatal flow of American reinforcements which was providing Foch with as many reserves a month as Germany could recruit in a year.

The fateful attack began at 4 a.m. on 15 July after four hours of artillery preparation. Its object was to encircle the Montagne de Reims, the chief bastion of the line of communications between Paris and the eastern front on the Meuse, and to extend the German hold on the Marne from Dormans as far as Châlons. There were two converging attacks, one on the twenty-six miles of front which Gouraud held east of Reims between Prunay and Massiges, and the other on a twenty-two mile line south-west of Reims between Vrigny and Fossoy on the Marne above Château-Thierry. For each attack Ludendorff used fifteen divisions, with others in reserve. On both fronts he found Foch prepared to counter the tactics which had been so successful in the earlier stages of the offensive. The first line was lightly held, and the Germans were shaken by a skilfully arranged bombardment as they crossed the zone between it and the real French defences. Upon these in Champagne they made no impression whatever. Prunay, Prosnes, Auberive, and Tahure were yielded at first, but recovered by counter-attacks; the French lost no guns, and their casualties were insignificant. Gouraud more than anyone else had frustrated Ludendorff's last offensive. South-west of Reims the Germans were rather more successful. They pushed across the Marne to a depth of some three miles between Mezy and Dormans, and in three days advanced up it past Châtillon towards Épernay as far as Rueil. Similar progress was made eastwards on the line between the Marne and Vrigny. But the gate-posts were firmly held at Fossoy with American assistance, and at Vrigny with that of the British and Italian divisions which under Berthelot did some of their best fighting in the war. By the evening of the 17th the Entente forces were successfully counter-attacking all along the line, and at dawn on the 18th Foch delivered the blow which converted the German advance into a retreat, and began a triumphal progress which did not stop until four months later the enemy sued for peace.

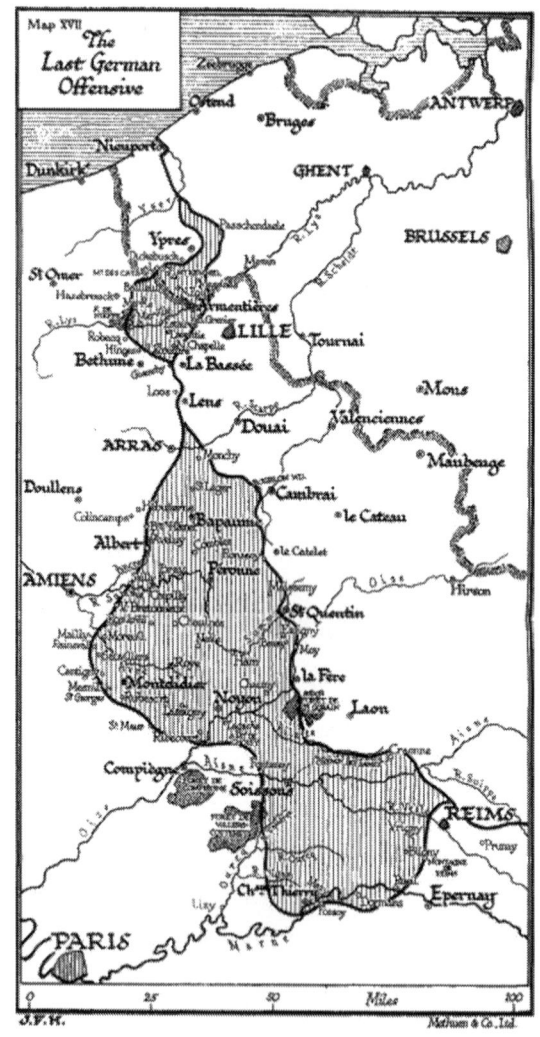

The Last German Offensive

CHAPTER XIX

THE VICTORY OF THE ENTENTE

There were a few people in England who had some inkling on 18 July that it might prove a turning-point in history. Foch's simple piety had led him into what was almost an indiscretion; he had asked for the special prayers of the faithful, the request had spread to conventual schools in England, and by the 16th it was guessed by those who knew the fact that a special effort was in contemplation. But his great counter-attack owed its importance to what had gone before and what was to follow; and victory was due to more complex and comprehensive causes than the valour of the troops engaged upon the Marne or even the strategy of Foch. Greater efforts were made at other times on both sides than during the last fortnight of July 1918, and the destruction of the salient the Germans had made since 27 May was merely the last ounce which turned the balance of power and the scales of victory. There were many ounces in the total weight, and the pride of each belligerent points to the different contributions which it made. To the Americans their divisions at Château-Thierry seem the decisive factor, to the French it was Foch's genius. The British point to the fact that the greatest weight of German force was still in front of Amiens and not on the Marne, and an Italian prince has declared that it was Italy who won the war on 24 October; while Ludendorff has maintained that American troops counted for little, and that the crucial factor was the revolutionary propaganda which had begun to undermine the moral of German troops as early as 1916. None of these partial explanations contain more than an element of truth, and a more comprehensive view is suggested by the likeness of Germany to the "one-hoss shay" of Oliver Wendell Holmes' ballad, a vehicle so skilfully compacted of durable materials that each part lasted exactly as long as every other, and that the whole eventually crumbled into a heap of dust in a single moment. German resources were vastly inferior to those which were slowly mobilized against her, but she organized them with such skill that they resisted the wear and tear of the war for a period to which some observers could discern no end. The strength of materials is, however, limited, and no organization can make them last for ever. The German armies began to give on 18 July, and the decay went on increasing because she had not the means with which to make repairs. The wonder is not that the machine broke down, but that it bore so great a strain for so prolonged a time. The Germans could not command success because they defied the conscience of mankind, but from the military point of view they certainly deserved it.

In spite of Ludendorff's attempt, natural in a Junker, to debit revolution with his failure, it was American reinforcements which turned the scale. Few of them were as yet in the battle line, and there was no great disparity between the opposing forces on the front. But the mobilized strength of the Allies was growing to three times that of their enemies. Foch had an inexhaustible reservoir which enabled him to take risks which Ludendorff could not afford, and gave him a freedom of action which no Entente general had yet possessed. The extent of his command and his resources released him from the bonds of limited offensives. He could crush the German salient on the Marne without prejudicing the prospects of his plans at Amiens and Arras, in Champagne or at Verdun; and fear imposed on Ludendorff the dire alternative of weakening his powers of resistance to future attacks elsewhere, or starving his immediate defence. His plans for resuming the offensive at Amiens had already been ruined by the drain of his attacks on the Aisne and on the Marne; and his defensive prospects on the Amiens front were now to be jeopardized in the effort to avoid disaster in the salient he had rashly made along the Marne. For, except on the assumption that Foch was unable to attack on the western flank of that salient between Soissons and Château-Thierry, the German thrust deeper across the Marne was a wild adventure (see Map, p. 362).

Foch, however, had made his plan and his preparations. Concealed by the forests of Compiègne and Villers-Cotterets, he had assembled in the angle between the Oise and Marne reserves of which the Germans denied the existence. From the Aisne near Fontenoy southwards to the Ourcq Mangin commanded an army containing the pick of French colonial troops; and thence to the Marne Degoutte had another which included five American divisions. Before them ran the German flank weakly guarding the line of communications with the German front on the Marne. Led by a vast fleet of French "mosquito" Tanks something like the British "whippets," the French early on the 18th broke through the German defences on a front of twenty-seven miles and advanced from two to five miles towards the Soissons-Château-Thierry road.[4] Mangin reached the Montagne de Paris within two miles of Soissons, and Berzy-le-Sec on the banks of the Crise, while south of the Ourcq Dégoutte got to Neuilly St. Front and the Americans captured Courchamps, Torcy, and Belleau. Sixteen thousand prisoners and fifty guns were captured, but there was nothing like a German rout. They stubbornly defended their main line of communications for days until the bulk of their forces could get away; and they evacuated the salient slowly and in good order. There was, of course, no further hope for them south of the Marne, and by the 20th they had regained the northern bank without very serious loss; it was not till the 22nd that the Allies crossed the river in pursuit. On the 21st the Germans had abandoned Château-Thierry and the Soissons road as far as the Ourcq, but north of that river they held the road for a week, and Buzancy was not captured till the 29th. By the 23rd Berthelot was making progress on the other side of the salient, and the German centre had to relinquish the forest of Fère and Oulchy on the 25th. On the 31st the Americans drove in their centre at Seringes, and on 2 August the French forced their way

---

4   An error made in the British réchauffée of the French official news represented Mangin as having advanced eight miles on the 18th to the Crise on a stretch of five miles east of Buzancy. It was a mistake of nord-öuest for nord-est which was never corrected, and has got into most of the summaries and histories of the war, although it makes the subsequent French fighting in that area unintelligible. The history of the German evacuation of the salient would have been very different had the French got east of Buzancy on the 18th. As a matter of fact, it took them eleven days to secure the territory credited to them by this error on the 18th.

into Soissons. By the 3rd the Germans had been driven across the Vesle and the salient had been flattened out.

Even the best of the critics in the French press had little idea of what was to follow. The Germans' latest offensive had been foiled, and they had lost the more adventurous part of their gains in May; but Foch's success was regarded as merely a promising detail, and men discussed the locality of Rupprecht's counter-attack. But the signs of the times did not point in that direction. On 4 July Americans and Australians fighting side by side had captured Hamel below the Somme. On the 19th the British had recaptured Meteren at the apex of the German salient across the Lys, and Merris fell on the 30th. On the 23rd the French between Amiens and Montdidier had advanced two miles on a four-mile front and captured Mailly-Raineval, Sauvillers, and Aubvillers in the Avre valley; and on 4 August the Germans withdrew from all their ground to the west of that river. Two days later they attacked and recovered some of the ground they had recently lost near Morlancourt. Both the withdrawal and the attack were signs of nervous anticipation, but neither broke the force of the blow which Haig struck on 8 August on a twenty-mile front from Morlancourt to La Neuville on the Avre. The troops were mostly British under Rawlinson with a French army under Débeney cooperating on his right. Their success first opened the eyes of the public to the change in the situation on the front, and on Ludendorff's own testimony deprived him of his last vestige of hope. It was no weak flank that was attacked, but the sector of the front that was most strongly held by German armies. The drive was straight along the great road from Amiens to St. Quentin on which the Germans had made their westward thrust in March; and the first day saw them seven miles back at Framerville. To the south they lost Moreuil, Mezières, Demuin, Cayeux, and Caix, and to the north Morcourt, Cerisy, and Chipilly, while 7000 prisoners and 100 guns had been taken by 3 p.m. On the 9th those totals had risen to 24,000 prisoners and over 200 guns, while the British continued their advance to Rosières and Lihons, and the French to Arvillers and Beaufort. Nor was that all; for south of Débeney, Humbert interposed with another attack between Montdidier and the Oise. By the 11th the Germans had lost to the French most of their gains in the June offensive, and to the British further ground between Albert and the Somme.

On that day the German line ran in front of Bray, Chaulnes, Roye, and Lassigny to Ribecourt on the Oise. They had brought up reinforcements to make a stand on that shortened front, and they stubbornly contested the French advance on the Lassigny massif. But its capture was completed by the 15th, and the number of prisoners had risen to 33,000 and of captured guns to over 600. The Germans were also being pushed out of their salient on the Lys, where Merville fell on the 19th; and Mangin was forcing his way forward in the angle of the Aisne and the Oise between Soissons and Noyon. But the next great blow was struck north of the Somme by Byng between Albert and Arras. The Germans sought to evade its force by a timely retreat across the Ancre, and there was no such rapid advance as marked the first day of Rawlinson's offensive south of the Somme. But it was less interrupted, and day by day some progress was made. Byng's attack on the 21st was along a ten-mile front north of the Ancre, and the first day gave him Beaucourt, Achiet-le-Petit, Bucquoy, Courcelles, and Moyenneville. On the 22nd he extended his attack from Albert to the Somme and advanced two miles to a line between Albert and Bray. On the 23rd his left was advanced another couple of miles to Boiry, Ervillers, Bihucourt, and Irles, while on his right the Australians captured Bray. The German centre at Thiepval was thus outflanked on both sides; it gave way on the 24th, and Byng pushed on to the outskirts of Bapaume. Bapaume held out for five days longer while Byng pushed his right forward along the Somme towards Péronne, and extended his left attack northwards beyond the Scarpe.

Byng's addition to the pressure the Germans had to bear from north of the Scarpe to south of the Oise imposed upon them a retreat as extensive as that of March and April 1917; but now they could not make it at their leisure. On the 27th they had to abandon the line south of the Somme on which they had stood since the 15th, when they recovered stability after Rawlinson's offensive. Roye was relinquished that day and Chaulnes and Nesle on the 28th. Noyon followed on the 29th, partly in sympathy with the northern withdrawal and partly owing to Humbert's pressure on the north-western bank of the Oise, but also because it had been outflanked to the south by Mangin's advance between the Oise and the Aisne. Beginning on the 17th with an attack on a ten-mile front between Tracy-le-Val and Vingre he had steadily pushed on until by the 23rd his left flank held the Oise as far as its junction with the Ailette and his front faced the latter canalized river as far as Guny. By the 29th he was across the Ailette and threatening to turn the whole German position south of the Somme at Chauny. Bapaume fell on the same day as Noyon, and it soon became clear that the Somme would not protect the Germans any more than it had done the British in March. For on the 31st the Australians stormed Mount St. Quentin the bulwark of Péronne, and Péronne itself fell into their hands on 1 September. Simultaneously Byng's army pressed forward from Bapaume to the Canal du Nord which runs north from Péronne.

But this after all was ground we had held for a year in 1917-18, and the Hindenburg lines might serve the Germans as well in 1918-19. More significant of the coming debacle was the success of Horne's First Army, which now intervened and extended the line of Byng's attack. Already Canadian and British troops, by the capture of Vis-en-Artois on the 27th, Boiry on the 28th, and Haucourt on the 30th, had seized ground which the Germans had held since 1914; and on 2 September in one of the outstanding actions of the campaign Canadian and British troops broke the Drocourt-Quéant line on a front of six miles between Étaing and Cagnicourt. On that day the British army fired 943,857 shells. No single engagement caused greater depression in Germany, but the impression was somewhat fallacious; for behind this sector of the Hindenburg lines were waterways which were even worse obstacles to our tanks, and although the Canadians pressed on to L'Écluse, Écourt, and Rumancourt, they were hemmed in on their left by the Sensée and in front by the Canal du Nord, which protected Douai to the north and Cambrai to the east. The advance here was checked for some weeks, but it went steadily on along other fronts. The salient on the Lys was melting away: Bailleul fell on 30 August, Mount Kemmel on the 31st, and Ploegstreet wood on 4 September. Lens was evacuated on the 3rd. South-west of Cambrai the British were approaching their old lines, and east of the Somme the Germans were retreating to St. Quentin. On the 6th the French took Ham and Chauny, and on the 9th they were once more across the Crozat canal. Mangin was pushing his way towards the St. Gobain massif, and French and American troops were driving the Germans back from the Vesle across the Aisne. It looked as though winter might come with the line of battle much where it was before the German offensive began in March.

But the latter half of September gave a novel aspect to affairs. A great deal, no doubt, was due to Foch and the unity of command; but that unity did not extend to the East nor account for the debacle of Bulgaria and Turkey. It was, however, partly responsible for the extension of our offensive in France beyond the limits of the year before and for the timing of the American attack in the Woevre. In the hour of his Allies' need President Wilson had consented to the brigading of American with French and British troops, and to the employment of American divisions as supports for French and British generals. But with the American Army growing equal in size to the French and the British and acquiring an independent skill in war, there could be no hesitation about an American command on an equal footing with the armies of Haig and Pétain; and to the Americans under General Pershing had been allotted the right wing of the Allied front, the British forming the left and the French the centre. Some critics talked of Pershing's armies being used as the spear-head of an invasion of Germany through Lorraine; but this would have been an eccentric operation, and there were obvious reasons for restoring Lorraine, if possible, to France undevastated by war. North rather than east was the natural direction for an American advance, and in either case an indispensable preliminary was to eliminate that strange wedge at St. Mihiel which the Germans had held since September 1914. The task would also be a useful apprenticeship for an independent American command. The attack was made on both sides of the salient on 12 September, but the principal drive was from the south on a twelve miles' front between Bouconville and Regnieville. Part of the defending force was Austrian, but the whole salient collapsed under the blow; 15,000 prisoners and 200 guns were captured, and a new front was formed on a straight line from Fresnes to Pont-à-Mousson. The strategic purpose was to free the American flank and communications in view of a bigger offensive northwards, and on the 15th Austria and Germany began their overtures for peace, to which President Wilson at once returned an unsympathetic reply.

Anticipations as well as achievements counselled that diplomatic move, and Austria in particular had reason to fear developments on other fronts than the French. The Balkans had been quiescent during the summer, although the Greeks had on 30 May given an earnest of a better future by a victory at Skra di Legen, west of the Vardar, in which they captured 1500 Bulgarian and German prisoners, and on 18 June the fall of the pro-German Radoslavoff Ministry indicated that Ferdinand wished to present a less Teutonic appearance to the world. Italy, too, in pursuance of her assumed protectorate over Albania, thought in July that the time had come to assert herself, and with the assistance of some French troops began an advance towards Elbasan. The Austrians were taken by surprise, Berat was captured, and the country overrun as far as the Semeni and beyond the Devoli. The effort was not apparently serious; in August the Austrians returned to the attack, recaptured Berat, and drove the Italians back to their starting-point in a retreat boldly described in an Italian official pronouncement as of no military importance. It helped to discourage Italy from taking an active part in the coming offensive against Bulgaria, but political motives were the principal reason for quiescence. Italy had a tenderness for Bulgaria arising out of her antipathy to Jugo-Slavs and Greeks, and while proclaiming that Austria must be totally destroyed, she exclaimed against the wickedness and folly of imposing on Bulgaria a second Peace of Brest-Litovsk (see Map, p. 151).

The success of the Balkan campaign did not, however, suffer much from the lack of Italian push. Franchet d'Esperey was commander-in-chief, and he was ably seconded by the Serbian Marshal Mishitch. The Serbian Army was the spear-head of the attack, and it had with it an equally eager and effective force of Jugo-Slavs; with them cooperated the French on the west of the Vardar, while east of it were the Greeks and the British with the arduous and somewhat thankless task of facing the impregnable Demir Kapu defile and Belashitza range. The offensive began on 15 September, and the main attack was on the Dobropolie ridge in the angle between the Tcherna and Vardar rivers. On the first day the Bulgarian line was broken on a front of sixteen miles, an advance was made of five, and 4000 prisoners and 30 guns were taken. On the morrow the front widened to twenty-two miles, and the advance increased to twelve; and within a week the Serbians had cleared the angle between the rivers and crossed the Tcherna on their left and the Vardar above Demir Kapu on their right. This cut the main Bulgarian communications with Prilep on the west and Doiran on the east, and compelled a general retreat along a hundred miles of front. On the 23rd the French occupied Prilep; on the 25th the Serbians captured Veles and Ishtip and pressed on towards Uskub, while their cavalry were at Kotchana almost on the Bulgarian frontier. The British, whose first attacks had been checked, had actually crossed the border at Kosturino on the road between Doiran and Strumnitza. Bulgaria had put her whole trust in the strength of her front, and with it she collapsed. An armistice was requested on the 25th, and Franchet d'Esperey's terms were accepted on the 30th. It was the most dramatic overthrow in the war, and within a fortnight the whole situation in the Balkans was transformed. The Serbians were bitterly disappointed at having to stay their avenging hands when almost at the gates of Sofia; but the elimination of Bulgaria made the recovery of their country a triumphal procession varied by the occasional defeat of Austrian rearguards. On 12 October they and their allies occupied Nish, and a week later they had reached the Danube. Nor was Serbia alone concerned. Austria had relied upon the Bulgarian buckler, and when it crumpled her entire hold not only on the Balkans but over her own Jugo-Slav subjects in Bosnia, Dalmatia, and Carinthia was relaxed. A general uprising of Jugo-Slavs in favour of union under the Serbian crown more than doubled the size of that kingdom which Austria had begun the war to crush.

Nor did this exhaust the effects of Bulgaria's capitulation. The terms of the armistice included the Allied occupation of Bulgarian railways, and this brought their military front up to the borders of Rumania on the north and of Turkey on the south. Presently Marghiloman's Ministry, which the Germans had imposed at Bukarest, fell, and Rumania prepared to resume her part in the war. Bulgaria, too, was willing to revive her quarrel with Turkey. The famous corridor had disappeared, and Turkey was an isolated unit. It was no wonder that the "Easterners" looked up again, and the Prime Minister's henchmen in the press began to tell stories about his single-handed and far-sighted championship of an Eastern campaign as the solution of the problem of the war. But the collapse of the Balkan front was ultimately due to the collapse of its German foundation. Berlin journalists talked of the German troops which would soon bring back Bulgaria to her senses and to the Teutonic fold. But they were mortgaged to the Western front, and instead of a German expedition to assist her under Mackensen, Turkey was faced with ruin at the hands of Allenby.

His blow had followed swiftly on that of Franchet d'Esperey, and four days after the Balkan campaign had opened, British forces began the battle which was to prove the most perfect operation of the war. Preparations had been in progress during the summer, and little had been done to modify the British line running a dozen or fifteen miles north of Jericho, Jerusalem, and Jaffa to the sea. A Turkish counter-attack on 13 July had even met with some initial success; but the Turks had been unable to maintain their strength, the Germans could not assist them, the Arabs were perpetually harassing them along the Hedjaz railway, and what reserves they had were sent on a wild goose chase for the recovery of Turkish dominion in Caucasia and Persia and along the shores of the Caspian. The pursuit was rendered attractive by Russian impotence and anarchy: Armenia was regained and subjected to a final and more extensive massacre than ever; Northern Persia was overrun, and even the long and adventurous arms which the British Empire stretched out in August from Mesopotamia and India to the southern and eastern shores of the Caspian failed to save Baku from the combined efforts of Turkish troops and Bolshevik treachery on 14 September. But Allenby, the luckiest of British generals, brought down these airy Turkish castles with a single blow. He had been largely reinforced from India, which mobilized during the war nearly a million men and bore the chief burden of the Palestine and Mesopotamian campaigns; he had got a magnificent force of cavalry, and with it the terrain and open fighting wherein to exhibit a model of that traditional strategy from which the glory on European battlefields had departed for ever.

On 19 September his infantry drove the Turks from a sixteen-mile line between Rafat and the sea back a dozen miles to the railway junction at Tul Keram, while his cavalry burst through to the right towards the gap south-east of Mount Carmel and the plain of Esdraelon. It was a rare ride: on the morrow they were forty miles north and north-east at El Afuleh, Nazareth, and Beisan; and then wheeling south-east they cut off the retreat of nearly the whole of the Turkish forces. On the 22nd Allenby reported that 25,000 prisoners and 200 guns had been taken and counted, and that the

Seventh and Eighth Turkish armies had virtually ceased to exist. The Fourth was pursued across the Jordan, and mostly mopped up between its pursuers and the Arabs to the east. On the 25th we were round the Lake of Galilee, and the number of prisoners had risen to 45,000 and of captured guns to nearly 300. There was nothing left to stop our advance, which was joined by some French battalions, while the Arabs kept pace on the other side of the Jordan. On the 28th we effected a junction with them at Deraa, and Damascus fell on the 30th. On 6 October cavalry, advancing between Mts. Lebanon and Hermon, seized Zahleh and Rayak between Damascus and Beyrut, which the French occupied on the 7th, while the British took Sidon. On the 9th we were at Baalbek, on the 13th at Tripolis, and on the 15th at Homs. On the 26th Aleppo fell, and on the 28th we reached Muslimieh, that junction on the Baghdad railway on which longing eyes had been cast as the nodal point in the conflict of German and other ambitions in the East.

Allenby played the leading part in Turkey's destruction, partly because Marshall's attention in Mesopotamia had been distracted towards the Caspian. But in October he resumed his interrupted march up the Tigris: on the 25th his troops captured Kirkuk and forced the passage of the Lesser Zab; and on the 28th they took Kalat Shergat, and after a six days' battle forced the Turkish army on the Tigris to surrender. Turkey had taken a lot more beating than Bulgaria, but the end was the same. On 30 October an armistice was signed, which permitted the Allies to occupy the forts on the Dardanelles and Bosporus and make free use of the Straits. Marshall entered Mosul, and presently British ships commanded the Black Sea and British troops were holding a line across Caucasia to the Caspian and connecting with the chain of forces established between Krasnovodsk and India. An end was thus put to Germany's dreams of a Teutonic-Turco-Turanian avenue into the heart of Asia, but the search for an eastern front in Russia against the Central Empires was elusive. For the Bolsheviks, in spite of the murder of Count Mirbach the German ambassador at Moscow on 6 July, grew ever more friendly to the Prussians, and the Entente had to go to Vladivostock for a basis of operations, and rely largely upon the romantic achievements of the Czecho-Slovak prisoners who had enlisted in the Russian armies and refused to lay down their arms at the Peace of Brest-Litovsk. At first the Bolsheviks promised them a passage via Siberia to the Western front, but then, like Pharaoh hardened their hearts and refused to let the infant nation go. Thereupon the Czecho-Slovaks set up for themselves, seized the Siberian railway from the Bolsheviks, and after much hardship and fighting established contact with the motley Entente forces advancing from Vladivostock. With their assistance an anti-Bolshevik government, of which Admiral Koltchak afterwards made himself master, was set up in Siberia, while Entente forces, mostly British, were sent to Archangel and the Murmansk coast to prevent the Germans establishing their authority there as they had done in the Baltic provinces "liberated" by the Peace of Brest-Litovsk.

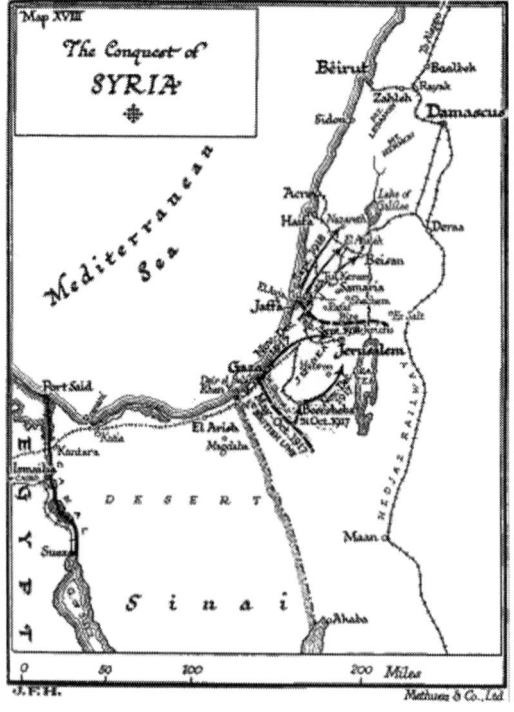

The Conquest Of Syria

But this Eastern front, which as late as August was regarded in high but civilian quarters as indispensable to the Allied success, failed to pierce the protection which the Bolsheviks gave to Germany or to penetrate farther west than the Urals; and Germany had after all to be beaten by professional strategists on the Western front. There was little fault to be found with their progress, and while Bulgaria, Turkey, and Austria were collapsing in the East, the Germans were being steadily driven towards disaster on a widening field of battle in the West. Simultaneously with Pershing's destruction of the St. Mihiel salient the British were thrusting the Germans back to the Hindenburg lines between Cambrai and St. Quentin, and Mangin was pushing forward towards the forest of St. Gobain. The Germans attempted to stand at Épehy, but on 18-19 September they were driven back with the loss of 11,750 prisoners and 100 guns; and from the 27th to the 30th was fought the first phase of the battle for Cambrai and St. Quentin, in which the British First, Third, and Fourth armies took 26,500 prisoners and 340 guns apart from the gains of the French. The object was to complete the breach of the Hindenburg lines on the strength of which public opinion in Germany was stayed; and it was a critical operation. The lines themselves were reinforced by the Canal du Nord protecting Cambrai and the Scheldt-St. Quentin canal between Cambrai and St. Quentin.

The southern sector in front of the Fourth Army was the more strongly fortified, and an intense bombardment began on the night of 26-27 September which continued till the 29th. This tended to divert attention from the First and Third armies, which on the 27th forced the Canal du Nord south of Moeuvres and then spread fanwise along the eastern bank. By the end of the day they were more than half-way from the Canal du Nord to Cambrai, and on the 28th the advance was continued across the Scheldt canal at Marcoing and broadened from Palluel on the north to Gouzeaucourt on the south. On the 29th the Fourth Army began its attack on the canal to the north of St. Quentin. It was well supported by several American divisions, and the great episode of the day was the capture of Bellenglise by troops who crossed the canal equipped with life-belts, mats, and rafts. East of Bellenglise, Lehaucourt and Magny were also stormed, and north of it Nauroy and Bellicourt. Meanwhile the Third Army captured Masnières and penetrated into the western outskirts of Cambrai while the Canadians threatened to outflank it on the north. On the 30th the Germans had to withdraw their centre at Villers Guislain and Gonnelieu, while the Fourth

Army extended its gains southwards by the capture of Thorigny; and, thus menaced, the Germans had to abandon St. Quentin to the French on 1 October. On that day, too, New Zealanders and British troops took Crèvecoeur and Rumilly south of Cambrai, and the Canadians Blécourt to the north of it. The Hindenburg line, apart from its tottering supports, had gone at the moment when Bulgaria was capitulating; and on the same 30 September Count Hertling and all his Secretaries of State resigned.

The British victory, while the critical movement on the Western front, was but one of the four operations which Foch had concerted with Haig in the middle of September. The other three were a Belgian attack at Ypres, an American advance on the Meuse, and a French offensive in close connexion with it in Champagne and the Argonne. The Belgian attack was an agreeable surprise, and nothing did more to illumine the change from 1917 than the contrast between its rapid success and the painful crawl of Gough's campaign. The cause was that which also accounted for the Germans' failure elsewhere; they had not the forces to sustain their vast and crumbling front, and they attempted to hold the line in Belgium with no more than five divisions. The attack began on 28 September on a twenty-three mile front, and in one day 50 per cent more ground was covered than had been gained in three months the year before. The whole of Houthulst forest, which then had hardly been touched, was taken at a stroke; and on the 29th Dixmude fell and the Belgians were across the Roulers-Menin road. As a consequence of this and of Haig's advance the Germans had to evacuate the rest of the Lys salient and draw back their front towards Lille and Douai. Armentières was recovered on 3 October, La Bassée and the Aubers ridge were abandoned without a struggle, and the Germans surrendered the remaining section of the Drocourt-Quéant line, withdrawing to the Douai, Haute Deule, and Sensée canals which protected Lille and Douai.

The French and Americans had a sterner task in the Argonne and on the Meuse, for here was the pivot of the Germans' whole position in the conquered territory. A possible retirement to the Meuse had been contemplated in 1917, and in September 1918 the Germans would have been glad to surrender everything west of it in return for safety on that line; hence their withdrawals and feeble resistance in Flanders. But the Meuse from Verdun to Mezières was an indispensable flank for any German front in Belgium; it had now become more to the Germans than even that, for it was the only shield behind which their armies could escape disaster and get back to Germany at all. Whatever else might have to go, this flank must hold; if it gave, the Germans would have to capitulate or suffer the wholesale destruction of their forces. Hence the stubbornness of the defence the Americans encountered; the terrain gave it every advantage with which art could supplement nature; and a singular and serious breakdown of their commissariat added to the difficulties under which American troops fought with intrepid skill.

The attack was launched on 26 September. The American front ran for seventeen miles from Forges on the Meuse, eight miles north of Verdun, to the centre of the Argonne, whence the French extended it to Auberive on the Suippe. Pershing's First Army advanced an average depth of seven miles and captured Varennes, Montfaucon,—for long the Crown Prince's headquarters,—Nantillois, and Dannevoux. Gouraud's progress was less rapid but better sustained. His greatest advance was only three miles, but it extended along a wider front and developed during the following days, while the Americans were held up by defective organization. Somme-Py and Manre were taken on the 28th, while on Gouraud's left Berthelot began to move from Reims, and farther west Mangin pursued the Germans across the Aisne. Progress along the whole French front continued in October; Gouraud's right pressed on to a level with, and then in advance of, the American left towards Challerange and Grandpré; his centre advanced towards Machault, and on his left Berthelot took Loivre, Brimont, and forced the passages of the Suippe at Bertricourt and Bazancourt, and of the Aisne at Berry-au-Bac. The Moronvillers massif was thus outflanked, and by the middle of the month the Germans were evacuating the whole of their ground south of the Aisne. This retreat, coupled with the French advance east of St. Quentin, endangered the great apex of the German front in the St. Gobain forest, and by the 10th its abandonment was begun. On the 11th the Chemin des Dames was relinquished, on the 13th the French were in La Fère and Laon, and the Germans were retreating to the line of the Serre.

Nevertheless, the advance of the right wing of the Allied front had not quite come up to expectations. The prolonged maintenance of the German bastion in the Argonne and on the Meuse enabled their centre to withdraw more or less at its leisure and thus avoid the colossal Sedan with which it was threatened; and, the French centre having been cast for a part subsidiary to those of the two wings, the brunt of the fighting fell upon the British, whose advance was not so fatal as similar progress would have been on the other wing. They were greatly assisted by American divisions serving with the Third and Fourth armies, by the Belgians and French on their left, and by the French on their right; but the check to the American advance enabled the Germans—unfortunately for them, as it turned out—to transfer reinforcements from the Meuse to Cambrai and Valenciennes.

Cambrai did not therefore fall until another series of actions had been fought in the first nine days of October. The Scheldt canal to the north of it had proved a formidable obstacle, and Haig determined to press the attack from the south, where the Fourth Army had prepared the way on 29 September by destroying the Hindenburg line at Bellicourt and Bellenglise. On 3 October Rawlinson attacked again between Le Catelet and Sequehart and captured those villages, Gouy, Ramicourt, and the Beaurevoir-Fonsomme line. On the 4th and 5th further progress was made by the taking of Beaurevoir and Montbrehain, while north of Le Catelet the Germans were driven from their positions east of the canal, which were occupied by the Third Army. On the 8th the final phase in the battle for Cambrai began. The chief fighting was on the line secured on the 3rd. An American division captured Brancourt and Prémont, and British divisions Serain, Villers-Outreaux, and Malincourt north-east of Le Catelet. New Zealanders south of Cambrai took Lesdain and Esnes, and three British divisions Serainvillers, Forenville, and Niergnies, penetrating the southern outskirts of Cambrai, while to the north of it Canadians captured Ramillies, crossed the canal at Point d'Aire and entered the city on that side. During the night the whole of it fell into our hands; the Germans were driven back in disorder to within two miles of Le Cateau; and Bohain was reached ten miles east of Bellicourt and a similar distance south-west of Le Cateau. By the 10th the advance had been carried to the line of the Selle river, on which the Germans made another stand, while farther south the French pushing east of St. Quentin, cleared the Oise-Sambre canal as far north as Bernot.

On the 10th Le Cateau fell, and by the 13th the British had gained the west bank of the Selle as far north as Haspres.

A great wedge had thus been thrust into the German line, leaving pronounced salients to the north of it round Lille and Douai, and to the south-east of it between the Oise and the Aisne. It was the policy of the Entente to eschew the destruction which fighting in cities involved, and it was particularly desirable to compel the Germans to retreat from Lille and its industrial neighbourhood by threats of encirclement rather than by frontal attack. To complete the process begun on the south, the advance in the north was now resumed; and on 14 October Belgian forces with a French army under Dégoutte and the British Second Army under Plumer attacked the whole front in Flanders between Dixmude and the Lys at Comines. Their success was even more striking than it had been on 28 September; the Belgians and French carried Courtemarck, Roulers, and Iseghem, while the British pushed along the north bank of the Lys until on the 16th they held it as far as Harlebeke, farther east than Ostend and even than Bruges. On the 15th the Belgians captured Thourout and the British Menin, crossing the Lys at various points and taking Comines on the 16th. The effect of this advance was to precipitate a comprehensive German retreat both north and south. The coveted Belgian coast had at last to be abandoned: Ostend fell on the 17th, Zeebrugge and Bruges on the 19th, and by the 21st the Germans were twenty miles from the sea, striving to stand on the Lys canal in front of Ghent. To the south the withdrawal was no less complete: both Lille and Douai were entered on the 17th; Tourcoing and Roubaix soon followed; and by the 21st our Second and Fifth armies had advanced to the Scheldt on a front of twenty miles, forming nearly a straight line with the First, Third, and Fourth on the Selle.

There the battle had been renewed on the 17th, as soon as our advancing lines of communication had been sufficiently repaired to bear the strain. The attack was made south of Le Cateau by the Fourth Army, employing British and American troops in co-operation with Débeney's French armies on our right. The country was difficult and the fighting stiff, but by nightfall on the 19th the Germans had been driven across the Oise and Sambre canal at all points south of Catillon, and on the 20th the Third and part of the First armies took up the struggle on the Selle north of Le Cateau.

Here again it was severe, especially at Neuvilly, Solesmes, and Haspres, but the whole of the Selle positions on both banks were secured, while north-east of its junction with the Scheldt the First Army had occupied Denain. On the 23rd a combined attack was made by the Fourth and Third armies, though progress was limited to the front north of the bend of the Sambre at Ors. Between that point and a few miles south of Valenciennes our troops advanced six miles up to the outskirts of the forest of Mormal and Le Quesnoy in spite of the intervening streams which had been swollen by rain, of the wooded country, and of the stubborn resistance of the Germans. These battles of the Selle between 17-25 October yielded to British armies alone 21,000 prisoners and 450 guns, and on the 26th Ludendorff resigned. Meanwhile the French were gradually squeezing the Germans out of their salient between the Oise and the Aisne back upon the Serre. Chalandry and Grandlup, near that river, were occupied on the 22nd, and east of the Aisne some progress was made in the Argonne by the capture of Olizy and Termes on the 15th; but till nearly the end of October the Americans west of the Meuse were held up by their commissariat difficulties, though east of it they had captured Brabant and Consenvoye and pushed forward their line to a level with that on the western bank.

It was only on the Meuse and on the Lys that the enemy front showed the last vestiges of stability at the end of October. The surrender of Bulgaria had been followed by that of Turkey, and Austria was on the verge of collapse. Her hold on the Balkans had gone, her southern provinces were rising in sympathy with the Serbian and Jugo-Slav advance, in the north the Czecho-Slovaks were preparing to join, and even Hungary was refusing to supply the starving capital with food. Unless Italy struck quickly, Fiume and Trieste and the whole north-eastern Adriatic coast would pass into the hands of the insurgents. The moment had come to forestall the Jugo-Slavs and deliver a blow which might overthrow the Hapsburg Empire before it collapsed of itself. Since the repulse of the Austrian offensive on the Piave in June, the Italian front had remained quiescent during the critical months of the war, though picked Italian divisions had done good fighting with the French at Reims, and the Italians in Albania had pursued the Austrian forces after they had been beaten by the Serbs and French and abandoned by the Bulgars. On the night of 23-24 October the Tenth Italian Army, consisting of two British and two Italian divisions commanded by Lord Cavan, attacked the island of Grave di Papadopoli in the Piave and completed its conquest on the 25th and 26th. Simultaneously Giardino's Italians with a French division attacked in the region of Mt. Grappa, but retired to their original position after taking a number of prisoners. On the 25th they were more successful, capturing Mt. Pertica and repulsing Austrian counter-attacks on the 26th. On the 27th the decisive movement began with Cavan's crossing of the Piave, and on the same day the Austrian Government requested Sweden to transmit to President Wilson an offer which was equivalent to surrender. At the front the Austrians continued to counter-attack very heavily at Mt. Pertica; but on the Piave they completely collapsed, and the breach of their line on the 27th was followed by a disorderly flight. The booty was colossal, the heterogeneous troops of the moribund Hapsburg Empire surrendered wholesale, and on 3 November their dying government submitted to the terms of an armistice imposed by General Diaz. On that day Italians landed at Trieste, where insurgents had taken over the government on 31 October; but an Austrian Dreadnought at Pola which had hoisted the Croat revolutionary flag was sunk by the daring act of two Italian officers.

Germany now stood alone, and any defence she might otherwise have made on her frontiers was hopelessly compromised by the position of her armies on their far-flung line in France and Belgium. Nemesis for the invasion of Belgium had at last overtaken the invader. The problem of withdrawing in safety was rendered insoluble by the battles of the first week in November and the consequent convergence of the Allies on Germany's remaining lines of communication. The decisive blows were delivered right and left by the American and British wings. Towards the end of October the Americans had surmounted their difficulties of transport and organization, and were breaking down the German resistance, which had been weakened by the transfer of troops to the British front, between Grandpré and the Meuse. On 1 November the German line was broken and the Americans advanced three or four miles. On the 2nd they doubled that distance and were in Buzancy; on the 3rd they repeated their success, while the French on their left cleared the Argonne and reached Le Chesne. German resistance also broke down on the east bank of the Meuse, and the Americans made for Montmédy. But their advance was most rapid on the west bank, where on the 7th they leapt forward to Sedan. The Germans were thus deprived of their great lateral line connecting the eastern and western sectors of their front, and were driven back against the barrier of the Ardennes; and a great French offensive into Lorraine was being prepared under Mangin. This provision somewhat weakened the less essential advance of the French in the centre between the Aisne and the Oise, but the progress of the American wing left the Germans no option but retreat in the centre, and three French armies under Débeney, Mangin, and Guillaumat were rapidly converging upon Hirson. The remains of the Hunding position were taken on 5 November, and Marle and Guise were captured farther north-west. Vervins, Montcornet, and Réthel fell on the 6th. Hirson and Mezières were reached and the Belgian frontier crossed on the 9th. On the 10th the Italians entered Rocroi, and on the morning of the 11th the Allies were converging on Namur.

This rapid pursuit of the German centre had been made possible by the coup de grâce given to the German armies in the battle of the Sambre. Haig regarded the capture of Valenciennes as an essential preliminary, and on 1-2 November corps of the First and Third armies attacked a six-mile front to the south of the town. The line of the Rhonelle was forced and Valenciennes fell on the 2nd. The line of the Scheldt was thus turned, and besides falling back in front towards the forest of Mormal the Germans had to begin evacuating the Tournai bend of the river. But the decisive blow was still to come. It was delivered on 4 November by the First, Third, and Fourth armies on a thirty-mile front, between Valenciennes and Oisy on the Sambre, which was continued by Débeney's army southwards to the neighbourhood of Guise. In Haig's restrained language a great victory was won which definitely broke the enemy's resistance. Nineteen thousand prisoners were taken on the British front and 5000 on the French. On the first day Landrecies and Le Quesnoy fell and half the forest of Mormal was overrun; and the remaining operations consisted of a pursuit. On the 7th Bavai was captured, and Condé during the following night; on the 8th our troops were twelve miles east of Landrecies in Avesnes and on the outskirts of Maubeuge, which fell on the 9th. On that day also Tournai was occupied, and the Second Army crossing the Scheldt on a wide fronting reached Renaix. On the 10th they were close to Ath and to Grammont, and early on the 11th Canadians captured Mons.

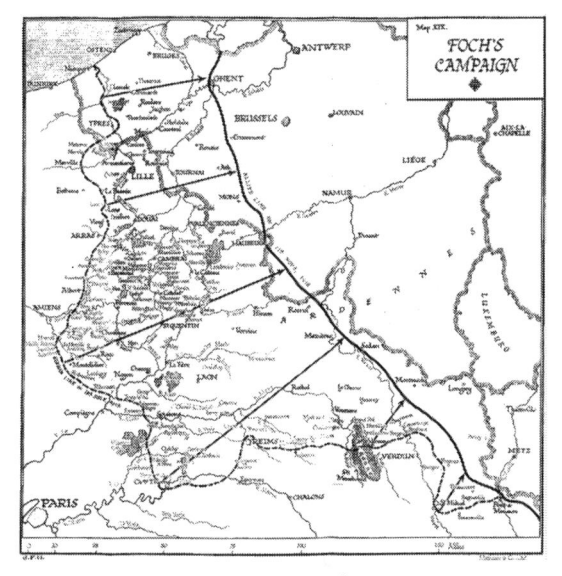

Foch's Campaign

The British Army ended the war on the Western front where it had begun to fight, and at 11 a.m. on that day the struggle ceased from end to end of the fighting line in accordance with an armistice signed six hours before. Its terms were severe, the immediate evacuation of all the conquered territory and withdrawal behind the Rhine, leaving the whole left bank and all the important bridgeheads open to Allied occupation, and a neutral zone on the right bank; the repatriation of all the transported inhabitants and Allied prisoners of war; the quashing of the treaties of Brest-Litovsk and Bukarest, and the withdrawal of all German troops from territories formerly belonging to Russia, Rumania, and Turkey; the surrender of thousands of guns, locomotives, aeroplanes, of all submarines fit for sea, and of the better part of the German Navy. The Germans had no choice: their armies were in flight along roads choked with transport towards an ever narrowing exit, and they could only escape if given time, which they could only obtain by surrender. They yielded to avoid a Sedan which would have destroyed their armies as a fighting force. But they gained one at least of the objects for which they had fought. The Fatherland was saved from the abomination of desolation which the Germans had spread far and wide in their enemies' homes; and except for a corner in East Prussia and another in Alsace, German soil had remained immune from invasion.

The surrender might have had the saving grace of common sense had it not been delayed so long; but it required the imminence of military destruction and an intimation from President Wilson that peace could not be concluded with those who had made the war, to provoke that revolution which competent observers had from the beginning declared to be an inevitable result of a German defeat. It was precipitated by an order to the German Fleet to go out and fight. That again had been anticipated as a counsel of despair, but few foresaw that the order would be disobeyed. The German genius for organization had tried the strength of its human material beyond the limits of endurance. The crews mutinied, and the spirit of revolt spread in the first week of November to Kiel and other ports, and thence throughout the whole of Germany. Every German throne, grand-ducal or royal, toppled into the dust, and on the 9th the Kaiser abdicated, fleeing like the Crown Prince to Holland, and leaving it to a government of Socialists to sign the terms of surrender. With the imperial crown went that imperial creation, the German Navy; and the crowning humiliation was its peaceful transference to Scapa Flow on 21 November, to be scuttled by its crews on 21 June 1919. Navies had gone in the past to the bottom, beaten and wrecked like the Spanish Armada, or battered to pieces and sunk as at Trafalgar; but never yet had Britain's sea-power led home a captive fleet without a fight. The curtain rang down on a fitting scene, a proof beyond all precedent of British command of the sea, and a yet more solemn demonstration that the ultimate factor in war consists in a people's spirit and not in its iron shards.

CHAPTER XX

THE FOUNDATIONS OF PEACE

Destruction is easier and more rapid than construction, and it needs a wiser man and a longer labour to make peace than war. War begins with the first blow, but peace is not made when the fighting stops; and months were to pass in the troubled twilight between the two, with millions of men under arms, with budgets more suggestive of war than peace and men's thoughts more attuned to a contentious past than prepared for a peaceful future. The first act of the British Government was, indeed, to transfer hostilities from its foes abroad to those at home, and to rout its domestic enemies at a general election. The Parliament elected in 1910 had, after limiting its existence to five years, extended it during the war to eight; and the argument for an election and a fresh mandate for the Peace Conference would have been irresistible had any Ally followed our example, had the Government during the contest given any indication of the terms of peace it contemplated, and had the British delegates not been hampered rather than helped by the foolish concessions which ministers made to popular clamour for the Kaiser's execution and for Germany's payment of the total cost of the war. There could, indeed, be little discussion on the platform, because on principles all parties were substantially agreed, and details were matters for the Conference; and the election was fought to defeat opposition, not to the Government's policy, but to its personnel. In this the Coalition was triumphantly successful: three-quarters of the new members had accepted its coupon, and of the remainder the largest party consisted of seventy Sinn Feiners who were in prison or at least pledged not to attend the House. The Labour group returned some fifty strong, but Mr. Asquith's followers were reduced to thirty. This result was, however, a triumph of political strategy manipulating a very transient emotion, the evanescence of which was shown in a series of bye-elections before the Conference reached its critical points. It was well for British influence in the councils of the Allies that it did not depend upon the vagaries of popular votes, and it would have been well for the repute of British statesmen if they had not had the occasion or the temptation to indulge in the hectic misrepresentation and profligate promises of which their electioneering speeches were full.

The weight which the various Allies exerted at the Conference depended upon the services they had rendered to the common cause and the force they had at their disposal. At the conclusion of the armistice the British Empire, in addition to its overwhelming naval preponderance, had over half a million men in arms more than any other belligerent. Its total military forces, including Dominion and Indian troops and garrisons abroad, amounted to 5,680,247 men; France had 5,075,000; the United States, 3,707,000; Italy, 3,420,000; Germany about 4,500,000; Austria, 2,230,000; while Bulgaria had had at the end of September half a million, and Turkey at the end of October some 400,000. Great Britain and France had also been fighting since the beginning of the war, while Italy had joined in May 1915, and the United States in April 1917. On the other hand, all the European Powers had reached, if not passed, their meridian of strength, whereas the United States could with a corresponding effort raise her forces to over ten millions. Potentially she was the most powerful of the associated nations, and only the existence of the British fleet brought any rival up to anything like equality. Together the United States and the British Empire were irresistible; and so long as they were agreed, any concessions they might make to others would be due, not to fear, but to their sense of justice, desire for peace, and consideration for the susceptibilities of others. The responsibility for the issue of the Conference rested therefore upon them to a very special degree; and in spite of unspeakably foolish and ignorant chatter in reactionary quarters, it was an inestimable advantage that the British Empire could look to the United States and President Wilson to bear most of the odium of insisting upon sound principles and telling unpalatable truths. America was in the better position to play the part of the candid friend, because she had no territorial ambitions to serve and no axe to grind save that of peaceful competition in the arts of industry and commerce; and if European allies occasionally grumbled at American interference, the reply was obvious that they should have won the war without waiting for or depending on American intervention.

In spite of a somewhat weak pretence to public diplomacy, the secret history of the Conference is not likely to be known to this generation; but its decisions were promptly published, and the attitude of the various Powers to the principal problems with which they had to deal was easily discerned. President Wilson had made a personal survey of the ground by a visit to Europe, unprecedented in the history of the Presidential office, in December, before the Conference opened at Versailles on 18 January 1919. It was largely owing to his presence and prestige that in the forefront of the programme and performance of the Conference stood a plan for an international organization for the future avoidance of war, settlement of disputes, and regulation of labour conditions. The idea of a League of Nations had made rapid progress as the war increased in extent, intensity, and horror. At Christmas 1917 the British Government, at the instigation of Lord Robert Cecil and General Smuts, had appointed a committee to explore the subject, and it had reported in the following summer in favour of a scheme in which the main stress was laid upon the avoidance of war. The French Government had also appointed a commission which likewise reported favourably in the summer of 1918: the principal difference between the two was that the French commission advocated the establishment of an organized standing international army. President Wilson preferred to proceed by means of more informal discussions with committees not appointed by his government; and the American stress was laid rather on the organization of an international council and tribunal. The fruitful idea of a mandatory system was first publicly advocated by General Smuts.

Lord Robert Cecil was charged with the principal share in accommodating such divergences as existed between the various governments on the matter, and remarkable progress was made, which resulted in President Wilson's production before the Conference, on 14 February, of a Covenant embodying the scheme for a future League of Nations. It was subjected to a good deal of criticism, and party-spirit in America sought to make capital out of the proposed abandonment of the self-sufficient isolation of the United States and the subordination of the Monroe Doctrine to the interests of the world and the common judgment of mankind. In Great Britain there were also those who preferred the guarantee of a predominant British navy to the security of any scrap of paper, and somewhat ignored the fact that the war had been fought to establish the sanctity of international obligations. In France, with her vivid recollection of painful experience, there was similarly a tendency to make the most of our military victory and to base the stability of peace upon the establishment of military predominance and the possession of conquests guaranteed by a permanent anti-German alliance. Italy was frankly out for all she could get irrespective of the principles of nationality and self-determination. A rigorous censorship, not merely of news from other countries, but of serious and moderate Italian books on history and politics, had combined with an ingenuous self-esteem to produce the popular conviction that Italy had been the main factor in the victory of the Entente, and that the Conference was therefore bound to concede whatever rewards she might demand in return for her services. She contended that her sentiment for Dalmatia was as sincere as that of the French for Alsace-Lorraine, and ignored the difference made by the fact that Dalmatia was peopled with Jugo-Slavs. Italy therefore had little sympathy with the Fourteen Points which at President Wilson's instigation had been accepted as the basis of the armistice and the principles of peace. Finally, Japan had a special grievance in the reluctance of the United States to accept the maxim of racial equality and a special interest in the acquisition of Chinese territory; and prejudice against her racial claim prejudiced the Allies' defence of Chinese territorial integrity.

These were some of the fundamental difficulties of the Conference which could only be settled in part by self-restraint and compromise. Much had to be left over to the patient labours of the future League of Nations in an atmosphere less charged than the Conference with the passion of war; and it gradually became evident that, instead of the League of Nations depending upon the excellence of the peace it was to guarantee, the permanence of the peace would depend upon the capacity of the League of Nations to remedy its imperfections. The League emerged as the cardinal factor in the situation which was to make the vital difference between the work of the Conference of 1919 and that of the Congresses of the eighteenth and nineteenth centuries. Reflection tended, moreover, to mitigate some of the objections to the Covenant, though various of its details were modified in response to criticism. Public opinion in the United States rallied to the argument that America would be stultifying herself if, after entering the war to win it and make the world safe for democracy, she refused to participate in the only means of making the peace tolerable and permanent; and it was recognized that the Monroe Doctrine was not so much being superseded as expanded from America to cover all the world. British reliance on sea-power was likewise somewhat impressed by the determination of the United States, if the League of Nations failed, to build a navy at least equal to our own, and by the recognition of the fact that the maintenance of even a two-Power standard would consequently involve us in a race for naval armaments more severe than that before the war and pregnant with an even greater disaster to the cause of civilization. French opinion, too, was gradually modified by the realization that Great Britain and the United States could not be expected to sanction a militarist settlement resembling in its spirit and its motives the German terms of 1871, or to guarantee a peace of which their people disapproved; and a halting trust in a League of Nations was fortified by a more specific guarantee of protection by Great Britain and the United States against an unprovoked attack by Germany. Italy, the youngest of the Great Powers among the Allies, the least mature in its political wisdom, and the most subject before the war to the influence of German realpolitik, carried her obstruction to the point of temporarily leaving the Conference in April; but her delegates returned on finding that the rest of the Allies were prepared to make peace without her participation.

Apart from these conflicts of point of view, the Conference had infinite trouble to deal with territories which had been conquered and peoples which had been liberated from autocratic yokes. The problem of races and lands in Africa and in the former Turkish Empire which were admittedly unfit for self-government had been simplified by the happy thought of the mandatory system which again depended for its efficacy upon the idea of a League of Nations. It had long been the claim of the British Empire, that so far as it was an empire and not a league of free States, it was a power held in trust and wielded not for the benefit of the Government, but of the governed. It was now proposed to formulate and expand this idea by treating these conquered lands not as the freeholds of the conqueror, but as lands to be held of the League of Nations by a mandate, for the execution of which the mandatory would be responsible to the common judgment of the nations. There was some objection to the proposal on the ground of national pride and resentment at the idea of being held responsible; but a juster appreciation led to the reflections that irresponsibility was a Prussian ideal of government, that a better cause for national pride arose from the general confidence in a nation's integrity implied in the conferment of the mandate, and that only those whose deeds were evil need fear the intrusion of international light upon their methods of administration. To be able to do what one liked with one's own was a baser ambition than to satisfy the conscience of mankind that one was making the best use of the talents with which one had been entrusted; and the general approbation with which the idea of mandates was received testified better than other proceedings in the Conference to the growth of a sense of common responsibility for the welfare of mankind. In this way the administration of German colonies in Africa was to be entrusted to Great Britain, France, and the Union of South Africa; Pacific Islands to Japan, Australia, and New Zealand; Mesopotamia and Palestine to Great Britain, Syria to France, and parts of Asia Minor to Italy and Greece.

More difficult was the self-or other determination of those parts of Europe which had escaped the iron hand of the three great Empires of Germany, Austria, and Russia. Alsace-Lorraine would revert by common consent to France, which was also given the Saar district for a term of years, not as a conquest but as a means of recovering the vast stores of coal and iron of which the Germans had robbed the French during their occupation. Belgium claimed a small strip on her frontier inhabited mainly by Belgian people; the self-determination which Bismarck had promised the Danes in Schleswig in 1864 was at last accorded them; and Heligoland was dismantled. The principal difficulties lay on Germany's eastern frontier, where the racial mixture between Germans and Poles was complicated by Poland's claim to a port and access to the sea, and by the fact that the cession of Dantzig and the Vistula to Poland would sever Germany from East Prussia, which was German in population and had been under German rule since 1524. Dantzig had been part of the Polish kingdom down to the first partition of 1772, but like other towns in Poland it had for centuries been inhabited and municipally governed mainly by Germans and Jews. For Poland was a kingdom which prolonged feudal conditions into the eighteenth century; it was a nation of serfs and landlords, and its commerce and industry, and therefore its towns, had been left for German and Jewish immigrants to develop. The corridor to the sea with most of Posen was eventually given to Poland, while parts of East Prussia and Upper Silesia were subjected to plebiscites which promised a similar result; but, like other territorial arrangements in central and eastern Europe, it was a settlement which could never prove satisfactory until racial antagonisms were modified by good government, and it became possible for different nationalities to live together in a State in Europe with as little sense of injustice and exploitation as immigrants in the United States of America.

As some offset to these losses of alien subjects, Germany hoped for an increase of population by the accession of German Austria (including the Tyrol) and the German fringes of Bohemia. The mountain ranges which ringed in Bohemia to the east, north, and west had, however, always been her boundaries, and were too natural a frontier to be surrendered by the new State of Czecho-Slovakia, the future independence of which had been recognized in 1918 as a testimony to the services rendered to the Entente by the Czecho-Slovak troops in Siberia and Russia; while conflicting views in German Austria, combined with the reluctance of France to see Germany aggrandized, postponed this reunion of German-speaking peoples, and left German Austria the weakest of the central European States into which the Hapsburg Empire dissolved. Hungary became entirely independent, but was shorn of her Rumanian, Serb, and Croat appanages. Rumanian troops held Transylvania, most of the Bukovina, and a slice of Hungary. Croatia and Carniola, like Bosnia, Herzegovina, and the previously independent Montenegro had already combined with Serbia to form a great Jugo-Slav kingdom stretching from north of Laibach to the south of Monastir, and from the Adriatic to the Danube. The Trentino, Trieste, and Pola had been occupied by Italy, but the future of Dalmatia, Fiume, and the islands in the Adriatic was the greatest bone of contention at the Conference, and their disposal was almost indefinitely postponed.

The gravest of all the problems which confronted the victorious Powers arose in connexion with their former ally, Russia, whose condition presented almost as many obstacles to peace as it had done to the successful prosecution of war. There was, however, one countervailing advantage of incalculable value. Had the imperialist Tsardom emerged triumphant from the struggle, the reactionary forces at the Conference would have been enormously strengthened; little would probably have been heard of the independence of Poland; Constantinople would have fallen into Russian hands; the Balkans and Asia Minor would have become, in fact if not in name, Russian protectorates; and there would have been found little scope for self-determination along the shores of the Baltic or in Eastern Europe. The great war of liberation would probably have resulted merely in the substitution of Russia for Germany as a greater menace to the independence of little nations and to the peace of the world. Nevertheless, the problems imposed upon the Conference by warring factions in Russia proper, by discordant races emancipated from Russian domination and pursuing their own conflicting ambitions, and by the folly of the Allies themselves in ignoring the principle impressed upon them since 1917, that it was legitimate to assist Russians against the Germans but not against one another, were harassing enough. The half-hearted, disingenuous, and misguided military efforts made by the Allies in Russia introduced alien irritants into the domestic situation and prolonged that painful process of internal evolution which could alone produce a satisfactory solution in a stable Russian government. If the responsible Allied statesmen had studied the history of previous attempts to impose particular governments on independent peoples by the force of arms, they would have been even more reluctant to attempt a repetition of the experiment in Russia. As it was, their efforts were hampered by their own subjects and Allies. The United States stood aloof; French soldiers and sailors refused to fight against Bolsheviks at Odessa; Italy did nothing; and the burden of an unwise policy was left to Great Britain, where not even the systematic manipulation of news from Russia in the interests of intervention could induce public opinion to condone more than perfunctory help to the cause of restoration.

The fairest guise this policy could assume was defence of the principle of self-determination, and the assumption was maintained that the Russian people were opposed to the Soviet government. There would have been better ground for assisting Finns, Letts, Esthonians, and Ukrainians against Bolshevik imperialism; but it was to Koltchak, Denikin, and their north Russian friends, rather than to the little peoples that help was sent, and a powerful motive in the discrimination was the pledge of the Russian conservatives to resume responsibility for Russia's debts to her Allies, particularly France, which the Bolsheviks had repudiated. Whatever success might attend this policy would not be due to its wisdom, and events were to show that the British Government misjudged the Russian situation in 1919 as much as European monarchies did that of the French Republic in 1793. The crimes and follies committed by the Soviet and the Jacobin governments were equally repulsive, but they did not make foreign intervention in either case a sound or successful policy; and the Allies would have been wiser to confine their military action to the defence of the nascent States which had asserted their independence of Russia and claimed the right of self-determination. The clearest case was that of Finland, which had always since its acquisition by Russia in the eighteenth century protested against its loss of independence. In Esthonia and Latvia, which had passed under the Russian yoke during the same period, the native movement was complicated by the class ambitions of the German barons; and there was a confused triangular struggle between German, Russian, and native influences, in which the interests and the principles of the Conference obviously lay on the side of the native party. The situation was more obscure in Lithuania. It had been bound by a personal union of its sovereign with Poland since 1370 and by a legislative union since 1569. There had been no conquest on either side any more than there had been in the personal and legislative unions of England and Scotland in 1603 and 1707; and the problem was rather one for domestic arrangement than for decision by the Conference. The Ukraine, on the other hand, had first been conquered by Poland and then seized by Russia during the successive partitions of Poland; and it required the constraint of a superior authority to check the predatory claims of both those Powers to their dubious inheritance.

The prospect of dealing successfully with the manifold problems which confronted the Conference depended to a large extent upon the order in which they were tackled. Manifestly they could not be handled simultaneously, and the first thing to do was to lay down the principles not only of the peace, but of its future adjustment and modification by establishing a League of Nations. When that Covenant had been provisionally accepted by the Conference in February, the next step was to settle with Germany; for no provisions for general peace or the security of new nations could be satisfactory until Germany was bound by material and moral guarantees to accept and to respect them. It was therefore both a logical and a practical necessity which constrained the Conference, after enunciating the principles of peace in the Covenant, to deal next with their application to Germany.

The terms were eventually settled in April and presented to the German delegation, which had been invited to Versailles for the purpose, on 7 May. The conditions were harsh, in parts vindictive, and in others manifestly inconsistent with any natural interpretation of the Fourteen Points which all the belligerents had accepted as the basis of the armistice and consequent peace; and they were not such as any Power could be expected to sign without an effort to get them amended before peace was concluded or a mental reservation to procure their modification as soon as might be thereafter. The German delegates, with Count Brockdorff-Rantzau at their head, did their best to expose the inconsistencies between the Allies' professions and their performance, and to secure a reconsideration of the more distasteful terms. An elaborate protest and counterproposals were delivered early in June and promptly answered by the Allies. A few minor points were conceded, but the terms as a whole were maintained, with an intimation that unless they were accepted at once as they stood, the Allies would draw the sword again. Count Brockdorff-Rantzau thereupon resigned, and Scheidemann's government fell on 20 June. He was succeeded as Prime Minister by Herr Bauer, and Herr Müller was sent to replace Brockdorff-Rantzau at Versailles with a mandate to sign the dictated peace. It was signed by Germany and by all her enemies, with the exception of China, on 28 June, five years to a day since the murder at Serajevo; and early in July it was ratified by a two to one vote of the German Assembly at Weimar and by the German President Ebert.

The Treaty, which filled a volume of over four hundred pages, had no precedent for its importance or its bulk. It was an epitome of the affairs of the world, and its predecessors, the Treaties of Utrecht and Paris, which ushered in peace early in the eighteenth and nineteenth centuries, were miniature in comparison. The German terms were an unsatisfactory and comparatively unimportant part of the Treaty except in so far as they bound Germany to accept the principles for which the Allies had fought the war and upon which they were determined that the future government of the world should rest. They were, indeed, not so much a pact of peace as a punishment of war; and an idealistic scheme of government by consent started by imposing on the weaker party conditions with which it could not but violently disagree. Millions of Germans in Alsace-Lorraine, Bohemia, Poland, and East Prussia were transferred to alien domination; millions of others in German Austria were denied the right of self-determination in the form of union with Germany; cities like Dantzig and Memel, which were admittedly German, were severed from Germany on the grounds that neighbouring districts were not, and that the economic interests of foreign States required the severance; and where German lines of communication crossed those of the Allies and their friends, the German lines were cut in order to provide what was regarded as an indispensable continuity for those of their rivals. These and like provisions were due to Allied distrust of Germany and lack of confidence in the efficacy of their own principles. For if the League of Nations succeeded in establishing that freedom of intercourse at which it professed to aim, there would be no need for this transfer of control or for the enforcement of access to the sea at the expense of the principle of self-determination; and these arbitrary arrangements on Germany's eastern frontier were the counterpart of the special alliance of Great Britain and the United States to afford France a protection which the League of Nations did not immediately or adequately provide. The judgment of posterity, which rarely coincides with that of the parties to a dispute or to a treaty, is likely to agree with the declaration of General Smuts, after signing the Treaty, that real peace would not be found in it so much as in the machinery it created for its own amendment, and in the spirit which would in time tone down the passions and products of war.

But that hope would have been vain without the crushing of Prussian militarism, and the best justification of the terms imposed upon Germany is that they sealed the defeat of that spirit and annulled its works in the past since the days of Frederick the Great. Here at least the Allies worked with a will and without susceptibilities to conciliate. The German army was reduced to an internal police force of a hundred thousand men, and meticulous care was taken to prevent the evasion of this exiguous limit. Her fleet was restricted to six battleships, six light cruisers, twelve destroyers, and twelve torpedo-boats; and she was denied submarines and air-forces altogether. Conscription—despite the war-time plea of our own conscriptionists that it had nothing to do with militarism—was abolished as the head and front of Germany's offence; and her armaments and munitions were limited to diminutive proportions. Much of what Germany had won by the mailed fist—Alsace-Lorraine, Posen, and West Prussia—was taken away, while the presumptive Belgian lands of Eupen and Malmedy, the indubitably German Saar district, Danish Schleswig, and disputed territories in Upper Silesia and East Prussia were reserved for determination by plebiscites held under the auspices of the League of Nations. But the purely German lands which had been conquered by Prussia's sword, Holstein, Hanover, Westphalia, most of Silesia, and half of Saxony, were left where the sword had brought them, presumably on the ground that popular acquiescence had condoned the barbarous arbitrament of war. Reparation was to supplement restitution: ton for ton the shipping sunk by submarines was to be made good out of existing German tonnage and future construction; and two thousand million pounds were to be paid in two years as a first instalment towards the repair of damage done by the German army in Belgium, France, and elsewhere. German colonies were held forfeit on the double but discrepant counts of the fortune of war and the failure of Germany to govern them according to the standard professed by all and practised by some of the Allies. The gain to their inhabitants consisted to no small extent in the fact that they were to be administered by mandatories whose responsibility was to be enforced by an annual report to the League of Nations.

Finally, Germany was required to acquiesce in whatever conditions the victors might impose on her defeated Allies, and to surrender for trial whomsoever of her nationals the Conference might select to charge with crime in their conduct of the war.

In earlier times a treaty of peace was commonly styled a treaty of peace and amity, and the whilom belligerents swore eternal friendship to date from the ratification. Here there was no pretence to amity, and the terms of peace were penalties imposed upon a prisoner at the bar. The justice in the peace was criminal justice, justice ad hoc rather than impartial equity. Other nations than Germany had waged wars of aggression; and if the breach of 1914 was a crime, the jury which adjudged it so had criminal records of their own. Even the British Empire and the United States had not attained their vast proportions or acquired their subject populations by the force of argument or in self-defence. There was no law against aggression in 1914; all nations were responsible more or less for its non-existence, and all except Belgium had themselves as well as Germany to thank for what they suffered in consequence. These, however, were precisely the reasons for making a law which was lacking and a peace for which there was no precedent. It was Germany who had taken advantage of the weakness of international law and done most to prevent its growth; and it was fitting that Germany should pay a corresponding penalty. There is a wholesome prejudice against retrospective legislation, but the benefit cannot be claimed by those who obstructed the legislation because they wanted to pursue the conduct which it would have made criminal. Occasions arise which imperatively require the creation of precedents, and the time had surely come in 1919 to enforce the principle that States must observe a moral code in their relations with one another, and to assert the responsibility of governments to that code by imposing penalties for its breach. For that the Allies had contended throughout the war, and the repudiation of that issue by the Germans was no ground for their immunity after their defeat.

Their claims were not, indeed, consistent. If there was no international code to which they could be held responsible, there was none to prevent the Allies from crying vae victis and using their victory as the Germans had hoped to use theirs. Their delegates first pleaded the absence of this code in order to absolve their former rulers, and then urged its existence to escape from punishment themselves. It was a specious plea that their revolution had acquitted the German people of the crimes of the German Government; but even more pregnant for the future welfare of mankind than insistence upon the responsibility of governments to their people was insistence upon the responsibility of peoples for their government. If the government of Germany was a criminal government, the fault could only be charged against the German people; and it is only when peoples realize that they will have to pay for the sins of the rulers they choose or tolerate that there can be any security in a democratic age for decent conduct in the relations of governments to one another. For fifty years the German people had been content to profit from the aggressiveness of their government, releasing it from responsibility to domestic opinion and denying its responsibility to any other tribunal. That negligence on the part of the Germans to guarantee the respectability of their State cost the world thirty million casualties and thirty thousand million pounds; and the debt to humanity could not be discharged by simply dismissing the agent who had incurred it. Germany herself could not undo the harm she had done nor restore the more precious losses she had caused. Repentance was something, and good conduct would lighten the burden she had to bear and shorten the term of her isolation. But judgment could not be evaded; and the majority of the German people showed good sense in their acceptance of the terms and in the rapidity with which the treaty was ratified.

From German affairs the Conference turned to those of Austria, Bulgaria, and Turkey, the minor importance of which was indicated by the departure from Versailles of the principal delegates who had determined the Covenant of the League and the terms of the treaty with Germany. President Wilson returned to America to secure the reluctant consent of the Senate to the settlement he had made; Mr. Lloyd George came back to England to the less arduous task of obtaining parliamentary sanction for those parts of the treaty which required it; and the further work of the Conference was left to the foreign ministers and other experts rather than to Prime Ministers, though M. Clémenceau remained to preside, and the Italian affairs in dispute were vital enough to require the presence of a full Italian delegation. These were concerned with the liquidation of the Hapsburg Empire, but not with that fragment of it to which Austria had been reduced by the recognition of Czecho-Slovakian independence, the transference of Galicia to Poland, and the union of Croats and Slovenes under the Serbian crown. Deprived of German support by the German treaty, this little Austria was but a suppliant at the Conference, and its efforts were mainly bent towards reducing its share in the liabilities of the Empire of which it had once formed part. Hapsburg Government was defunct, and it was difficult to apportion its liabilities fairly among those who acquired its assets; for some of them, like the Czechoslovaks and Jugo-Slavs, had exonerated themselves from complicity for Hapsburg malfeasance by rebelling against their government and fighting for the Entente. The problem was complicated by a further revolution in Hungary where a Soviet Government was established, and Bela Kun endeavoured to rule after the manner of Lenin. The Russian Bolsheviks were, however, unable to help their Hungarian pupils, in spite of the hesitancy shown by the Allies in dealing with the situation; and early in August Bela Kun's government fell before domestic reaction and the advance of the Rumanian army, which occupied Buda-Pesth. At last Rumania had her revenge, and it required energetic protests on the part of Versailles to induce her to recognize its restraining authority, refrain from reprisals, and regard the spoils of war as the common assets of the Allies instead of her own particular booty. She had ample compensation in the settlement through the redemption of Rumanes not only from the Hapsburg-Magyar yoke but from that Russian yoke in Bessarabia which had dulled her ardour for the anti-Hapsburg cause.

These diversions delayed until September the presentation by the Allies of their final terms to the Austrian Republic. Its territories were reduced to the limits of Austrian lands before the Hapsburg Empire was created four hundred years ago by the Emperors Charles V and Ferdinand I; parts even of their inheritance were lost, though the ecclesiastical lands like Salzburg acquired during the Napoleonic secularization were retained, and the future of Klagenfurt was reserved for plebiscitary determination. Instead of an Empire Austria became the fragment of a nation, divorced from the rest of the German people by the fears of the Entente, required like Germany to forswear conscription, denied all access to the sea, and left with regard to the size of its territories and weakness of its frontiers in much the same situation as the Serbia she had attacked in 1914. Protest was as idle as delay, and the treaty which was presented on 2 September was signed on the 10th.

Nine days later Bulgaria learnt her fate, and the draft treaty presented to her delegates at Versailles on 19 September condemned her to pay an indemnity of ninety millions, to reduce her army to 20,000, and to lose the town and district of Strumnitza and the whole of her Ægean coast. Strumnitza was given to Serbia, but the Ægean coast was reserved for disposal with the rest of Thrace and the remains of the Turkish empire. Bulgaria herself received a fraction of Turkish territory on the river Maritza, and her frontiers with Rumania were left unchanged. In the Balkans, as elsewhere, the Allies applied the principle of self-determination only to conquered countries; none but an Ally was allowed the privilege of retaining Irelands in subjection, and in the Balkans at least the victory of the Entente increased the populations under alien rule. Guarantees respecting the rights of minorities were, indeed, imposed on the lesser States, but they would have been more effective and less invidious, had the greater Powers subjected themselves to the rule they made for others.

The Conference found it easier to dispose of its enemies' lands than to compose the rivalries of its friends; and the blunders of Italy's statesmen combined with the blindness of public opinion to reduce her to a position of almost pathetic isolation. Signor Orlando's abandonment of the Conference in April failed to shake the resistance of the Allies to her extravagant expectations, and on 20 June, by a remarkable vote of 229 to 80 in the Italian Chamber, his government was driven from office. Not only in Italy but in Allied countries, Italian communities abstained from celebrating the peace with Germany, and grave indeed would have been the difficulties of the Conference if the conclusion of that treaty had depended upon Italy's signature. There was friction amounting to bloodshed between French and Italians at Fiume, and an Albanian rising against the protectorate which Italy had proclaimed. Her resolve to establish Italian domination along the eastern coasts of the Adriatic evoked opposition from all the native populations, who strongly appealed to the sympathies and principles of the Allies; and her dependence upon them for the necessaries of commerce and industry made defiance an impossible policy. Gradually her new government under Signor Nitti sought to withdraw from an untenable position; but D'Annunzio's raid on Fiume in September once more inflamed popular passion, and Dalmatia, the islands in the Adriatic, Albania, Epirus, and the Dodecanese were apples of discord between Italy and the Balkan States which distracted the Allies throughout the summer and autumn.

The settlement was also delayed by the enormous difficulty of liquidating the Ottoman Empire and the reluctance of the United States to accept the obligation of mandates in Europe or Asia. The curious spectacle was afforded of the two great branches of the Anglo-Saxon race indulging in a rivalry of retirement and endeavouring to saddle each other with fresh acquisitions of territory; and between them Armenia was almost abandoned once more to the Turks and the Kurds. France was less retiring in Syria, the inhabitants of which were believed to prefer to French rule any one of three alternatives, Arab independence, a mandate for the United States, or one for Great Britain; and the anxiety of great Powers to leave countries where their presence was wanted was only equalled by their determination to stay where it was not. French soreness over the lack of appreciation shown by the Syrian people was increased by an independent arrangement between Great Britain and Persia which gave us as complete a control over Persian administration as we possessed in Egypt during the eighties; and it was somewhat pertinently asked why Persia should be allowed to dispose of her government in this way, while Austria was sternly forbidden to unite with Germany without the consent of the League of Nations. The sovereignty of Persia had, however, been recognized at Versailles, and the League could not entrust a mandate for its government to any other State. It was therefore left for Persia to secure assistance in its administration by private treaty dictated by Lord Curzon and traditional views about India, Russia, and the Persian Gulf. Our patronage of Koltchak's government prevented him from making any protest.

Russia remained the sphinx of the situation, and the obscurity of her future darkened the counsels of Versailles. Early in the war the Entente had acquiesced in all the imperialist pretensions of the Tsardom to Constantinople, the Dardanelles, and Asia Minor; and even after the Revolution the web of the old diplomacy entangled the feet of the Allies. Fear of Bolshevism threw them on to the side of Restoration, and Restoration at the hands of Koltchak and Denikin implied a revival of the Russian Empire at the expense of independent fringes. The Ukraine, Lithuania, Esthonia, and Latvia, and even Poland and Finland, looked askance at such a policy, and naturally could not be brought into a crusade to carry it out. The straightforward line to take would have been to recognize these emancipated States on the principle of self-determination and limit our action to their defence. Hatred and haste had, however, betrayed the Allies into armed intervention in the domestic politics of Russia proper, and committed them to supporting a cause which had doubtful chances of success and, if successful, might produce greater embarrassment for them than defeat. From success they were saved by Koltchak's failure. Having mastered Siberia and made a brave show of descending on Bolshevist Russia from the Urals in the spring, he was routed in July and August and driven back to Omsk, while Bolshevist forces rose up in his rear. His defeat ruined our plans in North Russia, and at last convinced the Allies of their folly in seeking to impose a government on the Russian people; and evacuation became the order of the day. In South Russia Denikin, unassisted by foreign legions, met with more native support and greater success. The Bolsheviks were driven from the shores of the Black Sea, and the Ukraine recovered Kiev. Students of Russian history drew interesting parallels with the Russian Time of Troubles in the seventeenth century, but rather neglected the fact that they lasted thirty years; and the foundations laid at Versailles had long to wait before the temple of peace was erected upon them in Russia.

The Allies themselves were slow to ratify the terms they dictated to others, and months passed after the German ratification before its example of promptness was followed by the Entente. The British Empire had to await the separate decisions of all its Dominions; and the Senate of the United States was led, by the fact that a majority in it was politically opposed to the President, to make an even greater use than was customary of its constitutional powers of obstruction in foreign policy. Italy ratified the treaty on 7 October; Great Britain, her four Dominions having assented by 2 October, ratified on the 10th, and France on the 12th. But the Adriatic and the Baltic, Russia and the Balkans, Turkey and Syria, still defied a settlement and delayed the peace; and the Powers at Versailles discovered that their apparent omnipotence was impotent for many purposes. Not one of their peoples was willing to go to war to enforce the decisions of the Conference, and the submission of Germany removed the one possible exception to this rule. Almost against its own will the Conference was compelled to act on its own principles and find other methods than those of military force to settle the problems with which it was faced; and this situation provided ample scope for diplomatic recalcitrance and delay. The advantage was that practice was thus acquired in the exercise of such economic and other peine forte et dure as the League of Nations would in future have to use to reduce its unruly members to order. Proceedings at Versailles therefore took less and less the character of a conclusion to the war and more and more that of an endless introduction to a new era. The work of a temporary Conference to settle terms of peace was merging into that of a permanent League of Nations for maintaining it; and the world happily got into its international habits while its individual governments and legislatures were still debating whether they would fit. Just as before the war the appearance of peace was deceptive, so the clouds of a storm that was passed obscured the clearing sky, and filled the weather-prophets of the platform and the press with a gloom which the people declined instinctively to share. There were indeed symptoms that we, like our forefathers a century ago, were destined to tread the downward path from Waterloo to Peter-loo. The ties of nationality and the stimulus of patriotism weakened; the home-fires which kept brightly burning in the war threatened to end in smoke through dissensions over coal, and men reverted to their ancient anarchy of class and craft. Mr. Lloyd George's House of Commons, which owed its existence to past events and to a passing mood, soon forfeited the confidence of a fickle public, and the impotence to which it was reduced left the country prone to the temptations and a prey to the turbulence of direct and unrepresentative action. In the absence of effective opposition and incentive in Parliament nothing constitutional appeared to move the Government, and an evil example was set when a few hundred soldiers in January demanded in Whitehall and obtained their prompt demobilization. The Premier himself, who had been on Pisgah in September 1914, descended to a lower level and a dusty arena in his general election speeches; and animosities which had been concentrated on the Huns were dissipated in domestic directions.

Distance alone will lend discernment to the view, and only time will reveal the ascent of man during the five great years of war. There will be much backsliding to measure and record, and the intense agitation of war brought out the worst in the bad as well as the best in the good. Much that came to the top was scum, while often the salt of the earth went under. Treason blotted the pages illumined by heroism, and profiteering tarnished peoples redeemed by the devotion of their sons. Wastefulness and corruption ran riot even in government circles, while hundreds of thousands of humble men and women voluntarily stinted and starved themselves beyond the rigid requirements of the law. Lip-service was paid to the principle of equality in sacrifice, and some efforts were made to enforce it. But they failed to remove the inexorable inequalities of human fate, and the war which brought death and distress to millions, brought to others ease and honours, wealth and fame. These are the common property of wars; and if men did more evil in this than in any preceding conflict, it was not because they were worse than their forefathers, but because the war was more comprehensive and they had ampler means of working ill. Even the cruelty with which it was waged by the Germans created horror mainly because they sinned against the higher standards of modern times, and because their cruelty found more scientific and effective methods of expression.

All the nations which fought believed in the justice of their cause and fought as a rule with a courage which belied the alleged degeneracy of the human race. None of the Powers save Russia fell short of their previous fame. France strove at Verdun with a fortitude in adversity unequalled in her annals. German discipline and determination would have evoked unstinted praise but for the cause in which those qualities were displayed. Belgium exhibited a national spirit new in her history, and Serbian heroism was a revelation which earned for the southern Slavs the greatest relative gains in the war. The people of the United States became a nation of crusaders moved by motives at least as high as those which inspired the hearers of Peter the Hermit, Urban II, or St. Bernard; and the British Empire eclipsed its own and all other records. History tells of many a shining example of ancient valour in individuals and in the elect; but here we had heroism in the mass and courage in the common man. Human memory recalls no parallel to that uprising of the spirit which led five million Britons to fight as volunteers for the honour of their country and the liberty of other lands; despite its shortcomings the Conference of Versailles achieved higher ideals than those attained by any preceding congress of peace; and if during the war for its common weal the world paid, in flesh and in spirit, a price greater than that ever paid before, it purchased a larger heritage of hope and laid a surer foundation for its faith.

BIBLIOBAZAAR

The essential book market!

Did you know that you can get any of our titles in large print?

Did you know that we have an ever-growing collection of books in many languages?

**Order online:
www.bibliobazaar.com**

Find all of your favorite classic books!

Stay up to date with the latest government reports!

At BiblioBazaar, we aim to make knowledge more accessible by making thousands of titles available to you- *quickly and affordably*.

Contact us:
BiblioBazaar
PO Box 21206
Charleston, SC 29413